The Farmer's Friend

Drawing from her life as a rural midwife, Fiona McArthur shares her love of working with women, families and health professionals in her books. In her compassionate, pacey fiction, her love of the Australian landscape meshes beautifully with warm, funny, multigenerational characters as she highlights challenges for rural and remote families, and the strength shared between women. Happy endings are a must.

Fiona is the author of the non-fiction book *Aussie Midwives*, and lives on a farm with her husband in northern New South Wales. She was awarded the NSW Excellence in Midwifery Award in 2015 and the Australian Ruby Award for Contemporary Romantic Fiction in 2020.

Find her at FionaMcArthurAuthor.com

Also by the author

Red Sand Sunrise
The Homestead Girls
Heart of the Sky
The Baby Doctor
Mother's Day
The Desert Midwife
The Bush Telegraph
Aussie Midwives

FIONA McARTHUR

The Farmer's Friend

MICHAEL JOSEPH
an imprint of
PENGUIN BOOKS

MICHAEL JOSEPH

UK | USA | Canada | Ireland | Australia
India | New Zealand | South Africa | China

Michael Joseph is part of the Penguin Random House group of companies
whose addresses can be found at global.penguinrandomhouse.com.

Penguin
Random House
Australia

First published by Michael Joseph, 2021

Cover image by Alexandra Sophie/Arcangel
Cover design by Louisa Maggio © Penguin Random House Australia Pty Ltd
Typeset in Sabon by Midland Typesetters, Australia

Printed and bound in Australia by Griffin Press, part of Ovato, an accredited
ISO AS/NZS 14001 Environmental Management Systems printer

A catalogue record for this
book is available from the
National Library of Australia

ISBN 978 1 76104 066 5

penguin.com.au

With gratitude, awe and appreciation to the Rural Fire Service, a team of everyday volunteers who defend our people, homes and livelihoods.

Chapter One

Gracie

The October wind twirled coffee-coloured willy-willies south across the Queensland border. Spirals spawned into dust beings where hot road tar met dry, desiccated dirt.

Gracie Olivia Sparke stared out of the passenger window beside Jed, christened Joshua Edwards, watching the funnels of dirt and dreaming of her new home. Her fingers rested on Jed's warm, jeans-clad thigh in the battered F250 utility he'd bought cheap.

The old ute towed the horse float easily, a makeshift trailer Jed had panel-beaten back into shape, though it still looked like an origami tube of crinkled paper. Inside the float, furniture groaned and shifted, even when it had been jammed with pillows, and suitcases of clothes jostled the carefully positioned second-hand baby cradle as it rocked. Everything swayed and made music like a retro theatre company serenading tyres on bitumen, with the fencing equipment as the baritone, and Jed's tools as the countertenor to Gracie's mezzo-soprano kitchen implements.

'We're singing our way into New South Wales,' Gracie said.

'Yoddelaee,' Jed sang, not in tune but happily. His excitement for this new venture made her mouth twitch and she pushed away the precariousness of their finances that was weighing on her mind – if not Jed's.

Outside, a funnel of grit passed across the truck's bonnet in a swirl of crackling gravel rain and pattered over the roof of the cab.

'I like horse floats.' Jed flicked his gaze up to check the rear-view mirror. 'Floats fit everything. And they keep the dust out better than a trailer, too.'

'Yes, Jed.' She'd wanted to hire a trailer from a petrol station, self-haul and return, and not outlay capital expenditure. Not to mention yearly registration costs. But Jed had spouted how useful floats were, and she'd given in.

He shook his head in admiration for the lumbering box behind them. 'Maybe we could get a few floats and hire them out at our new store?'

Oh boy. He was starting already. But Gracie had to smile because his exuberance was one of the traits she loved about him. 'Let's just get the store going first before we add a new venture.'

'Did I tell you Featherwood's on the plateau, Gracie? The surrounding countryside's in drought, but we're on the edge of a fertile belt that almost always stays green. There's a creek that's still running behind the house and higher there are waterfalls in some of the gullies out of town. There are big falls somewhere out past Featherwood that we'll have to find for a picnic. Even in summer the creeks are cold and boulder-filled, though a bit slow at the moment. I think you'll love it.'

She would love anywhere with Jed. Gracie's gaze shifted from the front of the vehicle to the big man who still made her heart jump into a four-beat gait like a runaway horse. She tried to share his absolute belief that this venture would make their fortune, but couldn't quite keep her fears at bay. Having been destitute once, it wasn't something she would ever forget. Sadly, Jed couldn't appreciate the horror of that state. You don't, until it's happened to you. Despite that history, Gracie didn't need a fortune. She just wanted to pay the bills and be secure. For the baby. And for Jed and her.

Still, they'd bought a tattered and derelict stock-and-feed produce store, called of all things the Farmer's Friend. Diverted from her insolvency woes, Gracie smiled again at the name. 'Isn't a farmer's friend a weed that sticks to your socks?' she teased Jed.

'Sure is. A weed that doesn't give up easily. Like us.' She could tell Jed thought it a great name. 'Like the way farmers stick together. I like it. And I looked it up. They call it cobbler's pegs, too. *Bidens pilosa*, with herbal antibiotic qualities. It's good for lungs, and digestive and urinary-tract infections.'

Jed had looked it up to use in defence of the name. Gracie laughed. Every day he made her laugh. Oh how she loved him. 'True story?' He came up with the weirdest stuff. She was a nurse, a midwife really, because that's where her experience lay, and she'd never heard anything like that.

'True story.' Tickled she hadn't known, he stared straight ahead, his mouth kinked up in one corner. 'You pick the leaves and infuse it as a tea or add it to a soup.' He flashed his white teeth as he gave her a full grin. 'Or a green smoothie.' He glanced her way with his beautiful mouth now pretending to be serious. 'Though not sure about pregnant ladies drinking it.'

His gaze returned to the road. 'A town needs a good produce store.' He was off again as he waved his fingers in a small circle. 'Featherwood's a village really, but that's a good thing, Gracie.

And there's still passing traffic to Armidale.' Jed's big labourer's hands tightened with excitement on the wheel. Like they did every time he thought about their new home.

She felt the wry smile at the corner of her mouth as she studied the hand closest to her. Despite the roughness from hard manual labour, Jed's strong hands were always so gentle and caring with her. They were scarred too, with one hand oddly misshapen from a broken ring finger he hadn't stopped working to get properly aligned and had healed bent.

She felt a common sadness for that finger. She'd healed bent, too. From the past. From being a penniless and pregnant teen who'd lost her baby.

'You'll see it all today.' He smiled at her, as if sensing her melancholy. 'How was your last day at work?'

Gracie hadn't had a chance to tell him because it had been such a rush this morning. Sadness from leaving her job welled again. 'I was so pleased Jesse gave birth before we left.' Gracie had been waiting for her final client to go into labour and thought she'd miss the event due to their move. 'At six am. Phew. And she was wonderful.'

She'd had to work right up to the final moment and leave all the last packing to Jed, because she'd had such a rapport with Jesse. She just couldn't leave the circle of Jesse's pregnancy and labour incomplete.

'I'm glad,' Jed said, but she could see he was drifting away again in his mind, thinking about his new adventure. 'Everything worked out well, then.'

As if their fortune were set, which of course it wasn't yet. They'd talked about taking chances, but Gracie feared it was only she who felt the chasm of risk in small business that was about to open under them. Jed was the eternal optimist. That was a good thing, she kept telling herself. But she'd been penniless before and optimism could give the sorts of hunger pains Jed hadn't experienced.

He nodded his head as if he'd just had a silent conversation with his inner self. 'There's opportunity for growth without competitors close to the village. It's a big valley with farming families, so the prospect for new customers is there.'

Except Australia had been experiencing the longest recorded drought and nobody had money to spend. And it was in New South Wales.

As if he heard her thoughts, he slanted a look at her. 'It's not far over the border.'

But it was still down in New South Wales. She'd vowed never to return to the state where her life had crashed and burned. Twice.

Jed gave her a big, apologetic grin, his black curls falling into the crinkled skin around his eyes, and he brushed the nuisance hair away. 'You still okay with that?'

Bit late now, we bought it, she thought. But damn, she loved him. 'I can't remember, were there any other shops in the village?' She hoped there'd be a hairdresser. She'd have to cut his hair if they didn't have one in this tiny township. Her own as well. She wasn't a princess, but hopefully someone had a good pair of scissors. Please.

'A post office general store, and the pub. There might be a part-time barber behind a house, if I remember. That's all the businesses running apart from us.'

'Featherwood sounds wonderful, Jed,' she said. 'The fact that the rural store comes with a house, our own house, has a lot going for it.'

That part was true. Their own home. She'd wanted her own home so desperately after renting forever. It was worth the depletion of her tiny, hoarded nest egg for them to scratch enough together to do it. Which was no easy feat when no bank would touch them for a loan with both of them only having casual employment.

'It's worth moving if we own it lock, stock and barrel.'

Yes, it is. Still, there were rates and insurance and power and water, she thought, but didn't say it. Jed had banked his payout from the pastoral company and Gracie had her savings from before they'd met. She was the one who managed their finances. Added up the bills for the year, divided by twelve, saved that each month and put aside savings. No matter how small, she always put aside savings. Ever since she'd read that book, the one with the alpacas, she'd taken control back from poverty and debt.

Pooled together, they'd had just enough. Both house and sheds were run-down, Jed had said, so they were cheap. Gracie didn't believe anything came cheap. Or at least not without a reason.

'Tell me more about the house.' Unconsciously, she crossed her fingers. She'd been fantasising a little, too.

'It'll be fine.' Jed waved it away, his mind still on the store. 'It has more neglect than real problems.'

She could guess just how briefly he'd examined the old house that came with his precious produce store. It wasn't Jed's passion, but it would be hers. She'd find out soon enough.

Jed already loved the store; she could tell by the eagerness in his voice. It must have been better than he expected.

'It has so much potential.' Jed believed in fairytales. Gracie did when it came to birth and women and now, in finding love.

6

Not so much with finances, though. She'd tried to since she'd met Jed.

He took his hand off the wheel briefly again to wave expansively. 'The feed sheds are massive, and there are two small ones out the back and the shop itself is joined on the side. It's great. One of the blokes I met in the pub reckons we'd get a loan just on the sheds if we don't get one on the business,' Jed said.

Gracie hated loans.

As if he'd heard her, Jed said, 'We need a loan to restock the store. It needs rebuilding from the ground up. We'll make it into the best rural produce store ever seen. The shop part will be great. And there's even a tiny upstairs area we could make into a creche for the baby.'

Jed's eyes shone like blue headlights, something she hadn't seen for a while since the drought had turned tragic, and she did rejoice in that shining. Being the more pragmatic one, Gracie could see some battles ahead when Jed wanted to build a bigger-than-Bunnings boy-store with an empty bucket of money, because she still held the cheque book. All the same, though, he was animated now when he'd been low before. It wasn't an image she ever wanted to see again. Her big man dry and shrunken like the land. Like all the men watching cattle going down on their knees in front of them.

He'd lamented the lack of rain that cracked the dirt around Roma, seen the beasts fail, and the tough, resilient men he worked with go quiet. Watched his outdoor, joyful job wither and shrivel with the pastoral company profits. And disappear. The drought had crushed everyone but especially those on the land.

She breathed in and silently made a pact with Jed and herself. *Their new venture would work*. Jed had the background and experience from many farms and stations all over Australia. He was a hard worker. Full of ideas. A man with 'vision splendid', like in the poem. It would be good for him to be his own boss.

And he'd be a good boss. Her man was honourable and always honest. Sometimes, and her mouth twitched at the thought, he was too brutally and undiplomatically honest. But he was a strong, solid, generous man and she loved him and his qualities, even though sometimes he was like a child in his simplicity of thought process.

Right wrong. Black white. It was always Jed's way or the highway. Unless you were Gracie and knew the back roads and the sensible path through the woods. Quietly, and sometimes even silently, Gracie refused to budge until Jed cottoned on. She was no pushover.

She sat back with her head turned to watch his profile. 'So, what do we sell in a rural store?' She should have asked all these questions before, but they'd been chasing their tails since he'd seen the For Sale advertisement in the *Land* newspaper.

Jed's face lit up with the exuberance of that kid with the new pony, but his eyes stayed on the road ahead. Since they'd found out she was pregnant, Jed had dropped ten kilometres off his usual driving speed and he watched like an eagle for danger towards her or their baby. Sweet man. Gracie could look after herself. She had made sure she would never be a victim again. But it was still sweet.

'What can we sell?' That hand lifted again as he waved. 'Everything. Pumps, poly pipe, posts, wire, everything a hardware store sells. Then the produce stuff. It's a drive-through feed store, so stock feed, horse, chook and dog feed. Fertilisers. Seeds. Hay. There's a forklift, so you'll have to learn how to drive that.'

She laughed. 'Not until later.'

'True story. No heavy lifting for you. And when the baby comes, we'll have our own house to make the nursery. We can make a real go of this, Gracie.'

'Yes, Jed.' A rollover movement in her belly made her suddenly more positive. The baby thought so, too.

Gracie watched an eagle rise from a suspicious lump in the field. 'It's dry here, as well, poor things.' They'd come around the back way into Featherwood down the New England Highway instead of in from the coast and the M1.

Queensland lay behind them as they drove past paddocks with brown patches of dead, stubbly grass in well-grazed clumps. 'At least there're patches of feed,' Jed said. 'It isn't a dust bowl like in Roma.'

But they didn't see signs of rain. And they were coming close to their destination as they travelled down the ranges.

Water restrictions shouted in red from road signs, with the heritage town of Tenterfield counting the days until it ran out of water completely. Gracie stared sadly at dry ornate gardens, the brown grass, the long-faced people on the footpaths who didn't look up as they drove through and out the other side. Drought sucked. Period.

They passed an arid expanse where black cattle milled around a muddy waterhole. The edges of the dam were soft and torn and the cattle pulled one sinking foot after the other through the mud until they could reach the centre where the last of the orange water lay in a bowl of clay. Gracie sighed. 'That one's almost dry.'

'And the cattle will stick and die if someone isn't watching.' A grim edge to Jed's voice reminded her he'd seen too much of the drought.

'You said there's a creek through Featherwood?' she asked to divert him.

Jed blinked, wrinkled his brow and then his forehead cleared. 'Lots of creeks and a big one down the mountain that becomes the river when there's flow. Between Bellingen and Featherwood, the pocket of mountain top is one of the last to feel drought in New South Wales. Just an hour down the mountain as the crow flies and it turns into the Bellingen River, where you can paddle to the sea. A real snake of a waterway. Though they said it stopped running in places last month for the first time in years.'

'Where do you pick up this information?' Gracie shook her head. 'I've never met a man who could strike up a conversation like you can, Jed.'

'That was from Molly, the schoolteacher in the village. She'd dropped some cakes into the pub when I was there. She reckons the house will come up good and offered us help. I can't wait to show you.'

He'd mentioned the house. Positively. Gracie felt excitement stir in her belly along with their baby. She couldn't wait either.

The sun had passed overhead and was now behind them.

Since they'd turned onto the Guyra road that apparently snaked past Featherwood, towards Dorrigo, Jed's hand had lifted as each car or truck had passed on the road to their destination and the other drivers had waved back.

'Just like you and me are locals,' Jed said.

Now they were on the Waterfall Way and getting close. The last car, one they'd passed ten minutes ago, had been a blue BMW in a road tunnel of trees waiting to turn into a gate. The woman hadn't waved, but that wasn't a sign. Featherwood, the village, would be a friendly place.

As they approached the last rise, the overhead tree tunnel opened out into clumps of olive against the hills and pink cockatoos cawed in the sky in front of them as they swept the bend. A valley spread before them. Unbelievably, it was tinged with green.

'That's it!' Jed's face split in delight.

Featherwood fanned out below as they rattled down the hill. Houses and a church spire. The creek wriggled like a worm on a mission through a wide creek flat with the browns and greys of drought edged one side, while on the other, spotted cattle grazed hopefully across the still-green-in-places paddock of the flats. Gracie guessed that when it rained those same flats would be vibrant and lush.

Closer ahead, the spread of houses lay on each side of the one main road. Their new town. They crossed a bridge.

'Welcome to Featherwood,' she read aloud from the white board. 'The sign looks new.' Her gaze followed the road into the scatter of small buildings, some timber, some brick. Chimneys over all of them, as if winter meant woodfires and warm clothes.

But it was nearly summer and hot air rushed into the cab as Gracie wound down the window and let freshness blow her hair from her face. The breeze breathed the scent of their new home over them. Eucalyptus and dust. Cows. Cracked mud. Bottle-green bushes with waratah flowers.

The village started with the school on a flat pancake of land to the left of the bridge, with the two small brick buildings edged in white timber. The main classroom was a long, white timber verandah standing on short pylons with a ramp leading to the door. A row of small backpacks hung on the wall. A wide sports oval lay behind the buildings and she could imagine small, straggling cross-country runners gasping for breath. 'Featherwood Public School,' Gracie said with a smile. 'Our baby will go there.'

'I can see you in the tuckshop making lunches,' said Jed.

'Does that mean you'll do the meetings at night for fundraising?' Gracie teased him. Jed had been on the committee for the Roma Cricket Club and the rural fire brigade. He could drive the big fire truck when needed. A team player, he was a sucker if someone asked for a favour.

On the opposite side of the road from the school lay a white-fenced rodeo-cum-cricket-ground – sporting a small grandstand overlooking the field. It appeared as though it had even been used as a dirt racecourse. The cricket pitch resembled a brown sticking plaster on a dirty knee inside the fence. But at least Featherwood had a cricket pitch. Jed would be happy.

Then came two boarded shops and a big hall on stilts that proclaimed, '*Meetings held first Monday of the month. Progress Association*'.

Gracie guessed with the drought, Featherwood hadn't made a lot of progress recently. Jed would end up in the meetings, full of ideas, and occasionally getting up people's noses.

Gracie slanted a glance at her man. 'You're going to be busy.'

Jed rolled his eyes. 'Let's sort our world first.'

That was a good sign. Sensible.

A small, white church presided atop another knoll on the right. With one tall belltower square, it was solid looking with narrow arched windows and was surrounded by a painted picket fence. A matching gate led through to the graveyard on the right of that.

There were maybe two dozen old graves, but they were well kept. Gracie liked graveyards. She also liked what she'd seen of the village, but the rest would have to wait. They'd arrived and she doubted Jed had seen any of the things she'd noted.

Opposite the church sat the Farmer's Friend.

As they drove into the front driveway of the derelict produce store, her man's eyes were firmly fixed with a bright sheen of glowing anticipation.

He pulled up outside the shuttered, soiled shopfront with a noisy shudder as their belongings settled. He sat there with his hands on the wheel and stared at the mouldy building decorated with rampant weeds and spiderwebs and studied the scene with something like joy.

That wasn't quite the emotion Gracie was experiencing.

Chapter Two

Nell

Everything Chanel Truman owned, except her car, was second-hand and fitted in her tattered backpack. She'd been evicted from the white parental palace three years ago and now, at twenty-six years old, with no court date hanging over her anymore, she was driving away from Sydney as fast as the law allowed.

This would be her longest expedition in her barely used, pre-tragedy birthday car. It had been strangely liberating to push through the unexpected agoraphobia she'd acquired from her isolation as she left the city behind.

The adopted daughter of two eminent Macquarie Street dermatologists, Nell had pinned her sanity on buying this remote parcel of land when she'd sold the old shop in Petersham. She'd lived like a squatter upstairs while she waited for the scales of justice to squash her, but that hadn't happened. Although she still couldn't quite believe it, that was firmly behind her.

Soon she'd see the farmhouse for the first time. Like the stuff in the backpack, it too promised to be old and worn, but she'd grown used to that now. As far as she was concerned, she deserved old and worn, and quite frankly, it matched her resilience, which was old and very worn.

Five hours later, exiting at the M1 signs to Bellingen and Dorrigo – both new names to places en route to her bolthole – she allowed a little more accumulated tension out the window of the car and into the countryside.

In the distance, a plateau rose with a crenulation of steep faces dark with foliage and soaring up into the blue sky.

Below the mountain range lay the valley, eclectic in people and buildings, she thought, as she crawled through the little town of Bellingen. Her eyebrows rose at the varied peeps on the footpath; the surprising line of traffic inched slowly the length of the old-fashioned main street and gave her plenty of time to stare.

Apart from the unremarkable, smiling shoppers, there were occasional immaculately dressed and coiffed women who could have been any of her parents' North Shore neighbours, shoulder to shoulder with free spirits wearing archetypical dreadlocks, cheese-cloth items and no shoes. A plethora of health-food stores and organic convenience outlets jostled with designer homeware and artisan bread. Maybe she wouldn't stand out like a sore thumb here after all with her private school accent and her well-worn but unmistakably designer clothes.

She didn't see the man ducking out into the road in front until it was too late. Tall, sex-on-a-stick form in a black T-shirt and black jeans, he strode with purpose from behind the truck in front, with his coal-black crew-cut hair, hard, clean jaw and a death wish. He trod lithely, powerfully, on a mission, as if she wouldn't dare to run him over.

Nell hit the brakes hard, only just managing not to land on top of him.

Cold blue eyes raked hers through the windshield and something in his narrowed gaze – judging, assessing her – lifted her chin.

It wasn't her fault. She would have seen him if he'd paused before crossing, though he looked like he could stop her BMW with his shoulders, and there'd more likely be damage to her, not him.

'Sorry,' she murmured, too late. He was gone. Striding up the footpath as if he were storming through an enemy camp on some top-secret mission.

His contempt stung and flattened her mood, but her gaze was caught, like her car in the traffic, as his long, loping strides covered the ground big-cat fast up the footpath parallel to her.

People stepped out of his way on instinct and then turned back to look. He slid into a big, boxy blue utility with a huge backpack the size of a small elephant in the tray. Typical. He probably jogged fifty miles with it on his back. Tough-looking guy. Bad attitude. She'd met enough of them. People who made snap judgements of those they considered inferior.

In minutes she forgot Blue Ute, and began driving back in the countryside running along the river towards the approaching mountain. Along the valley base, she passed emerald paddocks with quaint houses and old sheds and agricultural oddities outside of her knowledge base of Sydney's North Shore.

Rows of trees, which she thought were avocado, patterned like plaid were splayed to the side, and the presence of white cows and green paddocks denied any evidence of water shortage. How could that be when ninety per cent of the state had floundered in drought?

Her car whooshed over a bridge and swayed along the snaking ribbon of bitumen leading the way up the mountain. Up. And up. And like the height above sea level, her mood lifted.

She zipped around tight corners with tree-studded sheer drops to the valley below and spotted, away in the distance to the right, a glimpse of the sea in the east. The higher she drove, the denser the emerald rainforest encroached on the road, a startling, lissom, layered landscape that soothed her soul and filled her with an awe and reverence she'd forgotten existed.

A truck crawled ahead up the steep incline and she slowed, oddly thankful it made her grind slowly past fern-decked forest giants and every little while, a tumbling waterfall to the side. Ah, she realised, hence the name, the Waterfall Way.

A rest stop ahead beckoned and she turned off to stretch her legs in a fertile fairyland she hadn't expected. Through soaring flooded gums, another waterfall was plummeting beside the road, down steep cliffs, sending liquid sounds and vapour swirling around her. The stream flowed under the bitumen to dive in ribbons down the valley, tumbling far below and skipping from boulder to boulder. Away to her left, the Tasman Sea blurred against the horizon.

The air chilled her lungs, fresh and crisp and redolent of leaf mulch, moss and native foliage. The rainforest echoed with the chirping and belling of birds, all another world away from the tiny rooms she'd hidden and huddled and hoarded her guilt in for the last three years.

Nell soaked in the splash of the water rushing past, watched leaves and twigs and bubbles fly over the edge to the next boulder below and wondered, if she stood here long enough could she, too, lose the burred-in filaments of debris that had gathered on her soul like cobbler's pegs to her socks?

Was it possible to allow pessimism to fall from her shoulders and plunge away? Could she be free? Could some of the shame and self-reproach strip from her soul and sail out over this precipice?

Could she let it?

A red sedan pulled in and a woman climbed out. The woman's big, pregnant belly came first like a slap in Nell's face. Nell winced and turned away, and all the old guilt and horror wrapped around her like cold, wet flypaper that engulfed her in clammy and caustic memories.

Back on the road, now that the slow truck had ground ahead out of sight, her mood struggled to even out. It helped that she still had to stop every few kilometres for the one-lane road to allow the passing of traffic because it forced her to see the green of the rainforest up close. It seemed in places the climbing pass had fallen away to the valley below and couldn't sustain two lanes all the way. And this was a major road? Who lived like this? Nell would! It was so different to the bustle and impatience of Sydney.

At the top of the mountain, her car popped out into the sunlight of the Dorrigo plateau, where more green paddocks stretched away. Everywhere she looked was so much greener than the dead, dry fields she'd spent the morning passing.

Down into the settlement of Dorrigo, she was getting close to her destination now and this would be her nearest retail centre, or so the map she'd studied had said.

Dorrigo. Derived from the Aboriginal word, *dondorrigo*, meaning 'stringy-bark', she'd read on Wiki. She liked the name.

A settlement steeped in the more recent past of timber getters and bullock drays with old-fashioned stores and a tall, lonely cenotaph looking out over the crossroads of town. The enormous Dorrigo Hotel stared at the War Memorial inscribed with names of local families who had given the ultimate sacrifice.

She would explore it all later.

Shop later.

Stop later.

Driving further west through winding hills and gullies, she could pick out steep farms that clung to the edges of drops and precipitous green cliffs. In between the green of the gullies, boulder-studded hills rolled away into the skyline. The land offered streams with tumbling stones, their water almost hidden in tufted grass, and she hoped there was something like this on her own little property.

Soon now, soon I'll find out, she thought as she passed into the final small village of Featherwood. A couple of dozen houses, a church and a hall. A couple of old commercial buildings, mostly derelict, and a post office, and then she was climbing out of the little valley again.

Nell hadn't slowed down in the village except for the speed limit. She was in no rush to be singled out as a newcomer yet. Villagers recognised people and gossiped, which was why she had decided to shop for her groceries in the larger town. She had no intention of stopping. Until, she came upon the hand-painted sign just over the hill outside the sparsely built-up area that declared, '*Last Pup for Sale*'.

The medium black dog lay tied up under a tree with a bowl of water, head on paws and nose on the ground. Unloved. Rejected. Like Nell.

She wasn't sure if the dog sign was a line to suck in a kind heart or a fact, but she stopped, got out and stared at the half-pup, half-dog.

The pup woofed at her. It was short-legged with intelligent brown eyes and a shiny nose and coat. It might not be loved, but it was well cared for. With its black fur all over to the tip of its wagging tail, it seemed older than the usual twelve weeks when they left the litter. It was maybe six months, and lost. Like Nell.

The wrinkled, crinkled older lady sitting in a chair under a tree at the top of the tree-lined drive inclined her head. Nell wondered how long she'd been sitting there today. It was hot. She had to be parched and it wasn't a busy road. Caved in like a deflated party balloon, the woman was dressed in maroon all the way from her bucket hat to her boots.

'He's good-natured, house-trained,' the woman said. 'But I've got four others and don't need another male.'

Nell stared at the dog, who lifted his head and thumped his black tail, once. Nell's heart cracked a smidge more.

'Good-natured,' the old lady said again. She stared and then blinked as if she'd had a petit mal fit. She looked vague for a minute before she refocused on Nell. Then she shifted in her chair and waved towards the village just out of sight. 'I need to get rid of the dog before my kid comes home from class. It upsets him to see them go.' She shook her head as if at soft-hearted kids.

She's eighty if she's a day, Nell thought, and she doubted this elderly lady had a child at school. She was lost in the past, perhaps? It wasn't Nell's business. She peered at the black bitzer pup. He rolled over onto his back and wagged his tail, begging for a scratch. Nell obliged and the little dog quivered with delight.

'I can't keep five dogs.' The older lady scrutinised Nell. 'The pup seems to like you. You look okay. Twenty dollars.'

Nell took out her purse and tried to look hopeful as she examined its contents – five credit cards, fifteen dollars and some shrapnel in change. She didn't think the old lady would take a card.

'Better leave you some coins,' Mrs Maroon, not her name but it fitted, said as she took the notes, and gave Nell an open bag of puppy food and instructions for 'half a cup three times a day'. 'Be kind,' she added. 'He's not a stupid dog. Buy more puppy food with the rest.' And with that she cackled – a snorting, delighted snicker – and waved Nell away. Clearly ecstatic to be rid of the extra mouth.

Crikey, Nell thought. She'd ended up in Wolf Creek. Or Deliverance. The woman had been a little scary.

Crazy place.

Except for the dog. He seemed sane.

A blue ute swooped down the road and pulled into a farm gate a few metres back towards town. A muscular bloke in a black T-shirt climbed out and opened the gate. He cast one grim look her way and then showed her his back.

That guy was odd, too, and she didn't need his bad vibes. 'Come on, dog, let's find our new home.'

Five winding kilometres of dense forest from the dog lady and roughly a hundred kilometres from either Coffs Harbour or Armidale, Nell waited to turn into her own gate.

A big old ute pulling a horse trailer had to pass first and the smiling people in the cab waved as if they knew her. By the time Nell lifted her hand to tentatively wave back, they were gone.

She stared after them. Someone else moving house? No one she knew, thank goodness. There'd been a big, black-haired bloke and a red-haired woman next to him. She shook her head. Their mistake.

Nell forgot them and pulled out the key from the real estate agent and slipped it into the big, bronze lock in the chain at the gate.

She'd arrived.

Her own land.

With her own dog.

Not Chanel Truman, but Nell Turner, a new surname, deed-poll changed, and a Christian name her parents had refused to consider shortening hers to.

The lock clicked, loud enough to echo in the soaring gums of stillness around her, and the heavy chain fell to the dry red soil with a soft *whoomph* and a puff of dust.

She was alone. With nobody watching. At least one more layer of the tension she'd hoarded for years slid off like a link from the chain at the gate.

She was about to enter into a new world that opened possibilities she hadn't dared dream about. It was such a change from tenement in Petersham to self-sufficient wilderness. *Welcome to the New England Mountains.*

No more hiding when she went outdoors in the city. From head down and sunglasses . . . to naked if she wanted. Why not? There was no one to see. For a second, she thought of the guy in the blue ute finding her naked. That would shock him! Where the heck had that come from? More oddness. She definitely wasn't going there.

This was about now. A new world. A new way of living.

She'd spent three years marking time. Staying out of sight. Saving because, heck, who wanted to buy anything except food if you were going to jail.

Waiting to be proven guilty. Waiting for a sentence that couldn't be any worse than the one she'd given herself. Permanent purgatory because she'd been weak, hadn't spoken up and someone had died because of her negligence.

All those endless days of existing above the hardware shop in Petersham, an odd inheritance from her father, doing the books for the shop she rented out below, a meagre wage to live on, and using the rental income to pay the bills. She had refused financial help from her widowed and bitter mother, who had denied access or support but offered money through a third party.

Her ex-private school friends had fled her disgrace. And the thought of calling her ex-midwifery colleagues made her cringe. If it hadn't been for the psychologist after the trial, she probably would have dwelt above that shop all her life. That could have been another fifty years or seventy-five if she lived to be a hundred.

She was too young to give up on life, the psychologist had said. And she was right. It was 'people' Nell had given up on.

The first thing she needed to do was make a sign to keep 'people' out. She drove into her new world and shut the gate.

The driveway proved to be deep, narrow wheel ruts that had her prissy car straddled with the breeze blowing under the chassis like Marilyn without underpants. It would be difficult in the dark, but she wouldn't be going anywhere at night.

The track took her upwards and was overhung by thick-trunked gums. Impenetrable scrub backed away to darkness from the edges, yet despite the drought that had sucked the soul from most of New South Wales, there was still some life in this tunnel of green. The real estate agent had said her fifty acres was at the very edge of the fertile zone. Any further west and the land was dry as a dead stick.

She rounded a bend in the driveway and the house yard welcomed her. It was tucked at the end of the gully with a wide, green paddock running downhill to a fence. High over the paddock nestled her rundown, two-roomed, home-built house with solar panels like two rows of shining eyes on the roof.

Nell stopped the car and allowed the thought of her home to marinate. *Nell's Farm*.

Forgotten emotions and flutters of anticipation she'd neglected – tendrils of dream roots – twitched like sprouting wild-flowers in her chest. Ownership, promise, direction for her life when she'd been without it for so long.

Four years ago, she'd thought graduating with her nursing and midwifery degrees had been the ultimate prize. Had seen the future as a glowing gold icon despite her parents' lack of enthusiasm for her chosen profession. Medicine would have been so much more sensible. Well, she wouldn't fall for that enthusiasm again. She would take it slow. Be wary. Tendrils and roots could get out of control. There was always disaster to bring you crashing down.

Her new dog bumped her hand with a wet nose. Gently, Nell pushed him back to the floor. Undeterred, her four-legged acquisition put his chin on her knee and gazed up. She would swear that dog had a grin on its muzzle. She frowned back at him. 'None of that.'

A wet, floppy, pink tongue licked her leg in a slurp of warmth and for the first time in years, Nell gulped out a short laugh. 'What? You want a name?'

The little dog acting ecstatic drew another unexpected laugh. His muzzle stretched, teeth showed in a snicker and he looked for all the world like a dog smiling in a cartoon. His tail thumped against the passenger door.

'You're a grinner. Maybe Grindy? Not Grinch, that's for sure. How about Grin? Rhymes with Finn and I have a friend with a dog named Finn.' Her mood dipped. 'Had a friend.' She pushed the negative thought away. She had to make this work. 'Grin it is, because that's your job. One of us has to. Let's go in, Grin.'

Two steps up and the front verandah creaked as she trod the simple wooden boards to the entrance. The screen door squeaked like nails tearing from wood and a kookaburra laughed, making her jump. She turned around but couldn't see the bird. In the sudden silence, it mocked her again.

She breathed deeply. Soon she'd start a list. *Fix the squeak with a spray. Laugh back at the bird.*

The front door proved solid as she pushed it and her nose wrinkled as dormant-for-months air shifted and exhaled over her face. A tinge of Eau De Rodent, though more mice than rats. She'd met enough dead rats in the terrace house in Petersham to know that aroma. Nose first, the house smelled dark and musty, and yet, as she stepped in more fully through the doorway, not unfriendly.

It was a good start. From the photos she'd seen, there was this two-bedroom shack with front and back verandah, the separate carport outside, and a four-walled, lockable toolshed, apparently with tools. The kitchen she stepped straight into had probably been outfitted with a second-hand kitchen module because it dated to the seventies and the house wasn't that old. But she liked the look. Red-speckled benchtops and shiny painted cupboard doors with curved handles. Old-fashioned again. It was cleanish, barring gifts left from hopefully departed mice, and apart from the smell, it felt welcoming.

She eyed the black puppy beside her. 'What do you think, Grin?'

The dog returned her regard, head tilted.

'I agree. We should open the windows.'

By the time she'd opened the windows and dragged the surprisingly springy mattress outside into the sun to the accompaniment of wailing shrieks from the wrought-iron bed – more oil needed – the house had begun to smell less infested.

The second bedroom sat empty, and the small lounge/dining had plain wooden furniture that she could wipe and add cushions to when she had some. The floor was unvarnished click-lock boards, but maybe she could stain or use a shiny sealer to toughen it into a hard shine. For the moment, she'd mop it and see.

The laundry had a concrete floor and held a small full-height pushbutton pantry cupboard. She opened it gingerly – who knew what had died in there – but to her surprise, inside lay such a dazzling array of cleaning products, brooms and brushes, sprays and wipes, that she laughed. Her mother's housekeeper would have been proud of it.

That made her blink. She hadn't thought of her matriarch with any amusement for a very long time. The housekeepers at her parents' home had been nice, though they'd never stayed long enough to become friends.

She left the laundry a little faster than she went in and headed straight for the sink to wash her hands, as if to rinse the thoughts of her always-disappointed-in-this-adopted-child mother away. The psychologist would have something to say about the need to cleanse.

She turned the tap, half expecting nothing to happen, but after the first three seconds of brown rust, it ran clear and freezing. *Note to self – check the level of drinking water in the tank so I know what I have.*

She struggled with the back door but eventually dragged it open – at some stage it must've been wet and jammed – and found the back of the house tucked into the hill. She wouldn't get a lot of sunlight on that rear verandah. Wood sat stacked to one side with a rusting axe asleep beside the pile.

Obviously, 'walk-in, walk-out' meant just that. It was as if the owners had been beamed up by Scotty to the *Voyager*. The real estate agent had said something about illness and heading off unencumbered.

Well, one person's junk is another person's treasure, Nell thought, and she'd take it all. And say thanks. Maybe trim it down, sell a few things, though that would be hard without talking to people to sell to.

But she'd think about that later. For the moment, she needed a fire in the kitchen stove for hot water and to work out the solar batteries before dark. She reached out and laid her hand against the doorframe. 'You're lovely. We'll do well together, house.'

Chapter Three

Gracie

Oh dear, the Farmer's Friend doesn't look like a friend indeed, Gracie thought. *More like a friend in dire, desperate need.*

Neglect hung in peeling paint strips off the wooden boards of the actual shop, though the shed was crusted dust on galvanised tin and when washed could possibly be shiny after a major clean.

So, this is what they'd bought. Their new life. A bunch of sheds behind piles of tangled wire and posts and wood heaps and rubbish. A sagging fence and rutted drive that went between the sheds in a big U, with the feed shed roof in the middle. She could see how a car could be parked in the middle and packed with goods out of the rain. If it ever rained.

The shop part leaned to the side of the big shed, though she couldn't see in through the dusty window at the front to anything inside, but there was a skinny, overgrown yard to the left. Gracie's eyes searched, her stomach tight and not from the baby, straining for the house behind the shop. The house that lay frustratingly tucked behind Jed's new adventure.

'Shift down a bit, Jed, so I can see the house.'

Obligingly, Jed drove along the two ruts away from the shop and towards the house and stopped again. He stared at the back of the store.

Gracie craned her neck. There it was. The grey residence on short stilts crouched in the middle of a large paddock with bracken that ran down to the creek behind it. It was a pretty spot if it didn't flood too high. But dangerous for kids if that was the creek back there, so they'd have to fence it off.

As a home it appeared bigger than she expected, more run-down than she'd hoped, narrow but long, going backwards, and . . . somehow sad. Unloved. She should have asked more about the house, she realised.

She remembered words from a real estate advertisement that had once made her laugh – although it wasn't funny when they were talking about her house – *suit a handyman*. Well, thank goodness Jed was a handyman. And she could learn.

Someone had mowed the front tobacco bush and thistles with a tractor and slasher, because the tractor was still parked there at the bottom of the steps. But now there was a short-cut drive from front cattle grid to the front door through the waist-high bush and lantana, and a fine growth of whisky grass.

A tunnel of weeds through which she could see the steps rose to a metre above the ground. The whole front paddock needed slashing. She shuddered at the snakes that no doubt would be very settled in their peaceful overgrowth.

The rusty bull-nosed verandah circled the house, and one roof corner sagged as if sometime in the far-off past, the drunken glory of rain had made it tipsy. Gracie didn't think the house had ever been painted; the walls stood naked in the spotted khaki-silver of old wood with grey posts holding up the elderly roof. The tin roof glowed oxidised red.

Three big brick-coloured chimney pots poked out of the roof, one on each side at the front and one further back, and she wondered for the first time if there was a modern stove – or if she'd be cooking on an old fuel heater.

Jed's eyes were still avidly roaming the shop. She could imagine his lack of interest in the house. Could imagine his nod as he said, 'Four-bedroom house, great!' Still thinking, *rural store, my produce store*, as he'd gone through the dwelling.

At least she had six weeks before their baby was due. Six weeks to make a home, and if she had to use some of her last-hoarded emergency funds to do it, she would.

'Is the house liveable, Jed?'

He tore his eyes from the shop yard. 'Hasn't been lived in for a while.' He finally noted the dismay on Gracie's face. 'Apart from the verandah roof, it doesn't leak,' he said, 'and the plumbing is fine though noisy. We have rainwater tanks and a fuel stove for hot water.' He brightened more. 'So, we're self-sufficient if the power goes off.'

Gracie's stomach dropped. Hot water via a stove. That meant an all-year-round woodfire. She'd noticed on the yearly weather chart that Featherwood rode the extremes of hot and cold. It wouldn't be fun with a fire in the kitchen in summer. And summer was around the corner.

His big hand stretched across and touched hers. 'That Molly schoolteacher, she said she'd come over before we arrive and sweep through the house. Said she'd get a couple of women to go through it with her and get rid of the cobwebs and dirt.'

He hadn't told her that before. Hadn't stopped talking about the shop. Gracie sighed with relief. Molly was probably the same person who'd arranged to drive the slasher and tractor up to the front door. 'Are we going there first?'

Jed was confused. 'Going where?'

'To the house.'

Jed frowned. 'Is that what you want?'

'Spare me,' she murmured. 'Yes. I think so. Maybe you could look around the store after we've got our bed set up and I can think about making something for dinner.'

'Righto.' Jed turned the ignition back on and waved at the piles of wire and wood as he drove past. 'I'll be back,' he said, like a famous acting hero, to the empty building.

The utility and trailer bounced and clattered over the cattle grid and they followed the drive to the bottom of the house steps. Gracie sat and stared, studying her new home. It was even more neglected up close, but with luck, it would be surprisingly solid.

Jed walked around and opened her door. The truck was tall and it was becoming more awkward to climb down as her belly grew. Jed gave her his strong fingers to help her out and they walked up the steps together holding hands.

Their gazes met and Jed smiled. A boyish, woo-hoo, delighted smile. Gracie's heart melted and he leaned down and kissed her, his beautiful lips warm and gentle on hers. She closed her eyes and sighed. They'd be fine.

Jed leaned forward and turned the handle of the door until it swung open on the hallway, then he grinned at Gracie. Reaching down, he swept her into his arms as if she were a red poppy and not more than seven months pregnant. She pushed the door with her feet as he angled in through the narrow entry.

'If you won't let me marry you, at least I can carry you over the threshold.'

She slid her arms around his strong neck. 'You big romantic, you.'

They smiled at each other.

He put her down gently on the other side and stood next to her in the central hallway that ran from front to back through the middle of the house, his arm warm about her waist.

Molly the schoolteacher had done well. She and her friends had swept and washed the wide wooden boards of the floor, so they were clean, though dull, and there were no visible cobwebs in the three-metre ceilings. The walls were a dirty coffee colour with age spots and the occasional peeling corner of old, suspect paint.

Jed narrowed his eyes at the flakes. 'I'll paint it first thing to seal it – in case there's any lead. I saw tins of cream water base in the corner of the store, old but in good condition. We can sort colours later once it has a sealing coat.'

Yep. Her handyman. 'I'd like that. Thank you.'

Even the windows had been given a wipe-over and sunlight streamed in through the green-and-red panels of stained glass that graced the bottoms of the wooden frames. The windows opened out sideways, not up, and more coloured panes glimmered at the front and back door. The reflected light highlighted dust motes and shifting circles of pink and green on the wide slats of the wooden floors. It was very pretty, and welcoming.

Jed took her hand again as they walked a few echoing steps down the central hallway, the tap of their feet pattering around the walls of the empty house like tiny voices. Or future children's footsteps.

'Nice running boards. Wide.' She inspected the boards between the floor and wall, where Jed was pointing.

They'd paint up well, Gracie thought. 'The best.'

The long wooden boards near the floor were at least a stretched-hand's-breadth wide and again more boards were head high as a picture rail. The ceiling looked like pressed tin though a couple of places needed reattaching. The light fittings and switches were old and crumbly black circles, and would need rewiring at some stage; hopefully it could wait. Though the house echoed with barren-ness, it murmured a history she wanted to discover with a sudden burning need.

The big kitchen lay first on the left and held the fuel stove, which, although it seemed clean and functioning, would be a lot of darn work. So would the vintage porcelain sink with three ancient taps, and the long wooden bench with turned legs and a single drawer. Gracie gave an inward sigh. Against the inner wall, a smaller wooden table with the same turned legs could possibly be a breakfast nook. An old-fashioned dresser was the only cupboard for kitchenware.

A tin bucket in the corner held a poker and a small fireplace shovel.

'I'll get that going as soon as we've had a walk through. You can have a hot shower, later.'

A treat, or a consolation, she wasn't sure which his eyes offered.

They stepped across to the sink window. The glass panes of the four wooden, push-out windows flooded the place with after-noon light and she could see Jed's store up the drive, and past that, the town.

The house sat well back from the road and probably any road noise. Back here, Jed could turn up the country music he loved without annoying anyone – except Gracie. Small mercies.

A door at the side of the kitchen led out onto the verandah that went all the way around the house, and she guessed there'd be a door in every room going to the outside. A security disaster in the city but not so much in the country with neighbours looking out for other neighbours.

They left the kitchen and poked their heads into the next room on the left, a concrete-floored laundry with one big stone sink, another door leading out onto the verandah. Next was a bedroom – no built-ins – then a bathroom with an original claw-foot bath and old taps dripping rust, plus the same-style vintage porcelain sink surrounded by bottle-green tiles. Nice tiles.

The bathroom floor was black-and-white squares of linoleum like the small separate toilet next door. So old, but clean from the life-saving lovely ladies. Gracie knew she had been very, very fortunate in Molly and her friends.

The next room was the master bedroom and spread twice the size of the other bedrooms with the red-and-green glass panels at the bottom of the windows facing out towards the creek. Because of the corner position, the room had one wall of windows and one with double doors to the verandah.

In her mind, Gracie could see their big wooden bed, which Jed had made, and the bargain white cane cradle sitting in the dimmest corner with their future baby sleeping.

On the other side of the hall were two more bedrooms, which were fine for kids or guests. The family room came second last, a large space twice the width of the smaller bedrooms with an archway leading through to the dining room with its own grate and fireplace opposite the kitchen. From the dining room, they looked out over the front of the house towards the town and again, the store.

The house was much bigger than she'd expected, with a lot of potential charm and quite a bit of maintenance work to keep it dust and spider free. The big family room and dining room each sported an ornate tiled fireplace in greens and reds and a big black grate which had been cleaned. .

She needed to find Molly and say thank you. Maybe throw herself on her neck and kiss her. Jed had done well there. 'It's so clean.'

'Lucky. Or I'd be in trouble.'

She grinned at him. 'Thank you for thinking of that, Jed.'

'Molly thought of it. Right after I said we were having a baby. I want you to love it. It's old, but I can see a family here, Gracie. Parties. Barbecues.' He raised his brows and said softly, 'A wedding in the garden?'

He never gave up. 'Sure,' she said. 'If someone wants to get married here, I'd have no problem with that.'

'Excellent. That would be me.'

'Jed,' she warned. She knew he wanted a ring on her finger before the baby was born, but it simply wasn't going to happen. He even had the papers ready because she'd said, 'maybe one day', and he'd wanted them set to go.

He held up his hands. 'What do you think?' Jed watched Gracie's face.

'The house? It's great, with parts that make my heart leap with joy.' She squeezed his hand. *But then there's the bathroom with the black rust stains in the old taps*, she added silently, *and the crumbling black-seated toilet that looks like it's been there since the early 1900s and might just crack if someone big like Jed sits on it.*

She walked across to the kitchen sink and turned on the tank-water tap. The pipes in the roof above their heads went *clunk-clunk-clunk* as they ran, but the water ran clean not brown, and she heard the pump outside, *tap-tap-tap-tap*, as it pumped water through to the house. The town-water tap worked as well.

'It has loads of potential, Jed.' She leaned up and kissed him. 'I love it.' And she did. She could see herself here, with their baby, with paddock views from every window and looking out front towards the store, where Jed would be in the day. She blew out her concerns and her body felt as if it smiled from the soles of her feet to her eyes. Home.

Jed walked back down the central hallway and opened the door out onto the verandah at the back and she glanced from the front door right through to the other end of the house. 'Imagine the breeze blowing through here,' he said. There was no such breeze today. Just hot, still air.

She followed him down the central hallway again and stepped out to the back part of the verandah, where they stood holding hands. They gazed companionably over the silver rails, the scent of jasmine coming from somewhere she'd discover later, and the melody of a family of butcher birds calling to each other in harmonious voices.

Behind the house, past the scrubby overgrowth, right at the end of their backyard and down a bank, the creek rested like a sleeping beauty. Shallow and slow-moving, it had balls of tumbled creek rock poking out of the thin water, one big weeping willow to the left and a barrel-trunked camphor laurel to the right. Other trees must've been cleared in front of the view from the house because Gracie could see directly across to the rising bank on the other side. 'I can imagine sitting out here on a rocking chair, or a swing seat, with you and the baby.'

Jed's face softened and he nodded. He walked to the left edge of the verandah and glanced longingly back at the shop.

'Not yet.' She waggled her fingers at him. 'Let's get the stuff inside.'

Jed laughed. 'I'll bring it in. You tell me where you want it.'

Chapter Four

Nell

One week after moving in, Nell Turner owned nine skinny cows and a fat Brahman in calf called Moo. She had bought them dirt cheap from the internet buy-swap-sell site and they had even come with a coop of chickens.

The farmer, five kilometres further west in the arid zone so different to the watered valley Nell's farmlet clung to, dropped them in a trailer as he left the land forever. She'd bank-transferred the cost and barely had to speak to him. He hadn't been chatty anyway, crushed by drought and deficient funds, desperate to leave the loss of his livelihood.

Prior to her herd's arrival, Nell had tightened up the saggy fences after watching a how-to on YouTube, grateful to the previous owners, Mr and Mrs Walk-in-walkouters, for the right equipment.

Now she was thrilled – yes, such a strong emotion – to look out of her kitchen window and see her little herd amble around the paddock. Because of the spring, there was still some running water and her herd being small meant enough feed for all so far.

Another week later, bovine coats had picked up a hint of shine and the bones on their pointy backs became less prominent. The online library shared cattle-raising and animal husbandry advice. Learning had never been a problem and Nell could study until her cows came home, so to speak. When the internet worked.

Of course, her dog, Grin, liked to chase them, and at first, she'd appreciated the fact that she didn't have neighbours to hear her yell and scream for him to come back. Eventually, she realised she needed to walk down and physically attract his attention by clapping her hands. He was having far too much fun to stop and couldn't possibly hear her in all the excitement.

If she walked down, he would see her, pause and smile at her. Almost a 'Did you want me?' look on his face and she'd shake her head and wave her arm and he'd come. The cows would stop running and look back in disgust.

She'd found lemon, lime and lemonade trees, mango, and most exciting at the back, six macadamia trees in the orchard. Macadamias were such impossible nuts. They hid in the grass looking shiny when they split – enticing beneath the thick shell except she couldn't open the prize until she found a hammer and a brick and smashed them to pieces. A messy but satisfying endeavour.

There were also stone fruit trees, but the crop had larvae and she would have to look up how to make a batch of something non-toxic to hang from the tree to deter fruit flies next year. Next year. It seemed so weird to be thinking about the future with her little farm and Grin and her cows.

She'd walked the fence lines of the property and even found a thin, sparkly waterfall that fell into her tiny cold creek at the back behind the house. The water disappeared into the ground and popped out of the spring hole down the gully, and although there wasn't much water running with the drought, at least it was there. A little piece of waterfall magic and the plants around the waterfall hung lime-green and turquoise with birds-nest ferns and grass trees.

Sadly, she had the feeling the black-barked green-spiked trees might be dying as the water evaporated from the air, and even the ground in the dense foliage of the hill had begun to dry out.

Late October mornings still made her cheeks cold, even though it wasn't as chilly now as when she'd first come. The air in the mountains on the plateau hung crisp and cold around sunrise and sunset, despite the fact that it was only a few weeks away from the start of summer.

Once the sun rose it turned hot and dry and she tried to stay in the shade when she worked on the veggie garden that she hoped would keep her mostly self-sufficient.

Utopian thoughts of peaceful solitude – forever.

Chapter Five

Mavis

Mavis Maloney, two days after her eightieth birthday, strode down the road wearing her favourite maroon trouser suit and maroon western boots with tassels. Mavis wore maroon like that sect of people who always wore orange – though Mavis was Catholic. She went to the church in Featherwood once a month when the priest came. The boy wouldn't come with her.

Her floppy bucket hat glowed maroon. She searched out the colour in footwear, jeans, tops and jackets. Even undies. She'd been doing it for so long that in the nearest town with a clothes store, Dorrigo, and even further the other way in Armidale, they put maroon garments in her size away for her, and she picked them up when she drove through.

Not that she knew how long she'd be driving these days with that medical review every year to say she was smart enough to drive. It was as if she'd become too old to have marbles. Apparently.

Apparently was another thing she liked. Something about the word appealed to her. Things weren't always real and didn't always make sense, but there was a chance they could be right. The way her drug-addicted granddaughter couldn't look after her eleven-year-old son and Mavis had taken him in after his mum had stayed with her briefly to detox.

When said granddaughter had mentioned she was going back to the city and the scared look had returned to the boy's eyes, Mavis had said he could stay if he wanted to, to live with her and the dogs. Ride his bike to school until next year, when he'd have to catch the bus into Dorrigo High School. He'd said yes so fast his mother had been offended. So it looked like Archie was with her for good. Apparently.

Today they had a new store open in their little town. Or an old store opening anew. That was an occasion for a place with only a pub, a post office and a once-a-month church. Everyone was excited about the Farmer's Friend's grand opening two weeks after the new folk had arrived, and Mavis would take herself in for a look-see. Her ancient, polished walking stick that her dad had tramped these hills with tapped on the road. Not that she needed a stick, but she liked it. She liked waving it.

She could have driven, but it was less than two kilometres from her farmhouse to the other end of town and she'd walked or ridden her horse there all her life. Cars were for driving to Dorrigo or Armidale. She hadn't been to Coffs Harbour for years. There were too many folk and fast cars on the ocean side of the mountain for her liking.

It was warm this morning. There was an extra bite to the sun, making her lips feel dry. She'd been out in the paddock early checking the cattle. She could hear her great-grandson scuffing rocks behind her, dragging his feet, unhappy to leave his computer games behind and go out into the daylight when it was a Saturday. Scandalised they were going to walk to town.

Young ones these days baffled her. What could he find to amuse himself staring at a computer? His mother had left him a dingle, or dongle, whatever that was, which lasted for a year. Internet waves, or something. The boy played games online. She didn't understand it.

Halfway through the village, the aroma of cooking onions glided towards her like a willie wagtail skimming up and over a fence, food fragrances sliding in and tickling her nose. She paused, turned back to Archie and furrowed her brow at him. 'Smells like sausage sandwiches.'

Archie's feet quickened and he pulled up next to her with a short jogging spurt of speed. 'Reckon we'll get one?' he asked.

'With a bit of luck they'll be free.' They grinned at each other. Then she stopped and frowned. Tried to remember where they were going and why. She'd been off somewhere. With the boy.

'We're going to the produce store, Gran,' Archie reminded her. 'They've got sausage sandwiches.'

Seems like a good idea, Mavis thought. 'Reckon we'll have to pay for them?'

Archie kicked a rock on the road and it skipped into the culvert beside them. 'Hope not.'

'Nice day,' she said, hoping for a smile from the boy. He looked annoyed for some reason. He huffed out a sigh and gave her a small twitch of his mouth. *Nearly a smile*, Mavis thought with relief. Good kid.

'It's a nice day, Gran.'

They turned into the driveway of the produce store. 'A crowd,' she said to Archie.

Three people was a crowd in Featherwood, all standing around a big, black-haired bloke wielding an egg flip and a pair of long tongs.

'Looks like someone's having a baby,' she murmured. A girl with a pregnant belly under a tent dress stood beside the black-haired bloke. She was holding a piece of bread in a serviette in her palm, ready to cradle the next sausage. The tomato sauce hung poised in the other hand.

Mid-height, wild red hair tied back in a ponytail but escaping everywhere, thin arms and legs and body except for the belly, fine features, big eyes, the young woman had one of those faces that shared sunshine. A glad-to-see-you face. Mavis liked those people. They made you feel warm. There weren't enough of them around.

She saw another smiling face. 'Dolly's here,' she said to Archie.

'Molly, Gran.'

She'd known it rhymed with lolly. Molly, then, she could never remember their names, but Molly was nice people. That's right. Molly Dolly. She'd taken one of the pups.

She heard the Molly bird call out, 'Hello there, you two. Here's Mavis and Archie.'

Archie waved at them and Mavis shuffled up closer while the aroma of barbecue soaked the air and made her mouth wet with anticipation. Lordy, how long had it been since she'd cooked meat? She really should buy more meat for the boy; he needed it to grow.

She glanced down at him, and blinked. Apparently, he was growing. She tilted her head. He was up to her eyebrows now and she was pretty darn sure he'd been short of that when he arrived.

Eyes were on her. Mavis realised she'd faded out again.

Molly said, 'This is Jed and Gracie, Mavis. They moved into the big house down the back as well.'

'Nice spot.' Mavis inclined her head as if she could see past the shop to the house behind. 'Last time I was there was maybe twenty years ago. We were picking corn.' She smiled at the friendly faced girl. 'Welcome to Featherwood. Good to see the old shop open again and a new family move in.' Her hand waved. 'This is my great-grandson, Archie.'

The girl did look delighted. 'Hello, Mavis and Archie. Lovely to meet you. I'm Gracie.'

Lucky she'd said that 'cause Mavis had already forgotten her name. She wanted to remember because she liked her on sight. She searched for a mental rhyme to help. Gracie-nice-facie? Mavis blinked as if stamping her brain. Got it.

The girl waved the slice of bread at them. 'Would you and Archie like a sausage sandwich? To celebrate our opening.'

'I wouldn't say no.' Mavis tried to look surprised. 'I'll have mine with onion, thanks, and Archie'll have his with sauce, instead.'

They all stood there in the sun on the swept pavement, munching sausage sandwiches, marvelling at the lack of rubbish and old wire, peering into the big, clean shed with stacked feed and fertiliser, the scent of hay mixed with cooked onion and tasty sausage on her tongue. Archie looked happy, with sauce dribbling down the front of his shirt and his fingers covered in red stripes of escaping goo.

Mavis chuckled and shook her head. Gotta love these young'uns. They could make a mess just by looking at it.

'Where'd you come from?' Mavis asked the question that no doubt everyone else had already asked.

'Queensland. Roma.'

Drought was bad up there. She read the *Land* newspaper every week. She nodded sagely. 'Even drier than here. People walking off the land.' She thought about that. She wasn't going anywhere.

'Gracie is a nurse and midwife,' Molly Dolly said.

That caught Mavis's attention. 'I could've asked you about Archie's splinter last week. Had such trouble getting it out. But it's too late now. It's good to know for next time. We used to have a St John's man here – he did all the first aid.' She smiled at the newcomer.

'I'm more of a midwife but happy to help with little things if I can, Mavis. Any time.'

When she finished her sandwich, Mavis wiped her hands on the serviette and dropped it in the big empty drum they had for a bin. She nodded at the smiling girl. 'I might just go and have a wander around in your new store. I need a new dog collar and keep forgetting to buy one in town.'

Gracie-nice-facie gifted her that beautiful smile. 'That's exactly what we want you to say.'

Mavis just nodded, but she was thinking, *Goodness me, the town is looking up if we have people like this moving in.*

Chapter Six

Gracie

Gracie watched the older lady move away. She was fast-moving for someone who had to be in her late seventies or early eighties. She'd better brush up on her first-aid skills, she realised. Mavis's great-grandson looked as though he didn't know if he wanted to follow or stay. 'Want another sandwich, Archie?' She waved the bottle of sauce. 'Seems a shame not to have two sausages.'

Round eyes switched on, porch-light bright, as he nodded. Gracie smiled at him. She reached for another slice of napkin-wrapped bread and Jed put a snag on it for her.

'How's your gran keeping, Archie?' The lad jumped at Molly's question, his flip-over blond fringe falling into his eyes as he began to edge nervously away. Even before Gracie could give him his serviette of goodies.

Gracie stilled and watched.

'She's good,' Archie mumbled and slid his gangling body further left.

'She remembering to give you dinner?'

'Sure.'

'If she gets sick, or you need another adult's help, I'm across the road, not far. You can knock on my door any time.' Molly spoke quietly and there was something in her tone that kept Gracie's attention. 'If I'm not there, my brother is. Liam. You met him?'

'Seen him. Thanks.' The kid reached back to accept the sandwich. 'And thanks.' Then he took off like someone was chasing him with a stick. He sat with his shoulders turned away from them outside the shop, directly opposite the door that his great-grandmother had gone in, studiously avoiding any glance back towards the barbecue.

Gracie recognised Molly's kindness, had seen it firsthand the night they'd arrived, with Molly at their door with a big dish of pasta and chicken right after an exhausted Gracie had thought about dinner. 'Are you worried about him, Molly?'

Molly compressed her lips. She was a small woman, just over forty and one of those indefatigable helpers who seemed to lend a hand everywhere. You could see her personality in the bouncy dark curls and her wide blue eyes showing her default optimism, and her vibrancy in the bright, homemade macramé earrings she loved to wear.

Liam, her younger brother, seemed her opposite. Tall, whipcord strong, recently ex-army, he looked as if he could run all day. He was mostly silent with hard eyes, as if he'd seen things. A bloke's bloke who liked hard work. And he liked Jed. He and Jed were an odd couple. He'd arrived in town the same day they did but his family were here so he wasn't really new.

Molly watched Mavis's great-grandson ease away. 'He's a good kid. I think Mavis is getting more forgetful. If the child wasn't there she'd probably be in a bigger mess. But then if Mavis wasn't there the boy would be living in some dive in Kings Cross with his mother doing ice. It all works in a strange way. But . . .' Molly visibly shook off the worry. 'There's a time limit on it. As a teacher at the school, I hear things and I like to check in on the kids, that's all.'

Gracie had learnt Molly's husband had died in a tractor accident two years ago. Childless, she had her mother in Armidale and her only brother staying with her to heal emotionally from his time in active service. She kept commercial bees and sold the hives to agricultural companies and farmers in her spare time. When she wasn't helping others. Molly cared about people.

Gracie's gaze rested for another few seconds on the young boy as he sat on the brick fence outside the shop, swinging his thin, freckled legs as he ate, looking over to Jed's pile of shiny farm gates and fencing wire. She'd keep an eye out, too, for Archie's unexpected needs.

'Another car's turning in.' Jed's voice held satisfaction and Gracie turned to look. Her man was excited. His eyes wide, his smile big. Yes. The store doors stood open and six people had been through in the first hour.

She could see another family walking down the road towards them, so there'd be more. She waved her hand at the folk. 'Better put on more sausages.' It was still early.

The Farmer's Friend shone with two weeks of polish and repositioning of old stock to clear and the new stock had arrived over the last three days in big Pantech trucks. Jed had been busy on the forklift after he'd serviced it and fixed the brakes. The outside tin of the big shed had been pressure-sprayed and the old wooden shop walls painted inside and out with water-based white like inside her house. He'd been hitting sixteen-hour days to get it done.

The stock they carried seemed a constant kaleidoscope of things Gracie had never known existed. And it kept arriving. She couldn't imagine the end-of-month bills for the orders. Fly-repellent paper, yellow lotion, pony balm, puppy and kitten shampoo, organic dehorning paste. Who knew?

Gracie had requested a kit for medical emergencies that they'd stashed under the office desk. It seemed that was serendipitous with Mavis's comment about first aid. She also had a resus bag and oxygen face masks in different sizes for serious resuscitation in a green sealed case, plus a small portable defibrillator, yellow, like those you saw in public buildings that hung on the wall. As well as a set of dressings and antiseptics and such for the minor stuff.

Jed had completed his first-aid certificate when he'd joined the Roma Rural Fire Service and Gracie had her nurse's training and midwifery. If they had the skills, then the least they could do was be able to provide help if it was needed. They were a fair way out of town and the nearest ambulance station was a good three-quarters of an hour away. But that was for another time. Today was store-opening day.

The big sheds stood half full of bags of different animal feed and fertilisers, which had arrived this morning, two days late, and all on credit. As well as supplemental feeds for horses and dairy, they had layer pellets for hens, working dog mix and organic ferti-liser pellets.

Jed had panicked that the big twenty-five-kilo bags of feed wouldn't arrive on time, so he had ordered more from some-where else, and then both orders had arrived simultaneously. He'd worked like crazy to forklift it all away in the tall shed before he started the barbecue.

Gracie's hands were raw and blistered from scrubbing shelves and windows and walls, but the house and store looked good. Jed and Liam had painted every house wall and done running repairs on the saggy bits in both places.

All their meagre belongings and furniture were in and unpacked, and the house had shifted to a half-furnished home with warmth and character. Gracie was happy with it unfinished, but Jed was scouring the garage-sale lists relentlessly.

They still had four weeks till the baby was due. In the shop, Jed had been working non-stop shifting the big banks of stock boxes while Gracie had been stacking the shelves and inputting the inventory in the old computer. After school, Molly had helped her with rearranging and bookkeeping skills. Her back ached, but that wasn't surprising. She'd bet Molly's back ached too.

Gracie wondered again what she would have done without the little dynamo she counted as her new friend. Despite the fact that Molly was ten years older than Gracie's thirty, she'd never lived anywhere but Featherwood, and both women had in common an inbuilt kindness towards others.

'Hello, welcome,' Molly called out to the newcomers. 'Come and meet Gracie and Jed.'

By the following Saturday, the gradual expansion of customers had transformed into busy most of the time. Jed was right. They were meant to be here. Gracie couldn't believe the ease with which her rugged outdoor man had morphed into the produce proprietor.

He admitted to a struggle with the till and the orders, but Gracie persevered, making him practise in the use of the 'search' button to find prices, adding goods to the electronic inventory and using the electronic payment system for the accounts. He scratched his head often and sighed.

Gracie could do it so much more quickly, but she made him persist because he'd have to manage on his own when the baby came. And he needed to know how to work the float at the end of the day and how to bank money and keep track of everything. Thank goodness they could deposit the day's takings in the post office across the road and didn't have to run into town and the bank.

This morning, standing out the front of the store during a quiet moment, she wiped the small cast-iron table Jed had found at the tip with its three heavy chairs. He'd pressure-sprayed the filigree and positioned the setting outside on the forecourt of the store.

She sat to ease her legs while Jed loaded another trailer with hay. The drought effects for the farmers worsened every day now and they could see it in the faces and worried eyes around them. Jed would need to buy more hay, but feed stock was becoming harder to source. They might even have to look at rationing bales to make it last for everyone to share. Jed knew a bloke who knew a bloke in Adelaide and one more shipment had been secured.

Gracie would really have loved to rest her ankles up on one of the other chairs because her legs had begun to ache, but she didn't like to look lazy at work. The table, meant for older patrons to rest or chinwag, often filled with up-valley farmers who needed to offload their worry, or bachelors with their dogs who could buy their feed off Jed instead of going into Dorrigo or Armidale. All were keen to enjoy a conversation with the produce bloke who seemed to understand the darkness of drought and yet had a smile to share.

Jed's bluntness meant they knew he'd walk away, just up and leave, if another customer came. Customers seemed to get it and would chat among themselves when left to their own devices. Gracie, however, found it harder to break into a monologue and make her excuses.

Right now, she couldn't see her man and his current customer but could hear the conversation in the drive-through where Jed worked. Charlie from up the dry end of the valley had returned for more hay. She could hear it thumping into the back of Charlie's truck. *Thwat, thwat, thwat* as each bale landed.

'Dam's dry. Had to pull two heifers out with the tractor.' She heard Charlie's voice and then silence. 'Don't know if they'll be much good.'

'The hay will help,' was Jed's quiet reply.

'Yeah, but do you waste it on them when they might not make it? Or give it to the others so they got a better chance?'

'It's a point.'

Another long, aching silence except for the *thwat, thwat* of the hay.

'How's the missus going?' Jed asked.

'Doesn't say much. Never has.'

Gracie smiled to herself as she heard that. Just last week, she'd been bailed up by a long monologue from Charlie. More than an hour. His wife, Ruby, a tall, angular lady who looked as if she'd ridden horses all her life, could hold a spirited conversation, but didn't get a word in if Charlie held court. Still, even Charlie sounded different this week.

Jed had called him Chatter Charlie. He'd met him at the pub that first time he came to see the shop. Charlie had been the fount of knowledge Jed had soaked in. Today, words were coming out in short, sad beats unless Jed nudged him. 'Haven't seen you since last week.'

Charlie said, 'Gotta save the petrol money for feed. You blokes are the first we've seen.' He lowered his voice. 'Your missus is getting ready to pop.'

Gracie wasn't his missus. Jed would hate hearing that. She could almost feel his wince. But Jed wasn't thinking so much about his problems as Charlie's.

'Same up there for everyone?' The change of subject suited both of them.

'Yup. Nobody's going out. We spend our lives feeding or shifting cattle. There's no money to drive to town let alone buy anything. One day stretches into the next with nothing in between. It's all we can do until the drought breaks.'

Jed nodded sagely. 'How many families you got up there on that arm of the creek?'

'Three families left on old holdings. Two single blokes from the big smoke left in the last month. Sold up what they could and walked off. Families on two other properties, and the new, young, snooty one running her place right at the back. No idea how they're all managing.'

Gracie's ears pricked up. New, young, snooty one?

'Seen any of them?'

'Nope. Occasionally, I'll see a car go past.'

There was silence again except for the sound of hay landing in the back of the truck.

'In Roma . . .' Jed paused to catch his breath and Gracie could tell by his voice that there'd been a lot of hay going into that truck.

'The rotary club were doing the occasional barbecue for farmers to get a few families together in the smaller outlying communities. We could do that. Gracie and I could supply the meat. I could bring my gas barbecue up and toss a few snags on next Sunday if you think people would like to have a get-together. No cost. Just a chance to get out without having to drive too far?'

'Well . . . It's a total fire ban, but Rural Fire Blue's up there. I've got the tennis court shed and table.' Charlie sounded a touch brighter. 'Don't like being told what I can and can't do and been told no burning off. But Blue's the brigade and he'd be there . . .' She could hear the smile now in Charlie's voice. The idea of Jed supplying a freebie food feast must have sat well.

Gracie remembered Blue was the sandy-headed bloke they'd been talking about last night. He was around sixty with bad knees.

Apparently, Jed and I are having a barbecue. She smiled to herself. She was starting to sound like Mavis, with the 'apparently'. Mavis had dropped in a couple of times in the afternoon this last week before school finished for the day. Gracie enjoyed Mavis's company, and sometimes she wasn't confused at all.

'Sounds good.' She heard Jed's acknowledgement. 'Blue can supervise us. And we'll have the requisite ten litres of water ready.'

'Good of you.' A pause. 'Why would you do something like that?'

Because he's Jed, Gracie thought.

Her man harrumphed, embarrassed. 'You fellas are supporting me. Sometimes just a get-together and talk helps. I'll ask around and see if anyone else is interested. Liam and Molly might come. So, you and Ruby would go?'

Gracie didn't doubt that Chatter Charlie wasn't sleeping well, would be eating less, worrying more without sharing to others.

'Too right.' She heard a slap. Probably Charlie on Jed's back. She'd seen him do it before. 'Supply the meat and we'll be there.'

It wasn't a bad idea from her big, soft man. Except for the cost, but they'd manage. Charlie would ask Blue. She and Jed liked Blue and Jill. And they'd talked last night about the downward mood spiral in the community since they'd arrived. And the rush on the thirty-day accounts she hadn't wanted to give, but Jed had insisted on, for the store. Jed had wondered if they could do sixty days' credit and Gracie had nearly had a conniption. Another Mavis word. She'd mentioned semi-calmly that they'd have to sell the F250 to meet their suppliers' bills and still have to leave the valley owing money.

But the people up the valley had bigger cash flow problems than even Gracie did.

Gracie remembered Blue's wife, Jill's, concern that Blue had shut down, though she said he was doing better since Jed had arrived. Chatting to Jed about the volunteers and how the brigade recruits had dried up helped to share the load.

People were boiling their tank water as the house tanks grew bottom-scummy, but nobody liked to truck the town water in for a top-up unless they had to. 'Tasted like crap,' was the general consensus, and they still had faith that it would rain.

She'd seen the mood spiral in Roma as well. She'd heard the concern from the pregnant women about their farmer husbands. And if half-a-dozen other families were retreating from society in the drier pocket, then maybe a barbecue gig would be worth the money and energy.

It would give her and Jed a chance to meet new people, become part of the whole valley and maybe run into others their age.

Hopefully, even the young, snooty one they'd mentioned because she, Gracie, loved eccentrics. And some younger company would be good.

Jed could source what people would like the store to offer and until the baby came, they had the time. Most of all, it might ease the isolation of those struggling with the drought.

Chapter Seven

Nell

Nell found the brown-and-yellow note in her letterbox and the world intruded like a bee in the kitchen. Buzzing into her brain when she walked past the little scrap of striped paper, where it stuck to the fridge. People.

Not that she hadn't done some internet surfing with the wi-fi on her phone over the last four weeks and caught up with world events – so she was communicating. Sort of. If she walked to the left of the front verandah and leaned over, she could get enough signal to scroll, swap, sell, or download library books. She could even make a phone call. But she hadn't had the need for one of those yet.

And she'd taken to driving into Dorrigo once a week for essentials. Sunglasses on and hat pulled low, not talking unless she had to. Really, she needed to go further east to Bellingen or Coffs, or west to Armidale and do a big supermarket shop. Maybe once a month to buy staples, because it was naturally limited at the convenience store.

A brief disastrous exposure to the wider world of people

had occurred not long after she'd arrived – a prime example of her inability to cope with outsiders as she'd begun to think of them.

The visitor had been a bouncy, bright-earringed woman from Featherwood who'd stopped her car at the mailbox just as Nell had gone down to check the mail. The shock of a person asking questions to her face, politely interested but still questions, had been so great she'd snapped and said she wanted to be left alone. Then she had stalked off muttering up her driveway. She probably appeared hare-brained. Or like a snob.

Then she'd spent the next twenty-four hours regretting her rudeness, but there had been nothing she could do about it because in the frightened red fog of her brain she hadn't heard the woman's name.

Now this week the letter had come. Inviting her to a drought-relief barbecue for the up-valley families on Sunday. Hosted by the people in the produce store at Featherwood, the little village near where she'd bought Grin, and there was a phone number and name to RSVP. No cost for the day. Bring a plate. Map on the back.

She'd stared at the spidery writing, thought about the lady she'd been rude to, talked it over with the dog, considered what her psychologist would have said. And she'd finally decided that she needed to start somewhere. But the idea had cost her a whole night's sleep.

It wasn't held at a house. It was an outdoor thing at an old tennis court. It would be a bit different to the yacht-club socials when she'd played tennis as a teen. She hadn't really enjoyed those, either.

This could be a good opportunity to prove she could meet a few people. She'd drive herself there and drive home, which meant she could leave at any time if she thought up an urgent excuse.

The plate could prove a problem when she didn't have much flour to make a cake, but she had plenty of produce to take. She could even decorate a basket to share. Fruit from the orchard. Macadamias. The chooks were heading for an entry into the Guinness Book of Records for prolific layers. She could make devilled eggs. Her mother's housekeeper had taught her that. And nobody knew her, so they didn't expect much.

Although she hadn't stopped at Featherwood at all, she had noted the changes at the new produce store as she'd driven past. This would be one way to broaden her horizons.

Gulp.

Chapter Eight

Gracie

'It's blinkin' hot,' Gracie grumbled to herself as she climbed out of the tall utility back at the house.

With only one day before the barbecue, temperatures hovered around thirty-eight degrees Celsius, or a hundred in the shade, as the old blokes said. It was more like a beef-jerky oven shrivelling Gracie's skin and drying the air in her throat.

She sipped the cool water from the fridge she'd brought with her, which had grown warm now. She'd heard that warm water hydrated you better, anyway.

The relief of the truck cabin's aircon as she'd driven the hour in and out to Armidale for her antenatal appointment had been a highlight, not so comfortable with her bigger belly pressing into the steering wheel, but she had been excited to pick up their order of sausages and minute steaks for twenty people.

She and Jed had assumed there'd be kids and they'd be hungry and Jed had said, 'Everyone loves onions on a barbecue, so a huge bag of onions would be good, too.' Now she'd have to peel onions.

Half an hour later, she watched Jed through the kitchen window stride across the paddock after the Saturday lunch-time closing and could just hear him singing. Something about outback utes.

Her man was happy. She smiled wetly at that.

The door opened and his warmth came up behind her at the kitchen sink. He'd put something down on the bench at the door, but she didn't turn to show him her puffy face and stinging eyes. She must be a sopping mess.

He peered over at her and sucked in his breath. 'Babe. What's wrong?'

'Onions.' She sniffed. 'Lots and lots of onions.'

Jed pulled her into his chest and stroked the top of her damp hair. 'You smell like an onion,' he said, drawing in another breath. 'My bad. Next time I'll do the onions. Did you get the bread? I was thinking maybe it would be stale by tomorrow.'

'Molly's going into town early tomorrow for church. She said she'd pass the bakery on her way home and bring the bread with her.'

'Nice.' He eased her out of his arms and turned her so he could look into her face. 'I bear gifts. For my poor, red-eyed beauty.' Jed's delight washed over her. 'One of the customers was off to the tip and he had this in the back of his ute. Said it works great, but it's noisy and his wife told him to get rid of it and buy a cheap, silent one in town.'

An ancient black fan sat on the table, heavy and bulbous with rounded fan petals catching the light on the shiny blades. His eyes were lit with mischief. 'I gave it a good clean, and checked it worked between customers, so don't worry. I fixed the squeak.'

It was actually a handsome piece of very elderly machinery and looked heavy and in wonderful condition. No wonder Jed liked it. He settled it into the corner of the room, plugged it in, and directed the angle of air towards Gracie.

Sure enough, a steady stream of silent breeze blew solidly towards Gracie and eased the stillness in the room like a balm against her hot skin.

She raised a hand to catch the breeze. 'I like it. It goes with the kitchen. And it's stronger than the little one I have over here. Thank you.'

Jed grimaced. 'It's hot in here.'

Of course it was hot. They had a blinkin' wood stove supplying the water heater in the kitchen.

Jed went on. 'I was talking to Blue about air-conditioning. You like Blue.'

Gracie wiped a drip of sweat off her nose. 'I like Blue.'

'Blue's gone back to being a part-time air-conditioning contractor. He asked if you'd like to have an aircon, 'cause he has a small unit that someone in town bought and decided it was too small. He said we could put it in a bedroom to have one cool room, and he might get more. What do you think?'

Gracie thought of one cool room she could lie down in, especially to get relief on a hot night if they needed to. She knew they shouldn't spend any money, but she was thinking of the baby in the heat. 'How much?'

'Two hundred for the unit and I said I'd help him do a fence – if he put it in for me.'

She had that in her savings. She smiled. 'I'm not sure when you'll have time, but that's a great idea. Thank you. I'd like that.'

'Great. He said he'll drop in and sort it when I ring.' He slid his big hands over her smaller ones and made her drop the knife. 'I'll finish this. You go have a cold shower, put on your coolest dress, and go sit on the back verandah with your feet up. I'll bring you a drink.'

She must look knackered. She felt it and could do with a rest. It would be a big day tomorrow and she wanted to enjoy it, not be worn out.

Baby gave her a big rollover in agreement and she pulled Jed's hand down to her belly. 'Baby agrees. But you're the one who worked all morning.'

'Baby knows best. You work too and now it's time for you to stop.' He kissed her and she sighed against him.

'Okay.'

The next morning, Gracie discovered that Chatter Charlie's tennis court and barbecue shed had seen better days.

She watched Charlie study it fondly and scratch his balding head. 'Years ago, the up-valley families played tennis every Sunday right after church. Most of the properties took turns to host. Most have an old tennis court somewhere near the gate.'

Nobody had played here for years, Gracie could tell, with the tin-roofed barbecue shelter rusty and buried in brown-layered spider webs and thick dust-covered ferns.

On the court, the tennis net declared absent, but the net poles were there and the ground lay flat and shaded a little where it backed under a towering liquidambar. The huge tree shimmered a green umbrella over the picnic tables below. The lower branches had been culled and the canopy hung leafy and soothing above Gracie's head as she wiped over a heavy wooden table and trestles made out of tree trunks with a disposable wipe.

Charlie's wife, Ruby, trotted back and forth. She reminded Gracie of someone but she couldn't think of who. She had such a long, almost equine face and occasionally broke into a canter as she brought table cloths, a drum of drinking water and a cardboard box filled with lamingtons.

Jed and Liam, Molly's brother, were lifting the gas barbecue into place and they had a fire extinguisher, a bucket of water, and a fire blanket on hand in case of any problems.

Gracie still wasn't sure if any type of barbecue in a total fire ban was legal, but apparently Blue had said as long as it was in the shed and no fuel was close by, it was fine.

'Not long till the baby comes now,' said Ruby.

'Two weeks,' Gracie agreed, 'if it comes on time, but it could be two weeks later.'

'Do midwives know any secrets that make babies come on time?' Ruby had a cheeky twinkle in her eye. 'My mum used to recommend castor oil.'

Gracie laughed. 'No thanks and I've no desire to go into labour while stuck in the ladies room. I especially don't fancy having belly cramps with contractions.'

'What do you suggest?'

Gracie winked. 'Oxytocin, the chemical in our body that starts labour and drives breastfeeding, is a *looovvve* hormone.'

Ruby drew her dark brows together and then her eyes twinkled as she understood. She sighed. 'That man of yours'd be nice to snuggle into.'

Molly, back from getting another basket of food from the car, snuffed a laugh.

Gracie sneaked a look at Jed, but he and Liam were concentrating over gas bottles and not listening, thankfully. 'He's a good man.'

Molly said, 'I like my men medium height and lean, Ruby. If you see one like that send him my way.'

'Will do, young Molly.'

Gracie changed the subject. 'So, tell me about the people I haven't met?'

Ruby turned back to Gracie. 'You've met Blue and Jill, she's a wonderful seamstress if you want sewing done. From curtains to school uniforms, Jill can whip it up.'

By the way Ruby shook her head in admiration, Gracie assumed needlework wasn't in her skill set.

'Your lamingtons are a craft in themselves, Ruby.'

Ruby blinked and a blush came and went. 'You're sweet. Anyway, of course, there's that young Nell Turner who's also coming, not that I've met her, but the letterbox says "Turner" and the sign says "Nell's Farm".'

'Been here about the same time as you and Jed,' Ruby said. 'Shy and likes privacy. Lives in the old hill house right up the back of Shearer's Gully with a dog she bought from Mavis and some skinny cattle she got from one of the walkouts.'

Ruby shrugged. 'I didn't think she'd come today, but Charlie went up and left a note in the letterbox and she rang him and said she'd be here. I'm right pleased to see her get out.'

Gracie sensed a lost soul. 'Why shy and private?'

'We might find out. She ran away when Molly tried to welcome her.' She turned to Molly. 'Didn't you say?'

Molly nodded. 'Won't have visitors. There's a sign on the gate saying, "Nell's Farm, KEEP OUT". She'd be about your age, Gracie. No man about that I've ever seen. Or woman, either.'

Ruby lowered her voice. 'I reckon something nasty happened, maybe a man.'

Molly shrugged. 'Could be. Or a bad time to buy in. It has to get lonely up there and it's getting drier.'

Gracie mulled over this new information. Nell had been in the valley the same time as her and Jed? She'd watch for Nell. Maybe she'd like to chat, because living alone was something Gracie had thought her future held until she'd fallen into Jed's embrace.

'Are there many kids coming?'

'Alison and Pete have four boys. All tearaways, they'll be here. Blue and Jill look after their granddaughter, Holly, she's six. Her mum died of breast cancer.' Ruby shook her head. 'Too young to go.'

'Terrible disease. And so sad for such a little girl to lose her mother. Do you and Charlie have kids?'

'Sure have. Three. All boys. All not interested in the farm.' She shrugged as if to say, *nothing you can do about that*. 'Breaks Charlie's heart that does, but there are grandkids coming up, and they might find the love of the land.' She pondered. 'Or I might get to move to town like I want to. At the moment that sounds good.' She glanced up the road to a ball of dust. 'And here comes the first mob.'

A battered Range Rover pulled up at the tennis court. 'That's Alison Timms and her husband, Pete, they have . . .' she lowered her voice, '*had*, the best Charolais bull in the valley, right at the end of the road halfway over the mountains. I heard they lost that prize bull last week in one of the creek beds up a gully and didn't find him until too late. That would have ripped Pete's heart out.'

Gracie shook her head at the story but was distracted by four lanky boys who tumbled out followed by a tall, thin, anxious man and a round, smiling woman of about forty. The boys were like steps and stairs; the tallest was about twelve and the youngest maybe eight.

There was a head height between all of them, so they obviously took after their dad in the height stakes, and they jostled at the back of the Rover to pull out a big bag that they dragged across to the court.

Before their parents had properly climbed from the car, Gracie saw they were putting up a tennis net, pulling out rackets and throwing balls at each other. She shook her head and smiled at their eagerness.

Alison, their mother, carried a big cane basket covered by a blue checked tea towel. Pete carried a battered blue esky the size of a half-grown poddy calf. He put it down beside Jed, Liam and Charlie, and the men all shook hands.

Alison glanced at the boys and trod calmly across to Ruby and Gracie with a smile. 'Hello there, I'm Alison, and you must be Gracie.' Alison heaved the obviously heavy basket up onto the picnic table as if throwing another calf to brand it. 'Thanks so much for arranging today.'

Gracie smiled back. 'You're very welcome. It was Jed's idea, but I'm so pleased to meet you.'

Alison had big green eyes with a hint of sadness, or tired-ness, or both, but her mouth curved in a delighted smile. 'I must say, it's really good to get out.' She flicked her eyes towards her husband. 'Good for him, too, to get in a chinwag with some blokes. Starting to get me worried, he was.'

She nodded at Ruby. 'So, what've you been up to, Ruby? Haven't see you for a while.'

'Same as everyone else, I guess. How's your cattle going?'

'Could be worse.' Alison inclined her head to the kids. 'The boys put out the first lot of feed before they go to school and fill the water troughs in the afternoon. We've lost cattle before in drought.'

'We were just talking about summer coming,' Ruby said. 'It looks like Jed's joining the fire brigade.'

Alison glanced across to where Jed towered over Charlie and Pete, his big arms and big shoulders moving as he talked, with Liam standing silently beside him. She tilted her head appreciatively. 'It'd be good to have someone who can lift the gear and not moan about his back. Who's the serious one?'

'That's Liam, my brother from the army,' Molly said. 'I'd say he'd have no trouble lifting anything, either.'

The women laughed, and if it was a little cracked and forced, at least it was a start.

'What would you like me to do?' Gracie waved at the table.

Alison pointed at Gracie's belly and then at the box of bread. 'The men can get the barbie going, so you could sit there and butter the bread.' They all knew she got the 'heavily pregnant-lady job' and they smiled at each other. Not saying it.

Alison was quite the organiser. *She'd have to be*, Gracie thought, *with all those boys in the house.* Alison flipped off her tea towel from the top of the basket and pulled out a potbelly-sized steel bowl with cling wrap trapping the contents. 'I cut up a heap of watermelon.' She plonked it on the table and retrieved a huge bundled cloth. 'And made a couple of trays of scones with jam and cream for after. Pete has the cream in the esky.'

Ruby lifted her own esky. 'I brought a big French onion dip and a heap of cut carrots and snow peas to dip in. And a drum of non-alcoholic punch with fruit. I reckon we set up a drinks station, with punch as well as water, and I brought a couple of thermoses with boiling water for tea later. It'll be good with the scones. I've got milk and sugar.'

Alison nodded. 'Pete brought a billy, but that's better.'

Before they could start, another car pulled up under the shade of a gum tree across the road. A white 4 x 4 with a tray back holding two dogs. A man, woman and little girl climbed out.

'Here's Blue and Jill and little Holly. Who else is coming?'

'Nell Turner said she'd come.'

'Wow.' Alison shut her mouth. The two older women looked at each other but didn't say anything. Gracie and Molly exchanged glances. Gracie had the feeling the bush telegraph had supplied all the details. Then she said, 'I haven't met her yet.'

'Well, here she comes.'

A dramatically dusty late-model BMW approached slowly and stopped behind Alison's car. The vehicle had been blue once, but the only blue Gracie could see showed in patches on the roof – the rest of the panels lay well splattered, in layers of dust and mud.

The girl who eased out slowly was around mid-twenties, with one long plait of brown hair reaching to her jean-clad backside. Despite the obvious wear of the clothes, the jeans hung perfectly and screamed designer, while a loose top draped stylishly and elegantly over her thin frame. The woman seemed absorbed in the big bag over her shoulder, as if she were in no hurry to greet the others.

The skin of her face and arms, and legs – through the stressed holes in her jeans – showed dark brown, whether from sun or heredity. As she came closer, Gracie silently whistled. Her eyes were dark brown, almond-shaped, framed by thick, dark lashes and solid, dark arching brows. Her mouth was full and rose-coloured above her determined chin and the whole picture shouted catwalk model doing outback shoot.

Rearranging the contents of the bag, she adjusted the weight on her shoulder, keeping her eyes down in front of her until she reached the side of the road. Shielding. Protecting herself.

'Snooty' wasn't the word that came to mind, Gracie thought, with a surge of sympathy. More like damaged.

Chapter Nine

Nell

Nell had to force her feet to tread the dirt. She needed to cross the road and meet people.

She'd had nightmares last night.

Thinking about this. People.

Again.

Flashbacks of disgust on faces, grief on others. Scorn and ridicule. The bitter disappointment of her mother after her father had actually died from the shock.

The creeping anxiety she'd begun to control at Nell's Farm had been back in full force this morning. She'd blown her reaction to the first overture of friendship and she needed to fix that. She'd made herself ring the Charlie on the note and say, *Thank you, yes!* Her psychologist would have been proud of her.

But now that she was here her muscles were tight, mouth frozen and her legs barely lifted through the rutted dust of the road as she began to drag herself towards the group of women staring at her.

She lifted her head briefly to see them . . . 'Damn,' she swore under her breath. The men were coming over to greet her as well.

She tried to smile, but it wouldn't come. *Which is why you are here today*, the determined self inside whispered. *Practice. You need to start going back into civilisation.*

Nell made it to the dry brown grass on the peopled side of the road and kept her chin up as she finally focused. She could make two faces out of the blur. One, a tall, dark-haired man about thirty looking down at her with hard blue eyes and no smile – oh yes, she recognised Blue Ute – and the other, unknown, a woman with the most welcoming, beautiful, non-judgemental smile Nell had seen in her life.

Nell smiled weakly back at her and felt her shoulders ease a fraction. Until she saw the pretty woman's belly. The last pregnant woman she knew had died and it was her fault.

A chorus of men said, 'G'day.'

Three other women, one the woman from Nell's front gate whom she'd been rude to that time, murmured a flurry of welcome, with smiles. *Maybe it won't be too bad*, she thought.

The blue-ute jock narrowed his eyes and nodded.

The pregnant, pretty one said quietly, 'I'm Gracie and Charlie here,' she gestured to a bald man, 'says you're Nell.' She pointed to the biggest bloke there. 'This is my partner, Jed.'

He had a nice smile, too, and Nell forced herself to hold still as everyone checked her over. She avoided looking at the belly. Nobody would have guessed she'd once thought nothing was nicer than a gravid uterus.

Charlie spluttered, 'Partner? Gracie? I thought you two were married?'

The lady next to him kicked his shin, and the man called Charlie winced, confusion pulling his jaw forward and bringing

73

his brows down. 'Ruby?' he muttered miserably. 'She kicks like a horse. What the . . .?' The attention shifted off Nell and she sighed with relief.

Charlie hopped and leaned on the table with one leg up, bewilderment suffusing his face as he stared at Ruby.

An unexpected giggle lodged somewhere in Nell's throat for the first time in a long time out of the privacy of her home. She saw the man named Jed straighten even taller beside Gracie.

'All good, Charlie. I've tried to marry her.' Jed's voice rumbled quietly. He glanced down at the nice but pregnant Gracie. 'I've tried to get a ring on her finger for two years now.'

'Maybe one day,' Gracie said as if to stop the conversation. 'Anyway, good to meet you, Nell. You'll have to come down and have a cup of coffee with Jed and me, or if he's busy, just me. And maybe Molly.' She pointed to the lady Nell owed the apology to. 'It's more fun with just girls.'

Gracie smiled at everyone and they all smiled back. Nell thought the power of this Gracie's smile could probably stop a war. The thought amused her and amusement wasn't something she'd considered she'd feel today.

Gracie went on. 'Next time you're in Featherwood, come see our store, the Farmer's Friend.'

'Of course.' It was an odd name for a store. Wasn't that the weed? Nell sent a quick glance around the group and shot a smile she hoped wasn't too strained. 'Good to meet you all, too.' She searched for the visitor lady's face and found her. 'Sorry about the other day,' she said quietly. 'Nerves.'

'No problem.' Molly waved it away. 'Glad to see you here. Might see you at Gracie's, too.'

Nell inclined her head and turned back to the pretty woman. 'I've been meaning to come in and see your new place, Gracie. Save me going into town for puppy food.'

'Saves all of us going into town,' Blue said heartily. Too heartily. There was an awkward silence after that. His cheeks went red like his hair probably used to be, if his name was anything to go by.

'Let's get this barbie going. I'll need your supervision, Blue,' Jed murmured. 'I wouldn't mind a hit of tennis after. Those boys look like they're having way too much fun over there and I'm missing out.'

Everyone turned to the boys on the dirt court and away from Nell again, which felt like a load off.

She saw Gracie send a soft, appreciative glance towards her man for the adroit way he'd directed the attention away from Nell. What a nice couple. Maybe she could get to know Gracie more before the day was over.

The men moved away, even Mr Macho of the blue ute, although he'd sent a cool glance over his shoulder at her before he went. She sneaked a skim of the cars at the road and now she could see his car tucked under a tree.

Gracie said, 'You play tennis, Nell?'

'Not for years. I'm not really a social person. Lately.' Now there was an understatement.

'Jed's the opposite. Mr Have-a-chat.' Gracie laughed. 'I'm happy to stay in the background and enjoy the show.'

Nell smiled inwardly at that, and inside was way better than not at all. 'Do you play tennis?'

Gracie scanned her belly. 'Not today. Maybe we can have a game when this baby of mine decides to grow a bit on the outside.'

Fingers crossed all goes well for you, but she didn't say it. Nell simply nodded and said, 'Impressive belly.' Which wasn't surprising considering the size of her man. Stupid fear wriggled in her belly and she had to force her mouth to say normal words. 'When *are* you due?'

'Two weeks. I'm having the baby in Armidale. We go to the antenatal clinic there.'

'Gracie is a midwife.' Ruby said it as if she was saying Gracie could do it all by herself. Nell's stomach sank and now she really wished she hadn't come. What if Gracie had heard of her? No, that was a stupid thought. She'd changed her name, and nobody here knew who she was.

Gracie slid her hand over her belly and her shirt shifted as the baby kicked, then rolled. She laughed. 'I think the baby's talking to you. Want a feel?'

Nell felt the terror rear. 'No. No thanks.' She stepped back. Sucked in a couple of fast breaths and told herself to settle, then glanced at all the food. Trying to ignore the sudden silence, she shifted her shoulder bag to the table and pulled out her fruit and vegetables. A container of the devilled eggs. Half-a-dozen avocados she'd traded for nuts, oranges and lemons, and six small cucumbers. Then she took out a pile of paper bags and some brown twine. 'I didn't know what to make, so I brought eggs and some organic fruit and veggies for everyone to take home in a bag.' She smiled shyly. 'Sort of like party favours.'

Gracie laughed. 'What a great idea. I love organic food, thank you. And we have tons to eat today, so that's perfect.'

Nell sensed the man come up behind her and she knew which one it was. Molly's brother, Liam. Blue Ute. She didn't know why, or how she could be so sure, but she knew. She didn't turn.

'Like being alone, do you?' The lack of expression in his voice was an insult in itself, yet there was something about that tone that cut through the timidity she'd acquired since the court case and made her lift her chin.

'I see you're one of those men who judge people.'

Nell's comment hung between them and she tilted her face further away from him.

His voice was whisper quiet at the back of her neck. 'Instincts save people.'

Now she swung and stared straight into his eyes, all expression wiped from her face. 'Or they can ruin people's lives.'

And as if that wasn't a dead giveaway that she had something to hide. *Stupid. Stupid. Stupid.* She stalked over to Gracie, more cross with herself than Liam.

Jed smiled at her and stood up from the chair he'd just returned to. 'Take mine. Gracie's probably sick of me. I'm up for tennis.'

'More likely you're bored with sitting,' Gracie teased him. 'Yes, come sit with me, Nell.'

The couple had such a warm rapport Nell wanted to bag it and take it home with her. 'Thank you.'

'Hey, Liam,' the big man said. 'Let's go for a hit while the boys are eating. Get ready for me to flog you on the court.' When the men walked past, Nell didn't look up.

'Fine-looking man, that,' Gracie said once they were out of earshot.

'Jed's lovely.'

Gracie laughed. 'That one, too. I mean Liam.'

'Not my type. He-man heavyweight.'

'Interesting word.' Gracie sipped her lemonade. 'Molly tells me Liam joined the army when he was eighteen and has served in Afghanistan and Iraq. He's home for three months because he stopped talking.'

'Must be a ball of fun to live with.' Not.

'I don't think so. But he's handy around the house, she says. And I can vouch that he's handy at the shop.' Gracie smiled at her. 'Now, Jed? He makes Liam smile.'

Nell felt the tension in her shoulders ease. 'It's the first time I've met you all, but even I can tell that Jed would make anyone smile. And Molly is nice. Did she tell you I was rude when I first met her?' Now why did she say that? As if she wanted to push Gracie away.

'No.' Gracie sat serene. 'I heard you were shy.'

Liam served the first ball and it whistled past Jed in an ace. Gracie smiled and shook her head. 'Liam is going to wipe the court with Jed.'

By the time the men were packing up the barbecue, Nell felt almost like a normal person sitting on the folding chair Jed had given her. They were all watching Alison and Jed, the last two tennis players, belt out a game of singles to finish the day.

The main food had been shared and packed away. Gracie had helped her tie bows of twine around the bags for everyone to take, and she'd even enjoyed the company of the young boys and the little girl. But she was tired from forcing herself to talk and answer questions, even though none of these people had tried to ask about her past or made her anxious. Maybe Molly had warned them against it.

Liam didn't offer any conversation, but every time she glanced his way, those cold blue eyes were on her.

She'd said to Gracie, 'He's always watching. As if I'm an unexploded bomb.'

Gracie had laughed. 'You've knocked him for six. You're stunning and where he's been there wasn't much beauty around.'

Nell closed her mouth at that.

After two hours of sharing barbecue space with all the men, Nell had relaxed a tiny bit towards Liam. She wasn't sure she believed Gracie's sympathetic version of why Liam didn't talk, but she could believe he was having difficulties being in a normal environment. So was she.

In fact, she hadn't felt this relaxed since before the birth.

Immediately, she stiffened. The word *birth* made the ghastly memories rush back. Her spine pushed against the chair as she planted her feet more firmly on the floor, and her fingers whitened on the edges of the chair's arms; her skin tingled and burned as the anxiety attack chewed like a rabid dog on her composure.

She felt Liam's eyes on her, as if he sensed something. Damn him. When she turned, his gaze was fixed on her, his brows pulled together, his relaxed stance gone.

'I have to go,' she said desperately. Damn it, she wanted to cry. Now she'd gone and ruined it all by bringing 'it' back to the front of her mind.

Gracie turned her face from the match and something she must have seen in Nell's face made her touch her arm, very, very gently, but still Nell flinched.

Gracie lifted her fingers as if she got it. Gracie would. 'Sure. It was so lovely spending time with you. Come to the shop or the house soon.' Gracie smiled. 'I don't think I'll be getting up the valley to your place for a while.'

Nell still couldn't believe she'd issued an invitation after Gracie had offered hers. She hadn't thought she'd ever invite anybody to her home, but she knew even in this short acquaintance that one day she'd see Gracie there.

'Can you thank Jed for the chair, please?'

Gracie nodded.

'And thanks to Charlie,' Nell directed at Ruby, 'for the invitation and to everyone who made me welcome.' Her mouth was rabbiting on, the words tumbling out fast. And that didn't sound like she was excluding Liam. Much. She tried to make a joke. 'Even if you all looked surprised when I ate meat.'

The ladies laughed. It had been pretty funny the way they all thought she'd be a vegetarian or even a vegan. She didn't kill her own animals, but could fancy a piece of meat from the shop every now and then. 'The sausages were fun,' she said to Gracie. Not something she would have bought herself. 'And the scones were amazing – please tell Alison. And the punch and dip and the lamingtons,' she said to Ruby. Gawd, she sounded like a schoolgirl reciting lines.

Softly, she told Gracie, 'Thanks to you and Jed for organising this.' *You're the first person I've felt a connection with in years,* she wanted to add, because connection was something she never thought she'd feel again.

There was hope.

Jed had suggested she go along to the next fire-brigade meeting and join. He reckoned if a few girls joined then the men might decide they should go too. A novel way of recruitment. It wouldn't be easy, she knew, but she should do it. She was part of the community and she needed to help others, also. Blue had told her how to find the training information booklet online if she wanted to know a bit about the service, trucks and fighting fires before she came to the meeting. That would be the easy part.

Nell slid on her shoulder bag, heavy with the food of strangers, and tilted her head to listen to the last sounds of conversation and children laughing. She cast one flat look at Liam, hovering for a minute, then nodded silently to Gracie and crept to her car to drive home.

It would have been a good day except for this last stupid panic. And him.

Chapter Ten

Gracie

Gracie waved but Nell didn't look back.

'She didn't seem as agitated as the last time I saw her,' Molly said. 'But she still jumps like a rabbit.'

'It's the first time I've met her,' Jill murmured, and watched the dust settle now that the car was out of sight. 'I went to visit when she first moved in, but the sign said "Keep Out". So I did.'

'She could have been scared?'

'Of me?'

'Of anyone.'

Jill looked thoughtful. 'That's what Blue said. Maybe she was hiding from someone and now she's getting over it.'

'It's not crazy,' Ruby suggested.

Gracie let them work it out their way, glad she didn't have to suggest anything. Though she agreed with Jill about the huge anxiety vibrating from Nell. She'd seen it before.

Something bad had happened to Nell.

'She was pretty brave to come down here and face everyone.' Gracie packed her own bag of goodies. 'And you ladies were lovely, so I bet she's glad she came.' She gestured with her arm to the shed, the glorious shady tree and the court. 'This is such a great place to hold the day, Ruby. Thank you.' She inclined her head at the two at the net, shaking hands. 'I think Alison just whooped Jed's butt on court.'

'Great game,' Blue called out.

'Beaten by a woman,' Liam offered, one of the few comments he'd made today. She'd noticed him talking to Nell that once, but mostly he'd just stood around with the men and stayed silent.

Gracie smiled at the teasing Liam could manage because it was directed at Jed, but she was tired. She couldn't help feeling relieved that it was over.

She said to the ladies, 'Don't let us break up the day, but I might get Jed to take me home so I can put my feet up.'

The women peered down at Gracie's swollen ankles and clucked.

'Good grief,' said Jill.

'You do that,' said Ruby. 'We're all packed up here, though the men will chinwag a while longer now they've started. I might make another cup of tea.'

Back on the road ten minutes later, Jed asked, 'Did you have a good day, Gracie?' Satisfaction shone clear in his voice.

'I did. I think everyone did. It was a great idea of yours, Jed.'

'I think so.' He sounded thoughtful.

'I was glad to have met Nell, too. I hope we can become friends.'

'She seems nice, if quiet. They're all good people and that Alison's got a great forehand.'

Gracie laughed. 'You went down to a woman.'

Jed grinned at her. 'I have no problem with that if she's better at it than me. Best way to improve.'

And that was Jed in a nutshell. 'You're a good man, Joshua Edwards, and I'm very lucky to have you in my life.'

Jed slowed the truck for the oncoming curves in the road, right down. 'Which reminds me . . .' His voice had changed, grown serious. 'Why is it you won't marry me?'

Gracie had known this would come up after today's awkward moment. 'Let me think about it.'

Apparently – she thought of Mavis with that word – it wasn't the curves Jed was slowing for.

He pulled over to the side of the road and idled, before he turned to face her. 'It's been two years. I'm wondering if there's something in me that worries you, Gracie?'

Not in Jed. 'There's nothing in you that worries me, Jed. It's something in me.'

'There is nothin' in you I don't love.' Jed reached over and took her hand from her lap and enfolded it in his big, callused ones. 'I'm willing and waiting. Our baby is almost here and we'll be connected always now. There's nothing to wait for.'

'I'll think about it.' It was a weak platitude, but she couldn't think of marriage before the baby.

Jed studied her face and nodded, but his lips had pulled tight. 'I'm the man you deserve. Not the others, Gracie. We would have a real marriage. I think you need to let the past,' he indicated the passenger door, 'fly out that window.' He put on his blinker and accelerated back onto the road a little faster than normal.

Gracie had to wonder why Jed was so determined to tie her to him, because that's what it was. Or was it just a mutual trust that she couldn't give?

Her head began to ache.

'I didn't think Nell was antisocial.' Jed changed the subject and her shoulders sagged in relief.

Gracie had to smile at his lack of subtlety. 'Apparently, she told Molly to get off the property when she first moved in. Ruby said she'd nailed a "keep out" to the gate with a no-trespassing sign. She doesn't talk to people in town. Drives to Dorrigo. Most of her food is homegrown or left at the gate. There are no house deliveries.'

'She's pretty brave to come out, then,' Jed said.

'That's why I love you.' Gracie leaned across and kissed Jed's cheek.

'I love you, Gracie, but I want you to be happy. I'm sorry I pushed.'

By the time they got home, Gracie's feet were so swollen she didn't want to put weight on them. Jed noticed instantly when he opened her door and he wouldn't let her walk. He just lifted her out of the car and carried her up the front steps, through the hallway, all the way down to their room and put her on the bed.

'You rest those feet. I'll bring you a cold drink in a minute.'

First, he knelt down on the floor and eased the shoes from her feet with gentle hands, drawing his breath in through his teeth in consternation. 'How come you didn't have your pressure stockings on?'

'Too hot, dude.'

'Not too hot, dude.' He pretended to glare at her. It was a rare thing when Jed did appear cross with her, and if it happened, it was usually about not taking care of herself properly.

'I should have,' she conceded.

'I'll get the drink.' He opened all the windows in the room and turned on the small fan they'd moved from the kitchen to the bedroom before heading for the door. 'Stay,' he commanded.

'Woof.'

Jed raised his brows at her. 'As if.' And with that he left.

Gracie smiled after him. She didn't know why she couldn't accept that her commitment to Jed was solid. She loved him, she'd chosen a good man and a wedding celebration of what they had would make Jed happy. But she just couldn't. She kept thinking, what if something bad happened to Jed, like it had to her first baby? And then to Carl and her mother? She'd told Jed all this, but he'd waved it away as silly.

She had the sudden thought that maybe she could talk to Nell about that and she had no idea why she felt the other woman would understand. But some deep instinct of connection stirred, and the idea helped her to relax. Then her mind drifted to the concerns of all the women today and the impact of the drought. The lack of water. The risk of fire.

Jed returned with two beaded glasses of lemonade cordial made from real lemonade lemons. The fruit had been dropped into the shop as a welcome gift from a family just out of town. Ice chinked in the glass as he handed it to her, then he pulled the chair in the corner beside the bed.

'You okay?'

Instead of answering that she said, 'How do we prepare our house if we get a bushfire through here?'

Jed sat back in his chair. 'I've been thinking about that, Gracie.'

She felt more strain drop from her shoulders and she loosened her neck by rocking her head. 'Of course you have, Jed.' She smiled at her man. 'So? Tell me what we need to do.'

'Well, I'll keep the lawn short, all the way around the house from the creek to the store. We need to clean some wood from behind the sheds.' He widened his eyes at her. 'Can't lose my store in a fire.'

It was a joke they had. She was having a baby and he was having a newborn store. Except his baby was growing faster than hers and reps were flocking to him in droves. She had tried really hard not to think 'easy mark'.

She did have a couple of young farming women interested in an impromptu antenatal class discussion – there was talk of one morning-tea meeting a week for an hour or two – but nothing like the growth of Jed's circle of acquaintants. Or his plethora of new products. It seemed every day he found something new and exciting to add to the shelves or the shed. Lucky he was selling his products, or his dreams would have bankrupted them.

Also, it was a shame that most of the sales through the till were on accounts to be paid later.

'Being prepared is important,' Jed said and Gracie pulled her thoughts back to the question she'd asked.

'We had a long discussion at the fire shed and again today about best defences. That's apart from the brigade responses.' Jed rubbed his head as he repeated the advice. 'Liam and I will both have a tank and spray system with hoses set up on a skid. We've ordered two little Honda engines, 'cause Blue says you can leave them in a shed and twenty years later, just start 'em up and they'll go. We'll have that whole system ready to lift onto the back of our vehicles by next week. That'll give us a mobile water tank and hoses for fast response in an emergency.'

He gestured to the ceiling above them. 'I'll clean out the roof gutters of any leaves, which I'll do this afternoon because if I don't, it'll be next week.' He checked his watch. 'We still have a couple of hours of daylight yet. I don't want you worrying through the week.' His eyes twinkled. 'You'll be able to lie here and hear me clomping around above you.'

She didn't say, *Don't fall off the ladder*, because that was asking for trouble. Her man did have a clumsy streak that gave her grey hair, but she couldn't have peace of mind without risk.

'I'll set up a sprinkler system with one on each corner to wash the walls and roof if we turn it on, and a hose so the water can run through the gutters,' he continued. 'That's here and the shop. Anything outside the shop will be steel and non-combustible.

'If it comes to that we'll push a rag in the downpipes if we need to fill them. We'll use the town water for fires if anything happens because it shouldn't turn off – or not straight away if a big fire comes through.'

Gracie drew in a breath. She hadn't imagined a fire so bad the town water would be turned off.

'The tank water we'll keep in case the town water does go off. It can run on gravity, so even if power goes, we can get water to survive,' he said. 'So, until we get rain, don't use that third tap in the kitchen for a while. It's getting too low. The sample came back from the plumber to say it's clean enough to drink, but I still think we should boil it.'

Gracie was right there with him about boiling the tank tap water now. And wow, the men *had* talked today, and Blue's brigade had certainly looked into this. When the drought broke, they'd get the tanks flushed and cleaned and start again.

He lifted his head to meet her eyes. 'I'm thinking we should cover in the wooden pylons under the house.'

She shrugged. She'd have wanted that done later anyway when junior started to crawl. That was safer for kids.

'It will still look fine. The fellas were saying today that embers blow under a house and start a fire, so mosquito wire will help stop that. There's a roll at the shop. We can make a door on each side in case we need to get under there. Toddlers won't be able to get in, either, when that time comes.' They smiled at each other. 'Liam said he'd help.'

Liam helped a lot. Gracie put down her empty glass and relaxed back against the pillows. She had watched the thoughts chase across Jed's face with his words, his big hands gesturing right and left, his voice a low rumble of determination. 'It all sounds great, Jed. I should've known you'd have it all in hand.'

'Blue's keen for me to go to the fire meeting on Tuesday night. You okay with that?'

'Of course. The women today were relieved that you were here to help Blue.'

He shrugged that off. 'I'm glad we asked Nell to go. Encouraging the ladies is a good way to boost numbers.' He winked. 'I'll chase more of the young blokes who don't usually turn up and the girls might make them keener.'

They smiled at each other. 'Maybe we can swell the numbers at least until after summer. Get a bit of training in now, even if they all drop off later.' Jed looked determined and confident. As if he'd read her mind he said, 'I'll keep you and our baby safe, Gracie.'

'You make sure you keep yourself safe, Jed. For me and the baby.'

Chapter Eleven

Mavis

Mavis listened to the brown grass crunch under her feet, snapping and grinding to dust like salt-and-vinegar chips on the kitchen floor. The sound drew her brows together. Everything felt too dry. More than fifty years ago, she remembered it being like this with the worst drought ever. Her husband had been alive. It had been the most terrible time.

Above hung a cloudless, relentless blue ceiling, and even at seven in the morning, the heat rolled like a blanket over the paddocks, making her sweat.

On the hill, the spare water tank cast a cool shadow down the brown slope and she thought about the black poly pipe lying like a snake in the brittle grass. They should really dig a trench and bury the pipe. If a fire came through, it might melt their spare water supply.

Just the thought of the trench shovel made her back ache and she turned her head to the house where the boy would be playing computer games this early on a Saturday morning. Maybe if she promised him a trip to the golden arches in town, he'd do it?

She snorted. He'd do it anyway; he was a good kid. They needed emergency water near the house.

Even the big fishpond, which was one of those fake Roman stone ones, really a plastic two-hundred-litre pot, usually stayed topped up. It caught the dew and rainwater off the roof from the hole in the gutter, but now it lay perilously shallow.

Poor orange fish were bumping into each other as the water got lower. She'd fill it with a hose from the tank on the hill to give them an extra supply near the house. At least they could bucket from there if needed. Maybe she should have got the town water put on when they asked?

In 2009, she'd had a nasty gully fire that had almost licked over her house, but she'd been lucky and plenty of people had come to help. Times had changed though. The drought had thinned the families out of the valley. The rural fire brigade was almost a one-man band, although they'd had a muster through the week, she saw. If Archie was still here when he was an adult, she'd send him up to join.

She'd been lucky compared to those down in Victoria with their Black Saturday that year. She shivered at the thought. They'd lost more than houses, too many lives, and she shuddered again despite the heat.

She had the boy to protect. She'd better get back onto those tablets that gave her nightmares. She'd given them up to stop her waking with a thumping heart in the night, but now, well, she needed to keep her brain straight. At least until the fire season was over. Blood pressure and bloody diabetes.

'Whatcha doin', Gran?'

She hadn't seen the boy leave the house. 'I'm thinking how I can con you into doing a big job for me.'

His smile grew. 'You don't have to con me, Gran, you ask and I'll do it.'

He was like a little old man sometimes with his wise young eyes. 'Good grief! Where's my Archie? What'd you do with him?' She stared owlishly as if trying to recognise him.

He grinned back at her, and a little of the worry eased. He might be young, but he had a big heart. She pointed with one bony finger and found herself distracted by the thin, wrinkled digit. When did she get so decrepit? 'I'll help, but it hurts my back. We need a trench.' She forced herself to concentrate. 'You see that black pipe that runs from the tank at the top of the hill?'

The boy followed the direction and nodded.

'It just sits on top of the dead grass, and if we get a fire through here it would melt. Then we wouldn't have anything to put out any embers around the house with.'

The boy turned slowly to scan the brown grass, the cloudless sky, the black pipe to the house and then back to her. 'You reckon that can happen?'

'Anything can happen. I'm not doom and glooming, but it wouldn't hurt to have an extra bit of insurance. What do you reckon?'

'I reckon you'd know, Gran.'

Mavis felt the warmth in her chest. An expanding, unusual warmth and she looked at the boy to check he wasn't pulling her leg. Nope. He was serious. He believed that she was smart. Yep. She needed to get back on those tablets. 'All right, then. How about I get that bacon out of the freezer? It's been there for a while and we'll use the last four eggs, cook up a big brekky so you have lots of energy.'

She needed to shop for food, especially if they got cut off with fires. It meant a big drive in the car and she was losing confidence there.

The boy said they could order from the supermarket in town on the internet and they'd deliver, so she might ask him again about that.

The boy grinned. 'Sounds good.'

Mavis turned back to the house. 'We'll take the tractor up to the top with all the stuff on the carry-all. You can drive.'

Archie must have tripped on a rock because he stumbled, then jogged to catch up. 'True?'

'You're almost twelve. If you can dig a trench you can drive a tractor. I'll teach you.'

After breakfast Mavis took Archie down to the shed where the big tractor sat like a rusty red rhoetosaurus. Her mum had told her about that dinosaur skeleton, found on Taloona Station, near Roma in 1924. She'd always felt a kinship to that one, not the tyrannosaurs the boy fancied; her tractor was a rhoetosaurus.

Mavis made sure the travelling mechanic came once a year and serviced the prehistoric tractor, but the machinery had been young when Mavis had been pretty. She'd shaken her head when Archie had skimmed through a YouTube video on tractor skill sets while he ate. She clucked her tongue. Next thing they'd be teaching you to fly a plane from a computer!

'Righto. Climb up. I'll talk you through it from here.'

Archie had been driving her ute, which had gears, around the farm, and he mowed with the ride-on. But this was more technical. 'It's got gears and a clutch in low and high range. You won't be speeding anywhere, so we'll leave it in low range, second. You've just gotta remember to lift the carry-all up and down when you start and stop.'

The kid nodded, his eyes shining like two pennies. 'The other thing you need to remember is to make sure the key is properly off when you've finished because that battery is a big blighter and it's too heavy for me to lift out and charge. Okay?'

The kid nodded so enthusiastically Mavis thought his head would fall off. She smiled. 'You're really excited about this?'

Archie nodded.

'As long as you're just as excited about digging the trench.'

They'd already loaded shovels and water bottles onto the swinging carry-all, wore hats and long sleeves and gloves, despite the heat. Archie followed her directions, checked the gears etched on the knob on the gearstick and pushed his foot down.

Once they got to the top, Archie pulled over slowly, lowered the carry-all and turned off the key.

Mavis nodded in approval. 'You got it in low range, second, and it's parked level, so it shouldn't roll anywhere. With the carry-all down, that helps as well.' She climbed down from where she was perched against Archie with her butt on the big wheel arch guard, and Archie bounced out of the seat. They stood beside the water tank and examined the black snake running downhill to the house.

'How come you never had it buried?'

'It's a replacement. One of those "gonna do" jobs. Now that I've got you here as a workhorse, boy, we can get all sorts of things done.'

Archie laughed. 'As long as you don't want it done fast.'

'I'd rather have it done slow and proper. Fast and shoddy's not gonna help in the end. You learn that,' Mavis shrugged, 'and your life will do well, boy.'

'That breakfast was slow and proper.'

Mavis felt her face crack in a smile. 'Too right it was.'

Chapter Twelve

Nell

A week after the barbecue, across the lower paddock, Nell saw the tall white Brahman tossing her sharp-horned head. She'd called her Moo, because the others had loud voices, and while she was the tallest cow there, the Brahman had this deep, quiet, rumbling *mooooo*.

She wasn't rumbling now. Moo stood, not following the herd as they headed out to their favourite morning search for food and Nell wondered idly, why. The big cow had stood there yesterday afternoon, too. Right up against the barbed wire fence. Not moving.

Nell had brushed over Moo's odd behaviour last evening; the cow was pregnant after all, and Nell had been exhausted from cleaning roof gutters and dragging tree litter away from the house after the fire-brigade meeting.

And she'd agreed to go and visit Gracie today. Her last girl chat with an actual friend had been such a long time ago, so her mind had been nervy.

Still, Moo's behaviour was unusual. Nell's eyes narrowed through the glare from the kitchen window, her hands stilling over the hamper she was packing to take to town. 'What if Moo's had her calf?' Her voice echoed in the quiet kitchen. She was doing that a lot, lately. Talking out loud. 'What if she's calved?' she asked Grin. 'The calf could have wandered to the other side of the fence and couldn't get back?'

Grin didn't answer. Thankfully. She was still sane.

Moo's foot could have caught in some wire or she could be ill? Moo wasn't dumb. In fact, Nell suspected the cow might be uncommonly smart.

The other cows looked back at the fence then swung on their way in a straggling line, leaving the big white Brahman in isolation. Which was very curious. Nell needed to check what was going on.

Walking close up to the large beast wasn't a worry. Moo was the first to eat scraps from the kitchen bucket when Nell threw them over the fence. A couple of the other cows she wouldn't be so sanguine about approaching if they'd calved. Still, more people were killed by cows with calves than by bulls, so she needed to remember that.

The herd reached the corner fence and turned left to increase the distance between the lone cow and the rest of the mob. She wondered if Moo needed water. Had the cow even been to the bare trickle of the creek spring in the last twelve hours?

One of the gentle, hornless heifers bawled softly, looking back at Moo, and then made another nasal call, used by the cows in low-frequency distress. Nell had read about that on the internet. Moo didn't budge.

Nell opened the kitchen screen door, startling two butcherbirds into black-and-white flight, but the heat slapped her and made her rethink as she pulled on her floral gumboots. It was too hot to make a couple of walking trips if she needed to take water, so she turned and headed for the lean-to carport. She'd take the car.

She tied Grin up first. Her dog would not be able to resist a little nip if he thought Nell wanted to round Moo up – that was the heeler in him. She refilled his bowl with water and patted her friend. 'I'm going to town, too, so I'll have to leave you here for that as well.'

She and Grin had already been out once this morning to the back boundary on the internal track that bisected her property. She'd made sure all the gates were open when she left, as Charlie had told her she should, in case animals needed to escape a fire. The car was still warm and started instantly.

She puttered slowly, careful not to startle Moo, though the cow immediately lifted her head and stared at Nell's approach.

She needed to avoid the occasional taller stalks of pale whisky grass that could catch under the hot exhaust pipe. There weren't as many spikes because the cattle were eating even that now.

Jed had suggested she get some urea blocks to boost the mineral content for the herd. Cattle needed the extra mineral with the poor grass quality during drought. The information she had in her brain these days. She'd pick up some lick blocks today before she left the Farmer's Friend.

Nell steered the car to the left, not directly at the fence, and that's when she saw the black furry calf. It was on the next-door neighbour's side of the rusty five-strand barbed wire. Right up against the fence, trying to get as close to its mother as it could without catching on the barbs.

Nell turned off the engine and climbed out, her mouth curving. 'Well, you're beautiful, aren't you? My first baby. But not real smart. Didn't inherit Mum's brains?' She studied the fence and the size of the calf. 'Now you can't get back to your mummy?'

Dilemma. She didn't want to frighten the newbie, but she wanted to hunt it through the fence, so she'd have to come around from behind to push it through the wire. All of which meant squeezing through the fence, and the barbs were rusty and sharp.

She grimaced at the calf. 'You've got a thick enough coat, so you'll be fine. I'm the one with the singlet top and bare arms.'

A high-frequency call, that long-distance mouth bellow cows made when they wanted to warn of danger, lifted Nell's head. One of the more militant cows had trumpeted her displeasure that Nell was near Moo's calf. The whole herd had turned around and they were trotting purposefully back to support their stranded mate.

Nell wasn't afraid of the cows, but she didn't need to be caught in the middle of a milling jam of worried mothers, some with horns, so she squeezed through the barbed wire fence towards the baby more quickly than proved prudent.

'Ouch.' Her shoulder sported a long red scratch and she thought for a moment about her last tetanus injection. It was two years ago, so she should be fine. She grimaced as a trickle of blood ran down her bicep, but she'd made it through the fence before the rest of the herd arrived.

The black, curl-covered calf stood up, shivering in fright, big eyes shifting between Nell and its mother. 'It's okay, baby,' she murmured quietly. Then she looked at Moo. 'It's okay, Mum.'

Slowly, alert for snakes, she stepped away in a wide arc around the calf so that she came in at ninety degrees to push it towards its mother. It only took two of Nell's steps forward and the calf panicked. Nell caught a flash of scrotum as it ducked and pushed through the fence and popped out beside its mother like a cork from a bottle. *So, you're a boy.*

Moo threw her head up and skipped sideways as soon as her baby rushed in, and the whole herd turned with her. Mother, calf and aunties all cantered away as if Nell was chasing them.

Nell put her hands on hips and smiled, satisfaction warming her. This was the good part about being alive: feeling like she had done something useful. The little calf kicked its heels and ran, its tail flying upright like one of those fluffy toys on a stick at the Easter show. 'Excellent. Now all I need to do is get back through the fence without tearing more skin off.'

That was when she smelled the smoke.

Grey wisps tendrilled from underneath and around her car like wraiths. Nell's heart thumped as panic surged up her throat like bile. This time she didn't feel the scrape of the wire as she pushed back through the fence and bolted for the car. Despite her head telling her it was dangerous, she knew the worst danger was not moving it and letting the small grass fire blaze catch onto the car and get away.

The smoke had filled the interior and she coughed as she climbed in. She started the engine and jerked the vehicle across to the stamped-down area, where Moo had been standing for the night, and switched off the engine. Before jumping out, she grabbed blindly over the back seat for the damp hessian bag she kept in the wet bag she'd packed this morning. Her brain screamed at her to get out of the car.

With the pack finally in her hand, she slid out hurriedly and ran back to the now crackling grass fire.

Already a few feet wide, red flames danced through the dry stubble like wine splashing into low-pile carpet where her hot exhaust must have roasted the tendrils until the stubble had caught. Smoke swirled and floated. Thank goodness the wind hadn't started yet.

She beat the building flames, brittle sparks of crushed grass shooting out as she did and smouldering in a new space, while her heart pounded in her chest. She beat and stomped with her boots. *Beat, beat, stomp*, until the flames were crushed under her soles, a black circle of inert charred grass reminding her how quickly it could get away.

When it was over, her fingers shook where they held the now filthy hessian bag. It had been so quick!

She rested her free hand on her chest over her heart. Crap-fest. Now she needed to get her car back over the rest of the paddock without the exhaust starting a new track of flames. She should have walked down to the fence.

Two hours later, Nell eased back on the pedal to slow her car around the long bend of tar into the fifty-kilometre speed zone of Featherwood. Through the whole drive in, she'd shivered at the shadows cast by the double boundary of ghost gums that lined the road. What if those soaring branches burst into flames one day?

Two days ago, Gracie had said she was sick of being pregnant and needed a visitor, and now Nell was doubly glad she had driven in because it had brought home that she needed to plan her exit strategy in a fire. And it would be good to debrief with Gracie about this morning's excitement as well.

Her foot shifted to the brake as she passed the first few houses, passed the one petrol pump and post office, and stopped briefly opposite the church at Jed and Gracie's produce store to buy urea blocks and drove out again. Jed was busy with customers coming all the time, so she'd bought them from Liam. They'd nodded at each other and she'd been curiously glad she had her nice clothes on. Still, she'd been in and out quickly and Liam hadn't smiled.

Jed had seemed genuinely appreciative that she'd be company for Gracie, a concept of value she hadn't felt for a long time.

Driving the short distance to the cattle grid, she bumped over the rattling pipes into Gracie's house yard. She noted the dozen skinny cows Jed had bought for the top paddock and spotted a new calf, similar to the one she'd seen this morning at her place, with its stumpy black tail in the air, oblivious to Nell. It gambolled and bucked and then shot like a dog across the paddock. It bounced up and down, a playful pup, and to her amusement all the young heifers suddenly burst into a run as well, arching their backs, waving tails, as they chased the calf around a big old fig tree. Nell noted the urea block. My, she was getting observant, just like a real farm girl. And a farmer's friend. She grinned at herself.

Even the cranky-looking milk cow with the white face started bucking and trotting. The milling mob made Nell's mouth tilt and she laughed a little out loud. It was a nice relief from the morning's stress.

She needed to get out more. Yep, she'd needed that smile to let go of the last nervousness. Even if Gracie was the least scary woman she'd ever met.

Nell admired Gracie and Jed's silver-grey farmhouse with its new coat of sky-blue paint glinting on the roof. She thought the aged walls looked good unpainted, as if content to be old and loved again as they sat on the brown lawn around the house. The grass had been cut too short, she noted as she switched off the engine, but she probably needed to do the same at her house if today was anything to go by. The shorter the grass, the easier it was to put out if it was set alight.

Gracie waddled out onto the verandah looking like she had three pillows stuffed under her dress. Her face shone red and damp, but the smile she beamed at Nell was warm and unruffled.

'Thank goodness you've come.' Gracie gestured her up the stairs. 'You've saved my sanity.'

Nell felt any leftover tension on her shoulders fall away, drifting in a long wisp, like an unneeded scarf to the floor. She climbed the steps with the basket of goodies under her arm. 'I brought morning tea.' She glanced along the verandah past the windows and doors and shaded bench to the paddock at the side. 'Your house is like you. Friendly and calm.'

Gracie's smile grew wider. 'I like the sound of that. One day, I'll find out all about the people who lived here. It has age and history. Sadly, we haven't stopped chasing our tails long enough to dig deep, yet.'

Nell smiled shyly. 'Me too. Every spare minute I'm trying to learn about farming and animals. And now rural-fire-brigade modules.'

'Love your energy. Go you.' The words were sincerely admiring. Gracie gestured to the door. 'Come out of the sun. We'll have a cold drink out the back. The creek's there. Not that there's much water, but it might make us feel cooler.'

Nell followed the direction of Gracie's arm and felt the colder dimness of the house brush against her skin with welcome relief. A long hallway stretched right to the back door and the outside world again, with intriguing doors all the way down.

'Go for a wander. I'll be in the kitchen. Look in the rooms. There's not much furniture.' Gracie laughed and the snorting sound made Nell smile. 'I'll get the drinks. Don't forget to find the bathroom,' she added, still with that teasing amusement in her voice.

Five minutes later, Nell put her basket on the table at the back verandah. 'It's a lovely house, lovely home. I adore your baby cradle.'

'I know.' Gracie's face creased and her gaze grew softer. 'I loved the white cane on a rocker. And the curved hood. It was a garage-sale find. I miss the browsing in other people's junk, but that was a past life. Though Jed seems to pick up stuff people are throwing out every day. How's it looking up your way?' Gracie gestured to the parched creek in front of them.

'Dry. The spring that feeds the gully dam is still running but definitely slower. I have an extra rain tank, both half full.'

Gracie said mock seriously, 'Good to see they're not half empty.'

Nell's eyes widened at the realisation that she had said that. Then she laughed. 'I don't think I've been that positive for months. You're obviously good for me.'

'Must admit I was excited about you coming today. Although we've been so lucky with Molly and Liam, it's nice to have a woman my own age to connect with.'

Nell considered the word 'connect'. She said slowly as she thought it out, 'That's what I did when I left Sydney. I severed all connections and wouldn't let myself make new ones here.'

Gracie didn't look surprised or immediately curious, as if she knew now wasn't the time for questions. 'Sometimes we need to do that,' was all she said, and there was a faraway look in her eyes. 'Do you have family?'

'No.' Family were people who supported you and believed you over others, especially when you were innocent. She didn't have a mother. Her mother had cut her off. And she was the second mother to do that. Then she stopped as another realisation hit her: she'd just lied to this woman who might become the only friend she had. 'My mother, adopted mother, is alive, but she doesn't speak to me.'

'I'm sorry. That must be hard.' Gracie nodded. 'Jed and I are orphans of the other kind.' She looked up from the drinks she was pouring and smiled. 'We were, until we came here. I think Molly's adopted us.'

'I don't know her well, just from the day at the barbecue.'

'You will. She's at the shop a lot, and so is Liam.' Gracie waggled her brows and Nell tried not to laugh with embarrassment. 'They're good people.'

'It's a strange time to meet people with everyone so worried about the drought.'

'Jed's worried about the people up the valley. He asked me this morning to check that you have a fire plan, or if you needed help with it?'

'Please thank him for me.' Nell hesitated and then blurted. 'I started the RFS modules as I said, but I nearly needed help this morning.'

Concern filled Gracie's eyes. 'What happened?'

It was genuine concern about her. Gracie cared and yet she barely knew Nell. The thought warmed her. 'A fresh calf went through the fence and I had to push it through to its mother.' She shrugged. 'I took the car, which wasn't so smart in retrospect, because when I parked some of the grass under the car caught fire.'

Gracie's eyes widened. 'Must've been terrifying.'

Later it was. 'I was too busy trying to put it out with the hessian bag I had in the back. Getting into the smoke-filled car to move it, that was terrifying.'

'And you were alone,' Gracie said as she slowly shook her head.

'My choice.' Yes, it was.

'Well, I think you're amazing.' Gracie handed her the filled glass. 'I'd be still shaking if that happened to me.'

'It took a while for the tremor to go.' Nell felt suddenly teary, which was stupid considering it was over. 'But it's nice to be able to talk now with you.'

'Of course. And you can phone us at any time.' She wrinkled her face. 'We might need to set up some sort of phone routine so I don't worry myself sick that something's happened to you.'

Nell stared at her. Why would this heavily pregnant woman care about her to that extent? They weren't even friends. Yet.

Something must have shown on her face. 'Now don't get all worried that I'm going to poke my nose into your business, because I won't,' Gracie said.

Nell felt the tug of the smile on her own face. Maybe they were friends already. 'Thanks. You can tell Jed I researched all the things I needed to do to make my house the safest possible. I'm getting through the list.'

'That's great. He also said if you need somewhere to stay to come down here with us. We've got three spare rooms. Emergencies happen.'

She was a stranger and they would open their doors. Nell couldn't imagine anyone she'd known from her previous life doing that on such short notice. 'Thanks, Gracie.' She wouldn't take them up on that, but it felt reassuring. 'Same to you. With the baby.' She waved her hand at Gracie's belly.

Her mouth opened and the last thing she expected came out. 'I was a midwife, once.' Her throat closed and shock made her feel faint. Nell sucked her breath in as nausea climbed her throat. She'd just self-destructed her one chance of friendship.

She must have gone pale, because Gracie's concern was palpable. 'Are you okay?'

Nell stood up. 'I've gotta go.' She could not believe she'd just blurted the one thing she'd sworn she wouldn't tell anyone, ever.

Chapter Thirteen

Gracie

'Can I help?' Gracie saw such distress on Nell's face her heart ached and she stretched out her hand – then pulled it back. She remembered the instinctive shrink from Nell last time she'd reached to do that.

Her new friend's eyes looked haunted with shadows of the past. What the heck had happened to this woman?

Gracie wanted to enfold her in a hug, touch her arm at the very least, but she suspected Nell would run if she did either of those things.

'Please don't tell anyone what I've just said.'

'Of course I won't. You have my word.' Quickly promising was the best she could do. 'But stay for at least a little while. You've driven all this way and don't have to say anything – or you could if it would help. No pressure.'

Nell's eyelids closed as if in slow motion and then she turned her face to Gracie. 'I can't believe I started this.' She swayed slightly, frozen in the moment of escape, pale and shocked, her body still turned towards the door.

'Just sit.' Gracie needed to think of a diversion, quickly. 'How about I tell you my story, instead?'

She watched the emotions cross her new friend's face. Alarm. Fear, even. Resignation and finally a spark of hope that Gracie would let her slip go. And, right at the back of all those emotions, a tiny, reluctant hint of curiosity.

Gracie had a few seconds to hook Nell into sitting down. 'I'll tell you about how I met Jed. And why I won't marry him.' She raised her brows. 'But after the first two, I didn't want another husband.' Gracie paused.

Nell blinked and sat down. As an opening line, it had worked.

'You've been married twice?'

Gracie smiled. Score. 'Almost. Would you like a biscuit?'

'No. I want to hear about your marriages.'

'So, you'll stay for a while? No jumping up as soon as I finish?'

Nell eked out a tiny smile. It looked like it was a tough call, but she did it. Gracie admired her for it.

Nell puffed out a long breath and sagged in the chair. 'I won't run away.'

'Okay, then. My first marriage, I was sixteen.' She shook her head. 'The wedding was nothing to write home about and certainly no fairytale. It was a rushed, backyard affair, forced by my poor boyfriend's parents. Bad contraception found us fertile.' Gracie sighed. 'My mother was a single parent and they were not having their grandchild born out of wedlock like *that* woman.'

'Did your mum feel the same?'

'My mum had enough trouble keeping her own life tidy. She was happy to see me tied to someone other than her. I knew that.'

'It looks like you and your boyfriend were outgunned.'

'We were. And then we were dropped into poverty as if we deserved it. Anyway, after the wedding, his parents said sink or swim. They weren't going to make it easy on us and probably wanted us to fail.' Gracie shrugged. 'We sank. Pregnant at sixteen and we were crushingly broke as two teenagers trying to make a living in the city working in takeaway chains. Prior to that, I had no conception how poor and hungry two people could get. Neither his nor my mother helped, and we just kept spiralling down until we lived in an abandoned house with drug addicts. At least they took us in. That type of destitution sorts out any ideals of love. I will never, ever, be without a nest egg again for emergencies.'

Gracie had a sudden, cold thought that she was there now with the bills the store was running up, and it was an effort to push it away. Jed had this . . . didn't he? She shook her head and settled herself.

She drew a deep breath for the next part. 'We lost our baby three months after the wedding, and I knew, miserably, that I had nothing in common with this bitter young man who didn't love me. For his part, he felt like his life had been stolen by a failed condom.' She spread her hands in a what-can-you-do gesture. It had been a sad affair all around.

A small silence hung in the hot air. She had subjected Nell to an info dump, but there had been something cathartic in blurting out the shame, blame and pain. Maybe Nell would find comfort in not being alone that sad things happened. Plus, she had wanted her to stay. She had wanted to recover the rapport they'd had before Nell panicked.

'I'm sorry for the loss of your baby, Gracie.'

Nell's quiet sincerity made Gracie's throat prickle. It wasn't the response she'd been expecting. 'Thank you. I've come to terms with that loss. I told myself it wasn't that baby's time to grow here. But I did love the fleeting period when the baby was growing inside me. I did believe the moments the baby was here were meant to be.' And she had given her life direction.

'But still sad,' Nell said.

Gracie allowed herself a brief dwell on that past heartache. 'There was this amazing midwife there when it happened. She stayed with me through the labour and after the birth. I called my baby Lindy, and my midwife always did too. She made this incredible little booklet with hand prints and footprints and helped me mother my baby for that brief time I had.' She could see the woman's face even now. 'Those hand stamps were smaller than a five-cent piece, that's how tiny Lindy was. I still have that book, of course. Tucked away and treasured. Anyway. I decided then I'd be a midwife.'

Nell was watching her, obviously engrossed, and affected. She reached out and touched Gracie's hand. 'I'm so sorry for your loss.'

Gracie lifted her chin. 'Thank you. It's a long time ago but she will always be my loved daughter.' She allowed the past to open a little more, not something she did often. Never, really. 'His parents began the divorce swiftly and I haven't seen him since.'

Nell sat back. 'Wow.' She blinked as if still trying to take it in. 'Though, I wouldn't be surprised if my mother forced me to marry, as long as the father was from a good, meaning wealthy, family.'

Gracie could hear the bitterness in the statement. 'You said you don't talk to your mother?'

'No.' She gave a shake of her head and shuddered. 'And, I'd rather hear about your next husband than talk about her.'

Gracie took a sip of the lemon drink, but it didn't wash away the past. 'The second wedding was cancelled the night before.'

Gracie winced at that horrid, ghastly time when the mortality of those around her had slammed in her face. And the guilt.

'Nearly ten years later, and this time, it was my mother pushing me on. My mother and I had an . . .' Gracie paused as she searched for a word, 'odd relationship. The guy was well off, apparently smitten, and Mum envisioned if I married Carl, she'd never know poverty again.'

Ironically, she never had, but Gracie left that truth to lie silent.

'Carl was a lawyer and my mother was ecstatic. We hadn't slept together because I said not until the wedding as I wasn't in love with him. I liked him, we laughed and enjoyed each other's company, but there was no sizzle.' Not like she had with Jed. 'I doubted the marriage would happen. I knew the best contraception in the world could fail. I knew that. What if I never, ever, learned to love him and we didn't get married in the end?'

'Wasn't he sexy?'

'He was handsome, but something wasn't right because he didn't push for intimacy. He was a wealthy, witty man with so many women dying to be in my place, and yet all the way up to the ceremony I felt the finger of impending doom.' Her gaze met Nell's. 'A horrid something's-going-to-happen feeling. Have you ever had that?'

Nell actually paled and whispered, 'Yes.' And Gracie lost her train of thought. *Good grief. Poor Nell, too.* Nell waved her on.

'Anyway, I tried talking to Carl, my mother, his mother, but nobody listened. Everyone said wedding nerves. To my shame, I stopped fighting. Carl wanted me and he would have me. I still didn't know why I was so important to him.'

And she would never know. Gracie took a breath. 'The night before the wedding, a two-car pile-up left three people dead. My future husband and the best man, shockingly – everyone else said – as lovers, in one car. My mother had been driving the other car. Apparently chasing them.'

Nell gasped. 'Oh, Gracie. That's horrible.' Her brows drew together. 'But not your fault.'

It was almost a farce, except for the funerals. 'Of course not.' But even Gracie heard the doubt in her voice. 'Notwithstanding, I vowed never to inflict my potent brand of bad luck on someone special. So no weddings.' She took another sip of the cordial. 'And I was never coming back to New South Wales.'

Nell raised her eyebrows and looked around the back paddock as if to say, *Looks like New South Wales to me.* 'And that's why you won't marry Jed?'

'Not yet. I'm pregnant again. I want my baby to live. And I want Jed to live. I'm not game to risk either of them. Superstition is a funny thing, especially when you're pregnant.'

When Nell sat back, Gracie knew she'd staved off her departure. *Hell of a way to do it*, she thought, but it felt a little less dire now that she had. She'd wondered if telling Nell would help her. It seemed that in some strange way it had.

Nell sat there for a while, no doubt mulling over Gracie's disastrous life, and finally lifted her head. 'Yet you came down here to have your baby? Where you don't know anyone? Don't you miss the people in Roma?'

Did she? 'I miss going to work. I truly loved being part of midwifery group practice as one of the caseload midwives. But I love Joshua Edwards more than a career I can do elsewhere. And I can't do that for a while because of our baby,' she shrugged again, 'so it worked out well.'

Someone knocked on the front door. Solid, assertive knocks. Gracie frowned. She'd just bared her soul and wasn't up to being too social.

Nell jumped up before Gracie could awkwardly move. 'Would you like me to get it?'

'I would. It's probably Blue. He was supposed to come later this afternoon. He's putting an air conditioner in my bedroom, bless him.'

Nell had moved to the screen door and she peered through it. 'It's not Blue.' Whoever it was, her expression said she wasn't happy about it. 'It's Liam.'

'Interesting. Will you let him in?' As if Nell could choose to ignore him at the door. Gracie couldn't help the teasing note. Nell actually poked her tongue out and Gracie laughed. Her friend was certainly more relaxed now than when she'd arrived.

'If he'll look away instead of staring at me the whole way to the door.'

'Liam likes to know what's going on. I think they call it being hypervigilant. From his time overseas,' she said softly. 'People's lives might depend on it.'

She saw Nell's sudden comprehension. 'Oh. Okay.'

Gracie heard Nell's voice as she let him in. 'Gracie said come in. She's out the back.' It wasn't the warmest greeting and she didn't hear him say hello, either. She could imagine his cool nod.

She wondered if Nell would just keep walking past him, out the front and get into her car now, but Gracie didn't think so. No, she'd be polite, especially after Gracie had shared some pretty personal stuff with her. She couldn't hear either of them coming down the hallway. Then she heard Liam's voice.

'Good morning, again.'

There was silence at first, and then eventually, 'Yes.'

Gracie stifled a smile. Who knew which of them was the most uptight? And when had they seen each other this morning?

Liam pushed open the screen for Nell, who came out first.

'Excuse me if I don't get up, Liam.' Gracie gestured to her feet. 'I'm all set up here.'

'All good. I've got Blue's air conditioner out in the ute. I told him I'd put it in for him.'

'Can you do that?' Gracie was impressed.

Liam raised his brows and gave a small quirk of his lips, which was a nice change instead of a flat line. 'Not much use saying I can if I can't.'

Nell looked like she wanted to smack him, but Gracie smiled at him until, finally, he smiled back.

'True story.' Satisfied, Gracie turned to Nell. 'We get to perve on a workman. Woo hoo.'

'I might go home,' Nell said.

'Oh, stick around. Don't you want to see Liam use his muscles?' Neither of them seemed enamoured of that idea and Gracie shook her head. 'My bad. I'm just teasing. Would you like a cold drink before you start, Liam?'

'No, thank you. I'll get my gear.'

Gracie glanced at her new friend, and Nell's loss of calm was palpable. Had she done that with her teasing, or was it just Liam's presence?

'Jed's stationed two comfy chairs down by the creek. Would you like to wander down and sit there with me while Liam sets up?'

The bedroom was directly behind them and the air conditioner would be attached to the wall they sat at. They'd have to move anyway.

Nell looked uncertain.

'I could tell you about how I met Jed?'

Nell narrowed her eyes. 'You are an expert at luring me with your stories.'

'Am I?' Gracie grinned at her, before lowering her voice. 'It's good for Liam to be around us. He usually stays with the men or with Molly. But we'll give him space if we go down to the creek.' Now it wasn't all about Nell.

'Okay, but if you tease me about him – I'm going.'

Gracie raised her hands in surrender.

Nell held her expression. 'And I'll hold you to the cute-meet-between-you-and-Jed story.'

'Done.'

Nell carried the food and Gracie took the two glasses and they moved down the back steps and across the well-shorn brown grass to the edge of the creek. The big camphor laurel offered an umbrella of reflected green shade at least five degrees cooler than the back porch. Jed had taken out the lower branches to create space. The faint trickle of water from the creek added to the illusion of coolness.

They settled with their backs to the creek and watched Liam. Gracie had arranged the chairs before Nell had arrived with the food, and the young woman had sat before she realised the direction they were facing.

Not giving her a chance to object, Gracie dived into the story. 'So, two years and a different state after Carl died, I met Jed. I saw this towering black-haired, big-smile bloke at the Roma Rodeo. He was hard to miss. His curls were bouncing so hard around his face because he was laughing that big-belly laugh. You know the one.' They'd both heard it at the tennis match up the valley. 'Seriously, he made everyone smile.'

Nell smiled with her. 'What was he laughing at?' Nell had a beautiful smile. It was good to see.

'There was this kid with a cowboy hat on his head riding a calf. It had a tiny halter around its black ears and black nose. White calf, probably a Speckle Park breed.' She shook her head. 'The boy had a tin cup on the ground for busking and this big guy crouched down with a ten-dollar note and pushed it in the cup. I remember thinking, *a ten-dollar note? The kid will think he's made it.*'

Nell shook her head, but Gracie could see she wasn't surprised.

'This big, beautiful guy says, "I reckon,"' Gracie made her voice river-gravel rough. '"There's a lot of hours of practice in there, mate."'

Nell burst out laughing at Gracie's impersonation and the bell-like sound peeled out over the yard. She put her hand over her mouth and closed her eyes; the sawing stopped on the verandah as Liam stared across to watch.

Gracie noticed but Nell didn't. Gracie shook her head. The memory warmed her every time. 'I saw it,' Gracie said. 'In him. Right there. His eyes were so warm and free of clouds, I was lost. Kindness shone from him like a light.'

Gracie knew her own face was soft and soppy. 'I read a line once – it said something about seeing the brightness of humanity. That's what I saw in Jed that day. His shining light melted my heart and the chatter of people and cows and the honking of car horns, it all seemed to fade to stillness as I stared at him.'

Nell's eyes were round. 'Wow. That's beautiful.'

'It was. He saw me. Stared. Wiped his hands down the side of his jeans and stepped across and lifted my hand. "I'm Jed."' She used her deep voice again and Nell grinned. '"Joshua Edwards. And one day I'm gonna marry you."'

'He did not!'

'He did. First words. First sight and the guy decided he was gonna marry me.' Gracie threw up her hands. 'That's when I thought, *Oh hell. That will never happen.*'

'So, what did you say?'

She'd put it out there. 'I'm Gracie and I don't do marriage. But apart from the M word, I could know more about you.'

Nell leaned forward, her eyes shining, wistfulness on her face, as if she'd just listened to a fairytale, but was right there with her. 'And after that?'

'He squeezed my hand and tucked it into his arm.' She lowered her voice into gravel again. '"We can work on that," he said.'

Nell sat back and smiled, shaking her head in disbelief – or envy. 'And you've been together ever since?'

'It wasn't all easy.' She thought about Jed losing his job before he got the hardware-store one. Growing quiet. Withdrawn as she was the only one making money. 'The drought killed off the profits for the conglomerate of stations and feedlots Jed worked for.'

Nell nodded. 'I read the Queensland cattle sector's been struggling with all the changes to the live-export industry.'

'Yep. With the prolonged drought, it was a death-blow for workers like Jed.'

'So, he was out of work before you came here?'

'I was doing my thing. Looking after pregnant women in group practice. Visiting their homes all through the pregnancy and labour. Jed finally got work in the hardware store.'

Nell appeared suddenly wounded. She said quietly, 'That's what I wanted to do.' She blinked. 'Not the hardware store. The babies.' She shook herself. 'But I'm not ready to talk about that. So how did you get here?'

'Jed got that job in Roma. We needed to build our savings if we were going to get ahead before the baby arrived. And Jed being Jed, he kept seeing ways to improve in his new employment and the boss hadn't wanted to listen. There'd been no future there.'

She waved her hand to the front of the house. 'Then he found the Farmer's Friend, a run-down store in Featherwood. It came with a house. There was no stopping those dreams once he'd envisaged them. Anyway, it's nice sitting here. Let's eat some of the herb scones you brought. Or the cinnamon cake Molly made.' She cast a glance at Nell and glimpsed the turmoil raging across her new friend's face.

Finally, Nell's shoulders drooped, and she lifted her hand as if to shield her expression. 'I'm sorry about before. I'm not usually a drama queen.'

Gracie would have said anxious, not dramatic. 'I believe you.'

Slowly, as if shifting her body caused pain, Nell turned her chair away from the house, breathed out and leaned back in the seat. She stared at the creek in front of her for a moment, licked her lips to speak and then closed her mouth again.

Gracie buttered her savoury scone and took a bite. After she'd swallowed, she said quietly, 'You don't have to tell me anything or talk about stuff you don't want to. I meant to ask you, did I hear you have a dog?' She offered her gentlest smile.

Nell stared at her for a moment as if she couldn't process the question. Finally, she said, 'I do. Grin.' More of the strain fell away from her face.

'Let me guess.' Gracie's voice stayed casual. 'She smiles?'

'He. I bought him from that strange old lady just out of Featherwood.'

'Mavis.' Mavis could be odd, but she was funny. And real. 'She's not strange, just aging. Sadly. Some days she's worse than others.'

'Of course.' Nell looked down. 'She told me she had a kid at school, so I thought she was delusional.'

'Understandable.' Nell wasn't judging, but information might help her when she met Mavis next time. 'I think having Archie there – he's turning twelve – she's better than she would be. Molly says Archie is better with her than with his mum, Mavis's grand-daughter, who has a drug problem.'

Nell nodded. Thoughtful.

'But tell me about Grin. Great name, by the way.'

'He's a bitzer, mostly border collie, but all black. I had a friend,' she paused, 'once . . .' She paused again, before shaking her head. 'Anyway, she had a dog called Finn, so I guessed I could call him Grin. Mad, I know.'

'I don't think you're mad.' Gracie sat back in the chair. She didn't try to push questions towards her guest, just waited to see if Nell would say anything more.

Nell concentrated on the bends in the creek further down and avoided eye contact. 'Grin's loyal, a bit keen to chase my little herd for the fun of it, but great company.'

'Bring him next time. We have a small shady dog yard beside the house. He can go there if you don't want to tie him up at home.'

'You'd have me back after that performance?'

'Past trauma isn't performance. It's real. I'm not anyone to judge. I've shared my trauma today.'

Nell's head dipped. Then she flopped against the back of the chair. 'I almost ended up with a criminal record.'

Gracie said nothing. She simply waited. *She too has regrets*, she thought and let the silence grow. Nell could talk about it or change the subject. Gracie was fine with either.

Nell heaved out a sigh. 'Both my parents are doctors. Were. My father is dead. Both were disappointed when I started my midwifery degree. I didn't follow the family tradition, but then I am adopted, and my mother has been disenchanted since they picked me up, I think.' She shrugged.

'I'm sorry about your mum. Mothers are people we should have on our side.' *But that doesn't always happen*, Gracie thought wistfully. Then she shifted focus. 'I thought midwifery was a great choice, too.'

Nell's eyes blazed for a moment. 'I loved it. Was over the moon about my studies. Actually,' she looked shy for a moment, pink growing on her cheeks, 'I topped the state in the final exams.'

'Wow. That's cool. You parents must have been proud.'

Nell scrunched up her face. 'They said it was wasted on midwifery and I should have done medicine.'

Idiots. 'Ha. You should do a PhD on breastfeeding or something, and then you'd be a doctor of midwifery.'

Nell actually seemed struck by that. Gracie said, 'I can't think of anything worse than six or seven years of research and writing, but that's how researched change comes about. Doctorates. I just want to catch babies and be hands-on help. Preferably in group practice.'

Nell nodded. 'I'd had a small taste of midwifery group practice during my practical placements. I loved it and wanted to go down that path.'

'So, you did that?'

'My preferred private midwifery practice already had a full staff. I was twenty-three and had plenty of time. They said if I found a place to gain experience, they'd put me on the short list for next time.'

Gracie knew how competitive finding a post-graduate position was for new midwives. Especially in the group-practice arena.

Nell chewed her lip. 'There was an opportunity to work with a private homebirth midwife. I was a little uneasy in case I didn't get on with the midwife, because she liked to work alone. I tried to get advice, but nobody was saying much, and I needed experience. So, I took that position.'

Gracie nodded. 'I did two years post-grad in a hospital in Brisbane before moving to Roma. I couldn't start in private midwifery practice, either. Finally, I found a casual place in the practice at Roma. They called it Babes on the Plain.'

'Cute name.' Nell spoke flatly in contrast to the words. Gracie had a bad feeling about Nell's time in her new employment. 'So, you know that two midwives go to every birth?'

Gracie nodded.

'I'd only been there two weeks, buddying all visits, and was already worried about how much the senior midwife hated the hospital system. The way she played down risks. My concern grew about the chances of an early transfer if we had an emergency. I should have left then . . .' She stopped.

Gracie felt dread coil in her stomach. This wasn't going to be good.

'I didn't have the knowledge to back up my hunch and I still wanted experience under my belt. We went to a house on the North Shore of Sydney.' Nell's voice grew quieter, so Gracie had to strain to hear her. 'They had a birth pool. The woman agreed with my senior that even if she asked for help, she wanted to be talked out of it. No interference.'

Nell shook her head, her eyes holding horror. 'They laughed about it. She said, "Even if I'm screaming for an epidural, don't make it happen."'

Nell dragged her hand over her mouth, before she cupped her chin, as if she could hold back what had occurred. 'I wasn't happy. Things change. Labours do the unexpected. I knew that much. But the husband was there and he agreed. They were professionals, they'd read all the books, done all the classes and had a lot of faith in my senior.'

Gracie kept her voice soft as she said, 'So, you felt you couldn't follow your instincts? Couldn't suggest a less dogmatic approach? Couldn't let the parents down as the second midwife by leaving?'

'All of those. I couldn't just walk away. That would be even more unsafe.' Nell's eyes were huge as she shook her head. 'A woman in labour. It would have upset the parents and I'd have lost my job.'

She waved her hand. 'No excuse. It was a long labour; the mother didn't ask for pain relief until right at the end. Then the baby was born. It was so dark in the birth room, everything seemed normal, but I could barely see in the gloom. I asked about postpartum bleeding, but the senior said hardly anything. Nobody turned the lights on. I was doing the observations on the baby and kept waiting for the senior to do checks on the mother, but she just sat there smiling.

'I offered to do them and she waved me away. She said she could tell all was fine. She touched the mother's wrist every now and then as if that was enough.' Nell narrowed her eyes at the memory. 'All was not fine!' She blew out a breath and consciously let her shoulders drop.

Gracie's hand had come to rest on her belly as if to tell the baby inside everything was all right. Because she knew her own heart rate had increased.

Nell's face had turned white. Gracie didn't know whether to tell her to stop for a few minutes or not. But maybe she wouldn't start again and Nell needed to tell this story, Gracie could see that.

'About twenty minutes later,' Nell's voice was so quiet Gracie had to strain more to listen, 'the mum said she felt terrible.' Nell's eyes were huge. Stricken. 'I lifted the baby away from the mother to give to the dad. Dried it off and the towel came away bloody. Before I could say anything, my senior called out that the mother had fainted.

'I turned on the bathroom light.' Nell's breath came fast. 'Gracie, the pool was a sea of red. Like tomato soup. She'd been bleeding and the senior hadn't noticed. We hadn't noticed.'

Her hand went to her mouth again. 'Her pulse must have changed. I grabbed her wrist but couldn't feel anything. Anyway, once the light went on and we all saw the blood, the husband fainted and I had to grab the baby.' Nell's voice sped up.

Gracie's stomach clenched as she listened.

'I dialled triple 0 even though my senior said, "No, everything will be fine. Stop the call." I did it anyway. It was that call that saved me later. The record of it. I had to put the baby on a towel on the floor to help get the woman out of the bath. When we did, she was like a white floppy doll with her eyes rolled back.'

Nell's horror shone all there on her face from the memory. 'I was so frightened. By the time help came, it was too late. She arrested on the bathroom floor and we'd been working on her for ten minutes before the ambulance arrived. She died.' Nell blew out a breath.

Gracie let the shock wash over her and drain away. She made herself breathe calmly and slowly as she watched the creek trickle past, letting the words and the pictures in her mind float away. She pursed her lips to consciously blow out the stress that was pouring off Nell.

Blimey and hell in a handbasket. Gracie had seen a woman die in the hospital, once. With the full arrest team around her. Though that had been an amniotic embolism. Still, she'd never forgot it. But to be without support? She couldn't imagine.

Finally, she broke the silence. 'I'm so sorry. For the woman and her family. And for you.'

Nell's eyes were huge and she turned her head towards Gracie slowly. As if she had to pull herself back to the present. 'It was a torrential bleed. Like a garden hose on full and no stopping it. She was gone before we could put cannulas in or anything.'

Gracie sat forward, but she didn't touch Nell. She wasn't sure it would be accepted. 'It's a horrible tragedy all around.'

Nel was shaking her head. 'I should have done more. Checked the mother myself and not just the baby.'

'You each had your roles,' Gracie said softly. She hadn't been there and could offer nothing.

'My cowardice in not ensuring those observations were done cost that woman's life.'

So many tiny tells become clear, Gracie thought. Nell's first horror at seeing Gracie's pregnant belly at the barbecue. Her horror at Gracie's offer to feel her baby move. Her wanting to hide, avoid people. The absolute, crushing guilt that made Nell feel like she was a failed human. Where had her mother been? Her midwifery friends?

Really, Nell had come a long way since they'd first met.

'There was a lot of media attention.' The words fell flatly.

Oh, my lordy, yes. There would have been a media circus. *Homebirth midwife allows mother to bleed to death*. Gracie could imagine.

Nell sat back. 'Nasty innuendo and hate mail. My father suffered a stroke and died. From the shame, my mother said. Of course, she blamed me and cut me off from contact. The only friends I had were ex-midwifery students and I couldn't talk to them. My senior told me not to talk to anyone. It was the last thing I wanted to do anyway.' She lifted her eyes briefly.

'One of my tutors did contact me early in the proceedings. She told me to keep my registration, put it on hold, keep doing online courses and give myself time. I did what she suggested, but I'll never go back.'

Gracie could understand feeling like that.

'Even before the court case, we both had our registrations suspended; after it, we were charged with manslaughter, although later the charges against me were dropped. My senior was deregistered, given a suspended sentence and placed on a good-behaviour bond. I got away scot-free.'

Not how Gracie would describe it.

'But no way can I see myself in midwifery ever again.'

Gracie waved her hand. 'There are other things you can do with your registration, but that's for later. How did you live, if you weren't talking to your mother and you weren't working?'

'I would have been on the street, no job, no prospects, but my dad had left me an old terrace flat. It had been his grandmother's home. It housed a tiny shopfront with a one-room residence upstairs in Petersham. It was run-down and ratty, but I went there and lived off the rent from downstairs. I know I was lucky to have that, but they were horrid years. I would have loved a dog. Or a cat.' She shrugged. 'I couldn't get a pet, because I might yet go to jail. It took three years for the case to settle. I didn't talk to anyone except when I had to for groceries. People left me alone. Or I chased them away, became a hermit.'

How had she stayed sane? Gracie felt like hugging her for the loneliness she must have suffered. 'You've never talked to anyone except lawyers about this?'

'Not until after the court case. I'd retreated so much the judge recommended I see a psychologist for six months. A few months later, when the sessions with her were over, a developer made an offer for the shop. Enough for me to buy some land up here and leave Sydney.' She shrugged. 'So, I sold, changed my name and came here. That's why you can't tell anyone about my past. I have to leave it behind.'

Chapter Fourteen

Nell

Nell felt like she'd been crushed through a sieve like a piece of garlic. Her emotions lay shredded and mashed, but inside, in the tight mess of her inner self, she felt just a little sprig of hope. A little cleaner and stronger. As if she'd slashed a purulent wound.

Crikey, Nell felt exhausted. She could barely lift her head. She'd bet Gracie was too. Poor Gracie. She forced a quick look at her and was surprised to see her face held no condemnation, or, thank goodness, pity. Just a gentle sympathy and a lot of understanding. Gracie hadn't tried to comfort her, or touch her, which was a good thing, but somehow Nell felt held.

'I'm so sorry that happened,' the sweet woman opposite her said. 'Losing a birthing mother during labour is a midwife's worst nightmare. Or a doctor's worst nightmare. It happens to them, too, you know. And in high level care as well. To have it happen without a hospital-code alarm to get fast backup is unimaginable. I can't guess how hard it is to finally talk about it. Especially with another midwife.'

Nell put out her hand as if to push that thought away. 'Another? You may be a midwife. I'm not.' She could hear the bitterness in her own voice.

'You were. And what happened to your client and to you is a tragic part of that. When women catastrophically bleed after birth it's a life-and-death emergency. One woman in one thousand dies in underdeveloped countries from postpartum haemorrhage.'

Nell knew that statistic. 'Australia is not underdeveloped.'

'We still lose women. Even here seven women in one hundred thousand die within forty-two days of the end of a normal pregnancy.' She leaned forward. 'We all learn that in our training. More than half of those deaths are related to haemorrhage, embolism or blood pressure.' She waved her hands. 'Even the hospitals can't save them all.'

'I should have checked the mother,' Nell insisted. 'I'd seen my senior didn't do enough observations earlier. I should have called her out for not doing the right thing after the birth.' Even as she said it, she wasn't sure how she could have done that, though. Perhaps she could have whispered it. With the father watching and the mother birthing? It had been far too dark to hand her senior a note. Nell had gone over this so many times in the last years.

Gracie filled her glass and gave it to her. 'It's tough. That's something you've learned in the hardest way possible. But people make mistakes, in all walks of life. They are negligent, stupid, arrogant or just drop the ball for a million reasons.' Gracie held her eyes. 'When health professionals, and I'm talking doctors, midwives and nurses, drop the level of care in the acute setting, it costs lives. And breaks our hearts.' She poured herself a top-up and took a sip. 'That's why hospitals and services like the ambulance, fire and police have protocols for emergencies. But even protocols in institutions don't always prevent people from dying.'

Nell listened and tried to believe, but she was so used to the shame and the shut-down. Gracie opened her palms wide as if asking her to hear what she was trying to say. It was so hard to even think about it all again.

Gracie continued, 'Homebirth with well-regulated midwifery practice has been proven, statistically, to be safer from complications in birth than a birth in a hospital. We've all read those scientific papers. Cheered them. But just like in hospitals, and any other profession, people slip through who shouldn't be practising.'

And isn't that the truth, Nell thought.

'You were a victim, like your client and your client's family, of someone else's mistakes. And you didn't even have your peer group behind you. That's tragic.'

Nell had lived with the guilt and horror for so long she didn't know if she could assimilate Gracie's points, but somewhere inside the first doubts of her absolute guilt began to creep in.

God, what was she thinking to dump all this on a woman who was as pregnant as Gracie? 'I'm so sorry. Can we talk about something else?'

Gracie's shoulders sagged with relief. 'Let's. I think I'll get a dog.'

'Gracie! I've finished.' Liam's voice floated across from the house.

Nell had completely forgotten about him being there. His tall frame moved down the back steps towards them in a smooth, unhurried gait that covered the ground quickly, eating up the distance between them. Like that day in Bellingen when she'd first seen him.

Nell lifted her hand discreetly and touched her cheeks. They were dry. Thank goodness she hadn't cried.

Gracie waved at him and as he drew closer she said, 'Did you want something to eat, Liam? We can come up to the house now and make an early lunch?'

'No, thanks.' He stopped beside them. 'I'll go back to the shop and see what Jed's doing now. There's a truckload of hay coming in soon.'

Nell felt his gaze on her face, no idea how, but in response her cheeks warmed. No way would she look at him. Goodness knew what emotions she was wearing at the moment with everything she'd just relived.

He must have seen something, though. 'Hey, Nell?' His voice was softer than she'd ever heard it. What had he seen? 'You coming to the fire brigade again on Thursday?'

She risked a glance up. He towered over her, his eyes kind not cold, and she looked down, quickly following his body to the ground. Funny how she still managed to catalogue his washboard abs, which were visible through the thin T-shirt. And even skim past his muscular thighs in the blue jeans all the way down to his workman's boots.

He was all man. Too much man up close, offering kindness, when she hadn't been kind to him. She couldn't face him right now, especially with her emotions so shredded.

Gracie must've noticed because she stood and put one hand on Liam's arm and steered him towards the house like a little tug towing a container ship.

'Nell will be inside in a minute.' Her voice floated in Nell's direction as the two walked towards the back steps. 'I'll just get you some of our cake to share with Jed when you go over.'

Nell sat and breathed slowly, evenly, allowing the sounds of the wind in the trees above her to blow away some of the tension in her shoulders. Gracie had been amazing, and it had been good to let some of the angst out. Good that she hadn't run away earlier.

And Gracie had had her moments of unusual interest in her life, too. Good grief. Who would have thought? And who would have thought that Liam would care what she was feeling?

Chapter Fifteen

Gracie

'We'll just go inside and leave Nell alone for a little while.' Gracie steered Liam across the grass.

'She looks upset.'

Now he starts to notice things! Bad timing, she wanted to tell him, but instead she said, 'She's better now. She was getting something off her chest.'

They climbed the steps. Liam got to the top first and Gracie puffed her way up.

'Show me what you've done here.'

'I had to put the motor out here,' Jed said, pointing nearer to the corner than to the door. 'Hope that's okay.' He looked at her. 'I can move it if you want it somewhere else?'

Gracie laughed. 'No, it's fine. You're amazing.'

'It shouldn't be too noisy.'

'I'm sure it won't be, but I don't care if it is.' She opened the back door and stepped through the hallway to her bedroom, which was already cool. Marvellously cool. She leaned against the doorframe, waving her hand inside the cold air. 'Oh my. You've done an amazing job, Liam.'

She examined the floor where she couldn't tell a major installation had happened. 'You must've found the vacuum because there's nothing to show that a workman's been here.'

Liam shifted his feet, clearly embarrassed. 'Hope you don't mind. I found it in the laundry.'

'Of course not. Thank you.'

'It needs a bit of white paint, but I'll bring that back later, or Jed can fix it.'

'You've done enough.'

They heard Nell coming up the steps and Gracie walked back out into the hallway. 'Nell. Come and feel the temperature in my room. Woo hoo!'

Nell appeared at the screen door and pulled it open. She seemed to be trying to jerk her lips into a smile up at Liam and he offered an abbreviated version back. Gracie felt like the third wheel. Then, of course, both of them pulled on their private faces and the walls went up. Maybe she could bang their heads together.

'Feel how cold this is, Nell.' Gracie waved her in. 'I'll be in here with the cool air and you guys will all be melting in the heat.'

Nell tilted her head. 'Knowing you, Gracie, you'll be too busy to lie down in here.' She stepped to the door and put her hand in and wafted it around. 'It'll be lovely in summer when you and the baby need to sleep.'

Nell sounds like a midwife, Gracie thought, but she didn't go anywhere near saying it.

Nell stepped back out of the room and headed towards the verandah door she'd just come in by. 'You're obviously more than a handyman, Liam.'

'If you need something done at yours, you could ask,' he told Nell. 'I like to be busy.' He turned to Gracie. 'What did you want me to take over to Jed?'

'I'll get it from the kitchen.' She slipped past the other two and walked down the hallway. They didn't follow. Maybe they'd actually have a conversation.

From the kitchen she heard Liam say, 'Have you got air at your place?'

'I don't have any power. Only solar with batteries.'

'Do you have a generator?'

'Nope.' Nell wasn't offering long answers and Gracie bit back a smile. They should have a contest about who could give the most information for the least amount of words. They were the total opposite to Jed, but at least they were talking. Except now there was a long, painful pause.

Finally, he said, 'I'll head off.'

'Bye.' Gracie heard Nell's voice and the sound of the back door opening.

One set of footsteps was coming closer, then Liam appeared.

'Here you go, Liam.' Gracie handed him a container with cake and savoury scones. 'Tell Jed to share.' She smiled at him and his mouth lifted. His eyes didn't smile, but he was trying.

Gracie followed him out to the front and waved him off, before she walked down the hallway to the back door again. She found Nell sitting on the swing on the verandah.

'I think Liam is getting better at the social stuff, don't you?'

Nell looked up in surprise. 'I thought it was just me?'

'Molly's fretting that she's lost her brother to dark moods and anxiety.'

Nell seemed shocked at that and maybe a little rueful. 'And that was me jumping to conclusions when I complain about others doing the same. I'm sorry to hear this.'

'Molly said he's turned for the better in the last couple of weeks.'

Nell muttered, 'I'd hate to have seen him before.' She stood up from the swing and came to sit beside Gracie.

'He's been spending the mornings with Jed in the store. Jed actually makes him laugh.'

'I remember you saying that. And you make me smile.' Nell poked her shoulder. An actual physical connection. Gracie grinned at her but didn't comment.

Nell clasped her hands as if she couldn't believe it, either, and needed to control her fingers. 'Tell me about owning the store. Have you and Jed run one before?'

Gracie laughed. 'No. But Jed's landed on his feet. We've been here just over a month and Jed's got a small men's circle going at the table out front. If someone's been here once, Jed knows their name, family and if they have acres or a house yard full of dogs.'

'I can't think of anything worse than that overload of social interaction. Can't imagine Liam enjoying it.'

'He works out the back. He leaves Jed to deal with the table at the front and the drop-in guys there.'

Nell nodded. 'That makes sense. I'm glad your store has started strong.'

Gracie showed her teeth in a grimace. 'We would be if it was cash. Sadly, the line of credit for the store and the number of "accounts" have grown since we arrived. Everyone's doing it really tough with the drought and a lot of those purchases go on their thirty-day account.'

'Do people pay?'

'Most do. The ones that can. I'm doing the books – which I am not good at, but Jed's worse, and it will be even more challenging when the baby comes. But it's getting trickier to pay the suppliers at the end of the month. Sometimes it's not an easy task to meet bills when the payments don't come in.' Gracie stopped herself. She hadn't told anyone her worries. Even Jed.

Nell chewed her nail. 'That's a dilemma. If you need accounting backup, now or after your baby's born, I can do the books. A day or two a week, even. I find it easy. As long as I don't have to serve customers. Chatting to strangers gives me palpitations.'

Gracie felt a flare of excitement. This was too good to be true.

Nell added, 'You could pay me in dog food.'

Before Gracie could jump up and do a pregnancy-limited jig, Nell put her hand over her mouth.

'Cripes. I just told you I nearly had a criminal record and then I offered to look after your accounts.'

'Yes, but you only want dog food for it. I'm happy.'

Nell still looked horrified, but she said, 'I did do the books for the shop downstairs for those years I lived there. I like numbers.'

Gracie laughed so heartily she had to hold her stomach. 'Are you serious? Guardian angel! Thank you. Dog food, urea blocks and dehorning paste if needed. I'll take you up on it.'

Chapter Sixteen

Nell

Nell was home just after lunch, with urea blocks. Two months ago, she didn't know what a urea block was.

Grin greeted her as if she'd been away for a week and she ruffled the dog's soft fur as she unhooked the chain from his collar. 'Did you have a nice day, Grin? Mine was good but not what I expected.'

She closed her mouth abruptly. She didn't want to think about how much she'd shared, but there were other things to analyse from that trip down to see Gracie.

It was nice to know that she could help Gracie and Jed by doing some bookkeeping. And a relief that it would pay for Grin's puppy food. Expensive things, dogs. Working a day or two a week doing accounts for the produce store might just cut down her monthly expenses noticeably.

And then there was Liam. She had made just one long downward sweep of his body as he stood over her and the whole picture sat ridiculously clear in her memory. Nobody should have a chest like that. Arms like that. Even muscled thighs like that, come to think of it. He effortlessly beat the gym junkies she'd known in a sleek, powerful understatement. But she wasn't putting herself out there no matter how good the package.

Except for some cursory eye candy in the last couple of months – actually, that had been Liam, too – this would have to be the rare time she'd even noticed a man and thought about some tactile proof of all that muscle. Not for three, lonely, miserable years had she even been vaguely interested in men.

It turned out, with major irony, the first man she really looked at was just as screwed up mentally as she was. Oh joy. They could share antidepressants. Maybe they'd suit each other. There wouldn't be any long conversations she'd have to worry about. She almost laughed out loud at the thought.

For now, she needed to push it away until she had to revisit it – which would be Thursday at the fire meeting; he'd asked. Speaking of fire, she needed to think seriously about the risk of dealing with fire on her own, after the fright this morning.

At least she wasn't a girl with many possessions. Apart from three changes of clothes, a camera and computer, there were just financial papers and her backpack. And Grin.

Nell stood on the verandah and looked down the paddock towards Moo and the herd. They'd settled again, the calf was asleep beside his mother and the trickling creek still had a centre puddle of water with two happy ducks. There was a camera shot there, a moment of stillness and serenity in the heat, but she had things to do.

She stepped off the verandah, backing away from the house so she could look at the roof and gutters. The house had been built on the side of the hill and there weren't any towering trees that hung over, but maybe she shouldn't have planted those fluffy rushes near the back door. She'd cut them right down to the ground for the next few months. They'd have more chance of survival than if she transplanted them in a drought.

She'd only cleaned the gutters out last week after the barbecue discussions. She kept walking around the small mudbrick house, crunching dry grass underfoot, looking at potential areas that would embrace red floating embers with open arms.

There was a tank tap at the back of the house and the hose hanging from the wall was long enough to reach to the small carport and toolshed. She couldn't help but see an image of standing there alone, a fire roaring like a train down towards her, heat, embers, smoke . . .

Stop it, she told herself.

She considered the tank on the side of the house. At least those taps would run with gravity, but they wouldn't be fast enough to put out a fire. Time to stop pushing people away? The thought shocked her. Because when it all boiled down to it, she did want to live.

With clarity, she remembered the faces at the barbecue Gracie and Jed had arranged. Ruby, the lady with the lamingtons and her husband, Charlie. They'd even asked her if she wanted to go see them next Sunday for lunch.

Then there was Jill and the little girl, Holly; she was only about six. They'd been friendly, too. At least Jill's husband, Blue, someone she knew a little better since he was the fire-brigade captain, didn't think she was useless. During her first real fire attendance on Friday afternoon after her first meeting on Thursday, Nell had sat at the side of the road monitoring smouldering wood with Blue.

He had been impressed that she'd done all of the first-stage online modules. There must have been twenty of them.

Their job had been to watch a slow-burning tree hit by lightning fall over and then remove it from the road. Blue had said it was too dangerous to cut down beforehand. It had taken four hours to burn enough to fall. But she'd learned a lot by listening to the older man. And he'd gone through the truck systematically with her until she could name and use every object or mechanism.

The time had actually flown for what could have been an incredibly boring afternoon as the fire had crept inch by inch through the tree, but by the end Nell had understood more about risks in bushfires and falling trees, and a lot about the truck.

Blue gave her confidence, as opposed to taking it away. Maybe she should ask him if he'd come and cast an eye over her preparations. Perhaps even offer her advice. Or she could ask Liam. He'd been at the meeting and knew what he was doing, too. He had fire qualifications from the army.

Liam, who 'liked to be busy' and who had said if she needed something done, she could ask. And had incredible abs and cool but gorgeous blue eyes. She'd think about it before Thursday and decide if she wanted to solicit a favour.

Interesting choice of word, *solicit*. She stifled a quiet laugh.

Chapter Seventeen

Mavis

'Those paddocks are a worry, Archie.' Mavis narrowed her eyes at the stubbled grass. 'I still think you need to mow as low as the ride-on will go.'

Mavis planned to fight a fire if it came. She and the boy had been trimming bushes and dragging any stools or combustible plant pots into one of the small, empty rooms in the house. The problem with that was if the house went then everything went.

For the moment, the best she could do was cut down on the places where embers could smoulder out of sight against the building. She'd told the boy, if the time came, she'd send him to Gracie's on the tractor with the dogs. They were having words – and no words – about that, but she'd get her way.

'Good job we got that pipe buried up the hill.' But she was beginning to think everything was out of her control. It would be luck, not preparation, if the firestorm came up her gully like it had last time. This had been no ordinary drought, and the early summer had been no ordinary heat.

Archie didn't comment. He was giving her the silent treatment.

She hadn't realised he had a stubborn streak, which he'd possibly got from her.

Reggie, her old faithful and father of all the puppies, sat beside her feet and looked up at her as he thumped his tail.

'We love this place, don't we, Reggie,' she said as she patted his big head. 'You and me both got white whiskers.' She stared out over the paddocks, appreciating how much she'd loved being able to provide a home for Archie. How much pleasure she'd been gifted from the kid, though they'd had their moments of unusual interest as he'd settled in.

He'd made her change, too. Take a bit more care of herself. She could probably do more but now wasn't the time. They were famous friends. Apart from the disagreement about who stayed and who went in the case of a crisis, the boy was smiling much more often.

She hadn't appreciated that she'd dumped such a load on his young shoulders with her stubbornness. She was never too old to learn, she guessed. And he wasn't too young to learn. He'd taught her that.

Chapter Eighteen

Gracie

Gracie wiped a drip of perspiration off her nose. She wondered how much of this heat she could take before her baby came. Her EDC, or estimated date of confinement, such old-fashioned wording, had arrived. She was due today, but she knew how unreliable estimating due dates was.

There was nothing to say her baby would be here any day. She'd be a big, round, dehydrated crust curled in the corner soon. The sky hung bleached and piteously free of clouds above her as she flipped clothes to spread over the verandah rail because she couldn't face going down the steps to the clothesline with the basket.

Outside, the sun seared the creek stones Jed had dumped and smoothed on the drive, now too hot to walk on with bare feet, though Gracie loved the shiny round pebbles to the gate. They rattled and crackled when disturbed, so she never missed the sound of a car if someone dropped in unannounced.

The water out the back resembled a dying drain more than a creek that would eventually run to the sea, with decreasing pools of shallow green water shrinking in front of her eyes.

The top-paddock cows were being supplemented with the scraps of dry feed Jed swept from the floor of the hay shed before each, incrementally smaller, new load of feed was trucked into the store. Their little herd looked thin, but they'd been emaciated when they'd arrived two weeks ago, so they were no worse off. She'd wondered to Jed whether or not it was a good idea to buy cattle in the middle of a drought. Jed had said the bloke selling them had been in a state and he hadn't been able to say no. And he'd given him top price for them, while dishing out discounts to others.

That was Jed.

Jed had phoned Nell and suggested she bring her little herd down as well until it rained and the increasing fire danger lessened. He knew a livestock transporter who could help her if she decided to take him up on the offer. Surprisingly she did.

Apparently, Blue and Charlie were shipping cattle out to the coast. Nell's cows had arrived last night and Nell's new calf and Gracie's were gambolling together now. That made Gracie smile.

She wiped her brow again. Thank goodness it wasn't Thursday. She only went to the shop on Thursdays now when Jed did the deliveries in the truck. Liam usually came in to lift anything that needed moving and Mavis wandered down for a cup of tea while she waited in the store for Archie to finish school. The older lady had been a casual worker in the old store over the years and she had amusing stories about some of the customers. As long as she wasn't confused. The vagueness and short-term memory loss that caused flashes of worry to cross Archie's face were becoming more frequent, though.

Archie helped Liam until Jed came back, the young boy and the ex-soldier seeming to get on well, companionably lifting any bags of feed or heavy liquids into the cars for Gracie, who gave the boy pocket money and Liam a smile. That's all he'd take.

Later, Archie rode his bike and Mavis walked home past the village to their farm. Those two, so different in age, seemed perfectly in sync. Except for Mavis's deterioration, which seemed more pronounced as the summer came in. The old and the young. It was wonderful how symbiotic some relationships could be. And it would be such a shame if this relationship was broken by dementia.

Or squabbles. At the moment, she and Jed were having some niggles in that area. Jed said it was because she was impatient for the baby. Whereas Gracie felt he was riding their finances too close to the edge to guarantee said baby had a roof over his or her head. Either way, they hadn't made up before they went to sleep last night and she was still stewing over it.

He'd given half their customers an extra month to pay their bills, but by then they would have run up double the amount. Nell's frown when she'd helped with the accounts on Monday had made Gracie's stomach ache and not from the pains she wanted.

Nell had pointed to the spreadsheet of the Farmer's Friend creditors and said, 'You need forty thousand dollars by next week. Do you have that?'

'Sure,' Gracie had replied. It would come in, but not unless every single debtor paid in the next week. They might have fifty thousand if the ones who still owed from last month paid. She'd told Jed he'd have to write to the extended ones and ask for half at least of what was owed. He'd said no way. She'd have to ring the suppliers and beg for time.

With her washing hung and safe back inside and out of the heat, Gracie leaned against the door of the baby's little lemon-and-peppermint room and tried to dream the dimpled baby dreams she usually did when she stood here. She wiped the back of one hand across her damp cheek and circled the heel of the other on her back.

'I'm really feeling your weight now,' she said to her stomach. 'Serves me right for falling in love with a man with big bones.'

A white-painted wrought-iron single bed, low to the ground, waited with its peppermint quilt inside the nest-room she'd created for toddlerhood. The tiny wooden wardrobe and chest of drawers shone with new lemon paint, matching the rocking chair Jed had sanded and repainted. He'd spotted the chair on the Progress Association noticeboard and had to have it for Gracie. What was fifty dollars, he said? Every fifty counted, she'd replied.

Yesterday, she'd packed the cupboards with tiny and newly washed outfits and printed muslin wraps. So many little parcels of hand-me-down clothes had arrived from their customers. Only things in wonderful condition and often brands she would never have been able to afford. It made her warm to her soul that people cared enough. Jed passed on that they all said, 'We thought Gracie might like that.' She didn't think the town had had a new baby for a while and there were only twelve children in the school.

The empty white cradle stood waiting in the main bedroom with new sheets and a quilted top rug gifted by Blue's wife, Jill. Jed had brought the hand-sewn gift home from last week's fire meeting.

The house was done. Two empty guest rooms, for who knew when they'd have guests, had matching wooden double beds and wardrobes Jed had found at a garage sale and couldn't go past. They'd even taken the camphorwood chest full of immaculate hand-embroidered sheets and almost a dozen pure-wool blankets the granddaughter of the deceased had wanted to be rid of.

New plumbing fixtures had been methodically installed by Jed and Liam on Sundays when the store was shut. Gracie's house thrummed with anticipation for her baby's arrival.

The tumbled stones rattled outside on the drive and Gracie looked up from her abstraction. 'Visitors, baby? Who's dropped in?' She trundled her weight through to the front door and smiled as Nell climbed out of her car.

'Have you come to keep me sane?'

'To keep us both sane. I have a question.' Nell smiled at her. 'Is now okay?'

'Yes, please.'

Nell took a moment to unhook her dog from the car seat. 'Sorry it's only a five-minute visit. I wanted to check Moo and the calf weren't upset by the change of paddock. And the chooks weren't driving you mad,' she said.

Nell studied the mixed cows with concentrated eyes. Gracie considered the city girl and her adaption to this new world. She was amazing. 'They all look good. Thanks so much for having them. Just bill me the hay costs.'

Gracie shook her head. 'Jed said no.'

'You know you need to.' She hesitated. 'Grin and I have been into town to stock up on groceries. I should have asked if you wanted anything.' Contrition crossed her face. 'I won't forget next time.'

Gracie waved that away. 'I've had deliveries. It's easier.'

Nell blew out a breath, relieved. Grin jumped down and headed to the back of the house. He knew there'd be a water bowl and possibly scraps waiting for him. 'After the fire the other day,

I didn't like to leave Grin tied up home alone when I went to town for food.'

Gracie shuddered. 'Of course. Kettle on or cold drink?'

'Cold water would be wonderful, thank you.' Nell disappeared around the side of the house after Grin and Gracie heard the clink of the small dog gate as she turned to go back inside.

She missed friends dropping in. In Roma, she'd had midwifery work meetings three days a week to keep up with the client load and had exchanged social visits with the other midwives around that. Plus, the loss of contact with pregnant women meant Gracie was especially glad of Nell's company. They'd had a few visits now, each more fun than the last.

Nell came into the kitchen, boots off, and washed her hands, and Gracie decided she almost looked as if she felt at home. They'd come a long way. Gracie smiled at her. 'Follow me when you're done. We'll go into the bedroom.'

Jed had suggested she take to leaving the air conditioner on low in their bedroom and closing the door, so that when she needed a cool oasis it was there.

Gracie had added a small round table and chairs beside the double doors. In the evenings they opened the doors, but when it was stinking hot like now, they could sit in the cool room and look through the glass to the heat outside.

Nell followed her in with a sigh. 'Cripes. It's bliss in here.'

'It's going to be a stinker of a weekend. Did you know the village races are on Saturday? At the little showground on the edge of town.'

Nell settled into her chair. 'They were talking about it at the fire-brigade meeting. Said it was nearly cancelled.'

'Yep, "apparently".' They said, 'Mavis,' in the same breath, then smiled at each other.

'Anyway,' Gracie said, 'it's been held in the first weekend in November for the last fifty years. The Progress Association, which Jed has joined, voted unanimously to go ahead.'

'Are you going?'

'Absolutely.' Gracie smiled. 'There are people to talk to, and Molly's made me a hat.' She waved her hand to the dresser and the large pink straw boater. 'It has tiny pink plastic storks on it.'

'Storks or flamingos?'

'Because,' Gracie said sternly, 'I'm a big, pregnant balloon, they are storks.' She cast a sidelong glance at Nell. 'Wanna come and put your picnic chair next to mine on Saturday?'

Nell, still staring at Gracie's hat in astonishment, chewed her lip. 'I told the brigade mob no.' She paused, before she broke out into a gamin smile that lit her whole face and shifted Nell from beautiful to extraordinary. 'But if you're wearing that hat, I might not get another chance in my lifetime to see something like that.' The smile disappeared as if she'd just realised what she'd promised. Her tone stayed light, but the effort was obvious.

Gracie waited silently, not pushing.

'And if I can put my dog in your yard.' Nell blew out a breath. 'Sure, but the idea of that many people freaks me out.'

'I know, but it's brave of you.' Gracie held her surprise. She hadn't thought there'd be any chance Nell would consider coming. 'It shouldn't be that crowded. How many people would it be? You can just smile and nod.'

'Okay. I'll be there to watch the horses stir up the dust, but I'm not wearing a hat.' She grimaced. 'Or not a fancy one, anyway.'

'I could lend you one of my storks. Molly insisted it's a must for all the girls. Unless I go into labour first.'

'It's your due day today, isn't it? How cool.'

'Yes. And I'm not in labour,' Gracie complained. 'What did you want to ask me?'

A pause. Gracie was getting used to Nell's pauses, and she'd learned to wait.

'Blue asked me to be treasurer for the brigade. I backed away, of course. I'm wondering if I should have said yes.' She winced. 'And if I did, do I have to tell him about my past?'

'You weren't accused of being a thief, so why should you?' Gracie tilted her head. 'Your midwifery past has nothing to do with being treasurer for the Featherwood Rural Fire Service. If you'd like to do it, say yes.'

Jed had mentioned Nell's attendance at the musters for new brigade recruits. There'd been several small spot fires the unit had gone out to and everyone was getting practice at some advanced skills to manage the outbreaks.

'Thanks. I'll think about it. Seems there's no one else with bookkeeping skills.'

'Just make sure Jed doesn't volunteer for it.' There was a little too much bitterness in the words and Gracie closed her eyes. Snarky wasn't like her.

Nell changed the subject. 'Races.' She breathed out. 'If I went with you, I could volunteer for an hour on the sausage-sizzle roster, I suppose. The first hour before it got busy. Just cooking. I'm not talking to people. I'll think about it.' Nell sat back and picked up her glass of iced water. 'Enough about me. How was your ante-natal visit yesterday?'

'The clinic in Armidale is great. Baby and I are well. My blood pressure's fine and they're not worried about the swelling in my ankles. I'm booked for induction in two weeks, the longest I could get them to wait for me to go into labour, so I just feel heavy and hot.' And cranky with Jed, which was so unlike her.

'Of course. Are you getting Braxton Hicks?'

'Am I.' Gracie blew out a breath and eased her shoulders as she thought about the usually painless tightening of the belly that mimicked contractions. It felt good to talk to Nell about something other than the finances circling in her head. 'Sometimes my belly's so tight it makes me stop, but if I sit down it goes away.' She laughed. 'If I get tight sitting down, then walking makes the contractions stop. It's so funny. I've been telling pregnant women for years to change the activity to decide if it's labour or they're having Braxton Hicks contractions. Now I can actually feel it happen, I understand what they were going through.' She rubbed her rounded belly. 'It's weird being on the other side of the maternity circle instead of being the midwife.'

'It's your baby. It's exciting.' Nell appeared almost as surprised as Gracie when she said that. She shook her head as if to jiggle the oddness away. 'Is Jed nervous?'

Gracie rolled her eyes. 'He's asking me a hundred times a day if I'm okay. To let him know if the contractions start. Most of the time, I don't tell him about the Braxton Hicks because he goes into panic mode.'

'Fair enough. Ring me any time if you want company. I can come down and I'll bring Grin in case you want me to stay until Jed comes home.'

They both drained their glasses of cold water and put them down.

Nell stood. 'I've gotta go. I'll do the RFS books. It'll be good to have that sorted. See you Saturday if not sooner.'

The day of the races dawned with a westerly wind hot like the wood stove, fan-forcing the heat into Gracie's skin. There was more than a pall of smoke in the air and yesterday's sunset had been a red ball she could look at for as long as she liked through the haze. She didn't like it though. That sort of red sun made her nervous.

The conditions made a lot of people nervous. Gracie stood on the verandah and watched Jed cross the paddock to the shop. There'd been a few more lightning strikes; most had been reduced from out of control to under control fairly quickly, but it took call-outs for the volunteers and energy to damp them down.

The consensus, among those who'd passed through the Farmer's Friend the last few days, sat with everyone wanting to forget drought and disaster and have a fun day catching up with mates at the races.

Even Jed was closing the store dead on midday – when usually he stayed open chatting and helping latecomers until around two pm most Saturdays. Maybe he should have stayed open and made some cash sales. The bills were due to be paid and he still hadn't asked the customers to pay.

At two minutes after twelve, Jed dashed into the shower while Gracie pulled on her Molly-made tent dress, a stunning number in green with little flamingos masquerading as storks, and they met in the kitchen by twelve-thirty. 'First race is at one-thirty,' Gracie said.

Jed buttoned his one RM Williams shirt, tucked it into his best jeans and stomped his boots – he needed new ones – then leaned to the hat rack and completed his attire with his Akubra hat.

Gracie straightened his collar and leaned up. She inhaled the man cologne he rarely used and felt that flutter of pride and gladness that he loved her, despite the financial worries that smothered them. She kissed him. 'You are one handsome country devil, Mr Edwards.'

'And you look like a delicious flock of storks, my love.' They smiled at each other, both pretending there wasn't any strain between them.

'I don't know how long I'll last in the heat.' Gracie wiped a bead of sweat off her lip.

'I left the aircon on in the bedroom for you. I'll bring you home as soon as you want.' He waggled his brows at her. 'We can both have a lie-down in the cool when we come home.'

'Joshua Edwards, are you propositioning me?'

'At least a cuddle with you looking so edible.' There'd been no cuddling in the last few days. It had been all back to back and neither of them sleeping well.

She snorted. He was terrified of more activity than that. 'I thought you were I-might-poke-the-baby scared?' she teased.

Jed blushed and Gracie snickered. 'Let's go see how Feather-wood turns on the fun and I'll seduce you later.'

He held out his big hand and she took it with a surge of warm happiness bubbling up her throat. She was so lucky and she wasn't doing anything to draw bad luck.

They ambled across the road, sticking to the shady side of the street, then across to the racetrack, which doubled as the cricket pitch. Already dozens of cars had pulled up in rows in the paddock.

The Progress Association had organised people to direct the cars, and the stream from town had Jed lifting his brows. 'Way more cars than I expected.' He waved to a well-dressed couple from the Dorrigo side of Featherwood who shopped at the store.

'Everyone's looking for light relief,' Gracie said. 'First race doesn't start for another forty-five minutes, so there's plenty of time to put your fifty-cent bets on.'

Jed liked to study the form and take on the wild tips he'd been gifted with through the week. Gracie liked the names of the horses, and they both bet tiny on the races, which was the minimum bet allowed. And thank goodness; a gambling problem was the last thing they needed on top of everything else. While Jed's flutter involved many races with the TAB, Gracie would do the four names she liked on the program for a win if she lasted that long.

As they walked through the showground shelter, filled now with bookies and food vendors, and out to the enclosure looking over the dirt racecourse, Gracie marvelled at the tables and chairs laid out on the grass and the festive groups setting up. Bigger and brighter than all the rest under a pop-up shade house, a white plastic setting with ten chairs read, 'The Farmer's Friend Table'.

Gracie cast a sidelong glance. 'Did you organise this, Jed?'

Strangely, he didn't meet her eyes. 'We made a donation to the committee and they gave us a table. You needed somewhere in the shade to sit.'

Goodness knew how much that had cost, they certainly couldn't afford it, but she was keen for a seat after the walk in the heat. She'd ask how much later, when they got home. There was nothing she could do about it now, but it was an indication of their problems that this was the first she'd heard about Jed's latest generosity. 'Thank you,' she said, fighting to keep her voice neutral.

The grass had turned to brown stubble that the race-club committee had tried to make a little bit greener for the day and already umbrellas were popping up. The sausage sizzle looked to be doing a roaring trade under a big blue pergola, and she caught a glimpse of Nell in a white apron through the crowd.

Liam stood next to her. *Oooh*, Gracie thought with a lift of spirits and a delighted kink to her mouth. *Fun*.

Chapter Nineteen

Nell

Nell squeezed the tongs in her hand and turned another sausage. She wasn't sure whether the heat was coming from the pitiless sky outside the tent, the barbecue she'd slaved over for the last half an hour, or the man who'd appeared right next to her two minutes ago. They'd nodded at each other but hadn't said anything, yet.

She'd been weary, hadn't slept much last night because of the smoke in the air and the worry that a ball of orange fire would sweep up her valley and she'd sleep through the approach. Nobody wanted to get fried in their bed.

Funny how the weariness had dropped away since Liam had arrived. It was a very small pergola. And he was standing very close. His shoulders were huge.

If she'd known Liam had volunteered at the same time as she had, she would've picked a different time but still she eyed him sideways. She didn't have the head space to think about sex, and Liam didn't need a screwed-up ex-midwife leeching onto him because he was the only available male around. He had his own mental health issues. Yet it didn't stop her from inhaling discreetly . . .

Ahhh. Over the top of a truly yummy men's aftershave, the scent of smoke drifted off him and it wasn't the barbecue kind.

'Have you been out fighting fires?' she asked.

He'd been rubbing in alcohol cleanser, but he stopped at her question and picked up another pair of tongs. Began putting new snags on the empty side of the barbecue. 'A couple of lightning strikes last night caused a nuisance.'

'What time?' She hadn't got a call.

'Just after four this morning. I was back by seven, but I went out again until eleven.'

He'd have to be tired. 'So why are you here?'

He gave her a didn't-think-you-were-dumb look. 'I put my name down.'

'Just saying we can manage if you're tired.'

His tongs lifted from the plate as he turned to her. 'Do I look fragile to you?'

He stood very close. Peacock-blue eyes caught hers and for a change his expression wasn't cold or even indifferent. Something lurked behind the usual wall of distance, and if she wasn't mistaken, it may have been a tinge of lustful amusement aimed her way.

What had he said? Fragile? This whipcord hunk who looked like he could wrestle a crocodile? She wasn't sharing that thought. 'No. You look quite fit.'

'Quite fit?' He stared.

She'd actually teased him. She was just as surprised as he was. *Please get the joke, Liam*, she implored silently and mentally crossed her fingers.

He smiled, and a tiny tickle of pride surged through her. He'd be human soon, and so would she. This Featherwood place was fluffing up her and Liam's people skills, and there might be hope for them, separately, yet. But she wasn't going for broke. She was already broken.

She thought about Gracie's comment – Liam having trouble finding anything that made him smile. She could be another friend to him. A platonic one would be sensible. As a loner, she needed more friends.

Gracie had helped there. Liam had Jed and Gracie, and he had his sister, but she could return the favour she'd been granted by others and befriend him. It was incredible how much difference one extra friend could make.

Liam as a buddy would be very different. And possibly difficult. But she wouldn't judge Liam, like Gracie didn't judge her. Heck, she'd stop judging anybody. She'd even judged poor old Mavis when she'd bought Grin and she hadn't been crazy or lost – just aging, as she was entitled to.

Which reminded her: she needed to keep an eye on Mavis today. The sun shone stinking hot and the old lady would parch like beef jerky in the open, especially if she had a few beers.

'What on earth is going on inside your head?'

Nell refocused. Living alone and in her inner thoughts for so long made for fade-outs. Liam was studying her like she was an interesting bug. There was that something else in his gaze. Perhaps a thought that she was even a pretty, attractive bug.

You know what? she thought. She could just say what was in her head. She didn't have to hide anymore. She could just be herself, and if Liam didn't like it that was okay by her. 'I need to remind Mavis to drink water today or she'll get dehydrated.'

He stared at her. 'Random.'

She smiled at him and his eyes widened. The lift in her spirits felt amazingly good.

'I'll get her a bottle of water,' he said.

'Two sausages, please,' a voice came from behind them and Nell remembered where she was.

When their stint at the barbecue tent ended, Nell found herself walking with Liam to the Farmer's Friend table, his long strides matching hers perfectly, their hips almost touching. She needed distance to keep this sensible and she eased a fraction more space between them.

When they arrived, another dilemma popped up. Where to sit? Did she sit next to Liam, or next to Molly or Mavis? Mavis sat with a beer in front of her and a wide smile on her face as she watched the crowd. And Jed was already sitting next to Gracie.

Archie had taken off with a bunch of kids that Nell had seen running in a pack around the outskirts of the field, and Liam's sister was sipping the sparkling wine they were serving at the bar.

'The workers have returned,' Jed said. 'Welcome. Take a seat.'

Liam pulled out a chair for Nell beside Mavis, so she sat, but he didn't. He just hovered behind her like a big-shouldered panther ready to pounce. Now she was getting fanciful. Australia didn't have panthers. And substituting dingo just didn't do it. She ducked her head and smiled at the table and tried not to imagine Liam as a big dingo. Nope. Panther.

The loudspeaker crackled. 'Finalists for the best hat are . . .' Jed waved everyone to silence and craned his neck. 'Quick, sit down, Liam,' he said. 'I can't see.'

Liam slid in next to her, strong thighs brushing hers for a sec, and the whole exciting, awkward, close-to-Liam sensation started again, like a well-oiled machine. *Darn it.*

'Could the ladies with the numbers two, ten, fifteen and thirty please come up to the stage.'

Jed cheered like a crazed footy fan and pumped his fist.

Gracie stood up and she and Molly grinned at each other. Liam caught Nell's gaze. His eyes were crinkled and she could feel the wide smile on her own face; as one, they turned to watch Jed. Jed's face looked split in half as he gazed at his love while she waddled to the podium. Nell could do nothing but share her delight with Liam as their eyes met again, his thigh continuing to press against hers.

'Come on, Gracie,' Jed muttered, his big fingers crossed in front of his chest as if he could magic Gracie's result, while his fixed intensity was drawing a smile from everyone at the table.

Nell grinned at Liam. This was turning out to be a fun day, she admitted to herself, and squeezed her own thigh back towards Liam as a look-at-Jed nudge.

Their whole table watched Gracie toddle her way to line up with the other hat ladies, and while some of the competitors had very pretty headwear, Gracie's storks waved and jostled with each other on top of the brim like they were elegantly dancing.

After three tense minutes when Jed barely breathed, the microphone came on again. 'Unanimous decision,' the man at the microphone said, 'the winner is number thirty, Gracie Sparke with a Molly Mears creation.'

Jed whooped so loudly people from other tables turned to stare and then smile at him. Gracie waved the tiny hat trophy and was helped down off the stage by one of the other contestants. Everyone was smiling. It was no surprise to their table that Molly's storks had won the title.

Jed lifted his beer to Molly. 'Great job, Moll.' He then stood up and helped Gracie into her seat as she plopped back in the chair.

'What excitement,' she puffed.

'We'll save a bottle of bubbles for after the baby is born,' Jed said.

'I'd settle for a cold water.'

Jed studied his lady because Gracie's face was pink from the heat.

'I'm not looking forward to that walk home.'

'Take my car,' Nell said. 'It's under a tree over there, not far. Jed can drive you home. Just leave the keys in it and I'll grab it when I go. I've got to collect Grin, anyway. But I won't come in, just in case you're having a rest.'

'I'm tempted, but then you'll have to walk in the heat,' Gracie said.

'I'm not nine months pregnant.' Nell patted her own flat stomach.

'I'll drop Nell back.' Liam's offer made her turn to look at him. His face bore no expression, though. It was so hard to tell what he was thinking and all the smiles had faded. He'd gone serious on her.

Nell decided she'd walk but save that announcement for later. 'Thanks.' She dug in her bag and pulled out the keys to the BMW.

Gracie looked torn. 'We should have brought the car, Jed.' Then she sighed. 'But yes. Thanks. You're all champions.'

Jed reached to pocket the keys. 'Much to my embarrassment, I'm ready to take you up on it.' He stood and gently took Gracie's arm. 'Let's get you home, love.'

Nell watched them go, suddenly unsure whether she wanted to stay. No. Running away wasn't going to help her long term. She hadn't even bet on any races, and with Gracie gone she should try her luck. 'I fancy a flutter,' she said as she stood up.

'I'll come,' Liam said. 'Jed gave me a tip.' He spread his hands to indicate the racecourse. 'I am at the track.'

A whole three sentences, Nell thought. She caught Molly's eye and Liam's sister waved her away as if to say this was doing him good. She nodded in acknowledgement to Molly, but she was not responsible for Liam's future social skills. However, she was responsible for her own, so she smiled and eased her shoulders.

She walked with Liam to the betting ring, where the bookies – four grizzled men and one woman – had tall black boards with dials to change the horses' names and odds.

The woman Nell chose took her five dollars on the nose for Winnersaregrinners, which she'd chosen because of her pup and despite the long odds. Liam's ten on Jennaleigh, Jed's tip, was accepted with glee.

Nell drifted to the rail to watch the next race and Liam disappeared for a few minutes without mentioning his plans. One second he was there and the next he was gone. She shrugged and tried not to be annoyed. He didn't have to tell her what he was doing. She didn't need him to have a good time, anyway.

When he reappeared, much to Nell's gratification that she tried to hide, he passed her a plastic glass of sparkling wine. He sipped his own man-sized insulated water bottle.

'Thank you.' She smiled up at him, then remembered Mavis. 'I meant to get a bottle of water for Mavis.' She turned to look across the paddock to their table.

'I just dropped one off to her.'

'You did?'

'You wanted her to have water. Easy.'

Good grief. That was kind. And observant and scarily efficient. 'Thank you.' Clearly, there was nothing wrong with his memory.

He shrugged and lifted his bottle. 'Cheers.'

The bell went and the third race began, and Nell understood the subject was closed. She was here for the horses, anyway.

Liam's mare took off like a rocket and Nell's gelding settled two from the back of the pack. Oh well. By the second lap, however, Nell's horse had passed the rest then edged up to Liam's. It almost pulled ahead.

Nell could feel the buzz of the surrounding people's excitement seep into her. Her face tightened in a smile, breath coming faster. A laugh bubbled, lurking just behind her throat. This was fun.

'I'll catch you,' she shouted above the din to Liam.

He raised his brows at her and took a sip of water, combat-faced. He was doing that on purpose, but she didn't care. She was excited.

Nell gripped the white wooden rail with her free hand. 'Come on, Grinner. Come on,' she urged, jiggling on the spot. Liam's gaze slid over her as she wiggled, but she didn't care. This made her feet itch to jump.

Her horse edged closer to the lead. Liam's horse hung just out in front but was visibly tiring and the two horses thundered towards their position on the rail, shoulder to shoulder, as the winning post drew near. They flashed past too close for Nell to judge the victor.

Photo finish.

Nell raised a fist. 'Yes!' She sculled her remaining half-glass of bubbles and lifted her brows at Liam. 'I'll buy the next drinks when they confirm my win.'

'Confident?' Liam leaned down so she could hear him. 'It might be my win.'

Nell made a rude sound. 'Mine.'

When the announcement confirmed Nell's horse as winner, she crowed a little and flashed Liam a triumphant smile. 'A beer?'

He shook his head. 'It'd send me to sleep if I did. Diet cola would be good, thanks. You want me to get them?'

'No. I'll go after I pick up my winnings.'

Blue waved at Liam and he nodded at the older man. 'I'll meet you back here before the next race.'

Nell agreed and pushed off to get her winnings and the drinks. Standing at the bar a few minutes later, she could see it was getting rowdier as more alcohol went down. A solid guy in a western shirt leered at her. 'I'll buy you a drink, sweetheart.' He swayed towards her, almost slopping his drink over her shoes.

Before she could say anything, Liam appeared beside her and stared hard at the man. He didn't say anything, but even through his alcoholic haze the drunk froze his forward motion and spun away.

The barmaid chose that instant to ask for her order and Liam stayed by her side as she placed it. The moment passed to make a comment on the tiny incident, and she noticed Liam's attention seemed caught on the horizon. She would think about drunks and protectors later.

She tried to follow his gaze, but she lacked his height. Liam certainly seemed fixated on something. When they stepped out from under the shelter into the paddock again, she thought it looked hazy and the sky had begun to change colour. Nell put her hand out to catch a tiny, dark floating leaf and realised there were more dark floating specks in the sky drifting from the west.

In fact, the sky seemed tinged with an orange glow and Liam was on his phone. She snapped a pic of the background.

The loudspeaker broke the hum of voices and the racecourse supervisor regretfully announced the cancellation of the last race because of the leaves. Black fragments began to fall more steadily now, and in the name of safety for the horses and the jockeys, all racing was terminated.

Liam's voice broke into her thoughts. 'You right to carry that glass to the car? We'll go.'

Without hesitating, Nell tipped the wine out and slipped the disposable plastic glass into her handbag. 'I've gotta drive home and check the house, so I better not drink more. It might be a long day if the wind picks up.'

He nodded and despite his lack of expression she thought she saw a glint of approval in his eyes.

She added, 'Just drop me at the road opposite the store. I'll walk across the paddock to get my car if you have to go.'

'Easy.' He unlocked his ute with the remote as they approached, then moved to her side and opened her door. She slid a sideways glance at him, but he was stonewalling her. Okay. He could be the gentleman. It was old-fashioned yet kinda nice.

'Thank you,' she said quietly as he closed the door once she was in.

Inside the cab, Liam's brand of cologne surrounded her. Manly, slightly exotic, and, if she wasn't mistaken, one she'd inhaled before. The memory surfaced. It was possibly when she'd flown with her parents. Not a cheap brand, which was why it had such aromatic notes. Ah, of course. Not Liam, just the cologne she was attracted to. Sure.

Liam opened his door and slid in. He started the car without delay and began to ease out of the paddock ahead of the main crowd, who were beginning to mill and shift en masse towards the carpark now that the races had been cancelled.

He shot her a look. 'You should stay in town tonight. Blue says there's a couple of small gully fires not too far from your house.'

And why did she not know this? 'Is he worried about them?'

'No. He's worried about a big one over west of Featherwood. Towards Armidale.'

'I'll be fine.'

'You should stay in town,' he repeated, more of an order this time.

Nell didn't take orders. 'Thanks, but you're not my dad.' Her heart winced at the pain of that loss. 'I'll be fine.'

He sent her a frown. 'Your choice.' But she could tell he wished it wasn't.

She wasn't annoyed with Liam. She knew genuine concern when she saw it. 'Gracie said I had a bed if I wanted,' she told him as a sort of reassurance. 'I'll come in if it gets hairy.' Hairy. That was Gracie's word. Nell suspected she stole it from Jed.

'See that you do.' He pulled in at the rural store and she slid out of the ute before he could open his door.

'Probably see you in the trucks.'

'No doubt.' He nodded and she shut the door. He didn't look

back. She knew he didn't because she watched him drive out of sight and that dark head didn't shift.

Back home, Nell slid out of the car into a world tinged heavily with the smell of smoke.

Grin slunk out of the back seat when she undid his safety harness, but he wasn't happy. Maybe she shouldn't have come home while everything was so unstable? She had the choice to stay at Gracie's.

Liam's words haunted her a little. 'You should stay in town tonight.' And . . . 'There's a couple of gully fires not far from your house.'

Dammit, she was staying, but she'd just check everything was ready if she needed to fight – or flee.

She unlocked the house but went back outside to walk around the yard again before dark to make sure there was nothing that would be a good place for an ember to settle. Then she put her suitcase in the car with her paperwork, computer and camera. As well as a small backpack with clothes. Finally, she put her phone in the bedroom to charge. She was sooo glad the herd was at Gracie's.

How on earth was she going to sleep tonight?

When the full darkness of night settled, she stayed sitting in the lounge room, watching the news of more fires on TV with the battery radio not far away. She'd have to go to bed soon or she'd be using all her solar power for the lights and electronics, but she'd make one more cup of tea before she tried to sleep.

At ten o'clock, a sweep of headlights brushed the tops of the trees to the left of the house and she heard the sound of a car coming up the driveway. She recognised the deep, throaty engine immediately from the noise, even though it was too dark to see the actual car.

Liam's ute.

Funny that his was the first car to visit, and the way her nerves were jumping told her she was glad to see him. She opened the screen door to the verandah as Liam slid lithely out of the vehicle.

Was the fire coming? Maybe Gracie was sick. 'What's happened?'

'Nothing. Yet. I texted but you didn't answer.'

He'd texted? She didn't know he had her number. Who gave it to him? 'Sorry. I didn't see it. I'm charging the phone.'

'You should keep it on you.' He gestured with his hand to the vague orange glow in the skyline. 'I've got a bad feeling about this. When you didn't answer I thought I'd come up and check.'

'Thank you. That's kind of you.'

He lowered his brows. 'I don't do kind. I do sensible.' As if she wasn't sensible. She lifted her chin. Then the first part of his comment sank in. Didn't do kind? Who was he kidding? He was kind to Jed, helping at the store, Gracie with his repairs, had time for Archie and she'd seen him install an air conditioner so Blue didn't have to.

'Right,' she said and crossed her arms.

He looked at her as if not sure what she meant. 'Now that I'm here, I thought I'd offer to stay the night in the ute. I brought my swag so I can sleep in the back. In case the fire comes this way.'

'That's not at all kind,' she noted dryly. 'Why would you want to do that?'

He rubbed his short hair. 'Because I can't sleep at home knowing you're here alone and if it gets "hairy", you might get trapped.'

'So . . . two people trapped is better?'

'Yes. At least with two of us we've got more chance of getting help.'

'Well, thank you for your concern. You're not sleeping in your car.' He lifted his head as if to argue with her, but she beat him to it. 'But you can sleep in the lounge.'

He shut his mouth, surprise in his eyes, and she wanted to laugh.

'Thank you. I was nervous.' She saw no reason not to be honest. 'Please come in.' She held open the door.

Watching Liam squeeze past with his strong body brought out all sorts of odd emotions. There was that drift of aftershave and hint of ginger that was fast becoming a favourite and made her ache. He seemed so big and she felt instantly so much safer, as if nothing could go wrong with this man looking out for her. *Don't get used to it*, she reminded herself.

This was very dangerous territory for somebody like her. Here was a man who saved people and put himself on the line. His body, his emotions, his very mental health had been sacrificed to protect his friends and his country, and she hadn't even been able to speak up for a vulnerable birthing mother once against one woman. She was such a loser.

Would he even be here if he knew about her past? She doubted it. She didn't deserve his kindness.

Nell pushed those thoughts away, closed the door after him and turned. She needed to let go of all that. Gracie was right, but it was hard and she was fragile, out of practice with trusting people. It was just that having Liam here brought home all the things that she was missing without somebody special in her life.

Liam had come here because he was protecting a woman he considered unable to protect herself alone on her land. It was a lack of faith she should be more upset about. But no, she shouldn't. Because she didn't care what he thought. Liam's psyche was looking after others. Hers was looking after herself. She could do self-sufficient. Yet danger must be escalating up the valley. Perhaps she should've stayed at Gracie's so he didn't have to endanger himself.

She needed to stop these pointless mind games. It was done. He was here. And damn if she wasn't going to savour it just a little, because it wouldn't happen again.

Liam stood, tall and rangy, leaning against her wall like an immovable tree, and surveyed her house. 'Nice place. I like the lack of clutter.'

Was he saying it was too sparse? She looked around and tried to see with his eyes. All wood and splashes of plain colours. She'd added a wooden pendulum clock she'd picked up from the second-hand store in Dorrigo with the hallstand. There were no patterns in the room, except on the old rugs of Persian design but questionable lineage, and there were no picture frames except for the antique mirror behind the wood heater in the lounge.

'Molly would have the place filled with cushions and knick-knacks. It's nice to see free space and clean lines.'

'Thank you.' Remembering suddenly she was a hostess, she asked, 'Would you like tea or coffee? I've got some Anzac biscuits here if you'd like one.'

'Black tea and biscuits would be great. But I don't want to keep you up.' He glanced at the round table and two chairs. 'Sit there?'

'Sure.'

Nell busied herself in the tiny kitchen, every now and then looking back over her shoulder at him. She couldn't quite believe he was there. A silent, sexy guy sitting in her solo house. She forced herself to say something as she placed the mugs on the table. 'What's the latest with the fires?'

'Contained but critical if the wind picks up. The one nearest to you is under control.'

Heck. That was ominous when they were expecting a record-high temperature tomorrow. 'The next few days sound like they could get hectic. We'd better drink our tea and get to bed.' What did she just say? Her cheeks flamed.

'I'm game if you are.' His face stayed deadpan, but there was a definite wicked spark in those electric-blue eyes. She felt the zap straight to her bones. He put his mug down and reached for the biscuit tin. At least he hadn't reached for her.

What could she possibly say to that? 'Good to know.'

For a second, she thought he was going to lean over and grab her hand, and the fine hair on her arms lifted as if arcing towards him. Her skin prickled. She stepped out of range unnecessarily, because he said quietly, 'I'm trustworthy. Don't doubt it. But I'd like to explore this after everyone is safe.'

Explore this? Explore what? Two people who live too much inside their heads to be in any fit state for a relationship? 'Again, good to know. I'll get a blanket and pillow for you. The Walk-in-walkouters left me well stocked. Then I'm going to get some sleep.' She bet she wouldn't, but there wasn't any more room in her mouth to put more feet, so she might as well go to bed.

Nell woke to the sound of running water in the kitchen. The first pale light pushed away the night and she climbed out of bed in her short-sleeved *Busy Sleeping* nighty and rubbed her eyes.

So much for not sleeping. She'd crashed as soon as her head had hit the pillow, as if Liam's presence had given her permission to stop listening for the sounds of approaching fires or even the sounds of the night and finally relax.

Walking quietly, she pushed open the bedroom door and stepped into the lounge. He was facing the kitchen window with a half-full glass of water in his hand, but the lack of shirt and low-lying jocks meant she saw his spine straighten as if he'd heard her.

He was a soldier. Of course he heard her.

He didn't turn, so she enjoyed the luxury of gazing at a strong man's back, truly spectacular shoulders, corded muscles and flat planes down to the crease between his firm backside. Crikey. She was hormone Sally this morning judging by the absolute butterfly explosion in her belly and chest. She swallowed to moisten her throat.

'Good morning, Liam.'

He turned and her breath caught. Not fair. Six-pack alert. He reached for his shirt that hung on the kitchen chair and pulled it on, leaving the buttons open. 'Sorry I woke you.'

'Don't be.' *Really, don't be.* Holy heck, he was amazing to look at. 'I had the best night's sleep I've had since I got here.' And she hadn't meant to say that.

She clicked her mouth shut and saw the tilt of his lips as if she'd said something funny. Her cheeks warmed and she forced herself to cross the room and pass him. 'Do you want something to eat?'

'No. I'll head back to Molly's. Are you going into town today?'

'Featherwood?'

'Yep. I'm not being bossy,' he said, as if he knew he'd got up her nose yesterday. 'I think tonight will be even dicier and you might need to rethink staying here. Just for a day or two.'

She reached over and flipped on the jug before she turned her head to look at him. 'I'll think about it.'

His eyes narrowed. 'I'm guessing I'll be too busy with fires to call in tonight.'

'I understand.' She breathed in his smoky scent and tried not to lean in because, darn, she certainly wanted to.

Up close he looked even rangier, if that was a word, all valleys and plains of muscle, man-mountain with bronzed skin and angular bones that shrieked strength and sinew and silent power. Warmth was radiating off him, despite the morning air still being valley cool. It was cool enough, anyway, for her to notice the difference in temperature in the air between them.

She lifted her chin to see his face and something in his hooded eyes made her heart beat faster and her skin tingle. The deep blue depths darkened to almost black as the connection between them lengthened. She could lose herself in those eyes.

His hand lifted and he stroked her cheek, his fingers feather-light yet jagged from the hard labour he never seemed to stop. She wondered for the first time if he'd been driving himself to exhaustion.

'I'm glad you slept,' he murmured.

She guessed he didn't. 'Maybe I can return the favour one day.' Now there was a thought. Watching Liam while he slept. She liked his version of pyjamas.

'I'm a screwed-up guy.'

'I'm a screwed-up girl,' she countered, putting her hand over his where it remained on her face. 'You're a friend now. I don't presume to have seen the things you have, but I've had my own disaster that I'm not proud of.'

His eyes narrowed further and she couldn't read the expression. 'I don't know what happened in your past, but the person I see is worth knowing better.' His head came down and his mouth touched her lips very gently. 'We'll get to that as soon as all this is done.'

And with that he straightened, lifted one finger in salute and walked out her door.

'No. We won't,' she said to the empty room. She couldn't let him. He deserved more than she was. She didn't go to the door. She watched through the windows and added into the quiet, 'You don't need my brand of trouble.'

Chapter Twenty

Gracie

Gracie hadn't asked about the donation to the Progress Association after the races because Jed had been so excited about her silly hat win. She loved that he'd been invested in her two minutes of fame. Once they'd arrived home, they'd both lain down in their air-conditioned room and fallen asleep, spooning.

And Sunday was the only day they had off together so she hadn't wanted to spoil it.

But this morning, Monday, after the pregnancy-induced nightmares, ones that had her knocking on doors in refuse-covered streets searching for a home for her baby, the word 'invested' reminded her that they needed to be frugal. Any new donations like Saturday's surprise needed to be discussed and postponed until they were financially secure. The end-of-the-month bills were coming.

'Jed?' Gracie studied her man as he skimmed the *Land* newspaper, probably for potential new products, before he headed across to open the produce store. 'How much was the donation you made for the races?'

Jed looked up – *too much like a roo caught in headlights,*

Gracie thought, and her stomach sank. Jed sat frozen, until his eyes slid away to the door and his muscles actually tensed for movement. As if he needed to escape.

Now Gracie's stomach dived like a bird after an escaping worm, swooping down in dread. *No, no, no*, was being chanted ominously in her head.

Jed's bottom teeth showed as he worried his top lip. 'Now, Gracie . . .'

Real anxiety skipped along her shoulders. 'How much?' The words were whispered. As if it couldn't be too bad if he also said it quietly. But judging by his behaviour, she suspected even Jed regretted his generosity. And Jed loved being generous.

'Five thousand dollars.' The amount fell into the silent room and even the birds shut up outside.

Gracie's mouth dropped open and nausea rose up in her throat like foam on the tide. Words failed her. Nothing came out. Not even stomach contents, thankfully. Finally, she managed, 'Sorry? Say that again?'

Jed squeezed his beautiful lips together until they were a thin line of remorse, as if he didn't want to say the number again. The silence lengthened.

Gracie didn't help him out. She was too busy trying to breathe.

Finally, he blew out a sigh and tried to smile as he repeated, 'Five grand. It was dumb, I know.' His hand waved as if they'd sort it out.

Gracie couldn't believe he'd actually smiled at her, as if this was a joke.

He must have cottoned on because his big hand lifted higher and he dragged it across his chin. 'That bloke up river came in and bought a set of those huge new cattle yards, cash, pulled the wad

out of his pocket. Twenty grand.' His eyes searched hers for understanding. 'Jack Walton from the association came in just after and
said they were desperate to pay the insurance for the races. So,
I gave him a quarter of the wad.'

Five thousand dollars cash because he'd felt sorry for Jack. 'We
have to pay for the yards, Jed. We have to pay for the ones we
haven't sold. Four sets you bought worth seventy thousand dollars.
In two weeks. Where are we going to get the money for that?'

He peered out the window towards the shop – not at her. 'We
might sell more?'

Panic made her voice sharp. 'In drought?' Sarcasm came from
thinking about his idiocy. 'Farmers are walking off their blocks.
Apart from that bloke up river with his rolls of cash, nobody has
money. We could actually lose this business if we can't pay our creditors.' She pulled her rising voice down a decibel with effort. 'Our
baby will be here soon.' Then even more quietly she said, 'We'd
lose our home.' Gracie's breath came fast now. Too fast. 'How
could you? How could you be so stupidly, ridiculously, criminally
generous, to others . . .' Tears filled her throat and she ground the
final words out. 'And not think of me and our baby first!'

'Gracie.' Jed stood and moved towards her, but she turned her
back on him, frightened. Frightened she'd say something really
terrible because she was terrified that Jed would make her worst
nightmare come true and she'd be destitute again and so would her
baby. Jed could lose it all.

Still with her back turned she said, 'You'd better go to work,
Jed. See if you can sell another set of cattle yards before we have
to sleep in them.' And for the first time ever, she didn't kiss him
before he went to work.

Chapter Twenty-one

Mavis

On Monday just before lunch, Mavis's house phone rang while she was in the blinkin' toilet again. She heard the boy answer.

Hopefully, it wasn't the school going mad. Stupid excursion. The boy used to live in Sydney and he didn't need to go bussing down there to see the sights and get those memories back. So, she'd said he didn't need to go and could stay home. And the Woolies truck had been coming with all the internet food he'd ordered, so she'd needed him, anyway. Lucky the boy had been here to help her work that out. Ordering food online! Who knew?

She rinsed her hands and came out with the towel, still drying her fingers. 'Who's on the phone?' She'd thought his mother might be, but no, judging by his face, she hadn't rung to see how they were going despite the fires up this way. Typical.

'It's Jed,' the boy said. 'He wants to talk to you.'

She took the proffered phone. 'Yes?'

'Ah,' said Jed. 'I need a favour.'

'You got it.' No hesitation. She knew already Jed didn't ask for silly things.

'There's a big fire west of Shearer's Gully. We're all called out. Gracie has to run the shop. I wondered if you'd come and help her and Molly? Stay with them till we get back?'

'Sure. Archie'll come too. The boy can do the lifting.'

'That's great.' There was definite relief in his voice. 'Thanks. I don't like to leave Gracie as she is.' The boy sounded worried. And sad?

'We'll keep it running for those that need things. No problem,' she reassured him, although she was wondering just how big this fire was to have everyone called out to it?

Jed added, 'I'll throw a couple of bags of dog food in for you.'

Mavis frowned. 'No, or I'll slap you. I don't need payment. See you soon.' Mavis replaced the receiver onto the phone, wondering if she should've got one of those mobile phones the boy kept pestering her about. Letting that conundrum go, she turned her thoughts to the young pregnant woman in the fires. That worried her. She reckoned that maybe Jed should move his young lady out pretty darn quick just for a week or so. Till it was safer or the weather cooled down. Or the baby came.

To be fair, she remembered a time when she'd stayed on with her husband and she'd had a one-year-old. How they'd fought the fires together with the baby left in the bedroom crying. Knowing the baby was scared and alone and there was not a damn thing Mavis could do about it. Yep, that had been her worst memory of a very long life.

That baby had been the boy's grandmother. And she and her man had been fighting the flames outside because if they didn't win, they all died. It had been too late to run.

Jed should send his Gracie away. 'We're going to help at the produce store,' she told the boy. 'You'll be a good help this afternoon. I reckon if Molly is there, we'll have food, too.'

The boy laughed and she smiled with him. He was good value.

'We've got food, Gran. You've been internet shopping.'

Chapter Twenty-two

Gracie

At lunchtime, Nell's car crackled the stones on Gracie's driveway. Gracie wasn't sure if she was glad for the company or if she wanted to stay miserable by herself.

'Just dropped in to see how you bounced back after Saturday's heat at the races,' Nell said. 'I'm glad to see you up and about.' Then she laughed. Not a big guffaw, but a woman's chuckle, not something Gracie heard often from Nell. 'It was worth going just to see Jed's excitement over your hat win.'

Despite the effort required to smile, which was a nice break from feeling miserable over the horrid fight she and Jed had had this morning, Gracie waved her in. 'I'll get a cold drink for you.' But as she walked into the house her throat ached with unshed tears and tightness.

Her phone rang, and the caller ID read, *Jed*. It was as though he'd heard her anguished thoughts. Gracie swallowed over her prickling throat and strained for a smile. She tilted her face away from Nell and forced light words. 'Speak of the devil, I'll just get this.' She took a step away from Nell.

Gracie listened to Jed's unusually serious tone, the graveness and his urgent request for her to get to the shop. All of which gave her heart rate a blip of shock. Then he said, 'Do you know where Nell is?'

'She's here with me.'

Nell tilted her head in question.

Gracie listened and her sense of dread ramped up. 'Okay, I'll tell her. And I'll come over to the store.' She ended the call and explained to Nell, 'There's been a lightning strike up your way. Jed's going out with Liam and he asked if you wanted to get a lift with them. We could keep Grin here for you? One less worry?'

Nell jumped up. 'How close to my house?'

Gracie suspected too close, though Jed hadn't specified. 'He didn't say. It's up that way. I'm to hold the shop.'

Nell picked up her keys. 'I'll take my car in case I want to stay at my place. Or in case Jed needs to go somewhere else.' Nell's face betrayed none of the anxiety Gracie felt at the thought of battling a fire. 'If you keep Grin here that would be great.' Nell scowled down at what she was wearing. 'Today I have shorts and a sleeve-less top.' She shrugged. 'They'll have proper gear at the meeting shed in spares, I hope.'

'I'll get you a bottle of water to take with you.'

Nell followed her through to the kitchen, and when she turned Gracie wanted to hug her and wish her good luck, because she looked so thin and elegant and fragile, despite the nice clothes. She handed her the bottle of water. 'Go. Grin will be fine. You look after Jed and Jed will look after you.' Which made her think about Jed in danger and she firmly pushed that thought away.

Nell hugged her. Surprised, Gracie returned the hug. 'We'll both be fine,' Nell said. 'I'm not worried. I've been to a few fires now, and Liam will be there, too.'

Gracie had a mental image of Liam. A man who'd seen a lot of emergency situations, one who thought with his brain, not his big heart like Jed. A man who got out alive. He'd get Jed out too, even though she still wanted to kill him. So she did feel reassured.

'Thanks. Yes. Well, make sure Jed rings me as soon as he can.'

Nell nodded and walked swiftly out the front door to her car, then stopped. 'You want a lift to the shop? It'll save you walking across the paddock.'

The sun sloped in and seared Gracie's head as soon as she stepped onto the verandah. Gracie realised she needed to go immediately as well. She had to man the store. Lucky she was dressed. 'Thanks.' She waved her hand at her head. 'Baby brain.' She patted her pocket to check she had her phone, then pulled the front door shut behind her.

Nell slipped away to check on Grin in the dog yard and came back to the car and climbed in. Gracie heaved herself down the steps to the vehicle.

The wheels crunched over the cattle grid towards the shop. They pulled up at the front of the store and Jed had the old F250 running when they arrived. Mavis was standing in the driveway with Archie.

Jed strode over, his face grave as held out his hand to help Gracie exit the vehicle, leaving his truck to warm up. His face searched hers and what he saw must have eased his worry. He leaned down and kissed her, his familiar warmth suddenly more precious, the hard words between them still stinging but less important at this moment. Gracie touched his cheek. 'Be careful.'

'My middle name,' he said, which made Gracie roll her eyes.

Jed touched her shoulder. 'Archie and Mavis said they'd stay with you.' He gave her a mock frown. 'Don't do too much. You've got helpers.'

'How did you manage that?'

He shrugged his big shoulders. 'I rang Mavis, and Archie's home today.'

'Just for company.' Mavis stepped up. 'And Archie will do our lifting.'

Bonus. 'No school today, Archie?' Gracie forced a smile.

'I had a school excursion for the weekend to Sydney and I didn't want to go.'

'Lucky for us.'

'Liam's meeting me here and Molly's coming down as well to help you,' Jed added.

'I've got a team around me,' Gracie said, but Jed's usually smiling face held lines of concern. He was already dressed in his bright yellow fire-resistant gear.

'Everyone's going to this one,' he said.

Those present looked grim. 'It must be a big one if you need to leave the shop,' Gracie said.

'It's a fair way away. But the wind's picked up and Blue's not happy.'

Two minutes later, Liam pulled in with a measured turn and stop. His ute barely disturbed the gravel or created dust, despite the speed. Dressed in yellow, he too appeared serious. 'We could see the smoke on the way. It looks big.'

'Gotta go,' Jed said, and dropped one more kiss on Gracie's lips.

'You boys,' she forced a smile as she watched Nell, who was getting back in her car, 'and girls, be safe.'

'Ring me if you go into labour,' Jed called out. That was the last thing he needed to worry about. She wanted his mind firmly on the job. This time he needed to worry about himself.

'We'll be fine. You go.' She waved her hand and watched Jed and Liam climb into Jed's truck.

Nell followed them out of the driveway in her car and the assembled impromptu shop assistants watched as the others departed, silently.

As she turned and walked back into the shopfront, Mavis and Molly surrounded her, with Archie trailing behind.

'Does this happen a lot in the summer?' Gracie asked.

Molly nodded and Mavis said, 'Not this bad for a few years, but it's been a long drought leading up to this. Lots of dry scrub. It needs burning off if we can just get through this couple of months without a major fire.'

Gracie stared at her. 'You think we'll have a big fire?'

Mavis shrugged. She rubbed her mouth in concern before she went on. 'Haven't had one for a while, but there's a lot of back burning that needs doing that hasn't happened.' She inclined her head to the tank stand. 'And not much water to put it out if it comes.'

The lack of water, abundance of hot weather and build-up of underbrush was a deadly combination. Gracie remembered the drive up here and the tree canopy over the road, the wide creek bed exposed by lack of flow with big boulders sitting high and dry. 'The ground was dry for six feet under,' Mavis had said, and she was probably right.

Mavis added, 'I saw a house on the television burn in Tenter-field the other day. It was lost because the local fire brigade didn't have water to douse it with. It breaks your heart.'

Gracie thought of her own house. The old timber, and the front paddock of dry grass that led to the wooden front steps. When she'd raised her concerns with Jed, he said he had it covered. But then he'd said that about the bills, too.

Chapter Twenty-three

Nell

Nell followed Jed's truck up the valley along the winding, tree-lined tar road to the brigade shed and parked. It was about halfway from Featherwood to her gate. Visibility had come down to an orange light muting the sky, reminding her of the races on Saturday.

Four cars were already lined up in the wide, barren clearing around the corrugated iron brigade shed. She recognised Charlie's and Pete's trucks. The vehicles were separated in a way to make sure if one caught fire the other didn't, and both didn't offer fuel to burn the shed.

The mountains to the right plumed with smoke and her chest tightened, despite having what she hoped was her calm face. She squinted, trying to pierce the haze. She couldn't see flames, which she supposed was one good thing. It didn't seem too near her house.

The *beep, beep* of a reversing warning signal from the larger of the two red brigade trucks backing out of the shed nudged her mind and she moved to the side of the big double doors as Blue eased the truck past her.

Nell hurried into the shed for a spare set of boots, jacket and trousers to pull on over her clothes. Hers were at home in the laundry and she didn't want to waste time. She should have packed them in her car so they'd be with her always. She'd remember that for next time.

The idea of pulling on more clothes over the top of her own outfit in the stinking heat wasn't attractive, but neither was burning embers floating down the front of her shirt.

She was the last to scramble into the truck, and as soon as her belt was fastened, Blue roared away from the brigade head-quarters. Nell bounced beside the window in the back and tried to settle her accelerated heart rate. The grey undergrowth of the roadside blurred to the left of her through the tinted glass.

Charlie and Blue sat in the front, with Jed's knees doing a man spread next to her, and Liam on the other side. This truck was a five-seater and they were meeting a leader from headquarters at the scene in the other two-seater truck. She'd met the senior fire officer, Ewan, at one of the training sessions.

Ewan was a stern man who reminded her of an obstetrician she'd met once during the investigation. That doctor had been one of the few who had been kind to her, and Ewan Marshall had the same air of calm competence and fine people skills. He would bring the latest update of the surrounding fires and a detailed plan as well as the mundane, like pre-packed sandwiches for everyone and drinks in case they were out for hours.

She hoped that wouldn't happen, a fire under control was a much better thing, but the smoky area seemed to be growing. With half an ear, she listened to Charlie talking about a blaze in the next town that had taken a house and half-a-dozen sheds, and she thanked God she'd moved her cows and Grin to Gracie's.

A kaleidoscope of the last few weeks, the sudden changes in her social circle and commitments and even her much-denied attraction to Liam circled in her head. It could all disappear in a wall of flames.

Her heart began to trip in her chest and she wondered how she'd got here in a blinkin' fire truck with semi-strangers heading to a bushfire. But no, this was a blessing, an opportunity she'd wanted to be a part of, to save other people's lives for a change, and to save possessions because she was a member of a team who would use their skills together. Perhaps she'd even help to save her own house.

In all these months, years really, of not caring about anything, it seemed she had found a world to care about, after all. Certainly, she cared about her herd, and the native birds and animals she was used to seeing around her yard. But also, she now discovered, her house and few possessions were precious, too. *Thank goodness*, she thought again, *that Grin and the girls are safe with Gracie.*

The smoke hung in the still air like a thick quilt as they drove and she almost missed the point where they passed the turnoff to her gate. Around the next corner, they came to a roadblock. This was the first time she'd seen traffic stopped from going further west.

Blue, as captain, leaned out his window. 'How's it going?' he called out to the RFS volunteer.

'Creeping up the ridge,' the man said. 'The bloke from head-quarters is up at Thompson's creek. He's setting up there. He'll have more information.'

'Righto. Thanks.' Blue pulled his head back inside and engaged the gears. 'Everybody ready for a big day?' he called over his shoulder.

The men around Nell grunted, and her squeaky 'Yes' seemed insignificant next to theirs.

'Remember. Keep your buddy in sight. Everyone checked their

walkie-talkies?' The communication devices were clipped to the front of their jackets and as one they all touched their chests.

They rounded the next bend to where a white brigade station wagon was parked across the road. Flashing lights on the roof were dim through the now thicker smoke. Getting out of the truck was one of the first things Nell had learned. It was nearly three feet off the ground and nobody wanted to be a liability with a broken ankle. Nell had no idea why they didn't provide steps.

Blue walked straight over to Ewan and they put their heads together until Blue stepped back, nodded and returned to them. 'Liam and Nell together, in the smaller truck. It'll be here in a few minutes with two more for the team. You're heading to the top of the ridge.' Blue gestured over his shoulder with his thumb. 'Jed, with me. Charlie, you go with Ewan.' He told the other men, 'We're going down the gully to a shack that's at risk.'

Charlie, even though he'd been a member of the brigade for many years, was basic firefighter level like Nell, so he needed to be paired with an advanced-trained firefighter. Blue, Jed and Liam were the only advanced trained in their brigade, apart from the leader from town, Ewan, so that left Nell paired with a senior, too.

Ewan followed Blue across to them, his shoulders pulling the yellow coat taut as he tucked his satellite phone back into his jacket. 'The priority is safety of people first, then dwellings in immediate threat. Native habitat after that.' He pointed at Nell. 'Monitor your radio when you and Liam head to the top of the ridge. Report on the creep of the fire this way and keep us posted on wind shifts. I'll liaise with headquarters. Bulldozers are coming in to set a fire break.' He glanced at his wrist. 'About twenty minutes.' He gestured with his hand as the small truck arrived.

Two young men jumped out to wait for the bulldozer to arrive. 'Right, Liam, you move out.'

Liam said, 'Jump in, Nell.'

She understood the need for someone to give orders and was happy to take them. The few times she'd worked with Liam he'd inspired confidence and she instinctively felt she could rely on him.

Not like the time she'd worried over a senior midwife.

She shied away from that thought and concentrated on climbing into the truck. It was higher off the ground than the other vehicle, so she wound the window down to be able to hear the conversation.

'There's a front creeping up the gully on the other side of the ridge, but the choppers will drop on that. Latest weather says there's a westerly wind coming. We'll get the McLeod tools running and secure the dwelling,' Blue said. 'Jump in, guys.' The larger truck rumbled away.

Twenty minutes later, a small bulldozer with rubber wheels, as opposed to the one with steel treads she'd seen last time, crawled along the ridge under them. The smaller ones seemed much slower to achieve the objective.

'They're more manoeuvrable on a slope,' Liam said, as he stood beside her on the ridge. They'd got out to make their report. He'd just lowered his binoculars.

There were six different plumes of smoke Nell could see and the helicopters had come and gone to refuel. 'How many brigades are out for this?'

'Ewan said eight. Each with about six firefighters. There are four contract water trucks for refilling the water tanks on each pump.'

That was a lot of people who should be at work on a weekday, giving up their time, sweating in heavy gear and risking their lives. She didn't know anyone from her parents' friends who would do this for free. The hot wind tossed loose hair into her eyes and she brushed it away. Her long plait was tucked down her back inside her jacket. A small black curled leaf floated down and stroked her hand. 'Wind's picking up.'

Another dehydrated leaf brushed higher up Nell's arm. She turned to look behind into the sky and saw a cloud of floating debris dropping like evil snowflakes. The sky had turned a deeper orange and very faintly she could hear a distant roaring howl. 'Westerly wind coming,' she said into the mic.

Another gust came from behind her. Different direction? 'Which way's that coming from?' She turned three-sixty degrees and realised they were surrounded by spot fires and a building wind. She stood, disorientated for a moment, and tried to figure out in which direction her house lay.

'Climb in the truck.' Liam's eyes narrowed towards where Blue and the larger vehicle had gone. 'I'm not liking the way the embers are falling over there and now here. More wind is coming. We need to get them out.' He pulled his walkie-talkie closer to his mouth. 'Truck six-o-two. Come in, Ewan? Blue?'

No answer.

'Come in, Blue.'

Still nothing as embers began to hit against the vehicle.

Nell crossed to the truck, not as fast as she should have, still awestruck by the crazy winds and the roar.

Chapter Twenty-four

Gracie

Gracie kept hoping for a call to say Jed was safe or to see his truck turn in the drive. They should not have been sharing harsh words at a time like this.

The store had been busy, with mainly women customers asking for news of the fire and stocking up at the Farmer's Friend. A lot of the men were out fighting fires.

Her phone stayed quiet.

Molly helped her pull down the huge roller door that blocked off the driveway at five pm. It took the two of them heaving. 'I don't know what I would have done without your help,' she told Molly.

'Pshaw.' Molly waved a hand. 'I've had fun. And Mavis was a crack-up.'

Gracie shook her head, and despite her worries about Jed and the others, she couldn't help the smile that tugged at her lips when she thought of Mavis. 'I can't believe how much she knows about the people and the products.'

'She could give Jed advice on who not to give credit to,' Molly added. 'Always been a farm girl, I guess. And Archie worked like a machine. Saved my back.'

'He's such a great kid. It worked out well.' Gracie glanced towards the big pall of smoke in the distance that seemed larger and more menacing with every passing moment. Nerves crawled over her skin now that she had time to think, and uneasiness hung heavy in her gut. 'I just wish they'd get home.'

Molly's face creased into a frown. 'I know. This is the worst part. Them being away fighting fires.' She scrunched up her face. 'I hate being left behind to worry. I spent years doing that when Liam went on active duty. Mum did it with Dad. She said you never get used to it. How about I come back to your house and wait there with you?'

'What about your place? Don't you want to go home?'

'I'd just be alone there. We're on the immediate outskirts of town. Not that I'd stay home by myself to defend it, anyway. If that fire comes near town the whole world will come in and help. I'm not happy leaving you alone until Jed gets back.'

Gracie felt some of the tightness in her chest ease and she nodded enthusiastically. 'I'd appreciate the company.'

'If I move Liam's ute down to your front verandah then Jed and Liam will know where I am.'

'Great. Thanks. We can take this bag of dog food home because I'd say Nell's pup is staying for a sleepover. Surely Nell won't stay at her place alone with all that going on.'

'You haven't bought a dog yet, have you?'

Gracie shook her head. 'I'm waiting till I get settled with the baby first.'

'Dogs are good.' Molly nodded. 'I hope Nell's place is okay.'

'Me too.' They both stared at the orange sky. 'I don't like the look of those embers.'

'What we need is some rain.'

'Fingers crossed. I wouldn't mind some drinking water in the tank as well.' Praying for rain was like asking to win the lottery around here.

They locked the last small door at the shop and climbed into Liam's vehicle.

Gracie thanked Molly silently that she didn't have to walk down the driveway, because it felt like an echidna had wrapped around her swollen ankles, poking quills in. It was just pins and needles, but it hurt to walk.

Molly drove over the grid and down to the front of the house. 'You right getting up the steps?'

Gracie laughed. 'I have to be. Jed's not here to carry me.'

Molly smiled. 'True.' Then she sighed wistfully over that. 'Has he?'

Gracie waggled her brows. 'That man is so strong.'

Chapter Twenty-five

Nell

Embers drifted and then began to rain down like confetti at a black-themed wedding. Nell climbed up into the vehicle, fast and hopping, like a spider climbing up a web after a newly caught insect. She was the last one in again.

Liam started the engine as soon as he closed his own door. 'They're still not answering.' One-handed, he put a call through to headquarters on the truck radio and officially logged loss of communication with their team. He also gave an update on the wind shift and increase of danger, then put the vehicle into gear.

His brow had been furrowed the whole time. It was more emotion than Nell usually saw on his face. 'It's probably just interference from the valley they're in, but I don't like them not answering.'

Nell didn't like it, either. She knew these men. She'd promised Gracie she'd look after Jed. A cold dread slipped down her neck despite the oppressive heat.

Liam steered them off the ridge with meticulous precision, which was no easy feat with the scored line of broken earth and scrub that the bulldozer had created to break the fire. Past the last of the ridge and back to the point where they'd first met the team leader and separated.

'Will they be able to get out?' She didn't expect an answer; she was talking more to herself.

'They know their own valley. They know it better than I do.' He squinted closely through the windshield. 'I've never seen anything like this.' His gaze narrowed on her. 'The problem is falling branches and trunks blocking roads and being surrounded by burning trees.'

Nell remembered falling trees from the time she'd sat with Blue. When they did tip, it was usually when you least expected it.

'If our boys get stuck it means they have to get out of the safety of the truck and clear it. If that happens, they need to be careful. To get back into the truck if necessary.' The words hung in the air between them.

'Flashover,' Nell repeated softly. She couldn't think of anything more frightening than being stuck in the middle of one of those.

They'd been drilled with everyone crouching on the floor of the trucks under blankets, imagining the crashing of a firestorm of leaves and branches, flames pelting heat through the windows, as the fire passed over them.

'I hope they don't do that.'

'I hope *we* don't do that,' Liam said dryly. 'That's why we practise it so often. If that situation ever arises, you have to know what to do without thinking. Fire, like war, forgives no one for being distracted.' His face was set, his eyes dark and full of past trauma and his mouth formed a hard line. 'A flashover is okay if it's in a clearing. It blows over fast.'

The sky grew black in the direction the other crew had gone and they both peered through the truck windows at the shifting trees ahead.

'That's a southerly wind.'

Nell nodded and passed that on to the control centre. 'Different direction again. Is the fire creating its own wind?'

Liam nodded grimly. 'Saw fireballs once from a firestorm. Like sky rockets on cracker night. It shot balls of intense heat and flames like bombs. Whatever it hit,' he waved a hand, 'just exploded.'

Nell did not want to see that.

Liam ducked his head in front of the windshield to see the sky. 'We'll stay here in the open.'

'Shouldn't we move?' Or close her eyes and pretend it wasn't happening? Maybe sleep. Or run. She had a ridiculous urge to open the truck door, jump down and flee.

A part of her knew that she'd most likely die if she did any of those things. Another part of her knew instinctively that Liam would reach out and restrain her from running. His big hand would come across like a vice and stop her doing anything so stupid, but still her heart thumped in her chest and she gripped the dash with white fingers.

A roar, so loud, so ominous and terrifying, thundered towards them. They had nowhere to escape to. The fire was coming.

Nell's eyes grew wide, her glance flicking from the left, where embers were now beating on her window, to the right, where trees were bending under the increasing howl of the wind.

'Too late. At least we're in a clearing here. Hopefully, it will pass fast and to the side.'

The first gust hit them. The truck shook, buffeted as if they were sitting in the middle of an open plain in a sudden violent storm. But the rain that came was blackened leaves and flying embers that burned and flew in a burst towards them like sparks from an electric welder.

Outside the windows the day turned to night as more glowing embers rained, searing against the glass like tiny devils trying to burrow inside to them. The truck creaked and shifted against the wind.

Nell tore her eyes from the outside turbulence and glanced at her watch. It was only five-ten in the afternoon, yet it looked like orange night out there.

Ten seconds later, a burst of twigs and burning leaves cracked against the window and bonnet of the truck. Nell jumped – more slapped against the roof.

Holy crap, it was going to pass right over them.

The wind roared and the temperature in the truck rose steadily. It was as if a giant being had poured a bucketful of coals from the sky onto the roof of the vehicle. Broken and burning branches slapped the outside panels with pings and thumps and crashes. Spot fires jumped up in the grass all around them and trees exploded into flames.

The fire ball erupted into view and overran them.

Liam activated the truck's protective water sprays. The reflected heat from the surrounding flames, all dancing higher than their windows, began to sear Nell's skin.

'Blankets,' Liam yelled over the noise. Nell reached for the folded thick wool cover and she scrambled to open it over herself and pull the protective blankets up over her head. Just as they'd done half-a-dozen times in practice.

Both of them slid lower in their seats and Liam's big hand came out and took hers. She gripped onto him and found a measure of calm in the wild storm.

The roaring maelstrom from hell seemed to last forever. Nell's ears were battered by the crack and slap of flying kindling hurled against the outside of the truck, the heat in the cab scorching the air in her lungs. The flames were an orange wall whenever she dared to sneak an eyeball-searing look.

Finally, after what seemed hours, the noise died down and she heard Liam calling out over the receding roar, 'It's passing. You okay, Nell?'

Her fingers felt crushed. She wondered if she'd driven her nails into his fingers. But she was alive. And so was Liam. For a few minutes there, she'd thought she'd die here with Liam. Had almost accepted it. Strangely, her greatest regret had been that she wouldn't see Gracie's baby.

She checked her watch again. How could it have been less than four minutes from when it started until the main force of the wind and flames had gone?

The noise remained deafening with the roar of the swirling wind and leaves and those frightening flames, but it died down as the front roared off. Water ran down the windscreen and Liam switched off the sprinklers over the truck to conserve water. Shifting from under the blanket, his big hand released hers and pushed through his tousled hair as he eased up beside her.

'That . . . was intense.' Liam's voice came out ridiculously calm, and suddenly Nell wanted to giggle or cry or hug him because of nerves and sheer freaking fright, but she didn't do any of those inappropriate things. She just nodded and licked her lips. Her whole face felt seared by the reflective heat.

'You . . . are not a bad bloke to be with in an emergency.' She took a sip from her drink bottle and it felt like heaven as it slid down her parched throat. 'I see why Molly loves you.'

He looked at her. 'It hasn't been easy for her. I'm bent out of shape.'

'Is it so bad?'

'Yes. It doesn't feel right. Sometimes I don't feel anything at all.'

'I'm sorry.'

He nodded, before he picked up the radio handpiece.

'I'm bent too,' Nell told him as she pulled down the silver reflectors on the inside windows she hadn't seen Liam put up, and she began folding the blanket. Neither of them said anything after that.

'You there, Blue?' Liam's calm voice echoed in the cab and Nell shook her head at his stoicism. Men.

'Blue,' he repeated. 'Even if you can't respond, there's a fire-storm coming down the hill. We just had a flashover, but it's passed now. Nell and I are both safe. Get into that truck and protect your-selves.' He clicked the unresponsive radio off.

'Do you think they're all right?' Nell couldn't help the tinge of panic in her voice – so much for matching Liam's calm – but she kept thinking of Jed and Charlie, Blue and the others. Real people she'd sat beside, and talked to. Their wives and families. Gracie and her unborn baby. The last ten minutes had been the scariest thing she'd ever seen, except for that night three years ago. Maybe that was why in the middle of the firestorm, she'd been so ridicu-lously accepting of death.

She hadn't forgiven herself yet and didn't feel she deserved to live.

Half an hour later, they still hadn't heard from the second truck. They moved slowly along the track behind the destruction left by the front. Seared black trees were somehow shrunken bones of themselves, as if any buried moisture inside them had been sucked out and the trunks squeezed to skinny poles with outstretched arms.

Ash lay everywhere in piles, mounds of it, in white and red and black. Every now and then she saw the charred remains, mostly ash, of small animals, though the heat had been so intense it was hard to tell what they were.

Liam held a long conversation with headquarters, his voice becoming more clipped each time he called on the radio to retry contact with the lost crew.

Please God, let it be just their radio that's dead.

Headquarters suggested he keep trying from each new position, as no other unit had heard from the leader and his crew, either, and air support remained hampered by the turbulent winds.

'How the heck do we know which dirt track they've gone down?' Nell's voice rattled around the cab.

'We don't. But we stay safe while we look.'

They eased past another burning, fallen tree, peering down dirt tracks in a myriad of dirt tracks in a range of gullies and hills, buried in smoke. Every now and then, they'd come across an inexplicably untouched section, as if the fire had swerved away, changed direction with the capricious wind that whipped it and left a scene untouched. Green oasis in a bomb blast.

Burning embers floated in the air as if they were after-thoughts from the front.

'Do you reckon I still have a house?' Nell asked in a small voice, but she knew that wasn't as important as finding the other men.

Liam looked at her. 'I don't know, Nell, but I don't think you're safe to stay there tonight if you do. You and Grin should stay with Gracie for a few days until this all dies down.'

Nell imagined trying to sleep at her house. Then at Gracie's as she waited to find out if her place had survived. She wouldn't sleep in either home. But there was no use others risking their lives to save her. 'I might do that.'

There was a sudden crackle from the radio and Blue's voice came through. 'Liam, you there?'

'Roger. I hear you, Blue. You have no idea how good it is to hear your voice. We were worried.'

'We've had moments of interest. Everyone made it back into the truck in time for the flashover, but I don't want to play that game again. You and Nell?'

'Fine,' Liam said.

Fine? Talk about brevity. A hysterical giggle of relief bubbled at the back of her throat, but she forced it down and sipped her water, instead.

'We're driving out now. See you back at the roadblock.'

She could hear the hint of relief in Liam's usually stoic voice and see it in his face and shoulders. He'd held it together so well.

'We'll meet them there and then we'll head to your place. That okay with you?'

'Absolutely.' Now that the current crisis was over, she felt sick with relief. And if her house was gone – *Please*, she crossed her fingers so tightly they hurt – so be it.

Both fire engines ground up Nell's driveway in a low-geared rumble. Liam didn't speculate and Nell sat forward in her seat. The gate and posts were gone. One side of the dirt track was the same as she'd left it that morning. Untouched.

The other lay in a smoking ruin of charred grass, black fence posts and gutted bush with still blazing bark on the trees. There was no way of knowing if the house would be there when they circled the hill.

The smouldering fence posts leaned drunkenly, wire snapped in some places, sagging in others, but thank God she'd moved the herd. She could have lost Moo. And her baby.

Nell craned her neck as they rounded the bend, and her breath caught, before it lodged in her chest. Even though she'd half expected it, her breath still jammed with shock at what she saw. All that was left of her little farmhouse was smoking debris and piles of ash and tin. Her new home was gone. Bizarrely, the carport and toolshed stood unscathed. And the water tank was singed but not broken.

She blew out a shaky sob of air and forced herself to steady her breathing. *In and out.*

Liam's hand came out and gripped hers. She barely noticed.

Her home. Consumed. Crumbled. A wreckage on the ground amid wisps of smoke. But she was alive, she reminded herself. And Grin was alive. And her cows and chooks. Crucially, the men in Blue's truck were alive.

She sat there in the silence with Liam just staring ahead, uncomprehending.

The radio crackled with Ewan's voice. 'I'm sorry about the house, Nell. We've had an order to meet the next fire and save the next property. Both trucks need to move out.'

Liam took his hand back to pick up the mic to answer.

She nodded. 'The animals are safe. There's nothing to rush for here. Let's go.'

'I'm sorry for your loss,' he said, before he pressed the switch to reply, 'We're right to go.'

Chapter Twenty-six

Gracie

The sky hung an even deeper orange and the sun skimmed the horizon like a dim discus. Gracie's phone rang at five-thirty.

Her eyes met Molly's as she picked up the phone.

'This is Central Fire Headquarters, passing on a message from Joshua Edwards to Gracie Sparke.'

'Yes, this is Gracie. Go ahead.'

'Joshua said to tell you they're all safe.'

She covered the phone. 'They're safe,' she repeated shakily to Molly.

The woman went on. 'Nell's house has been lost – she'll be coming home to you tonight.'

'Nell's house,' she mouthed to Molly. 'Back by seven, yes I heard you. Can you pass on that Liam's sister, Molly, is here with me? Thanks for the call.'

Gracie covered her mouth with her hand and met Molly's eyes.

'Oh my,' Molly said. 'Poor Nell. And she's not long moved in.'

And she was just getting her life sorted, Gracie thought. Of all the bad luck.

'That's a bit close to home for the loss of a house.' Molly shook her head. 'She's only five kilometres up the road. I might need to go get my emergency bags.'

'You should do that. Thank God we have her animals here,' Gracie said. 'Bring your dog, too.'

'She won't even have clothes.' Molly searched for her keys. Then she laughed a little hysterically. 'Nell – not the dog.'

Gracie nodded but was too shocked to smile back.

Molly glanced over at Gracie as if assessing her height. 'She's not your size. I've got some of Mum's outfits at home. She's taller and skinnier. Mum's a merry widow with a social life in Armidale. She stays sometimes with me and always leaves things. How about I run home and get some bits and pieces?'

'Thanks, Molly. You'd better pack a bag for Liam, too, just in case. You never know.'

'No, you don't,' Molly said and shook her head with a sigh. 'Poor Nell.'

Gracie had a bad feeling about Molly leaving. 'Be careful. And get out at the first signs of danger your way.'

'I'll be fine. The fire's miles away. I won't be long.'

'But it can move fast,' Gracie cautioned. 'I'll put something out for tea. Doesn't take long to defrost in this heat.'

Molly stopped and pointed a finger at Gracie. 'You put your feet up till I get back. I'll bring the corned beef I've had in the slow cooker. And I have potato salad in the fridge. I'll only be half an hour.'

'Are you sure?'

'You've been busy enough. Take a few minutes so you'll have energy later. I'll be back soon.'

Molly looked so determined Gracie gave in and watched her friend leave. Yes, a quick shower after being at the store all day would be good. And Jed and Nell would need one when they got home. She'd be more use to everyone if she was rested.

Gracie leaned her back against the kitchen door as the front door shut. They'd kept the house closed to keep it cool until a breeze came up, with the door to the bedroom open to let the aircon drift through.

At least she had a house. Poor Nell.

She heard Molly drive away and straightened. The first mild tightness across her lower belly felt like one of those flutters of the baby stretching inside. The house creaked around her in the heat and Gracie's fingers slid down over the mound of her stomach to the odd discomfort above her pubic bone.

It could be a Braxton Hicks contraction. As she'd said to Nell, she'd spoken about them to countless women as their midwife. But this felt different.

She rubbed the spot, which ached in a tightening, clenched-fist sort of way. So, just a little discomfort, probably still the Braxton Hicks that she'd been having up till now, though the previous ones had been completely painless. To feel her stomach go hard like a board with a twinge seemed odd but interesting.

Instead of easing away, the discomfort pulled deeper and harder.

No. This was definitely different.

She wanted to giggle with giddy excitement, but a glance out the door to the orange skies wiped that thought. The discomfort eased. Gracie consciously dropped her shoulders and blew out a long breath. What if it was labour? What if by the time Jed came back it was still going?

She went to the kitchen and took some cold water from the fridge. Sipping slowly as she looked out the kitchen window at the smoke and the glow in the west, the prickle of unease grew stronger. She touched her belly as the next one started. It was rock hard. She'd always wondered if she'd miss the beginning of labour. What a joke. There was no way she could miss this. It was ouchy.

She could remember countless women asking the same thing: *What if I miss it?* She smiled softly and patted her stomach. 'Well, baby, you could have picked a better time, but I guess you know best.'

She'd have to go and leave them fighting the fires. Everything felt ready. Her bag was packed, the car was full of diesel, and even Jed had a change of clothes and some emergency food. He'd hate having to step away from the fires and the people in town he felt so invested in. It couldn't be helped. But she'd wait to confirm the contractions wouldn't stop. Unlike Braxton Hicks, labour didn't go away, so she'd let it fully form before she shared her news.

By the time she undressed and climbed into the shower, the next pulling contraction had been and gone and a faint ache remained in her back. This was her first baby, she reasoned. It wasn't like she'd broken her waters. She had hours and hours of this before she'd have to go anywhere, but if she told Jed, she'd be in the car and ensconced in the hospital in the fastest time possible.

Gracie stepped from the shower and scanned her glistening belly, the huge mound moving slightly as the baby shifted. It was so beautiful and soon it would change. Her belly would be gone.

She looked down at the beads of water that ran in rivulets down her body and pulled downhill. Pulled by gravity like her baby.

Another contraction did some pulling of its own. This was labour for sure. She shook her head. 'Not good timing, baby.' The pain made her reassess her situation. Perhaps she didn't have as much time as she thought before she needed to leave. It was impossible to predict how long this labour would take. It could be a couple of hours if really fast. Or a day and a half if it took its time.

Her mouth curved upwards. It didn't matter. Her baby was coming.

The phone rang and she hurried to where she had left it on the kitchen table. Dunce. She should have taken it to the bathroom. Baby brain.

She expected Jed; instead she got Mavis.

'Gracie? It's Mavis.' The older lady sounded a little breathless.

'Yes, Mavis.' A line of gooseflesh ran down Gracie's arms despite the heat.

'The fire's coming,' Mavis said. 'I want to send the boy down. I'll follow soon if you'll put us up for the night.'

'Of course,' Gracie said quickly.

'Thanks. I'd stay by myself, did last time, but he says he won't leave if I do.'

'Yes. Come. We have tons of room,' Gracie told her as she simultaneously thought, *Good on you, Archie. No one should be left behind to face the coming horror alone.*

Chapter Twenty-seven

Mavis

Mavis put the phone down. 'It was a good day when young Gracie came,' she muttered as she hurried out the back door. The heat and the rising wind slapped her. There was a roaring like a train in the distance and she'd heard that once before. Once heard never forgotten.

The fire was coming.

She whistled loudly. Could hear the *thump, thump, thump* of the diesel engine as the boy started the tractor.

'You can hardly see the shed through the smoke,' she said to the three dogs that gathered around her in response to the whistle and she opened the rear door of her vehicle. 'Into the car, you lot.' They tumbled in. Three? She needed four.

An hour ago, in the orange-brown glow of the early evening, little black leaves had begun to flutter down on the grass around the house. Mavis had turned grim and begun packing a small bag for herself. She also sent the boy to get his computers and put them in the car. Even loaded up most of the internet-shopping food.

Since then, they'd been running round the house closing windows and wetting the walls. The tractor chugged into view through the smoke with Archie bouncing a little as he pushed the throttle faster than he should.

'Slow down,' she muttered, though she'd have to shout like a maniac for him to hear, so she just jerked her hand in a downward direction.

The tractor came to a stop. 'You drive down to Gracie's,' she told him. 'Park in the shop-parking area away from trees. I'll follow in the car with the dogs.'

He nodded.

'Go. I've just gotta get Reggie.'

The old dog had slipped back into the house again to hide under the bed. Reggie liked staying home, just like Mavis.

'I'll wait for you,' Archie yelled.

'I'm faster than you. Go now.'

The kid shook his head and crossed his arms. Stubborn little blighter. Mavis blew out a big breath, turned around and trotted back into the house to her bedroom. She got down on her bony old knees on the hardwood floor. Yep. He was there. She grabbed the dog's collar.

Reggie bared his teeth and pulled back.

Mavis paused in shock. Reggie had actually growled at her. She narrowed her eyes and lowered her head so she could see the dog's face. 'You. Come. Now,' she growled at the animal.

Reggie's greying muzzle trembled, but the dog inched forward and began crawling out from under the bed.

Mavis sighed with relief once the dog was fully exposed. She stood, picked him up with a loud grunt and heaved him onto her hip, turning away from the room that had been hers for more than sixty years.

Outside, it was even darker than it had been a minute ago. The wind had risen to a distant howl that thrashed hair into her eyes.

'Get moving, Archie!' she yelled.

The kid nodded and the tractor began to shift away. The falling leaves weren't black now. They glowed red, and some fluttered down while others whipped sideways. 'Blimey, we're in for it,' she said to Reggie.

Mavis reached out with one hand to pull open the back door of the car. Muttering 'Stay' to the three wild-eyed dogs inside, she leaned forward with her bundle, but at the last moment Reggie flipped, twisted his centre of gravity, flopped from Mavis's arms and streaked back into the house through the dog door.

'Damn it, Reggie.'

There was a glow at the bottom of the gully leading to the house, and the wind was whipping around her. As she glared at the dog door that slammed shut behind her old friend, Mavis knew there wasn't time to fight again with him. She yelled one last time. 'Reggie. Come!'

Tears stung her eyes and she coughed as the smoke increased. She slammed the back door closed and ran to the driver's side and climbed in as fast as she could. 'Thank you, Lord, the other dogs stayed.' Maybe the house would be okay. The gutters were full of water.

The roaring drew closer. Embers settled like black snow on the car now as she shut the door. After she pressed on the gas, her car bucketed up the driveway through the open gate until she caught up with the lumbering tractor.

Grief contorted her face and tears dripped into her collar as she drove. There was no way the house would stay and Reggie would be in it.

The tractor halted suddenly in front and Mavis had to jam on the brakes before she ploughed into it. 'Blimey, kid,' she yelled, but he wouldn't hear her.

Then she saw the obstruction across Molly's drive that blocked the gate. It was then that Mavis heard the blaring of a horn and she realised the wind must've brought down a widow-maker branch from the big gum at the entrance to Molly's gate.

A blue utility was parked on the other side. Trapped. Barred from making it to the road. Not a good place to be with the fire coming.

It was Molly's brother's car. Liam. Funny how since she'd started taking more care of herself, she could remember everyone's names.

Okay. The kid was coming in sideways with the tractor, bull bar towards the obstruction, but it was a big branch and he didn't have room to manoeuvre. He'd only be able to shift the bulk of it slightly.

Mavis climbed out of the car, her bones creaking and sore, and opened the boot. She hefted up the small chainsaw, her shoulder clicking in complaint. She was too old for this crap.

She heaved the chainsaw across the road as the kid pushed the tree, and once he'd shoved it as far as he could, Mavis started the chainsaw. She chopped off the last ten feet that were stopping the car from coming through, the vibrations and noise all part of a hellish afternoon.

The wood snapped as the chain cut through, Mavis's shoulders slumping with the weight.

'Gotcha,' she sighed when it was done, feeling the exhaustion flow over her, and suddenly the boy was beside her. He took the chainsaw off her as if it weighed nothing.

'Get back in the car, Gran. Let's get outta here.'

Mavis could drink to that. She scurried back to the car and shut the boot; the boy had thrown the chainsaw onto the carry-all of the tractor.

She climbed back in and pulled the door shut.

Molly squeezed through the space in the gate and pulled up behind her. The boy started the tractor and drove it far too fast over the bridge into Featherwood.

With a lot of luck, and it would take a lot, the creek would slow the fire coming into town.

The convoy pulled into the Farmer's Friend. The place truly was a friend at the moment as they all converged on it. The boy parked the tractor away from the trees on an open patch of ground, then jogged over to jump in beside Mavis, and they drove down to Gracie's house. Molly followed in her brother's car.

They parked a safe distance from the house in case an ember landed on a vehicle and started a fire. She'd tie the dogs around the back in a minute.

Mavis rested her hands on the wheel and bowed her head.

'You okay?' Archie asked.

The boy's concern lifted her chin. She opened her mouth but nothing came out. Instead she nodded.

'That there was crazy, Gran,' the boy said beside her.

'Good job at the tree, Archie.'

He stared at her. She guessed she rarely called him Archie, but he deserved recognition.

'You cut the branch.' He grinned at her, all crooked teeth and freckles.

'We're a team, mate. Let's go in and see what Gracie says. She probably has news.'

Archie climbed out and was nearly knocked over by Molly, who threw her arms around him. 'Thank you, Archie. You just saved my life.'

Archie looked nonplussed at the unexpected body contact and Mavis smiled. The kid was getting more positive feedback today than he'd had for a while.

Chapter Twenty-eight

Nell

At the fire front, Nell's whole body, even her face, felt numb as she followed orders, spoke on the radio and hosed down someone else's walls. Her house was gone. All the furniture and bed linen. Towels and blankets. Everything in the kitchen. Her few clothes except for those she'd packed. Though she hadn't had many and hadn't been interested in those for years.

They held more interest now that they were gone. It wasn't a tragedy, however. Possessions were possessions. She dragged back the sob that wanted to escape. *Stop it.*

When all this was over, she would still have a water tank. She could live in the toolshed until she rebuilt. Already she'd seen three homes turned into rubble. People who had lost everything.

Liam waved at her. She moved away from the small front she was working on, back towards the truck. They were all on alert, and everyone did exactly what they were told. This fire was a holocaust of heat and mayhem and it surged and seared flames at them at every turn.

Twice now, they'd been saved by the helicopter dropping water and she, like everyone else, was numb with weariness.

'That's it,' Liam yelled. 'In the truck. We're pulling out.'

She nodded and helped roll up the hoses. Once it was done, equipment stowed swiftly, she climbed into the truck. She and Liam were still together in the smaller unit. They had achieved a working relationship that didn't need words often. A look could say a lot. And neither were wordy people.

She pulled the door shut with the last of her strength and the outside noise died down. Her head rested wearily back against the seat.

'New crews are coming in. One from Wollongong and one from Ipswich. They've sent help from all over.'

'Good,' was all she could manage.

'We're to go home.' He stopped and shot her a piercing glance that held a touch of remorse. The thought clicked into her tired brain – Liam was realising she didn't have a home.

'I'm sorry, Nell.' He changed his tack. 'We're to rest, eat and come back tomorrow.'

She nodded.

They drove back through the eerie light and falling black leaves to Featherwood Brigade Shed and parked. She'd forgotten her car was there. 'I still have a car, too.'

Liam looked at her with something that felt a lot like admiration. 'Well,' he drew the word out, 'you're a lucky bugger.'

She snorted, too exhausted to laugh.

'Looking forward to Gracie's shower?'

'I'd have to fight Jed for it.' Nell tilted her mouth wanly. 'He'd win.'

'I could fight Jed for you.'

She had the feeling he would too. 'Nah.' The thought made her feel a bit faint, so she reached down and picked up her water bottle and took a sip. That was the problem. The heat sapped fluid from the body and she felt like a dried-out chip. An unattractive, dried-out chip.

Liam was right. She couldn't wait to get these hot clothes off and stand under the shower. Her stomach rumbled. And maybe eat something. Even though the sandwiches had been on tap all day, until now she hadn't been hungry.

'Gracie knows you're coming,' Liam said. She inclined her head again. 'I'll sort the truck with Jed, so you go on ahead. And make sure you leave Jed some water. Molly's there with my car, so I'll see you there.'

She wanted to reassure him. She had the feeling he felt worse about her house going than she did. 'I'm blessed,' she said.

Liam was a good man, they were all good men, and after today, almost brothers. Though she wasn't feeling brotherly about Liam. Probably just some sort of hero worship because he'd been calm all day and kept her safe.

Despite her house, she had somewhere to sleep and keep her dog and knew she was welcome. She hadn't felt welcome in someone else's home for a very long time. She truly was blessed.

Her face cracked into a smile for the first time in hours. 'I'll only be using the cold water.'

She saw Liam's face as he thought about standing under a cold shower.

'Hell, yeah.'

Chapter Twenty-nine

Gracie

Gracie opened the door to a tousled Mavis, who seemed far too pale despite the red flags in her cheeks. Archie's face bore streaks of sweat and he'd soaked both armpits of his shirt with perspiration. Behind them, a wild-eyed Molly swayed and reached out to hold the door.

'Look at you all. Is everyone okay? Come in.' Her last contraction had eased and was almost gone, so she could concentrate. She stood back a foot, but in view of her stomach that wasn't far enough, and she had to take an extra step back because she realised her belly still blocked the way.

Mavis slid past, followed by Molly because Archie had been polite and was now waiting for Gracie before he came in. 'You're a real gentleman, Archie.' She smiled at him and he ducked his head shyly before he followed the ladies into the hallway.

'Into the kitchen. Have a drink before you go any further. You all look like you need to sit down.'

'Archie just saved my life,' Molly puffed out, then took another breath, and added, 'Mavis helped with a chainsaw.'

Gracie stared. 'What happened?' she asked Archie, who blushed.

Molly slumped into the chair. 'One of those big branches from the tree at the gate blocked the driveway when I was trying to leave. He,' she pointed with a shaking finger, 'pushed it away with the tractor as cool as you please, and Mavis cut the end off so I could drive through.' She shook her head. 'I was terrified, embers falling, smoke making me cough, not game to get out of the car and run from the fire until I saw them coming down the road.'

Molly stopped and covered her mouth with her hand for a second. 'Archie heard my car horn and I don't know where I would have been if they hadn't stopped.' Molly's hand rested in the middle of her sternum now, as if to stop her heart jumping out of her chest.

Her friend needed a cold drink and maybe a sweet tea as well for the shock. Gracie waddled to the fridge, but as she grabbed the handle the pain clamped around her like a double vice squeezing her back and her front. She closed her eyes and breathed out slowly.

'You okay, Gracie?' Mavis hadn't missed her frozen stance.

Without turning she said, 'Getting a few contractions.' It came out a little breathlessly.

'I've only been gone an hour,' Molly said.

Gracie carefully removed the cold water jug and set it on the table. 'Pretty well started just after you left.'

'That changes things,' Mavis said and her brows drew down, a no-nonsense look on her face. 'After our falling-branch adventure, you'd better get going. There's a lot of trees between here and the hospital.'

'I'll wait to see what Jed says.' She smiled at the older lady. 'And get you all settled in a room first.'

Molly poured herself a big glass of water, sculled it in one long slurp and put it down. 'Which room? I'll do that.'

'The green one. Nell can have the baby's room.' Gracie smiled her thanks.

'I had to bring the dogs, Gracie,' Mavis said and the stricken note in her voice made Gracie turn and look at her.

'Of course. You okay, Mavis?'

'I had to leave one of them.' She glanced at Archie. 'I'm sorry, mate. Reggie ran back into the house and I didn't have time to get him out from under the bed again. The fire was coming,' she explained to the others, 'and the dog panicked.'

Archie, face white and strained with shock, stared at his great-grandmother, before he lifted his chin. 'Oh. I'm so sorry about Reggie.' He blinked back his tears. 'But you did the right thing. I couldn't lose you, too, Gran.'

Gracie stared at the boy, feeling tears prickle at the back of her eyes at the young lad's maturity and sorrow.

Molly spoke into the silence. 'I'm really sorry, Mavis. I know you and Reggie have been together for a long time. That means the three girls are here with you?' When Mavis nodded, Molly said to Gracie, 'My dog's in the car, too. She and Nell's are all from Mavis's Reggie and one of the girls. Archie and I can put the girls out the back with Nell's dog and mine. They'll all be fine.' She heaved herself out of the chair. 'Archie, do you want to give me a hand?'

Archie drained his glass of water and stood up. As he passed, very lightly, he touched his great-grandmother's shoulder and squeezed, then he was gone.

'He's a beautiful young man, Mavis. A real credit to you,' Molly said quietly as she followed him out.

Mavis sniffed. 'Yep,' was all she said.

*

Half an hour later, Mavis's gear had been transferred into the green room and a bed on the floor assembled for Archie. They might need all the rooms tonight. Mavis had been sent to have a shower and encouraged to put her feet up and read the local paper in the sitting room while Molly took over the kitchen. Molly had the other guest room and could share with Liam.

Mavis had brought food, and Molly sorted that into drawers in Gracie's fridge and spare freezer. Molly had brought the corned beef, waiting to be sliced, a huge salad and enough Idaho potatoes and sour cream to feed an army ready for tea. Plus, she had filled cold water bottles to freeze in case the power went out. That would take up the rest of the space in the fridge.

Gracie left her to it and packed the last of the toiletries she needed to collect for the hospital and watched for Jed.

Nell's car pulled up outside and Gracie could hear Nell talking to the dogs. Grin's happy yips carried above the rest. For someone who didn't have a dog, Gracie was well endowed with them at the moment. This thought made her smile despite the circumstances.

She heard Nell climb slowly up the steps onto the rear verandah and she slipped out of the bedroom to meet her at the back door of the house. Nell swayed a little as she peeled off her boots and fire-brigade clothes.

Gracie put her arms around the smoky woman. 'I'm so sorry about your house.'

'Hey.' Nell eased back out of her embrace. 'I'm all smoky and sweaty and I stink. No cuddling.'

Gracie shook her head. 'Well, go get showered and smell sweet. Then you have to let me give you at least one big hug after you're done.'

At least she'd managed to coax a small smile out of her, Gracie thought. And might get that hug later.

'You're a sweetie and all the men, including yours, took very good care of me. I've decided I'm going to adopt Jed as my big brother.'

Gracie laughed. 'I'm pleased to hear it. Mavis, Molly and Archie are here.'

Unexpectedly, Gracie sucked in a breath as a contraction grabbed her and twisted. This was the strongest one yet.

'You're in labour,' Nell said without hesitation. It wasn't a question.

Almost a full minute later Gracie blew out a sigh. 'I very much think so.'

'Well, you'd better get on the road. Why haven't you rung Jed? If I'd known, I would have stayed back to restock the vehicle and sent him home. Liam could have come in my car once we were done.'

'It's okay. I need time to get my head around it. Go have a shower and then Jed can jump in as soon as he gets back.'

Nell nodded then asked, 'You haven't broken your waters yet, have you?'

'No. Once a midwife, always a midwife,' Gracie teased, then could have bitten the words back as soon as they were out. But nobody was around. It was a sign of just how emotionally exhausted Nell was that she didn't even grimace.

'Seems so.'

Jed and Liam arrived fifteen minutes later. Jed took one look at Gracie's face and stopped. 'You in labour?'

'Yes. It's only just started. I was waiting for you to come home.'

'The road's just been closed,' he said in a grim voice that wasn't like him at all.

Gracie blinked. 'That was quick. There was no warning.'

'We had a lightning strike in the middle between here and town. The power lines and towers are down, so there are no texts getting through from the SES, but they're working on restoring some power. They were door-knocking to check on everyone and I said I'd clear our house.'

He blew out a breath and she could see how tired he was. And now worried. 'Gracie. It's gonna get hairy. You shouldn't be here in labour.' He ran his grimy hand through his hair. 'You shouldn't be here at all. I'll see if we can get a chopper to get you out.'

If it was gonna get hairy, Gracie didn't want to go anywhere, but she didn't say it because one look at Jed's face told her that he wouldn't be able to handle that thought.

'Yes, Jed.' She touched his sooty arm. 'I'll be hours yet. Go have a quick shower.' She'd been encouraging water sluicing to everyone. She hoped the town water kept running. 'Your clothes are on the bed.'

He nodded. 'I saw Mavis's tractor at the shop and her car out front.'

'Yes. Lots to tell. She and Archie came here. The fire was getting too close for comfort and Archie wouldn't leave without her.'

'He's a good kid, that,' Jed said.

Everybody congregated opposite the kitchen in the front room. From the dining area, they could see the town and the store.

Smoke was heavy in the air, catching in the back of their throats. The orange glow shone like a flickering monster behind the hills out towards where Mavis and Molly lived.

Liam sat with his arm around Molly and Molly wouldn't let go of his hand. It was a measure of how much his sister had been shaken up.

Nell looked marginally better in a pair of cut-off jeans and a short-sleeved T-shirt Molly had brought with her. She'd complained to Gracie quietly that Molly must have brought a push-up bra because suddenly she had breasts. The thought made Gracie smile.

Leaning against the doorframe, Gracie surveyed all the people in her house, whom she hadn't known less than two months ago. They were all important to her now. She chose not to sit down because the contractions were coming so frequently that it was more comfortable to stand up.

Seemingly, she had been telling the truth all those times she'd told labouring women that gravity was your friend. It made perfect sense being upright and it was certainly easier just to sway gently standing up when the contractions came. Doing it subtly so everyone else didn't notice was a little trickier, but Gracie didn't want to miss any of the conversation by leaving the room. She'd miss it all soon enough.

Here was another one. She began to gently sway and a big hand came behind her and rested warmly in the small of her back. As if he'd read her mind, Jed's big hand rhythmically rubbed the aching spot. When he stopped and moved forward to the doorway, the conversations in the room stuttered and ceased. As soon as she turned to look at him, her smile died.

His face had sculpted into tight lines. 'They've had half-a-dozen more lightning strikes with new outbreaks to the west and east. The two-pronged fire is cutting us off from Dorrigo and Armidale. Now it has several fronts and it's out of control. We're surrounded.'

He stared straight ahead, not looking at Gracie. 'They're going to try to get a chopper to airlift Gracie out. We'll take some cars down to the racetrack and put some lights out for them because it will be full dark by the time they get here. The rescue chopper is on another job at the moment and they'll call us when it leaves the base.' There was an unspoken undertone: *if it leaves base.*

Mavis asked, 'Have they heard if my house is still there?'

He shook his head. 'Nobody can get in, Mavis. The wind picked up and the firestorm carried over everything. They've dropped retardant around Featherwood and the two bridges.'

Liam stood. 'What about Moll's house?' His voice was grim, too.

Jed met his eyes. 'Nobody can deny or confirm. The driveway's blazing and your front fences have gone. But it could be still there.'

Molly sucked in a breath as she and everyone realised she'd have been in a spot if she'd left it too late to leave.

'Your driveway, also, Mavis.'

Mavis looked at Archie.

Low in her belly, Gracie felt the pull of another strong contraction grow; she tried to keep everything quiet as Jed explained the situation that he had gleaned from the two-way radio. Her belly grew tighter and tighter and the pain at the front and in the back where Jed had started rubbing again pulled low. The sudden unexpected tweak of pressure inside her jumped and released with a pop.

She gasped.

Suddenly, she was standing in a puddle of water. Embarrassingly, everyone was looking at her. Jed swore.

Jed never swore.

Chapter Thirty

Nell

Jed had verbalised the exact word that Nell would like to have used. She had been watching her friend for the last ten minutes and those contractions were barely giving her a minute's break between. She was in established labour, all right.

Praying for the helicopter had been the best they could do. Now, everything had escalated. There was no doubt that Gracie's waters had just broken.

It was highly likely that Nell's worst nightmare was about to happen. Gracie might be a midwife, and she certainly had knowledge, but she was the one having the baby. Nell knew, responsibility-wise, she was on her own until help arrived.

Not only that, everybody would find out about her past.

But that was something she couldn't worry about because right at this moment Gracie required her to step up. Gracie needed her to be the midwife until she could be airlifted.

That might happen. *Yeah, right,* her inner voice scoffed. *And a big rain cloud is going to dump water on the fires today and extinguish them all.*

And . . . pigs might fly.

Nell twisted her mouth. It was highly unlikely a helicopter was going to land and take Gracie away before she birthed. That was pretty darn obvious.

She moved forward to where Jed was looking with horror down at the mother of his child. Both his hands were on her elbows as if he was waiting for her to say, *No, this didn't happen.*

'I'm sorry, Jed,' she heard Gracie say. 'But I think I'm going to have the baby here. Soon.'

Jed took two steps backwards as if in denial and Nell, feeling extraordinarily calm because there really was nothing else to do except move forward and prepare, lifted her game. 'Well, we might just go get you in the shower, Miss Gracie, and Molly might find us a towel for the floor.'

Molly jumped up. 'Yes.' She shot a worried glance at Jed, who stood as if poleaxed. 'Great idea.'

Archie backed away to the far corner of the room and picked up the newspaper his great-grandmother had discarded. He put his head down and hid in it.

Mavis was watching everyone with an expression on her face of 'I've seen everything now' and a tiny smile.

Liam gave Nell an approving look and eyed Jed. 'I'll get onto control and push the helicopter.'

Jed looked like he wanted to pick Gracie up and run with her to the car, but there was nowhere to run to. He carefully licked his lips as if they were stuck together. Finally he said, without taking his eyes off Gracie's face, 'Thanks, mate. Do that.'

Taking Gracie's arm gently in hers, Nell steered her to the bathroom. Molly and Jed followed.

When Gracie handed Molly a towel from the shelf, her eyes turned to Nell. And Nell gave her a smile. A reassuring one, she hoped. 'Where's your equipment bag for your homebirths?'

'Could you get that for me please, Jed?' Gracie asked. 'It's in those tall cupboards in the laundry. Please put it in the bedroom.'

Jed spun on his heel and strode away. Nell followed her friend inside the bathroom and closed the door on the two of them.

First things first. 'Does everything feel normal?'

'Normal?' Gracie leaned on the wall and breathed through the next contraction. 'I don't think . . .' she paused and breathed, '. . . there's any cord . . .' pause '. . . falling out if that's what you mean. I'll check in the shower.'

The contraction faded and Gracie's shoulders relaxed.

'Last time I was at the clinic, they said the head was well down.'

'Excellent. That's a relief,' Nell said. Now the other important question. 'What do you want me for, Gracie? Do you want me to be your midwife? Or do you want me to just do what you tell me to do?'

They stared at each other, Gracie appearing troubled. 'Are you able to be my midwife, Nell? I know it's a big ask.'

Nell blew out a big breath, almost bigger than Gracie's had been. 'If we hadn't had that conversation, I don't think so, but I spent a lot of time thinking about it in the last couple of days and it's not like I've forgotten what a normal labour looks like. And for you, doing the birthing, you can't relax and let everything happen if you can't hand over responsibility. So. Yes.'

She saw the relief in Gracie's face. She didn't understand how, but Gracie had that faith in her.

'Wonderful. I truly hoped you'd say that.'

It was done, then. It was now her responsibility.

'We're going to have a nice, normal labour,' Nell said, her voice sounding rock solid. Not like her fingers. They shook.

Gracie nodded. 'And if the helicopter lands, I will go to hospital, but until then I would love you to be my midwife.'

Nell noted the burden of responsibility on her wasn't as huge as she would have thought it would be. The difference being she trusted her own instincts and she trusted Gracie. There hadn't been that trust last time because she'd been taking orders from someone with an unhealthy agenda.

'You should climb into the shower and let yourself relax. I'll get Jed to come in while I set up the bedroom.'

Gracie needed the heat of water against her back, before the next contraction began. She began to strip with fumbling haste and Nell helped her.

She didn't make it.

When she could speak, Gracie said, 'There's a spare shower curtain in the bathroom cabinet there. You could put that over the bedsheets. The linen is in the box at the end of my bed.'

Jed knocked on the door.

'Come in,' Nell said. 'I'll slip out and get the handheld monitor to have a listen while you two have a quick chat.'

She found the midwifery bag Jed had left on the bed and scooted back to the bathroom just before Gracie stepped into the shower.

She had to guess the place to listen. The heartbeat would be low in Gracie's belly near the midline, she hoped – they'd confirm position later. Relief flooded her as she was rewarded with the regular *clop-clop, clop-clop, clop-clop* of the baby's heartbeat.

The steady sound filled the room and all three of them sagged a little with the proof of a happy baby.

'Sounds beautiful,' Nell said, and had to look away from the intense glance between Jed and Gracie.

She took a couple of deep, head-clearing breaths herself. *Thank God, thank God, thank God,* she thought in time to the clopping heartbeats.

No baby with a cord prolapse would sound like that.

No baby unwell with anything would sound like that.

Everything would be fine.

The three of them listened all the way through the next contraction, both Gracie and Nell dreading the idea that the baby would slow the heartbeat from exhaustion after the contraction, but it didn't happen. In fact, if anything, the baby's heart rate sped up.

'Lots of energy,' Nell said as she stepped away.

By the time Jed and Gracie left the bathroom, Nell had been busy in the bedroom. She'd made a small towel-lined area for immediately after the birth. A flat area, safe, and clear for access if there was an unexpected hitch with the baby. Just in case, on the little round tea table Gracie kept in the bedroom. Being prepared was so important. Nell would have a workspace for the baby's resuscitation if she needed one.

Please, universe, don't let that happen.

There was no reason for the baby to need such a thing. The heart sounds had been strong and healthy in the bathroom as they'd listened. She'd tucked the table into the corner and added two clean face washers and a hand towel for wiping the baby dry.

She moved the two chairs to the opposite window to make a comfortable place for Gracie to sit, looking out, leaning over pillows propped on the chair. Jed would be able to sit behind her and rub her back if needed.

She expected Gracie to keep walking as much as she could because she looked much more relaxed as she swayed. But sometimes legs got tired.

It was so strange that all she'd learned returned to her. *Make a birth space that is inviting, offer comfort, offer options for position, and keep safe.*

On the bed, the pillows had been piled high, top covers had been stripped away and the shower curtain placed over the bottom half with Molly's help.

Molly was particularly excited and kept saying, 'Oh my goodness. Imagine. My goodness.'

Her murmured repetitions built until Nell wanted to laugh – or strangle her. But there was nothing funny about this situation. Everything had to go right. Nell had to believe that it would, and preparation was the key.

The baby would be fine. Gracie would NOT bleed.

Mavis was in the kitchen boiling up a pan of sterile water. Nell wasn't sure why, but Mavis was adamant. And hot water was always good for pain relief when applied with a washer or hand towel. Of course, Gracie had her birth kit for Nell to draw from and it sat on the dresser top now.

Nell unzipped the little pack, which was very similar to the one she'd been so excited to buy four years ago, with sterile scissors, plastic cord clamps and the disposable dish that sat in a bag for the placenta afterwards. She had a plethora of syringes and emergency drugs in case she needed more medication. Nell was seriously impressed with Gracie's emergency pack.

After assembling the small mask and resuscitation bag for a newborn, Nell tried it against her palm to confirm that it remained in working order. When she was satisfied with it, she placed that over on her round 'newborn' table.

Now Nell assembled the syringe, the needle and the ampoule of medication to increase the tone of the uterus, after the birth. Nell had suggested she should give it to Gracie for insurance, since there were no options for emergency help if Gracie did bleed. Gracie had seen Nell's need for the extra safeguard and consented.

The ampoule was not yet opened but it would be. When she gave it, the uterine-contracting properties would take three to seven minutes to work and last for thirty to sixty minutes. Nell knew this stuff. Boy, did she know this stuff.

As well as the shower curtain on the bed, Nell had placed one folded sheet and kept one for decorum if Gracie wanted to lie down to birth. And there was another space against the wall, near the bed, with towels on the floor if she wanted to kneel or stand.

The room was cool, not cold, because the aircon was on and the door was open for the moment, but they'd turn it off when the baby came.

Gracie came into the bedroom with Jed so close to her shoulder it was as if he couldn't let her out of reaching distance. She paused, looked around with a slow smile, and her shoulders relaxed even more. 'The room feels wonderful, Nell, thank you.'

'Isn't it great that Nell is a midwife?' Molly shook her head at Jed. 'Imagine us not knowing that.'

Nell deadpanned Molly. She'd had to explain why she knew what needed to be done, but had kept it brief. 'Let's talk about

Gracie,' Nell said, because if they started talking about her past, she'd end up throwing up in the corner of the room from nerves.

'How was the shower?' she asked Gracie. She could see by her buddy's slightly unfocused-looking eyes that the labour was progressing fast.

'The water's still coming away,' Gracie said, her voice seeming slower, almost detached, as if her own body was creating distance from the world. As it should. Endorphins were the body's natural pain relief that compensated for the discomfort of labour. It worked beautifully if fear was absent and synthetic pain relief had not been given.

'Funny, that, the way the fluid keeps slipping out when you don't expect it,' Nell said with a smile.

The two midwives exchanged a glance and Nell saw Gracie's shoulders drop a little more as she noted how calm Nell was. Nell slowed her own breathing more. She really was helping by being here and that gave her added confidence.

'Let's have a listen to your baby again,' she suggested, her voice low and calm. 'It's fifteen minutes since your waters broke.' She lifted the handheld ultrasound doppler again. As she turned the switch the device wailed and she quickly turned the volume down. *Oops.* At least she knew the batteries were still good.

She rustled around in the bag again and came up with ultrasound jelly. 'Could you take some of those pillows away from the top of the bed, please, Jed? Just leave it with one.'

'Well, if you're going to do midwifery things,' Molly's eyes were huge in her face but filled with excitement, 'I'd better leave.' She hurried to the door, muttering, 'Oh my goodness. Imagine this. Oh my goodness,' and shut it behind her. They could hear her down the hall, muttering as she went.

'She is funny,' said Nell.

'She told me once she always wanted a baby, but then her husband died and her baby dreams with him,' Gracie said, her voice distant. 'I feel like we're giving her a gift by having one with her here.'

'You could always wait to give a present after you get taken to the hospital,' Jed said gruffly from where he was carrying pillows to the chair.

Gracie smiled, but then she drew in a lungful and consciously began to breathe slowly again. The look she gave Nell said there was no way she was going anywhere.

'We'll be ready to go, or ready for your baby. Whatever happens,' Nell said quietly to Jed, but both women knew which would come first.

Once that contraction had eased away, Nell waved her hand to the bed. 'Let's have a feel of your tummy and feel for the baby's position before the next one comes.'

Gracie watched her with big eyes and nodded.

Jed was there, instantly, to help Gracie climb onto the bed, and she scooted down awkwardly with more of his help.

Nell knew she'd have to be quick before the next contraction built, but she also wanted to do it right. Swiftly and surely, as if her hands were driven by muscle memory, she felt the height of the fundus, both sides of the uterus, and down the centre of Gracie's circular belly, noting the anterior position, then around the baby with a quick dip into the pelvis through the abdominal wall to the pelvic cavity to feel the baby's descent.

The contraction started and the wall of Gracie's uterus went rigid. In a breathy voice, Gracie said, 'I can stay here if you want to hold it there all the way through the contraction.' She rolled over to her side to wait for the contraction to pass as Nell pushed the coin-sized head of the ultrasound transducer onto her belly and listened.

Gracie slipped her fingers into Jed's hand, and both sets turned white with the force of her grip as the power of the contraction grew.

The reassuring clopping of the baby's heartbeat lifted into the room like a little horse galloping around the ceiling.

Nell smiled. 'Do you want me to check to see how dilated you are?'

Gracie studied her man's face. 'Let's check and then Jed can tell the retrieval team.'

'Good idea,' Jed said.

Of course. Gracie constantly thought of others. It always seemed to be those who were waiting that needed to know the most, Nell mused. Poor Jed was a mess. Just looking at Gracie, Nell knew she was almost ready to birth, so it didn't matter if she was five centimetres or nine. It could change as soon as Nell had finished the examination, because the mum-to-be was almost there.

It only took a moment, but Nell stepped back with a smile. 'Nine centimetres. Where are you having this baby?'

'I have to stand up.' Gracie climbed off the bed as if it was hot and getting hotter. Being stranded on a flat surface didn't suit her at all. She moved instinctively across to the place where the towels were on the floor and remained standing. 'Hold me, Jed.' Her voice suddenly was crisp and sharp.

Nell narrowed her eyes. It was time to check everything was ready for the baby. She crossed to the little round table, drew up the injection for Gracie post-birth, rechecked the resuscitation bag and mask, and pulled on her new gloves. Then she called in Molly because she wanted a runner if she needed one.

She was ready.

Chapter Thirty-one

Gracie

When Jed's arms circled her, warm, loving and totally reliable, Gracie could let go. All of the remaining tension from the possibility of having to leave, to the money worries, to the fire descending on them, to forcing Nell to be her midwife because of the circumstances, it all had to go.

This was about being present and accepting. Acquiescent. To let it happen.

She allowed the fogginess of her body's response to pain, that distance from the worries of the world, to enfold her. Here, slumped against her baby's father, still on her feet, it felt good to fully relax into the overwhelming sensations – and release – with Jed taking nearly all of her weight.

The first inkling of pressure swept over her. Her eyes sprang open and she gasped. It was happening. The baby was coming.

She had to force her breathing to slow again. To let go of the fear that jumped out at her like a demon from nowhere. The anxiety that she didn't need in this moment.

She had this. Nell was here. And Jed would hold her.

The contraction built, twice as powerful but somehow different. Directional, overpowering, an out-of-body experience and she needed to let it have its way. Gracie sighed into it, into her lower body, grunting almost silently, allowing the waves to drag downwards, and feeling the sudden heaviness grow heavier as she breathed out.

A sudden panic flared as she came up against an immovable wall, her body feeling trapped, stuck somewhere in a place where no one could help her, and her chest fluttered with fear.

Nell's whispered voice came to the rescue. 'You're doing beautifully, Gracie.'

Yes. She forced the fear away, reassuring herself that she had this. She blew away the panic and sighed again into her lower back and thighs and legs, and imagined her baby, coiled, edging through the twisting canal of her centre, imagined the cervix pulling up inside her past the baby's head, and then that particular, grinding contraction eased away.

Vaguely, she was aware of Nell leaning in with the doppler, cold against her skin, and she heard the steady drumming of her baby's heartbeat. And felt the warmth of Jed's hands on her shoulders.

She inhaled the soapy scent of his chest with her nose pressed into that firm wall that she knew so well. Her hands clasped his hips to hold on to, his body as steady as a rock, her rock, the father of her child right where he needed to be at the right time.

The next contraction built and she drew a deep breath and sent it down. She felt herself squeezing, opening like a lotus in sunlight, the overwhelming urge, the surge, the purge of the baby from her. Knees bent, she sighed it downwards, and Jed held her.

'Beautiful,' Nell's whispered voice drifted to her. 'A tiny view of the head now.'

The contraction went away, and Gracie heard the swish of Nell moving and she opened her eyes. 'Molly's just turning the aircon off before the baby is here. Now, I'll have a listen.'

A few seconds later, again the sound of the baby's heartbeat filled the room. Soaring. Rhythmic. Clopping happily. Everything was right. Everything was safe. Gracie rested her forehead in the safest of places – against Jed.

In the silence of that moment, while they waited, a single, illuminating, shiny thought surfaced in her brain.

She should marry Jed.

She should stay in his arms for the rest of her life.

Then the pain came back and shiny thoughts were pushed away as she concentrated with the deepness and direction and determination needed. Now she revelled in the surge, pushing through the burning and feeling the weight and the stretching and the aching. Her legs began to shake, Jed tightened his grip and she let him have more weight.

This time when the pain went away, the burning remained. She heard Nell say, 'Do you want me to put the hot washer there for the stinging?'

She'd forgotten that. 'Yes,' she breathed. 'Let's try that. It stings.'

Jed's hands rubbed her shoulders, offering comfort, and down below something pressed against the stinging. Hotness seeped into her, the deep, easing, comforting warmth of the wet compress against her backside.

The relief was instant and soothing until the contraction began again and she willed her baby down, sighing deeply, welcoming the end of the very beginning in a last gentle exultation of birth. There was a rush, an explosion of sensation that made her gasp, another expulsion and then a sudden feeling of emptiness.

And then she heard her baby's first cry.

Chapter Thirty-two

Nell

Everything happened so fast at the end.

With the heat of the compress allowing Gracie to relax her bottom, the baby's scalp rose swiftly from within until the crescent grew into a thatch of dark hair, a crown of curls, until the head was fully free and Gracie puffed out a gasp.

From where Nell was crouched on the stool, she saw the little face swivel to realign with the shoulders, squashed nose and eyes tightly shut, until the baby was facing Nell as she hovered with the towel in her hands ready to catch.

First one shoulder and then the other dipped with gravity and the squashed chest was freed into the safe harbour of the waiting towel held under Gracie. The baby's belly slid and then there was a tumble of legs and feet that followed in a swish of movement and fluid and very little blood. Barely any.

The towel Nell held was full of Gracie's baby joined by a twisting coil of cord to its mother. Shocked by the cool of the room, the baby gasped and began to cry, and Nell felt the sting of tears in her own eyes. Her voice stayed calm, however, as she said, 'Back yourself towards the bed, Gracie. It's just behind your knees.'

Jed helped steer Gracie until she sat and then leaned back as Jed lifted her legs. He scooped her against the pillows while Nell followed with the baby in a towel.

All the while, the baby roared its disgust at the shock of the cold atmosphere, and in Nell's tight chest, air expanded as exultation rose. She could feel the grin splitting her face. She dried the baby quickly and placed it belly down, face to the side, warm against Gracie's belly skin and facing Jed.

Gracie's hands came down and reverently rubbed the tiny back, and Jed's hand came in over the top. Reaching for a clean blanket that had been wrapped in a hot water bottle, Nell settled the warmth over all of them while she waited for the cord to stop pulsating.

In the meantime, she checked Gracie's loss and gave her the injection. Thankfully, there was still very little blood.

By now, Jed's face was shocked and streaming with tears. 'What have you got, Jed?' Nell asked softly and lifted the cover and one little leg. The scrotum and penis flopped into view.

'A boy!' He laughed and put his face down to Gracie's. 'We have a son.'

Nell busied herself clamping the umbilical cord now that it had stopped pulsating, and when she had both clamps closed, one near the baby's belly and one an inch further along the mother's end of the cord, she offered the scissors to Jed.

'Would you like to cut the cord?'

Jed blinked. 'We've got a son.' He blinked again and his mouth opened and closed as if words had deserted him or his throat had closed.

'Yes, darling.' Gracie reached out a hand and stroked his arm with a tenderness that made Nell look away. 'Shall we call him Oliver, after your dad?'

They all waited for Jed to agree. He pressed his lips together as if to hold back a sob, then nodded mutely and brushed the back of his big, hairy wrist across his eyes and straightened.

Gracie seemed to have revived to alertness and was shaking her head indulgently at Jed. 'Then cut the cord.' She waved him on. 'The sooner you do that, the sooner we can cuddle our baby properly.'

Jed jerked and took the scissors from Nell. Then he proceeded to snip determinedly at the thick, meaty rope until it was separated into two parts and fell away with cord clamps attached, one length still connected to Gracie and one to the baby.

Nell lifted the infant up to Gracie's chest, their eyes met, and Gracie whispered, 'Thank you, dear Nell. For keeping us both safe.'

'My absolute pleasure. You were all amazing.'

Gracie suddenly frowned and grimaced at her. 'Last bit now, I think.'

Nell lifted the blanket and nodded.

A few minutes later Gracie was sitting up so naturally, so content-edly, gazing with pure devotion down at her newborn at her breast. Oliver's little chin bobbed as he drank, his dark eyes fringed with ridiculously long lashes, staring up at his mother like a tiny owl who needed to keep focus.

Jed's awe and wonder as he watched his family made Nell's eyes mist over again.

Gracie caught Nell's gaze and smiled that beautiful Gracie wonder-smile of warmth and now gratitude. Nell nodded and bustled away to tidy, her chest full of so many emotions she could hardly breathe.

Check Gracie. She needed to check Gracie.

Gracie was patient as Nell worked around the baby, pressed the heel of her hand below Gracie's umbilicus to palpate the contracting uterine ball below the skin and confirmed this mother's uterus was well contracted.

'Firm and central,' she murmured.

She also observed Gracie's blood loss was minimal and pulse normal. Then she checked Gracie's blood pressure on her free arm, with the blood-pressure cuff and stethoscope Gracie had in her kit.

Nell could feel the tension inside her easing. She'd examined the expelled placenta meticulously to ensure there was no danger of retained products of birth that could make Gracie bleed, and felt the relief when the sack and its contents proved whole.

She started a chart to record the contraction status of Gracie's uterus and blood loss, pulse and blood pressure every five minutes for the first half an hour; then she would feel better. Gracie had agreed, aware of Nell's need to overcompensate. Nell couldn't help that, though. But it was over. The baby was here. And she would be watching Gracie for post-birth bleeding until her eyes fell out.

Those outside the room were invited in to meet Oliver once Nell had straightened up.

Liam had notified the helicopter that they would be rescuing a mother and baby now, but the smoke was so thick there was no arrival time. Headquarters was talking about an all-terrain bus to shift any remaining townspeople if they didn't have cars and forming a convoy out if they did.

Gracie's face took on a mutinous scowl. Nell wasn't buying into that discussion; that would need to occur between husband and wife. They could make that decision without her.

Jed was back, having gone for an update on the fires. Everyone gathered around.

'Featherwood's cut off, barring one dirt track around the back of the main fire. It pops out at one of the smaller towns west of Armidale. They want to form a convoy to evacuate the town. Everyone has to go. A lot have already left, but it's getting trickier to get away. You have to go soon.'

'Everyone?' Nell asked, but just by looking at Jed's face she knew he wasn't going.

'I've arranged for Gracie and Oliver to be picked up with Molly. Mavis and Archie can travel with them.' He turned to Nell, who continued to look at him sceptically. He grimaced. 'Everyone is supposed to go.'

'I'm a basic but trained firefighter with no family. Are you staying?'

'Yes.'

'Then I'll stay.'

His face twisted. 'I was hoping you'd go with Gracie, help her and keep them both safe.'

Nell drew in a breath. Would she be more help doing that? Certainly, from Jed's point of view. She knew he would feel better if she stayed with Gracie and Oliver, but Molly was quite capable of minding the new mother and baby on the road.

The sick feeling of uncertainty descended with the thought that Molly couldn't help if Gracie began to bleed. Gracie and bleeding. The thought made Nell's neck go cold.

The first hour was the riskiest for bleeding, but the first four were close behind. She wanted to stay, but these people were asking for help. Jed had agreed to her being brought into their home. He as well as Gracie had been there for her. So she would be there for them.

'I'm staying,' Mavis said.

'If you're staying, I'm staying with you, Gran.'

Jed grabbed a handful of his hair and pulled. 'Gracie, all I know is I need you to go with Oliver and be safe so that I can think and not have to worry.'

Nell stepped away from the couple. She could see Jed's problem and she could see Gracie not wanting to leave. Nell wondered what it would be like to have someone like Jed, whose whole purpose in life seemed to be to make Gracie happy and keep her safe. She'd never had anybody like that and she doubted she would.

Yet her eyes searched for Liam's.

He inclined his head discreetly towards the door and she stepped out of the room to follow him. Was he going to lecture her about what she should do? No way was she taking orders from him. Her chin lifted.

'I understand why you want to stay,' Liam said. 'Of course I'll support you either way. What are your thoughts?'

'You're not going to say I should go with Gracie?'

'You listened to me in the fire. In this case, you obviously know about birth. So,' he shrugged as if it were obvious she knew what she was doing, 'I'll listen to you.'

She sighed. She'd jumped to conclusions again. She needed to stop doing that. There lay a whole other conversation she could have about this, but for the moment his trust warmed a cold part of her.

She gave in. Her decision. 'I should go with Gracie. The first four hours are the most at risk of bleeding, and while she's not high risk, it's still a possibility I can't ignore.' She raised and lowered her tight shoulders for relief. 'But when I want to come back, I'm scared the people manning the roadblocks won't let me back in.'

Liam's face remained expressionless. 'They probably won't.'

Nell wanted to grind her teeth in frustration. 'I want to be here. I'm part of the team.' She thought of Grin. 'My animals will be here with Jed, too.'

'Grin's with the other dogs. If you go, we'll keep the dogs safe until you get back. When you have Gracie safe, stay one night. I'll phone you tomorrow. If I can, I'll get you back here even if I have to slip out and pick you up.'

'You'd do that?'

'I will, if you do my friend Jed the favour of escorting his wife to the hospital.'

Chapter Thirty-three

Gracie

Gracie watched Jed's frustrated face. Her poor man. She loved him so much and they hadn't even had the chance to talk about the miracle of Oliver.

Today had to be the craziest day to give birth. Which reminded her to be thankful that everything had gone well and that Jed had even been here for the event. The rest was out of her control.

There was movement at the door and Nell slipped back into the room. Everyone else was still in there except Archie, who'd apparently looked green and said, 'Hello, Oliver,' and left.

'I'll go with Gracie,' Nell announced, and Jed nodded, trying to hide his relief. 'But I'll come back when she's settled.'

'Thank you,' he said quietly.

Thank God for Nell, too.

Her darling man was trying to keep everyone safe. Always trying to do the right thing. She was the last person who would want to make things harder for him.

Jed stepped back and scrubbed his head again, but she beat him to his next argument. 'Oliver and I will go to the hospital for a night and then find accommodation.'

Molly said, 'My mother will have us all when you come out of hospital. Then I could stay with you and Oliver, too, Gracie. I can cook and manage the extra housework . . . though I would have to fight Mum for it.'

'Will your mum take all of us?' Gracie asked.

'If she can't,' Jed said, 'it's only for a day or two. They have accommodation at the showground in town. Maybe you'll be able to come back here after the night in hospital if everything settles?'

Molly added, 'Mum's got a big house and only her in it. You'd have privacy with a bathroom when you come out of the hospital.'

Gracie and Jed exchanged a look. Molly's offer was a good option.

'There's room for Archie and Mavis,' Molly said and she turned to the older lady. 'If you did decide to come with Archie. That's if you'd rather squash with us instead of going to the showground.'

Gracie saw the easing of Jed's strain. Maybe she could help. 'Please. Come with us, Mavis, bring Archie with you. They want everyone to evacuate so they know where people are.'

Jed nodded. 'Liam and I will be all over the place and you'll be here in the house on your own. It might put us in danger if we have to come back and check on you here if the wind shifts.'

Mavis frowned. 'What about the dogs?'

'I'll tie them onto the work truck with me. I'll have the pressure hose and water tank, so I can get the spot fires in town. If I have them with me, I'll know they're safe. If Liam's not with me he'll be with Charlie in a fire unit. We'll keep in contact with headquarters. But we need everyone else to leave.'

Gracie felt the misgivings rise in her throat. 'Will it be safe to take Oliver in the evacuation vehicle? What about smoke and the possibility of spot fires blocking us off?' The more she thought about it, the more worried she got. Not for herself but her baby.

'The SES is coming in to get you. They'll get you out.'

Half an hour later, they were ready to go. The SES transport vehicle coming down the driveway looked as tough as a tank. That left Jed and Liam holding the fort at Gracie's house and Nell keen to get back as soon as Gracie was settled.

Standing in the front doorway, Gracie surveyed her home of less than two months. She thought about Jed carrying her over the threshold not long ago and reached out and touched the wooden doorframe. It felt like she'd always lived here. It was a very different house from when they'd arrived.

'Stay safe, house, and keep Jed safe.' She murmured that as a mantra as she carried Oliver against her towards the truck. It would be okay. She'd be able to come back here with Oliver in a day or two.

A mammoth SES officer put out his hand to help Gracie up the tall steps and Nell stood close behind her as she climbed awkwardly into the rugged vehicle. She nodded at the grizzly-bearded driver in his hi-vis outfit.

Jed had put her small suitcase of clothes for her and Oliver in the back. At least she was going near shops. She'd waited to buy things in colours until she found out if she could buy pink. It would be blue. But such things were so trivial now. This was not what she expected she'd be doing two hours after giving birth.

Molly climbed on with her suitcase that had been in the car. She'd left all the food she'd brought from home for the men. Mavis and Archie were coming because Archie wouldn't leave without his gran and his gran couldn't see him stay here. The older lady continued to grumble as she passed Gracie and moved down the back.

Cuddling Oliver against her as the engine started, Gracie caught one more glimpse of Jed standing on the verandah, his face grave as they bumped out of the paddock over the cattle grid.

Once out of town, they turned onto the bumpy forest roads in the failing light. Nell had made her take two mild painkillers and sit on a soft cushion to help with the bouncing for her still-tender backside. Her belly jiggled, but she was running on adrenaline to get her baby to safety.

Outside the windows, the firestorm had already been through here. The desolation stretched as far as she could see in the gloom of approaching night, an alien landscape of black trunks and bare branches, where before would have been leaves and grasses and bushy ferns. Now mounds of ash and broken fence posts, and smoking piles of fallen trees, were pushed to the side of the road by the clean-up crews who had gone ahead.

The up-valley families were in the bus. They'd been in Featherwood at the Progress Association hall deciding what to do. Ruby, Alison and her four boys, Jill and Holly were all on their way to friends in town or the showground. The last hour had seen a mass exodus.

The police had door-knocked through Featherwood and the last outlying stations had come in if they could. Surrounding farms that hadn't burned were cleared to confirm everyone else had evacuated.

Jed had been holding the police off until Gracie had a chance to shower and get dressed after the birth. Only Jed and Liam with Charlie and the fire brigades were to be left in town fighting to save the small settlement.

The phone company were working as fast as they could on the nearest ridge that had burned through, to put a new tower up so that communication channels could open again, but they too had to leave.

Gracie could feel the shakiness of adrenaline fatigue catching up with her and wished they'd get to town already, but the route they needed to take almost doubled the distance to avoid the fire.

Suddenly, it grew dark and embers began to fan the front of the windshield. The vehicle slowed and then stopped.

'Wind shift. We're turning around,' the driver yelled over his shoulder and spun the wheel to turn the big vehicle towards the way they'd come in the dark. He shouted, 'New fire's cut this road, too. There's safety in numbers. Back to Featherwood.'

The headlights bounced back from the smoke and the glow of orange fires in the dark distance of night seemed to be on every distant hill.

Nell and Gracie exchanged a worried look and Gracie hugged Oliver to her as they were jostled in their seats. She twisted to try to see the back of the bus, and noticed Mavis's concerned face and Archie's wide eyes. Jill and Ruby and Alison turned to look out the rear window, but the night blocked any view except orange glows in the distance.

They traversed the bumpy road even faster on the way back, and by the time they reached the lights of Featherwood, Gracie was wilting in her seat. Nell had taken Oliver and both couldn't wait to get out of the uncomfortable vehicle and be on firm ground again.

All the lights were on in the house and shop, and Jed's big shoulders showed as he hosed the front of the house. When they rattled over the cattle grid, he turned towards them with his shock reflected in his unnaturally pale face.

The big vehicle stopped beside the house and Jed bounded up the stairs of the bus. 'They can't stay here!'

'Road's blocked, they have to stay here for now,' the driver said.

Jed looked from the driver to Gracie with horror. Then he waved wordlessly towards the swelling orange cloud.

Gracie reached out to touch his arm. 'It's okay, Jed.'

'It's not.'

'The road's blocked, mate.' The driver threw his hands up. 'It's too dangerous to get through.'

'We'll be fine. We'll all be together.' Gracie squeezed his arm as he helped her down the stairs of the heavy transport. They both turned to stare at the ominous horizon.

'There are more of us now. Let's get inside.'

Jed nodded and helped Gracie up into the house, and Nell followed with the baby. Mavis and Molly and Archie were next, and Jill, Holly, Ruby, Alison and the boys trooped in after them.

The SES man roared away with the truck saying he'd head off to meet up with Blue.

Jed's face shone white under the house lights, his eyes tortured by the turn of events. And not just about them coming back. 'Has something happened?'

'Yes.' He lifted his shoulders, as if reminding himself to stand tall. 'We'll be fine.'

'Was someone hurt?'

'Later.' Jed avoided her eyes. 'Let's get you sorted first. Is Oliver okay?'

Something's happened, Gracie thought. But all she said was, 'He slept through the lot.'

'You should rest too, then. We might not get rest later.'

Although Jed hugged her to him, Gracie shuddered at the trickle of alarm that ran through her. Had someone died?

Chapter Thirty-four

Nell

Nell helped Gracie shower to ease the aches and feel fresh again. Now, dressed in loose shorts and a button-down top, sitting up in bed with all her lovely snuggly pillows around her, she seemed more comfortable. They'd both decided pyjamas seemed wrong when they might have to leave at any moment.

Medically, Nell was sure Gracie was fine, despite the rattling ride. Molly and Mavis would coddle her and they were over the four-hour period of most risk for bleeding.

Everyone had crowded into the room to hear Jed share the latest update. Standing room only and some in the hallway. Nell wanted desperately to head back up the valley to check on Liam and rejoin the brigade.

Gracie obviously needed to sleep, but she wanted to know what had upset her man and wouldn't do so until she found out. Nell wouldn't mind knowing either, and she hovered by the window looking out towards the hills. They were glowing.

'What's happening, Jed?' Gracie's voice was quiet.

'We're safe for the moment, but there are three main fronts, none of them contained. The fire's getting closer to town. The wind keeps shifting. For the moment, it's moving around us again.'

The orange glow had crept nearer and wider than it had been when they left. Nell was rocking the bassinet with Oliver inside dozing off after his feed. Now that it was night the shimmering red horizon felt ominous.

'Was someone hurt?' Gracie was determined to find out.

He said nothing.

'Dead?' Gracie stared into Jed's face.

Nell sucked in a breath. 'Who?'

'Guy called Skeeter Woods, war vet from Afghanistan. He comes,' Jed winced, 'came to the shop. Liam found him in his burnt-out car, blocked in his driveway by a fallen tree.'

Nell remembered him well. Skeeter had been quietly content without neighbours and lived an unassuming life in a secluded valley with his horses and his chooks. Pretty much like Nell had been living until Gracie had drawn her into her friendly fold. She'd seen him at the produce store talking to Jed and Liam. Poor Skeeter. And Liam would be devastated. A man left behind. A man lost.

Death by bushfire happened. Hell, it could have been her when she'd been adamant she wanted to stay with her farm. She hadn't thought so at the time, but Liam had seen the risk.

'It sounds terrible past Featherwood?'

Jed's face tightened. 'It's hell on earth. Dozens of homes like yours, Nell . . . gone.'

Nell felt the grab of loss again but forced a smile onto her face. 'I'm alive. And insured. I still have my car and I can sleep in that.'

'Most fences are down and burnt through. The lost cattle numbers are bad. I'm glad yours are here.' Jed frowned. 'There's a big herd that's just wandered into town. A couple of blokes on horses rounded them up from all over. They pushed them into the centre of the racetrack and locked them in.'

Nell crossed her fingers. 'Hopefully they'll be safe there.'

Gracie said, 'What else is happening?'

'Two more houses were lost up the valley. A family closer to Armidale barely escaped. One woman dived into a dam to save herself and another couple hid in a storm-water drain. They escaped with their lives, too.'

'That's crazy.'

'We're crazy sitting here, but we have no choice now,' Jed said, his expression not changing. 'They say this fire generates so much heat everything's scorched, and even the fastest of the critters haven't been fast enough a lot of the time. And when it's coming it makes its own wind to drive it along.'

He pursed his lips to blow away some tension. 'Stories are coming through of families slipping away by the skin of their teeth. I don't want to be one of those. With the roads cut it's impossible to leave, but we have to know where everyone is. No wandering off.'

There was a murmur of agreement.

'Fire crews from all over Australia have been deployed here, but now it's not just this shire involved. Some of them have to leave for their own problems.'

'Dangerous times,' Molly said. 'I heard on the radio that there are new outbreaks spreading down the coast, thinning the troops. They say there's a great pall of smoke across south-eastern Australia.'

Nell shuddered as she imagined being run down by a fire. She shut her eyes.

Mavis muttered, 'This is the third day they've been fighting it. The heat's wretched. I can't imagine how the firies can rest.'

'They take turns,' Jed said and Nell remembered how she'd gone to sleep when Liam had stayed over. She wondered if he had rested at all.

'Maybe.' Mavis didn't look convinced that they'd get any rest that way. 'Hanging their heads waiting for someone to shout and say we need to go again?'

'Probably,' Jed said. 'Blue, Charlie and Pete know their families are here and will come back here to stay until they can evacuate.' Then to Nell he said, 'We'll take turns on lookout tonight and watch for embers falling or a change in wind direction. At least the wind's dropped. It's nine o'clock. There are more adults and we'll do it in pairs. We can all do two hours at a time.'

'Let the women do most of that, Jed,' Nell said. 'Go to bed with Gracie and rest. You've had a big day. We'll wake you if anything changes, but you're one of the ones who'll be the busiest if anything happens and we might need you later tonight.' She looked at Mavis, who nodded. 'I slept well last night. I'll start with Mavis nine to eleven. We'll patrol outside. Then I can do another shift in the early morning.'

'I'll do eleven to one am with Ruby,' Molly said.

Molly had sorted the three other women and Holly to bunk down in the lounge room on the sofa and chairs, and the boys were in the dining room at the front of the house on the floor. Gracie's box of blankets was coming in handy.

Alison nodded at Jill. 'And Jill and I will do one to three.'

'I'll do the three to five,' said Mavis. 'I only sleep a couple of hours a night and I'll get the boy to sit with me. You'll be fighting fires tomorrow, too, Nell.'

'I will.' But Nell couldn't rid her mind of the fact that someone had died and it could have been any of them.

Chapter Thirty-five

Mavis

At three am, Mavis watched for Archie to come back onto the verandah from around the outside of the house. He'd been keen to be woken, but not quite as keen when the time came to get up. He hadn't complained though.

He's probably been out in the yard to see a man about a dog, she thought, and she wondered if she'd blown it badly by having him stay with her. What if the fire came through and they both died? Then it would be her stupid fault for keeping the boy.

She shook her head. No. This wasn't like her. The loss of Reggie must've rattled her brain because the boy hadn't been safe in Sydney, either. Hearing that young Skeeter was dead, too, that had compounded the shock.

She could hear the low murmur of voices from inside the house. The place was packed to the gunnels with people. Gracie and Jed were good folk to open their house to everybody. It was no doubt more than they'd bargained for with her house and Molly's house most likely gone, though that wouldn't be confirmed until someone actually went into the properties. She could hope. Who knew about Jill's and Ruby's.

Mavis was glad not to be in town, except for the boy. She could see him outside still wandering around, looking lost. Mavis felt a little lost herself. She didn't know if she'd need to build again. Frankly, she didn't have the energy. Maybe she should go into one of those old-people's homes and sit in the corner and knit.

The snort bubbled up from her chest and surprised her. Her lips quirked. She hadn't knitted a stitch in her life and she wasn't about to start now. If she went to an old-people's home, she'd have to send the boy back to his mother. And she'd have to get rid of the dogs. At least Reggie wouldn't have to leave. He was here, forever.

She could start again if the boy wanted to. She could give him a home base he could rely on. She'd leave it to him in her will when she died, and with luck, he might be a decent age by then if she hung around for another ten years.

Chapter Thirty-six

Nell

The next morning, just as the light of dawn began to filter through the smoky sky, Nell sat outside on the back step looking over the dry, stubbled grass to the creek. Gracie's massive camphor laurel seemed impossibly green after all the black skeletal stands they'd passed in the truck last evening before they'd turned around.

She shuddered to think what the day would bring. The air blew a hot breath on her neck and the smell of smoke, thick and some of it acrid, coated her throat. She got up and walked round the side of the house to see the dogs and check they had enough water.

Grin jumped up and down against the fence, and she leaned in and rubbed his neck. She couldn't be sure he wouldn't run off if she let him out, so it was best not to try just yet.

The water dish was full to the brim, so she guessed Archie had been out and seen to them or done it before he returned to bed at five.

As she walked to the back step, her gaze travelled along the edge of the house where Jed had closed the pylons in with fine screens to stop embers blowing underneath. Surely they could defend this house, considering there weren't any trees around it and there was only stubble to burn. They had Jed's emergency equipment ready to go in the back of his big truck.

Maybe all that beautiful green at the creek would go. Her gaze slid across the top paddock to the road, where the shop sat, and she saw a man walking down the drive to the house. She lifted her hand and he waved briefly back.

Liam's big, rangy body covered the ground fast, despite what seemed to be a lack of effort. As he drew closer, she saw the weariness in his shoulders and the dark smudges under his eyes, noticeable even against the ash-stained grimy skin of his face.

'Hello.'

'Hello,' he said, his eyes dark pools of fatigue. 'I heard you were turned back. Bet Jed's unhappy?' He didn't seem to expect an answer.

'There was nothing else to be done.' She pointed to the nearby step. 'You've had a tough day, too. Will you sit for a minute?'

He eased down on the steps and stretched his long legs in front of him. 'Happy not to face the others just yet. Is Moll okay?'

Nell thought about the indefatigable Molly. 'She's running the house in there. She seems happy.' And still raving about the birth.

'She would be. Gracie and the baby fine?' His eyes avoided hers.

'They're resting.' She didn't want to pry. She knew how much she'd hated prying. 'Do you know about Molly's house?'

'Probably gone, but nobody's been able to see it yet.' His voice was clipped.

'Mavis's?' She held her breath.

'Same.'

She blew out the shock. It was likely that there was just this house left for all her friends. 'Then I guess you're here with us. Bet you're hanging out for a shower.'

'Poor Gracie's bathroom's getting a workout.' He smiled tiredly. 'I might just strip off and roll around in the water in the creek.'

'There isn't much there . . .' She paused and tried for a smile. 'But I'd still like to see that.'

His next smile glinted a little more real. 'Good to know.' He had her there, repeating her own words back at her. He lifted one brow. 'So, until you were redirected here, how was that mountain road?'

Nell thought of their grind through the dark on the way out and the headlong rush to return. 'Rough, winding, dark. Then the embers hit the truck and he was forced to turn around. It was scary when we started going towards another orange glow. A glow at the front and a glow at the rear. We were glad to see here.'

Liam's brow furrowed. 'Two of the fronts are out of control and they're moving quickly. In the end, it might be good you got back.'

He shrugged out of his heavy yellow jacket, black smudges and the stink of smoke coating it. He stood up and tossed it across the rail on the verandah. 'Probably need that again soon.' He ran his hand through his sweat-damp hair.

She hesitated, but then stretched out her hand to his, because she wanted him to know she understood the angst he was feeling. 'You've had a rough twenty-four hours.'

Liam's other hand came in over hers and he squeezed her fingers as if he didn't know he was doing it. As if he needed to ground himself. 'I've had better days,' he said to their joined hands.

He hesitated. 'Finding Skeeter was bad. I've seen things like that before,' he said, his voice low and slow, as if easing the words out. 'But that was war. This is sheer Mother Nature reminding us that she's all powerful and we're just frail human bodies, capable of being burned to a crisp.'

Liam continued, 'That fire that got Skeeter travelled ten kilometres in half an hour. The wind lifted embers so easily because of the speed of the gusts. Blue said there were spot fires starting kilometres ahead. It makes me worry for here.'

'We have people to fight it.'

'True. If it comes the brigade will meet here and surround the house. We'll protect it with everything we have. Call in the choppers.'

Nell couldn't help the free hand that went to her throat. She could feel her pulse pounding, understanding now what he was saying. 'The stakes are high. A baby and five kids – no, six kids counting Archie, though after what he did for Molly, he's one of the adults too. Where do we go if it comes in a rush?'

'Under woollen blankets, I guess, Jed said they had a box full. Then, pray they drop water on the house. Hopefully, it won't come to that.' He turned his head towards her. 'It made me think of your place when it came through.' His eyes went even darker. 'I don't want to find you like that.'

She didn't either. 'It won't happen to me, Liam. I'll be careful. It won't happen to Gracie, or baby Oliver, or Molly or Mavis and Archie. Or the others in there. You and Jed and the brigade are going to keep us all safe. I'll help.' She shrugged. 'We're stuck here. We'll make the best of it and remember, it's people not possessions that count. I'm more philosophical than I was. Featherwood's given me back my self-esteem. The ability to lift my head and make friends and I'll fight for that.'

He pulled her closer, then tugged her down again to sit next to him. He took her hand in his big ones and held on. 'Active service happened to me. What happened to you?'

Their hips were touching. Just a pressure in the dim light. He reeked of smoke, but underneath she could smell Liam. It was the aroma of the trust she was building without even trying with this man. He was safe and real and as damaged as her, and she had the feeling that might be why it was easier to connect with him than anyone else.

But this moment? 'Do you want to do this now?'

His dark eyes met hers briefly before he looked away, lifted their joined hands and studied them. 'We might not get another chance.'

She didn't believe that, but maybe if she did trust him, she could let him know he wasn't alone in regretting the past. So she told him about that terrible night so long ago when a mother died because she hadn't spoken up. When she'd finished, he let go of her hand and pulled away.

Her heart sank. But instead of creating distance between them, he lifted his arm and draped it over her shoulders and pulled her even closer.

'That's hell, too,' he said. 'We've all given trust to the wrong people in our lives. We can only learn.' He gently bumped his head against hers and she smelled the strong smoke and sweat and male scent that covered him, but she didn't want to pull away. 'Thank you for trusting me with that.'

'You're welcome. Poor blighter having to hear my sorry tale.' She leaned in and kissed his cheek as a thank you and because, blow it, she wanted to kiss him.

He didn't push her away. She tried to shrug as if she didn't care. 'Everyone will know soon enough, when they know I was there for Gracie's baby.'

'Being brave wasn't meant to be easy,' he quoted. 'Sam Berns said that. That little guy was a hero and an inspiration in our unit.' His arm dropped and he heaved himself up, then he offered her his hand. 'Truly,' he said as he gazed into her eyes, 'it won't matter what they say. You've got mates who care.'

He was her mate. Her friend. One of the boys being kind. Good-oh. But she knew he didn't mean that. When they were both standing and she had to look up at him again she said, 'You need to sleep. Are you washing in that puddle over there or going into the shower?'

'We'll leave the creek for another day.'

'Promise?' Her mouth kicked up.

'You're on. Who'd've thought we could joke this morning?'

'Not me.' She gave him a little push. 'When you're clean I've got a bed and a bedroom. You're welcome to it.'

'You gonna lie down with me?'

'No. I'm going to watch out for you. I'll wake you as soon as you need to be up. You'll be able to sleep knowing that I'm watching for you like you did for me the night before last. I got a full night's sleep because of you, so it'd be nice if you let me return the favour.'

'I'm to trust you to wake me?'

'Yes. Trust is important. But Jed will be onto you like flypaper if he needs you to protect his family.'

*

After he'd spoken to Jed and used the bathroom, Liam was cleaner but even more exhausted.

Nell gestured around. 'Do I need to pay more attention to fire coming from the front or the back?'

'Out the front. It's just out of town and at the moment the wind is blowing it back on itself. But it's already changed twice. Let me know if it blows this way.'

'I will,' she reassured him. He stared into her eyes and nodded before going into her bedroom and closing the door.

Nell spoke to Gracie to check she was fine, and then Jed, to let him know where she'd be, then went out to the front verandah to sit on the chairs Jed had set up there. Mavis was already there watching the smoke. Nell sat beside her.

'So, you and I could be in the same boat,' Mavis said in that dry, crackly voice of hers, made huskier by the smoke.

'I hope your house is okay, Mavis.'

'Molly's place might be gone too.' Mavis blew out a breath between her teeth.

'We don't know for certain,' Nell said.

'We'd better make sure we keep this place safe or we'll all be sleeping in the street.'

Or dead, Nell added silently, but to Mavis she said, 'We've still got the Progress Hall and the barbecue area at the racetrack.'

'True story.' Mavis nodded and gestured with one bony finger. 'And then there's Jed's store.' She smiled grimly. 'It's got that little office up the top we could use. Interesting times.'

Chapter Thirty-seven

Gracie

Gracie woke to movement beside her when Jed climbed out of bed and slipped silently out of the bedroom door as if he didn't want to wake her.

Oliver had been tucked back into his bassinet less than an hour ago after a feed and it was only just morning. Despite her weariness, more than sleep she wanted her baby in her arms again, because somewhere inside her the fierce protective maternal instincts that were born yesterday along with her baby told her today would be a fear-provoking day for mothers.

Down the hallway, she could hear the murmur of voices, Jed's and Liam's.

Gracie lay there and stared at the ceiling and thought about all the people under her roof and those who had been a part of Oliver's birth yesterday. Jed had been the rock she knew he would be, which was probably what had led to that illuminating moment just before Oliver's birth when she'd let go of her fear of marrying Jed. She knew without a doubt now that they'd sort out their problems, even if she had to drag him to a financial adviser.

Then there was Nell, who had been so reluctant to take respon-sibility but who had braved her fears and been there unhesitatingly for Gracie. She remembered Nell saying Mavis was boiling water in the kitchen – she couldn't tell them why, 'just in case' – and Molly bustling and lifting all household worries from them all as she murmured, 'My goodness.' She'd certainly been blessed by her friends.

Now they had others under the roof in this harrowing time and she prayed that everyone would stay safe. Today, men and women would come and fight beside them if the time came. From the things Jed wasn't saying, she suspected the risk was great.

The fear ramped up again despite the fact that she knew Jed would die protecting her, and there would be a lot of strong-minded people with skills she didn't have surrounding the house. It was unacceptable that she didn't know what to do: she and the rest of the women would learn those skills for next year.

Jed had told her the volunteers, the heroes out there all night in the brigade, would surround the house with their trucks and their hoses. How, if needed, they'd call helicopters and fixed-wing aircraft to dump water and retardant respectively over the fire-affected area.

In truth, there was no point packing anything precious because where would they run to? She wasn't getting back into another bus to head into the bush and it didn't look like they were getting out.

Featherwood was it.

Gracie climbed from the bed, wincing a little from the aches of yesterday but surprisingly whole and well. *As you should be,* she reminded herself. *You're designed to give birth, you know.* She smiled at that thought and crossed silently to the white bassinet, which was tucked into the corner nearest to her side of the bed.

Her baby lay sleeping. Pink cheeks, dark hair across his pale baby skull, a tiny drop of milk nestled at the side of his mouth. Inside Gracie, deep in her chest, such a swell of love and joy escalated – just before the fear rose again.

He whimpered as if sensing her distress and she pushed the trepidation away as though it was a solid wall that wanted to fall on her. Of course her son detected her anxiety about their safety. She so didn't want his little body to absorb her worry. She would have to have faith and be brave, but it wouldn't be easy with Oliver so vulnerable.

Staying busy was the key until she could do something concrete.

She gathered her clothes and dashed to the bathroom for a welcome shower. A wild-eyed woman stared at her from the mirror and she frowned. This wouldn't do.

Relax. Breathe deeply. Loosen your shoulders. Smile, she told herself.

'I am well,' she said aloud to the face staring back at her. 'My baby is well. We will survive.' Never underestimate the power of the spoken word, she told herself as she'd told countless women in her work. She lifted her chin and stepped into the shower.

When she stepped out, a different woman stared into the bathroom mirror. And yes, she was a dramatically different woman from the one of yesterday morning and she felt surprisingly good. Human again. And blessed.

The kitchen, when she stood at the door looking in, seemed teeming with women. Mavis wasn't there, however. With the food everyone had brought, there was a side of bacon and dozens of eggs sizzling on the stove.

Alison was creating a toast mountain and across the hall Ruby stood setting the dining table. A chorus of 'Morning, Gracie' met her and some of the load she was carrying allowed itself to be shared.

'Good morning, all. Where's Nell and Mavis?'

'Out on watch,' Alison said. 'Archie and the boys are taking the dogs for a walk. Jed made five ropes because we weren't game to let them free in case they bolted or chased something.'

'They needed to get out of the pen before they turned the grass into a bomb zone,' Molly added.

Gracie smiled and saw Jill and Holly across the hallway folding blankets and putting the rooms back to rights after all the sleepers. Everyone was pulling together. Gracie had never seen anything like it. Certainly not in her family.

Hang on, yes, she had seen this before. Up the valley at Jed's barbecue, it had been like this. A surge of pride in her community grew and pushed out some of the anxiety. It was hard to understand that all these women had possibly lost precious possessions, maybe their houses and animals, and yet here they were working quietly, achieving through something that couldn't be changed.

'Blue and the men will be in soon,' Jill said, 'to talk to us about emergency plans. They expect the front to escalate towards us around lunchtime when the wind picks up. I think they're hoping the army will send one of those big, noisy helicopters to lift us all out.'

Chapter Thirty-eight

Gracie

The army helicopter, a Chinook, Liam told her, arrived at twelve-thirty as black smoke began to build to the west of town. They needed to board and go immediately once it landed, they'd been warned.

The sudden decision was a shock for the up-valley women because their men weren't back and they hadn't seen them since the day before. Blue, Charlie and Pete had been supposed to drop in after breakfast, hence the great pile of bacon-and-egg toasted sandwiches that waited for them, but they hadn't arrived. The emergency control centre in Dorrigo passed on that the men were aware of their families' evacuation and would be in touch later.

Gracie had handed out envelopes and paper for notes to be written. She took some for herself. She needed to say things to Jed that she hadn't said among the populace in the house. Things she should never have allowed to reach this point unsaid. Things she might never have a chance to say if the swirling mayhem of fire captured her Jed and he was lost.

My dearest Jed,

I love you. Thank you for being my rock. Not just during the miracle of Oliver's birth, when I was safe with you, supported as always by your wonderfully strong arms as he entered the world. But in our joint creation of our beautiful home, our wonderful store, and the network of friends we have around us now.

Thank you for loving me. Unconditionally.

I've realised it's my turn to do the same. Unconditionally.

I'm sorry for nagging about finances – we will sort that out when we're all safe and our Featherwood world is returned to near normal – together we will survive anything.

What I said about you not thinking of me and our baby first was wrong. You do think of us first and if the Farmer's Friend goes under, we will find something new. But I would like to stay in Featherwood.

More important than that, thank you for loving me despite my refusal to marry you and my show of non-trust that you have suffered over the last two years. It wasn't you I didn't trust, it was myself and lady luck who knew all along that my path was with you. And Oliver. And other children we may have.

What I'm trying to say, is, Joshua Edwards, will you marry me? Please? As soon as you can? So Oliver and I can share our name with you and hold it up proudly for the world to see. And we can be together, always, at the back of the Farmer's Friend in our home.

With all my love, Gracie xx

She slipped the missive into the wad without him seeing and wiped away a tear. He didn't glance through the papers as he took them. Jed would pass them on when he saw the men, and find his own, but it was time to go now. Her throat ached so much from suppressed tears that she felt her neck was torn wide open.

The *whoomp, whoomp, whoomp* of the approaching helicopter vibrated in their ears as it came closer and made Gracie's heart rate thump as well. When the massive machine landed in Gracie's front paddock she clung to Jed's hand, her own lost in his, clutching. He squeezed her fingers.

Jed was on a mission. He leaned down, kissed Oliver's dark head and then Gracie's lips. 'You'll be safe. I love you,' he mouthed, before he let go of her fingers and moved to meet the crew.

The huge rotors deafened the world and spun a tornado of fallen black embers across the paddock like twirling march flies. The noise decreased slightly but remained a roar that killed all other sounds. The rear tailgate lowered slowly to form a ramp. Three army personnel in fatigues jogged out towards the men.

All the women and children stood on the front verandah watching, the boys excited and the women silent.

Jed and Liam strode to meet the soldiers, where Liam exchanged information with hand signals. Jed turned to Gracie and waved her towards the aircraft and her heart sank. She had to leave. She had to leave Jed.

Unconsciously, Gracie's arms tightened around Oliver until her baby squirmed and she eased the pressure. It wasn't that she was afraid of flying herself, she was afraid for her child. But as a mother she had to go.

One of the female flight crew carried head gear, and as Gracie came up to her, she helped fit ear protection on Gracie and a small pair over Oliver's head. The muffs cut down the roar of the rotors by half.

She blew out a breath and walked forward towards the next person, who waited halfway between the house and the aircraft, and took her bag. Another crew member stood ready to help her up the ramp and the black maw of the aircraft opened ahead of her.

Gracie turned back to Jed and lifted her free hand, her heart breaking; surely this wasn't the last time she'd see him safe? Jed's face held such relief that she and Oliver would be taken away from this danger, she couldn't stop the tears in her eyes.

Molly's arm came around her and the weight felt good. Gracie turned away, lifted her head and moved forward to the soldier who waited inside to settle them into allocated seats. With one last look before she lost any view of the outside, she saw the end of the road glowing orange near the bridge into town.

Gracie had to stifle the urge to run back and grab Jed and tell him he had to come. To tell him that nothing material mattered and he needed to escape with her.

Molly's hand touched her shoulder, urging, and she shuffled forward.

Inside the belly of the beast, she moved down the end where two rows of seats sat, one on each side of the aircraft and facing each other. She sat on the second seat furthest on the left; the last held a helmet blocking it off, and she assumed a crew member would sit there.

Molly sat beside her. Alison sat opposite second from the end, her four excited boys next to her, with Archie on the end and

Mavis next to him. Ruby and Jill sat on Gracie's side with little Holly between them. Holly's eyes were huge but not frightened. She was as excited as the boys, her gaze travelling from floor to ceiling and around the cabin – her mouth a big O of awe.

When Gracie leaned forward to count everyone on board – there were six children, six adults and a baby plus four crew – she realised they'd only taken up half the space.

The aircraft crew climbed in swiftly and the back ramp began to close like the mouth of a whale, and any chance of changing her mind disappeared. Gracie's heart clenched as the noise increased. The crew members split and checked down the line, ensuring seat holsters were correctly applied. One handed Gracie a baby restraint and showed her how to connect it. *Just like a commercial flight*, Gracie thought with a hint of hysteria she quickly clamped down on.

The rotors thumped to a roar, even through the noise-cancelling headgear, and the vibration increased until her teeth rattled. The crew strapped themselves in, and the female crew member sitting next to Gracie reached and confirmed the placement of Oliver's strap.

Gracie pushed herself back against the seat and they lifted ponderously into the sky.

The trip didn't take long. Although it seemed only a dozen minutes, Gracie knew it was longer than that. She'd had her eyes shut most of the way because Oliver slept, and now they were landing at the airport in Armidale where a minibus waited for them.

Another SES vehicle waited to take Gracie and Oliver to the hospital first for a check-up, and Ruby was going with them because her sister was the current nurse manager of the hospital.

Alison and Jill and their children were going to friends in Armidale. Molly, Mavis and Archie would head to Molly's mother's house.

Gracie wanted to go with them. She didn't know anyone here at the hospital. The antenatal clinic wouldn't be open. Her fear for Jed would be a hundred times worse if she was alone in a hospital bed. It hadn't been so bad while they'd been coming here – her first priority was to get Oliver to safety – but now that they were safe, she couldn't help worrying.

'I don't want to go into hospital overnight, Ruby.' Gracie hugged Oliver to her. 'If we're all together we can hear the news together. I can turn my phone on and not upset other patients. Jed can call me any time.'

'We'll go through the emergency department,' Ruby soothed. 'We'll ask. Hopefully, there's an obstetric registrar and they can come check you out and give us the necessary clearance.'

'Fingers crossed.' She wondered if Nell would have let her tell the hospital she was a midwife and that she'd been checked. But Nell wasn't here to ask. Maybe she could say Nell was a doula – a labour supporter. She was that, too.

'Let's see if we can find someone to make that happen.'

Gracie's anxiety bloomed again, and Oliver whimpered; a reminder to her that she needed to calm down. To be calm for her baby. Calm for Jed. Her man had enough on his mind in the big picture, and if she had to stay it wasn't a tragedy. She wasn't having any real tragedies. No way.

But she needed to talk to Jed, to let him know they were here and she needed to know that he was okay. The last she'd heard the fire crews had all pulled back to Featherwood to make a stand.

She'd tried once but the call had failed. The phone company couldn't get in to restore the towers that had been burned in the outlying areas, but on higher points phone communication still happened sporadically. Gracie tried again, but she couldn't get through to Jed's mobile; she suspected he wasn't answering, more than not getting the call. She'd have to wait until after she was seen.

Gracie and Oliver were cleared of any complication of birth and half an hour later their taxi pulled up to Molly's mother's home, where Gracie got out, hardly believing her luck. Ruby went off to her sister's house to stay until they could go back into the fire zone.

When Molly came to the door and ushered her in, a blast of cool air-conditioned air stripped the outside heat from Gracie's body like a cool cloth.

Molly's mum, Christina, a lively seventy-year-old, had purple hair and a house full of macramé. She looked ten years younger than her age, energetic and happy. The merry widow, Molly had called her. According to Molly, Christina had a great social life, being a widow of twenty years with no interest in marrying again who loved to salsa with different partners.

'The macramé's a new thing,' Molly said over her shoulder. 'She's selling it at markets and making enough to keep her in nice wine.'

Gracie's mood lifted. Christina was obviously a doer like her daughter. All over the house, knotted rope and coloured twine had been turned into plant-pot holders, wall hangings in all the colours of the rainbow, and Gracie kept blinking at hanging shelves, lampshades and even macramé dolls.

When Christina turned to hurry across from the kitchen stove, purple hair flipped from blue eyes that matched blue twine earrings that swung from her ears. Macramé jewellery like Molly's? It all made sense.

'The new mother. You poor thing. Goodness me. Imagine.'

Gracie smiled. 'That's what Molly says. You're her mum all right. And thank you for having us, Christina.' Gracie showed the older lady her baby's sleeping face.

'Oh, an angel. How beautiful.' Christina reached out and very gently stroked Oliver's cheek. She jerked her fingers back suddenly as if she shouldn't have. 'My absolute pleasure, dear. Goodness me. Never thought that would happen. Imagine having a brand-new baby in my house after all these years. There're fire-affected families moving into houses all over town and I get the new baby.' Her tone said she was the lucky one.

Mavis grunted at the table. 'And an old woman and a teen.'

Christina tutted. 'You would always be welcome, Mavis. Don't know why we haven't caught up.' She explained to Gracie, 'Mavis and my older sister went to school together. One of her brothers was a good friend of my late father, but that was a long time ago.'

She gestured to the house. 'I'm happy to have these empty rooms filled up with people instead of just hanging baskets.' The smile fell from her face. 'And you all need a place to sleep while these horrible fires are happening.' She gestured to Gracie. 'Now follow me. I'll show you to your room. I'm thinking you need a rest after your last twenty-four hours.'

Gracie had the feeling she was going to be cosseted and spoilt by her eager hostess, as she followed Christina down the hallway, and it wasn't a bad scenario to live through. Better than what Jed was doing.

Christina turned back to look over her shoulder. 'And you've been living in drought. We're on town water here. You can have a lovely, long shower when you're ready and get into some cool pyjamas.' Gracie didn't tell her she had town water, too. She just hoped the said running water stayed viable for Jed and the rural fire service as they fought the fires in Featherwood.

Christina showed her into a room at the back of the house. It was blessedly cool with the heat outside behind the drawn blinds. A double bed waited with sheets turned down. A rocking chair sat in the corner and the bottom drawer was missing from the set under the window.

'Molly's packed your things away in there.'

The missing drawer sat on two chairs pushed together, seats touching, making a raised bed for Oliver that was tucked beside the big bed so she would be able to reach out and touch him when she was lying down.

Gracie stroked the sheets on the tiny drawer-shaped cot. They were crisp, cool cotton over some soft material used as a mattress. The most exquisite quilt with white ducks in a blue pond sat on top. And it was all turned back, waiting for her baby. Her bags had been unpacked and she had a comfy bed. This was a safe place and she sighed with relief. It was so much better than the hospital.

As soon as she could climb into bed she'd try again to ring Jed. She'd breastfed Oliver at the hospital and changed his nappy after the registrar had examined him. The idea of tucking him in his own little safe drawer bed while he was sleeping was enticing. As was the idea of resting on the comfortable-looking pillows after a shower.

Christina's head tilted to one side. 'Now you look exhausted. Tuck him in, I can sit here while you have a shower if you want. I won't touch him. Just watch until you come back.'

Gracie laughed. 'You keep anticipating my deepest desires. Thank you. I'd kill for a shower after the smoky trip in and being checked by the doctor.'

'There's the towel. Off you go.' Christina hadn't finished. 'There's bottled water beside the bed and some painkillers if you have those horrid after-cramps.'

'You've thought of everything.' Gracie shook her head.

Christina's eyes shone. 'Stay as long as you like. I'll be sewing like crazy until you leave and you'll have a baby bundle to take with you.'

Chapter Thirty-nine

Nell

Nell, fully dressed in boots, uniform trousers and fire-retardant jacket, watched the Chinook take off with mixed feelings. Liam had suggested she go with the women. Of course she'd just raised her eyebrows at his chauvinism, being as trained as the rest of the rural fire servicemen at her level.

Then again, she wondered if she was mad standing here with these two men because two months ago, she'd been hiding in an upstairs flat in the centre of Sydney with no usable skills to her name except for the purely brain-powered ones.

An RFS truck turned into the yard and crunched up the pebbled driveway towards them. Nell accepted that regrets had no place with her team – she was proud to work with these selfless men and women and do her part. She remembered Liam's Sam Berns quote: 'Being brave wasn't meant to be easy,' but these people made it look so.

Blue climbed out and turned to watch the disappearing helicopter before coming across to them. Charlie and Pete jumped down from the back. 'We missed them,' Blue said. The aircraft was out of sight already in the smoke.

Jed nodded. 'The army won't hang around.'

'It's for the best. It looks bad out there.' Blue glanced back at the other men following and raised his hands in a 'sorry' gesture.

Jed patted his pockets then pulled out the envelopes the women had left and handed them to the others. Nell saw him stop and take one of the envelopes and turn it over. His eyes closed and he tucked the envelope back into his own pocket.

Shaking her head, because Jed should have read it now, like the other men were, Nell trotted up the steps into the house. She grabbed the brown paper bags each packed with two bacon-and-egg toasties and handed them out. 'Your wives left these for you, too.'

That lightened the atmosphere a little. 'Man – bacon and eggs. Thank the Lord,' Pete said.

'You can eat between here and the bridge.' Blue almost smiled, then his face went grave. 'The fire front's come down the main road in a different direction to what we expected.' He waved his arm to the beginning of town. 'You lot ready to head out to the bridge with us?'

Liam looked at Nell and she inclined her head.

'We'll try to hold it at the bridge, but once it jumps the creek we'll keep falling back down through town and protect what we can. If it overruns us, we'll get in the trucks and protect life.'

They all turned to watch two other RFS trucks roll down the road with red lights flashing through the smoke. 'That's as much help as we'll be getting, and we're thankful for that, the way this fire is breaking out up and down the coast. We've got ourselves a perfect storm.'

Jed waved back at the water tank, pump and hoses on his old

truck. 'I'm set up here best I can and I'll follow in my truck if that's not a problem. Nell and Liam will go with you and I'll meet you at the bridge. If I have to come back to protect the store and the house, I've got transport.'

'If that happens,' Blue nodded his head, 'we'll be beside you if we can.'

Liam stood back to allow Nell to climb into the large vehicle and then swung in next to her, scooting her along the seat to the next person.

It seemed they'd become a joined-at-the-hip team. She hoped it would be an even sharing of responsibility and not Liam being protective of her. As long as she wasn't lying to herself. She had to be ready to deal with the fire coming at her. He needed to look out for himself.

The men climbed in and they rattled over the stones of the driveway into the thick smoke blowing down the road. Once out of the driveway, they turned right past the store and the other houses towards the outer edge of town where Molly's and Mavis's homes might have been lost. Towards where Nell's house used to be, a long way back behind that wall of flames.

Once they reached the bridge, the smoke grew thicker until they could only see a hundred yards in front of the truck and the sky hung a malevolent brick red in the thick sky.

On the Featherwood side of the bridge, they pulled up next to the two other trucks and climbed down. The air burned hot and heavy as it rasped into her lungs. It was like standing too close to a bonfire, it hurt to take deep breaths as heat pulsed in on her so forcefully that she almost staggered.

How had these people been working in this through the night

and all morning? Inside her protective clothing, her arms stuck to her sleeves with sweat, yet she wanted to be buttoned right up to her neck because the embers were flying across the far paddock towards the town and burns would be worse than the internal humidity.

They beat at the spot fires that were jumping up, hosing the ground, circling the first of the houses. Nell blinked and then the wall of fire was coming, at an angle, not directly down the street, but so as to cut the corner off the town. Where they stood, they were in the path.

Right where the smoke and dead embers were flying, she glimpsed the shift of something at the side of the road. Maybe a wombat? They'd been finding animals and snakes and birds the last few days in the bush. Some burnt, some coming back to see what was left, and some dead. Whatever this was, it hobbled on pained feet.

Nell stepped to the side of the road towards where it had stopped, making sure she could still see the men as she moved through the smoke to the shape. She hoped she didn't need to carry a terrified and wounded animal.

It was a dog. Limping. With injured paws and singed hair. 'Oh, you poor thing,' she crooned, but it wouldn't hear her through the roar of the fire. And she didn't have much time to cajole it.

Big, dark eyes peered up at her from behind a grey muzzle. 'Come on. I'll take you to Gracie's. My puppy is there. You'll be safe.' She patted her hip. 'Here, boy.'

The dog's eyes were weary, pained, assessing, and she thought for a moment it wouldn't come. Then the dog limped towards her and fell in beside her, and she slipped her fingers around its collar.

That's when she realised she couldn't see the men. The wall of flames was thundering like a train at full speed. Roaring.

Her brain overloaded. No amount of water would stop an inferno the height of two men, despite the lack of fuel across drought-shorn paddocks, and now balls of flame erupted like missiles from the centre of the conflagration and shot ahead, exploding into whatever was in their path.

Nell's eyes widened in horror as she saw a shed that had been standing tall in the smoke suddenly erupt into flames as if hit by a Roman candle. As she watched, the roof blew in as the walls blew out and debris scattered to be gobbled up by the flames.

Her limbs froze and her mouth gaped. The blast of heat and roll of thick smoke had reduced visibility. Suddenly, she felt as if her blood was boiling as the heat ramped up. Her insides felt on fire. It was coming.

The wind roared and the embers flew as flames jumped up on each side of them, and at the same time Liam grabbed her arm out of the smoke and pulled her towards the truck. She pulled the dog. Jed was running for his truck and she screamed at him, 'I have a dog!'

Jed turned, saw Nell holding the collar and scooped up the dog like he was a feather pillow and tossed him into the ute, before he jumped into his vehicle and tore off down the road to his store.

Liam pushed her up into the fire truck and scrambled in after her as Blue and the other captains ordered everyone into the trucks and to fall back. Once all personnel were inside the vehicles, Blue, who looked exhausted and pale, blinked rapidly with his bloodshot eyes and began counting his people. She saw his shoulders release when he confirmed all were in.

They moved down the road away from the main front, faces grim and stunned. 'We were lucky. If that changes direction and comes with the wind behind it, we stay in the truck,' Blue ordered in a no-argument voice. A chorus of agreement followed his words.

The self-created maelstrom of wind that churned the fire pushed the main front just past the town, collecting outlying farms and sheds and anything else that was standing in the way. Trees exploded, animals had no chance, and all the brigades could do was watch and pray it wouldn't turn this way. Their way.

Spot fires sprang up where the embers swirled and the troops decamped from the truck to put out the small fires that wanted to catch and dance through the village with malicious mischief. Half-a-dozen houses crackled and burned, the fire taking hold with glee in the heat. The men winced and put their heads down as if they'd failed. Nell wanted to hug them all. She who didn't hug.

The three trucks moved on to those homes that had a chance of being saved, and to begin fighting the spread from the rest. A loud boom and whistle of a flying gas cylinder from one of the burning houses near the bridge had everyone stop and watch as a second one punched through a fence and into the house next door, which began to burn.

Jed's paddock blazed between the gate and the house, but Liam was already there. He'd peeled off to man his own vehicle, which was parked there, and he seemed to have it under control, while Jed fought flames outside the Farmer's Friend. Two spot fires were licking at the shopfront.

Nell stayed with Blue and the boys beating at flames, following orders, silhouetted in the inferno of the fire like everyone else. Glad that Gracie and the children were out.

Chapter Forty

Gracie

Showered, dressed in PJs despite the fact it was still afternoon, Gracie needed sleep, but she wanted to hear from Jed more. Her phone rang at the same time as she lifted it to try again. Jed's voice came with instant relief.

Thank goodness. 'What's happening, Jed?'

'We're safe for the moment. I've driven up on the knoll behind the church to get service. The spot fires are still giving us grief. The firies are down here and reinforcements made it through just before the road shut. I can see the store. It's still there.'

Safe for now? She imagined burning buildings surrounding her man. *Oh, my heavens.* Her breath froze in her chest. 'You should get out of there, Jed.'

'I'm fine. The main front has moved past for the moment. We've got the sprinklers on over the shop, and the house, for further embers, but they've both been singed to the edges. It's a monster, Gracie. Pity help anything in its way. We rigged up the generator to pump from the creek. It's filling our personal ute tanks because we need to hoard the council water.'

Gracie couldn't imagine what the previous hours had been like. 'Where's Liam?' she asked.

'Below me at the shop, making sure all the sprinklers stay on.'

'And the dogs?'

'Here, beside me. Mavis's four with me, the other two with Liam on his ute. Nell found another one, too. They're sitting down as if it's a normal day on a work ute. If we have to move, then at least they're here ready to drive off. The rest of the brigade are at the school. They kept the fire away from the main buildings, but the back fence at the school and the toilet block have gone. I'm going down there now.'

'Have many houses gone in town?'

'At least half. Most of the fences. We worked our way along with the hoses from the trucks and saved where we could.'

'The people are safe?'

'Yep.'

'Did we lose fences? What about the cows? Nell's herd?'

'The fire burned up to the edge, one side of the dog yard is gone, but we stopped it before it reached the house. The cows are down in the creek. Safe for the moment unless it comes back. Hopefully, the house and shop are safer because there's nothing around us to burn, now.'

Except for the flying embers, which could smoulder and explode anytime a wind blew on them. But Jed knew that.

'You and Oliver okay?'

'Snug.'

'Great.' He sounded relieved that she was settled. 'I've gotta go.'

She didn't want him to go back into danger. She didn't want to lose him. He hadn't even mentioned the note. But she was the one who had left it to the last minute.

Chapter Forty-one

Nell

Nell moved with everyone else down to the school, extinguishing spot fires edging towards the outbuildings. The church stood unscathed on its little knoll, which was lucky, or divine, because they were running short of hands to save it.

The sweet *thump, thump* of the helicopter overhead had everyone step back out of the blackened area beside the school as the chopper dumped water and drowned the blaze they'd been trying to extinguish.

After that, control was wrestled back from the fiery beast, and as the hot flurry of craziness eased, they took a moment to survey the damage. Men and women in uniforms leaned against anything not burning and sagged with temporary relief.

The ground was leaking tendrils of smoke from ruins and piles. The fire had been fickle in choosing this house and not the next, then crossing the road in random zigzags. The church, post office and the school had survived, as did Jed's Farmer's Friend. The pub lost half of the beer garden and the laundry at the back, but the rest was saved.

The fire leader pulled out a crate of water and food and slowly half the combatants ate and drank and then exchanged places with the other crews to see what could be done on newly flaring hotspots. It would be a long night as new spot fires flared up from sleeping embers and smouldering stumps, but for the moment the wind had dropped and they had control.

Late in the afternoon the town water stopped running and the power stayed off. The local council had set up water tankers a few days ago, before the road was cut, to draw from for the fire trucks if the town's supply was disrupted. All the communication towers were down now. Two satellite phones were handed out. One of the phone companies still had service to be found on top of the blackened ridge above the town.

Behind Jed's house, half of the creek trees had been destroyed as the embers had caught and held; the camphor laurel looked like black bony fingers reaching to the sky, with black poles and mounds of white ash. Every few feet, smoke rose and flickering flames danced on the wider-girthed logs. The coals and heat consumed the last of anything that could be touched.

Yet the pocket where the cows stood in a horrified, frozen huddle, bizarrely remained untouched. And the shady liquidambar, umbrellaing two comfy chairs covered in ash, stood green.

In the creek, any pools of water were coated in thick ash, with a centre of trickling clear stream, where the moving water left a stripe of unsoiled flow.

Nell, while her team was taking a break, had come through to Jed and Gracie's house to check inside and right around the verandah, and she marvelled at the untouched building. The spot fires there had been extinguished, but the grass was burnt to the edge of the house all the way around except for the dog yard. Maybe the bombs had kept it safe. She couldn't even smile at that, she was so tired.

Jed's sprinklers had stopped working with the house pump and no power, but they had done their job at the height of it all.

Liam came to find her, his big, yellow jacket thrown open at the throat, and she could see his strong, soot-streaked skin amid the few curling hairs on his wide chest. Black ash scored his cheek like face paint and dusted his hair. Those brilliant blue eyes were tired but fierce, as if he was aware of everything that was happening and had everything catalogued.

'We saved the dog pen,' he said. 'You saved a dog. Where is it?'

'Still with the other dogs in Jed's ute.' Nell couldn't remember being this tired and aching from the trials of the day. Now she'd have to dress the dog's wounds before she showered. That was fine. She could do that. 'I found him on the road. An old guy with burnt paws.'

'You okay?' Liam studied her and shook his head.

'I'm fine. You saved Gracie's house.'

'Don't tell Gracie Jed sent me here so he could protect the store.'

Nell laughed, but it limped out in a tired half-snort. Still, it had been a laugh. This man could amuse her at the weirdest moments. Then she thought about that frozen moment when she'd seen the smoke rolling towards them. Those orange missiles of fire exploding from the approaching front.

'Thanks for grabbing me down at the bridge.'

Liam scrubbed his hand through his soot-covered hair. 'It was either that or get grey hair watching you disappear into the smoke. Seriously, woman, you needed to move back when things escalated.'

'There was the dog. And it's politically incorrect to call me "woman".'

He made his own snorting sound, before he reached out with a big hand and tugged her closer. As he stared down into her face, their eyes met. 'You are amazing. But you are all woman.'

She blinked, slipped out of his hold and stepped back, pretending she wasn't affected by his closeness and the impulse she'd had to reach up and kiss those sooty lips of his. Despite the dirt. Despite the non-event their relationship really was. 'I was doing the same as everybody else,' she said.

'Everybody else is not a tall, gorgeous, long-haired model who makes even the overalls look good.'

She waved her hand. 'I'm pretty darn sure I'm not looking like a model at the moment.'

He nodded, then glanced over his shoulder as another truck went past. 'Just thought you needed to know that I think you look great. And I'm watching you.'

Did he mean watching out for her or watching her? She'd take both. Two months ago, she would have run a mile. 'Thank you.' He'd come all the way over here just to say that. Or maybe to reassure himself after all the excitement that she was still all right. She suspected the latter. That was okay, too.

'You look pretty good yourself,' she told him.

'When this is all over, we will have a conversation.'

'When all this is over, I'd love to.'

Liam's eyes darkened. 'Best get back to doing what I should be doing.' He leaned down and brushed her lips with his. Hot, intense, but far, far too short-lived. 'Stay safe.' He turned and walked swiftly back across the paddock to the street, where another fire truck was driving past, and flagged it down.

'You too,' she said and shook her head. Then she added very quietly, 'It's been a big day.'

Nell didn't remember much of the rest of that night. Charlie, Blue and Pete had moved into the room their families had been in. Liam took Molly's bed and they took it in turns to sleep because a change of wind could blow the embers back towards the town again and they might not be so fortunate the next time.

When dawn broke the next morning, it showed a monochrome landscape except for the tiny pockets that had escaped the inferno. In the bush nothing was left, just mounds of ash where living structures had stood. There were no visible signs of life happening now – except powder with the wind. Occasionally, piles of red ash or brownish-grey humps lay like low dunes at the beach in open spaces marking previous tree stands.

A wasteland of black sticks surrounded a once thriving village, but those who remained had their lives still and when the dogs barked or a cow lowed, the sounds echoed across the quiet while everyone stopped and listened. And smiled that life went on.

Nell had rearranged Gracie's freezer with a row of Molly's frozen water bottles across the top to keep it cold as long as they could without power, but already some food was growing warm without the fridge motors to prevent it from spoiling.

Jed had the generator running at the Farmer's Friend to protect the veterinary immunisations that required refrigeration and he'd slipped in the house milk to safeguard it.

The shop and post office had generators so supplies were available, though no new deliveries would be coming in until the police could escort trucks past the blocked roads. Most dangerous of all were the burnt and arcing powerlines on the road from town.

At breakfast, Jed pulled out his barbecue in front of the Farmer's Friend, just under the awning, and began to cook. 'It's closer to the street than the house,' he said to Nell. 'People will be able to come and grab something.' He gestured to the house. 'We may as well cook everything in the fridge because who knows when the power will come back on.'

Nell set up a long self-serve trestle table with sauce and bread.

When the first soot-stained faces appeared, she realised how many sported minor injuries. She'd sorted the dog back at the house with bandages. Maybe she should have gone down to the hall last night to see if any humans had needed tending to. Her midwifery prowess had brought attention to the fact she was medically trained, and men and women pulled her aside to ask if she could look at their injuries.

Burns, cuts, strained ankles and knees. After discussion with Jed, she raided the shop shelves for first-aid kits and bandages and set up another table and chair to treat the injuries. She cleaned with boiled water and covered burns with aloe vera gel for unbroken skin and burn salve for the more serious type. She dressed limbs, fingers, bellies and backs, in clean bandages or sealed adhesive dressings.

There were more selfless firefighters than she'd realised. They walked up the road to the shop as word spread, heads bowed sadly past ash and smoking relics of scorched houses and shattered, burnt oddments and curls of tin. The homes they'd saved in between kept them going.

Troops from three exhausted units who'd worked for nearly twenty-four hours straight didn't have a house to go home to in between calls, so they began shuffling to the Farmer's Friend from the Progress Hall where they'd slept, wrapped in blankets, rubbing red eyes. They held empty paper plates as the unmistakable smell of bacon and sausage and onion filled the air and word spread that a nurse was dressing wounds.

When Charlie stopped in front of her with a second-degree burn on his wrist, she gasped, 'Charlie! You should have told me about this last night.'

He mumbled something, but she didn't hear what it was.

'Sit down. I'll clean that.' His face was now contorted with pain. She frowned. 'Is the pain so bad?'

Charlie slid sideways on the chair beside her and clutched his chest. He would have fallen, because he was unconscious and not breathing, but Nell lowered him to the floor. She turned to see the shocked eyes of the man next to her. 'Get Jed.'

She rolled Charlie onto his back and began cardiac massage, not worrying about the breathing just yet. When she felt Jed near, she told him, 'Cardiac arrest.' No doubt Jed knew that by the way she was compressing his chest. 'Gracie said you had an AED?'

'Defibrillator?' She guessed shock had frozen his brain. He shook himself at the brief delay. 'Yes,' he said, then disappeared again.

'Stay with us, Charlie,' she whispered breathlessly, her forcefully clasped hands pushing rhythmically down on his sternum.

Jed was back in no time. He fell to the floor beside her with the small, bright yellow box of the AED in one hand and the green airway box in the other.

Nell shifted away slightly. 'You take over the cardiac massage while I put this stuff together.'

Jed crawled over and commenced a very efficient external cardiac massage, and Nell heaved a sigh of relief that she had good backup. Snapping open the box with the bag and mask, she quickly assembled the pieces.

Liam appeared beside her. 'Great.' She handed him the breathing equipment. 'Can you do the bag and mask? Thirty compressions to two while I assemble the AED. The faster we get this onto his chest and see if we have a shockable rhythm, the better.'

Liam nodded and calmly took the mask. He said to Blue who'd jogged over with him, 'Ring for helicopter retrieval.' As he spoke, Liam placed the mask efficiently over Charlie's nose and mouth and timed two breaths with Jed's movements every thirty compressions. He began counting down out loud until the next breaths were due.

'Stay with us, Charlie,' Nell asked again. 'Ruby will kill us if you give up.' Tearing open the AED box, she pulled out the sticky disposable paddles and ripped off the adhesive backing.

Jed said between compressions, 'I'd hoped to heck that we never used this thing, but Gracie was right. Thank God we got one.'

Nell agreed. She asked the others to stop and lift their hands for a second. She yanked up Charlie's RFS T-shirt and exposed his chest as Jed began again. She tore off the adhesive from the sticky pads and was thankful to find Charlie didn't have a hairy chest to interrupt the connection. She didn't have a razor anywhere even if he did.

She slapped the silver-paper paddle adhesive above Charlie's right nipple, working around Jed's big hands, and the other pad below where his heart would be. When she switched on the machine, the automated voice broke the silence. '*Stop CPR. Do not touch patient. Analysing.*'

Every person there held their breath, and the tension escalated in the big open-fronted shed as all focused on hearing the response from the machine. Most had their first-aid certificate but had never seen the machine in real-life action, and shock for a comrade down showed on their faces.

'Keep clear,' Nell said quietly as Jed's big hands hovered. She doubted saying it was necessary, but she wasn't trusting anybody. The machine would only help if Charlie's heart had fallen into a rhythm that could be corrected by an electric surge. If Jed touched Charlie's skin they'd have to start again, and the longer it took to shock Charlie the lower his chances of survival.

Liam spoke quietly to Jed. 'If it says "shock", don't touch him. Then as soon as the shock's done, we'll recommence CPR for another two minutes.'

Jed nodded.

'*Shock advised*,' said the machine.

'Stay clear,' said Liam as the yellow box began the warning sounds of imminent charge until Charlie's body jerked with the surge of electricity.

Charlie's sudden gasp made Nell jump, but it was worth her nervous response to see his chest rise on its own. He dragged in another shattered gasp, and his eyelids flickered but didn't open.

'No more CPR?' Jed checked.

Nell said, 'No, he's nearly conscious. We need to watch him until he can be airlifted out.'

Liam added, 'They'll be on the way. No matter what! This is one of the firies down.'

'Okay.' Jed sat back and eased himself to his feet.

Liam slapped him on the back. 'Good job. On having the equipment and on some impressive CPR.'

'Glad I wasn't running the show,' he said.

They both looked at Nell.

Nell blew out a big breath and settled more comfortably beside Charlie, who had stirred and now groaned. His eyelids flickered. He would be sore after cardiac massage from Jed's big hands.

She closed her eyes for two beats and felt Liam's hand rest on her shoulder, as if transferring strength. She lifted her own fingers and tapped his. 'Thanks.'

What more could this day bring? They were so cut off from the rest of the world, with a raging inferno still moving away and major destruction between them and their families.

Did the rest of the world even know how they were faring?

The medical retrieval team arrived via emergency helicopter an hour later. They landed on Jed and Gracie's front paddock on a patch of charred grass, and Jed hailed them from the shop where Charlie was resting with Nell in attendance.

The medical personnel swiftly assessed, cannulated and medi-cated Charlie, and when he was stabilised, they moved him to a stretcher in preparation for retrieval. Conscious as he left, though uncomfortable, Charlie managed to wave to those around from his bed as he was transferred to the chopper. The doctor had promised to inform Ruby of his arrival once they landed at Armidale Hospital.

The aircraft took off immediately and Liam and Nell watched as it disappeared from view. Only then did Nell sag a little with the relief. 'So glad Charlie's okay.'

Liam's big arm came around her. 'You did an amazing job.' He hugged her briefly. 'There's so much inside you I still have to discover.'

She could feel her cheeks heat at the compliment. She really wasn't used to all this positive feedback. 'You and Jed were great, too.'

'What a team we are. Everyone's fed, Charlie's in safe hands, and now it's time to go back to putting out fires.'

As evening drew in, the first of many supply trucks arrived full of bottled water, bread and easy-to-assemble food, all donated. The truck was flanked by police to keep all who travelled safe and ensure only essential bodies arrived. Anyone who'd been trapped in Featherwood and didn't need to be there was escorted out for safety.

The transport had taken a full day to chainsaw and push aside burning logs that blocked the road. The more dangerous work was having to navigate felled powerlines that still arced and snapped at the side of the road. The personnel in Featherwood were told that trees were still burning most of the way and the road was closed except with police escort. Strictly no incoming civilians.

The power company men and women were working around the clock to isolate danger and re-establish power to the village, but it would take three to four days of non-stop, hazardous work to achieve that. Cheers to the sheer determination and grit of the power workers to have it happen that quickly, was the consensus of opinion from those in Featherwood.

The police brought two more satellite phones and some specialist helpers. To Nell's relief, an advanced-skills nurse practitioner and two assistants arrived to set up an emergency clinic to deal with further injuries and sudden minor illness. Nell was extremely happy to hand over a responsibility that suddenly had been declared hers.

News came through that Charlie was stable with a hopeful prognosis, and if Blue hadn't put a blanket ban on alcohol for all rural fire service personnel, there would have been a mass exodus to the pub. Only because Blue promised a real shindig when the town was off alert status did the crews wistfully agree.

Chapter Forty-two

Gracie

That first night, Gracie felt like she and Oliver were on another planet, impossible light-years away from Jed. She hadn't been separated from him for an extended time for the last two years. And certainly not with harsh words still hovering between them.

Although, she had to admit, living in Christina's house was like having the mother she'd always dreamed of having. Every couple of hours, and goodness knew how she had the time because she seemed to be doing everything else, Christina would appear with a new article of clothing that she'd created with love and almost magical perfection for Oliver. Oliver would be the best-dressed boy in the bush by the time Christina was finished.

While the comfort of being cared for so lovingly was wonderful, the unfamiliar cosseting a delight and the creative talents of her hostess a continual amazement, in Gracie's heart, she worried ceaselessly about her big man risking his life.

She tried not to show it, didn't speak of her concerns or rail against the lack of verbal contact, but Molly and Christina knew. As army wife and sibling, they'd had years of experience worrying about their menfolk, waiting for news. Twenty-four hours was nothing, but their sympathetic eyes read her thoughts with a too-easy perception.

What she really wanted so badly was to be there with him. It should have made it easier that she was helping Jed by being safe. Except, it didn't help at all. The worst thing was not hearing Jed's deep voice or even reading a text from him as they waited for communication to be restored.

She didn't know if he'd seen her note, her last-minute, desperate marriage proposal, and she wished she'd been brave enough to blurt the words out before she left.

What if something happened and he never knew?

No. She hugged Oliver close to her chest in her pretty bedroom. Nothing would happen. Jed had support from incredible people. He would be safe.

Jill had passed on from Blue via the RFS that things were critical but not extreme, downgraded from catastrophic, like they'd been the day she'd been flown out. The current report was passed on to Christina's house, and Molly kept in contact with the other families stranded in town with any news.

They'd all been shocked by Charlie's heart attack, but Ruby's latest message had confirmed that he was improving hour by hour.

'Ruby wants to squash them all in a huge hug.' Molly laughed. 'Reckon Jed's the only one who will manage it with poise, but Nell and Liam better be prepared for it.' Molly's voice held a relieved note after the latest update about Charlie's recovery.

Gracie laughed. True story. 'Jed's always happy to get a hug.' The thought made her tear up again. She would dearly like to give and receive a hug from her big, beautiful man. She turned away, embarrassed. Fortuitously, Oliver cried at that moment, the sound carrying from the bedroom, and she moved fast to get to him before Christina heard and swooped in to steal him. Oliver would allow her to hide her face.

By the time she'd changed his nappy and resettled him against her shoulder, Gracie had recovered her composure. The tears were probably the post-baby blues, a day early – now, why hadn't she thought of that? She felt a little less silly at that realisation.

She brought her baby back into the room and sat down to feed him in the comfy lounge chair. It had become quite a routine. Molly always made sure she had a glass of water next to her and Christina provided a small treat, like a scone, or a biscuit or even a sweet lolly.

Gracie worried she'd be a size bigger by the time she got back to Jed, not that he wouldn't love her as much, but she couldn't eat like that every time she fed when she got home.

Christina bowed and placed her treat, then went off to her sewing machine. And Molly set the glass down. Gracie could tell her friends liked the new routine.

'I worry how Nell's going,' Molly said as she settled herself comfortably again. 'For someone who wanted to live a peaceful, isolated lifestyle, she's been thrust into close quarters in Featherwood.'

Gracie agreed. She imagined that Nell might be overwhelmed with all the extra responsibilities, but she had faith in her friend. 'Jill told me Blue and Pete are in the house with Jed and Liam. She's the only woman. My house will be glad she's there, though. I know I am.'

'Nell was amazing during Oliver's birth.' Molly's eyes lit up as she remembered that incredible event. 'And then to save Charlie! We're so lucky she arrived in town when she did.'

Gracie thought so, too. She wished she could hold Nell up and show that horrid mother of hers that her adopted daughter was a hero. She hoped Nell understood she was valued very much by her friends, even if her lacking parent had no such sense. 'I think she and Liam are good together.'

'I noticed that.' Molly dropped her voice. 'Haven't mentioned it to Mum. She'd be over the moon if Liam fancied someone and I don't want to get her hopes up.'

Hope? Gracie had hopes of going home. Soon. As though he felt her yearning, the phone rang and it was Jed.

'Gracie? I borrowed a sat phone. Just for a minute.'

'Jed. You're alive.' She sagged in relief at hearing his voice.

'Everyone's fine. I can't talk now, but just to say we're okay. Look after Oliver and you. I'll ring soon.' And then he was gone.

It all crashed in again and tears trickled sideways from her eyes and down her cheeks. But he had rung.

Nell phoned Gracie that night because a new tower had been erected on the hill above the town and her mobile was working again. Gracie, the Featherwood women and Archie were sitting with Christina in the lounge area. Gracie clutched her mobile in gratitude for the call. They still hadn't received any news of the town. 'Nell. Thanks so much for calling. I'm fine. How are you? How's Jed?'

Everyone in the room swivelled to face Gracie and she knew

how they felt. Starved of news. They'd all been cut off from the drama and isolated from the place they wanted to be.

Gracie listened to Nell's answer. 'She said she's fine,' she shared. 'They all are.' The women nodded with relief. News of Charlie's heart attack had shaken them. 'What's happening? Everyone is here. Can I put you on loudspeaker?'

Nell agreed and the room crackled with tension as everyone pulled their chairs closer and leaned in while Gracie changed to speaker. She turned it up as much as it would go.

'Hello, everyone.' Nell's cultured voice rang clearly.

'Hi, Nell,' they chorused. A short, awkward pause followed.

Mavis heaved herself out of the chair and stood up, took two steps towards Gracie's chair and straightened her spine. 'It's Mavis, Nell.' She spoke slowly and clearly as if to a person who was deaf, lifting her chin high. 'Has someone been out to my place? Have I still got a house?' She was gruff and to the point.

Everyone stayed silent so they all caught Nell's blow-out of breath. 'No. I'm sorry, Mavis. Liam said your house is gone. There's nothing left except the tank on the hill.'

Mavis compressed her lips until they disappeared. Huffing out a 'hmmm' and nodding, she glanced across at Archie and shrugged. Her eyes were dry and she kept her chin up as she sank slowly back into her chair.

'And mine?' Molly's voice shook a little as she raised it so Nell could hear her from where she sat. She stared across the room at Christina as she waited. Then she added, 'It's Molly.'

Another pause. 'Yours is gone, too, Molly,' Nell said. 'I'm so sorry. Liam says he can rebuild, but you'll have to start from scratch.' A beat later she said, 'Some of the bees survived.'

Molly put her hand over her mouth and went to perch on her mother's chair to put an arm around her shoulders. Christina patted her daughter's hand, but it had been Christina's home, too. Both women sniffed.

'But everyone's safe,' Gracie said quietly into the phone, hoping for good news.

'Yes. Oh . . .' Gracie heard the smile in Nell's voice and wondered if her friend had caught the desperate wish for cheer. 'Yesterday, in the middle of it all, I found a dog. It was pretty hairy. The fire swirling around, I mean, not the dog, though it's hairy, too. Or it will be when its fur grows back.' She laughed a small, cracked laugh. 'Parts of him are bald, but the pink skin underneath isn't badly burnt.' Nell made that odd, almost-laugh sound again. 'He's singed and miserable. And pretty old, but he's okay and I've added him to the pen full of pups we have. He gets on fine with all the other dogs.'

Mavis looked up. 'Archie?' The boy's chin had been in his hands and he'd faded away, thinking dark thoughts, Gracie suspected, judging by his expression. He may even have been thinking about having to go back to Sydney to his mother because Mavis's house was gone.

At his great-grandmother's call, his head lifted and he refocused on the room. Mavis said, 'Nell's found an old dog, with burnt paws, coming out of the fire.'

Archie's eyes widened. He glanced once at Gracie's hand holding up the phone and flung himself at the instrument, skidding to a stop with his mouth almost on the cover. 'Nell! It's Archie. Has he got a collar with a tag? Does it say Reggie?'

'Reggie? Yes.' Nell's voice sounded uncertain, surprised.

Archie's breath hissed out and he sagged with delight.

Nell went on, 'He's lying here on the verandah. Hang on. I'll send a photo.'

The phone dinged a moment later and Gracie handed it to Archie. Archie's face broke into his crooked-toothed smile and he flung his arms out in disbelief. He showed the picture to the room. In the photo, the old dog's head rested on his wounded paws, but his tail was up. As if he'd wagged it.

Archie turned slowly to face Mavis. 'It is Reggie. He's burnt but looks okay. Oh, Gran.' He handed Gracie back the phone and concertinaed onto the floor beside Mavis's chair, his head leaning against her. Tears ran down his face and they matched the ones on his gran's cheeks. 'Reggie's alive.'

Chapter Forty-three

Mavis

It was day three in Armidale and Mavis was climbing the walls. She'd never been one to sit and twiddle her thumbs.

Christina's girly house and determination to look after everyone as she fought her daughter for the privilege was driving Mavis mad. Christina's eldest sister had been like that at school, sixty-five years ago.

She'd mentioned to Christina that she'd have to get herself some clothes, and even that had been a struggle. Why had she needed to fight to keep her favourite shade of maroon? Christina wanted her to look like a flippin' lorikeet with all the blinking colours and stripes she tried to get Mavis to wear.

Thankfully, her usual shops had been putting away some outfits, and when big-mouth Christina told them Mavis's house had burned down, the discounts had been generous. At least now she had a few changes of clothes.

And she'd seen the doctor. She had to come back next month and see him again. He'd changed her tablets when he'd heard about her nightmares. Christina had offered her a bed at her place whenever she needed to come to town.

Molly had been responsible for arranging the consultation and the appointment with the special old-people's doctor. A nice young bloke, he'd adjusted her tablets and given her a lecture about drinking more water every day. The doctor had said if she got too dry, she'd get confused. It was nice to find that out this far along. It could've saved her from worrying about losing her marbles a lot earlier on. Molly had heard and now everyone knew that when Mavis went vague she needed to drink more.

The boy was to fill up the big lemonade-sized bottle in the morning and she had to drink it all every day. Two if she could. She'd be living in the ladies', but she had to admit her brain was getting clearer every day and she wasn't so tired. Worth it to see the boy smile.

But she was soooo bored brainless sitting here. She wanted to see what was left of her place. She wanted to discover if anything was left. To work out if there was any way they could shore up the house and squat there until they could build a shed or something. And she wanted to hug Reggie. Ruddy, miraculous dog.

The doorbell rang and Mavis jumped. The boy, reading the local rag next to her, snickered. She jumped every flippin' time that bell rang. This house was like a train station for coming and going, and she'd kill for her nice, quiet farm. Funny how much it helped having the boy here with her.

She could hear Christina chirping at the door. She was a good old stick, but like the flippin' Energizer Bunny, for goodness sake.

Christina had with her two people, a tall man and short dolly bird, both of whom seemed to be in their sixties with nice, smiley faces. The neighbours. Christina had introduced her to them over the fence. Imagine having people right there living over your fence? It still made Mavis shudder. Who'd live in town?

Mavis plastered on one of those polite faces she'd needed so blinkin' often since she'd come here, stood up, and held out her hand. 'Hello.'

Christina's face blazed with excitement, maybe even more than usual. 'Jim and Jocelyn wanted to talk to you.'

Mavis was confused. Apart from the fence introduction, she didn't know them from Adam. 'I remember you from next door, but have we met before that?'

The jolly man shook his head. 'No. We just wanted to say sorry about your house. Um . . . we have an old caravan in the backyard, nothing flash, and it needs a new mattress.'

Mavis looked at him, then at Christina. Did she want Mavis and the boy to move next door?

The man went on. 'We didn't know what to do with it. We wouldn't get much if we sold it, but . . .' His wife nodded encouragingly for him to go on. He drew a breath. 'It would mean a lot to us if you took it. Back with you to Featherwood. Use it till you can get your house rebuilt? Keep it forever, of course.'

The words sank in, but Mavis's face felt set in hard wax. Like an old candle dripping in winter.

'It's free,' he hastened to add in case she thought it wasn't.

Mavis hadn't wanted to cry for a lot of years, but right now her eyes were stinging, her throat had closed, and she couldn't answer 'cause her voice wouldn't work. She struggled to swallow the big lump blocking her vocal cords and then, hopefully, she could answer.

'That's very kind of you.' Her brain was screaming, *You don't take charity*, but her heart was saying, *You could go home*. She and the boy could go home. Soon. And stay there. Just like that.

'I've never taken charity in my life,' Mavis said in a small voice. Archie had stood up when she had, but he was nodding like one of those fake nodding dogs in the back window of a car. Nodding so much his head might fall off.

'But it's very tempting.' She felt the heat in her cheeks. Yeah, well, she wasn't really good at accepting help from strangers.

The happy man said, 'We do understand. It's not charity. You'd be doing us a favour. We've got plans for that spot in the backyard. And if you take it, then we wouldn't have to sell it to people we don't know. We've got a couple of friends in the same boat as us and we're having a working bee to clean up some old vans lying around. Christina said there are a few people up there who could use a van.' He smiled at his wife. 'We had lots of fun with that one when the kids were little. It'd be nice to know it went to a good home.'

The woman, Jocelyn – Mavis needed to remember their names, these lovely people – spoke for the first time. 'Jim will tow it up there for you when the roads open. Set it up and get you going. We reckon you could get one of those port-a-loos just until things start to get rebuilt.'

Mavis's mouth opened and shut a couple of times like a stupid fish.

Archie touched her arm, his young face excited. He whispered, tugging at her, 'Say yes. And thank you, Gran.'

Archie's face was shining, his eyes happy when they'd been so worried. He rubbed his hands together as if he couldn't wait.

'Thank you,' she told Jim and Jocelyn. 'That would be great.' Even Mavis couldn't look that gift horse in the mouth, and the boy hopped foot to foot like he wanted to run rings of joy.

'So,' Archie said quietly, 'I won't have to go back to Sydney? Even if we don't have a house?'

Poor little mite. Mavis had been worrying about that, too. It'd be interesting to see if he still wanted to live with her after they were in each other's faces in a tiny van for a few months.

'Not if we don't fight in the van,' she said, and he grinned at her.

'We won't fight.'

That afternoon, the boy took to riding Christina's pushbike down to the shops and bringing back odds and ends from all the second-hand stores to outfit the new little house, as he called it.

Of course, Christina was a doer. She'd already started curtains and cushion covers. She'd even given her a sheet set. Blimey.

Molly had her ears open for a caravan for Liam at the family farm and another for Nell. She had had too big a fright at the gate that day and she was thinking she'd move into town with her mother.

Chapter Forty-four

Gracie

When communication had been restored properly two nights ago, Gracie had lain on the bed in her bedroom with Oliver tucked into her shoulder and the door shut, and video-called Jed.

Jed lay on his big, empty bed with his bedroom door shut in Featherwood drinking in the sight of them on the tiny screen of his phone. Since then, they'd spent many night-time hours on the phone.

He'd found her note, it was the first thing he'd told her apart from the one quick call, and her big man had cried. Her heart had broken. 'Oh, Jed, I'm sorry I didn't say it in person.'

He'd wiped away the tears and his voice gruff and broken at first, he'd told her he loved her. He was so sorry he'd been a goose to give away money without talking to her first. And yes, please, he'd love to marry her as soon as possible.

Yesterday, Jed had told her he'd been busy on the phone organising the priest to marry them as quickly as he could. Gracie could just imagine Jed wheeling and dealing with the priest and she shook her head at the thought. It was funny how ridiculous her reservations seemed now.

They'd talked of Oliver. Gracie had sent the everyday photos she'd been taking and couldn't send until then, sharing the little moments. And they'd even talked of her sadness at missing him, especially on day three after Oliver's birth.

'I'll be home soon,' she promised every night.

Finally, it was time. And oh goodness, it had taken a full, excruciatingly long week before the anxious evacuees were allowed back into Featherwood – and Gracie's heart pumped like a steam engine attacking a hill. She was on her way to Jed.

The out-of-town volunteer RFS men and women had moved on to the next threatened town, so the little village waited with open but singed arms for the evacuees to come home.

Gracie sat in the back of Christina's car, next to Oliver's baby restraint borrowed from one of Christina's dancing friends. Molly and Christina sat in the front with Molly driving. Mavis and Archie were coming behind them with Jim and Jocelyn, Christina's kind neighbours. Their big car towed the new-old van to Mavis's farm.

In Christina's car, her suitcases piled in the boot, Gracie ached with impatience. Her son had a suitcase larger than hers full of exquisitely sewn clothes. For herself, Gracie had been treated to three lovely, hand-sewn, crinkle-free day shifts with button-down fronts for breastfeeding. The material sat cool and swishy and made her feel spoilt and feminine, despite the messiness of a new baby.

She couldn't wait to show everything to Jed.

She couldn't wait to see Jed.

She wanted Jed.

She was dressed in one of her new outfits, and the day shone very warm, even though there were scuttling clouds in the brilliant blue sky.

They drove past drought into the bushfire area of the green belt, first on the ridges where all the green lushness had been stripped and replaced with dark crevices and spiky trunks of denuded trees. At the sides of the road, piles of chain-sawed forest obstructions had been pushed aside and mounds of ash lay around every corner in the previously green tunnel she and Jed had driven through all those weeks ago. Everything was covered in ash, the trees naked, silent and black, reaching for the rain that hadn't come.

They passed Nell's place, a charred stump the only sign of where her gate had hung. Now you could see into the driveway as it disappeared in a curve of skeletal dark trunks.

The next bend and the next, they saw more of the same incinerated landscape and ruined fences. There were no cattle anywhere, only mounds of ash.

'Jim and Jocelyn are turning into Mavis's driveway,' Molly said, her voice strained as she checked the rear-view mirror.

Gracie suspected Molly was distracting herself from what she'd find at her own gate. Christina must have thought the same because she lifted her hand and patted her daughter's arm.

'Oh my goodness.' Molly's voice shook, because up ahead, a charred stump marked where her own entrance had stood.

Gracie couldn't imagine the grief pulsing through Molly, and Christina, too, at the damage to their farm, as well as the loss of the house. Molly had told Gracie she'd lived there for as long as she could remember and it held all her memories of her husband, also.

'Just as well to drive past and breathe, before going in,' Christina said sensibly. 'People are the important thing.'

Molly was dropping Gracie at the Farmer's Friend before picking Liam up from the shop and going home. Liam had wanted to be there for his mother and sister when they were confronted with the ruins of the family farm.

Jed would be at the store, because they'd spoken this morning and he'd said, 'You know where to find me.'

Gracie had laughed. She'd see him soon. Her heart thumped half with excitement and half with horror at the relentless marching black of the burnt world as they drove closer to Featherwood.

The bridge stood singed at the edges with a seared creek name, a burnt rail, but usable. Unlike the tangled wire and stumps of fence posts that lay like a ghostly highway to the bald ridge top.

The *Welcome to Featherwood* sign stood barely readable, with the bubbled paint missing several letters. All the fences were gone, the first two houses were rubble, but the third stood proud, surrounded by burnt grass, and no fence.

The post office and shop had been burned to the edges, but all the cola and ice-cream advertisements still glowed with bright trademarks. No bubbles of burnt paint there.

The front fence of the church had gone, but the grass inside and the lovely white tower still stood serenely at the top of the knoll. Jed had been so relieved the church had survived. The thought made Gracie smile softly.

There was the Farmer's Friend!

It had charred grass and singed edges, but it was whole and alive. And there stood Jed, tall and excited, at the front with his hands on his hips. His big face lifted towards her with a smile so wide she could almost feel the warmth. She wanted to reach out and touch him.

Soon. *Dear, dear Jed. My love.* 'We're home,' she whispered to the baby strapped beside her. 'We're home.'

The car stopped and Jed was at her door, opening it and almost lifting her out of the car into his arms. He buried his face in her hair, his big arms cradling her as if he'd thought he would never see her again. She never wanted him to let her go. He felt so wonderful holding her.

'Gracie.' His voice was low and cracking. He said again, 'Gracie,' then put her away from him so he could see her face. She lost the warmth and feeling of safety against him. But she could breathe him in. Jed. He kissed her soundly and she closed her eyes and lost the world for a few moments.

When he pulled away, he said so very quietly, 'I love you.'

Oh, she'd missed him. Gracie sniffed. 'I love you, too.' She stepped back. 'Let's get your son out of the car so we can really be home.'

She didn't even need to see the house. Jed said it was there. She'd come to know with certainty that this man was more important than anything. He was her future and she would take as much as he offered.

'You want me to drive the bags down to the front door?' Molly said as she and her mother exchanged amused glances.

Gracie shook her head. 'No, you need to get to your place, but do stay with us tonight if you need, Molly. You too, Christina.'

Though goodness knows where, Gracie thought, *and how many are staying*. It didn't matter. 'Jed will get the bags now. He'll take them down later. I'm not leaving him for the rest of the day.' She turned to her man. 'Jed, come meet the amazing Christina. She's our fairy godmother.'

Chapter Forty-five

Nell

Nell heard the purr of a car out the front of the store. Then the cry of a new baby as it echoed through the Farmer's Friend. 'Now that's the sound of the new hope and new life that everybody needs.'

She stood out the back shed with Liam counting hay bales – not that that would help the dwindling supply; there were a lot of hungry cattle out there. But it was good to know just how low Jed was in stock.

'Sounds like Gracie's arrived.'

Liam raised his eyebrows. 'Reckon it's X-rated out there?'

'Jed missed her.' Nell smiled at him. Their eyes met and held, and Liam's were warm with delight for his friend.

Liam inclined his head slowly, as if deep in thought, trying to remember. 'I might have noticed that, seeing as Jed mentioned it about four hundred times a day.'

They'd both seen the shadow and sadness in Jed's eyes and his frustration at missing the first week of Oliver's life. Nell would be glad to see the old smiling Jed back, now that Gracie was home.

She glanced around the stripped store. 'He still managed to look after everybody who came into the store.'

They exchanged another look. 'He might have looked after them too well. Lucky you're keeping the records, or Gracie would have come back to bankruptcy.'

Gracie's comment weeks ago had been right. Jed was hopeless at anything to do with the accounts. When the electricity failed so did the till, computers and the EFTPOS. Every new person had a valid hardship and no money and desperately needed supplies. Of course, Jed just said, 'You can pay me later.'

Nell had been less certain that Jed and Gracie's creditors would be so generous. Of all the things those in the valley needed, repairs to their houses and fences if they still had them were high, and Jed carried that stock. His other stock, produce, they needed for their remaining farm animals.

She'd created a handwritten sales document, then stuck the sheet to a wooden board with a pen on the end of a string. If Jed couldn't find a pen, he'd just wave the idea of recording the sale away.

She'd insisted that Gracie would like him to write down the name of the product, the amount, and the name of the customer. Nell would enter it all later in the computer when the power was restored. She'd started inputting the spreadsheets on day four when the lights came on.

She'd noticed the impending disaster fairly early, so hopefully there was only a day or two of missed outgoings, and with luck, those people would pay anyway. But over time, word got around that Jed was an easy mark and couldn't do enough for people. The less scrupulous reappeared, cashless, and frequently.

But now, the government grants were trickling in, and people were starting to pay. So she felt confident that the store would survive. Perhaps even prosper.

'Maybe we should sleep somewhere else tonight?' Liam was joking. A new trait that had been seeping into his repertoire over the last few days.

Like either of them had a house to go to. 'Nah. She just had a baby.'

'Damn.'

Another joke? Already? Nell had noticed, she couldn't help it really, that she and Liam had started to exchange looks and smiles every time Jed spoke wistfully of his family. Sharing their appreciation of the dislocated family man had drawn them closer together. Along with the snap, crackle and pop of possible future sex, she suspected.

'You know, yesterday I phoned my psychologist for a consult over the phone. The one from before I left Sydney.'

Liam looked up. She'd rarely spoken about Sydney. And she'd been stonewalling any advances he'd made to further their relationship. She'd been finding it dreadfully difficult not to become involved with Liam, because, she suspected, she liked him too much to ruin his life.

'And?' Her man was one of few words.

'The psychologist said, as long as you and I had an honest, open and consistent relationship with good communication, it was a great idea. That healthy relationships support good mental health.'

Liam watched her, his dark eyes hooded.

'So, I'm communicating.' She waved her arms, blushing. She reminded herself that Liam had been putting himself out there and she'd been backing off. 'I'm being open. Telling you I had misgivings that I wasn't good enough for you and would ruin your life.' *Phew.* She sagged. The psychologist had also asked, 'Have you thought this was from the feelings your mother left you with?' Psychologists never told you anything. They always asked questions.

Liam blinked, slow comprehension clearing his serious expression.

'Well?' she asked. 'I communicated.'

'So, you think maybe you're not going to ruin my life if we get together?' There was teasing, and maybe a touch of relief in his voice.

She smiled at him. 'I don't think we'll ever chatter, but if we both learn to speak up and share when things bother us, it beats social isolation hands down for mental wellness.'

'I can think of something else that can *increase wellness*.' His gaze travelled over her with an extra ten degrees of warmth and she blushed again.

Yes, well, Nell thought, *time for a new direction of mind*. 'Gracie's home. We've given her enough time to greet her man, and I want to see the baby.'

'And I need to see my sister. She's picking me up. I'll go with her and Mum.'

'I'm sorry about your farm.' Nell reached out and touched Liam's hand. 'You were there the first time I saw my destruction. It made a difference.'

He stared at her as if startled, and then he dipped his head. 'I'm glad.' He turned and walked out to the waiting car.

Nell's attention was caught by the small pile of hay. They were hoping that with the road opened, more would come in today. Her herd still roamed Jed and Gracie's burnt paddock with the Sparke-Edwards cows, sharing the little there was to eat. She'd remedy that soon.

Yesterday, Liam had accompanied her to her little farmlet to help erect electric fences so she could bring her cattle back, because Jed didn't have enough feed for her herd and his. The front paddock grass was burnt to ash, the trees shared no leaves a cow could reach up for. Even though the lack of fences allowed displaced cattle to roam miles of roads, everything was covered in ash and the fodder was scarce.

She'd been more fortunate than most.

Nell had one long, lucky lane of paddock that was a healthy green, a freakish oversight by the fire, and a saving respite for Nell's cows. And the spring of creek water still trickled sluggishly through the ash.

She still had to wait for a space on the list for the cattle truck to shift her herd, however.

The best news had been that Molly had found a small caravan for her, which could keep Nell out of the rain – if the skies ever opened – and could be locked if she went into Featherwood. It would arrive tomorrow.

She'd spent the last few days waiting for the road to open and the chance to go out and stock up on essentials. This morning, she'd tidied and polished Gracie's house when the men had left, and then helped Jed and Liam in the store until her arrival.

Gracie was back and Nell could go home tomorrow. Her promise of looking after Jed while his love was away had been fulfilled.

Yesterday afternoon, she'd cleaned out her still-standing toolshed at Nell's Farm to move back into. The plan was to set up a camp kitchen. She'd come a long way from her mother's tennis-club afternoons and would manage to live quite successfully if not comfortably. She had more than a lot of others.

She still had a tank stand with a tap, and Liam had added a roof gutter to her toolshed to catch rain for her tank now that the roof of her house no longer existed. They were still waiting for the rain.

The lack of solar power would be a nuisance. Jed had given her one of the precious, single-cell, folding solar panels to charge her mobile phone so at least she would have contact with the outside if she needed it. When she could get service. She'd put her own name on the clipboard invoice to pay.

Nell heard Gracie laugh. She put down her clipboard and moved towards the sound. *Dear Gracie.*

'Nell!' Gracie called and held out her arms. Her smile looked as big and beautiful and welcoming as always. As if Nell was a most important person she'd wanted to see.

'Hello, Gracie. It's lovely to see you home.' They hugged, she'd known she'd have to, and it felt surprisingly familiar to be hugged by Gracie. 'Where's your beautiful boy?'

'Jed has him. Of course. He said you've been looking after him. At home and at the shop.'

'He's been looking after everyone else, at the shop.'

Gracie must have heard something in Nell's voice because she rolled her eyes. 'I heard you made him write down sales.' Gracie patted Nell's shoulder. 'Thank you,' her voice heavily sincere she added, 'my friend.' They smiled at each other. 'We'll talk about that in a minute.' They strolled back to the front of the store and out onto the driveway.

Nell waved at a familiar face. 'Hello, Molly. It's lovely to see you back. So sorry about your house.'

'Yes, well. You of all people would understand how I'm feeling about that.' Molly waved her hand to introduce her mother. She couldn't be anyone else with those features. 'Christina, this is Nell.'

Nell shook the older lady's hand, thinking, *This is Liam's mother*, and trying not to blush because she fancied this woman's son way too much. 'Jed says you've been looking after Gracie so well.'

'I will miss them,' Christina said. 'Though Molly is coming home with me, so that will help.' She glanced up at Liam. 'I wish my son would come home, but I know he won't.'

'Too much to do here, Mother,' he said.

Nell liked the way he said 'Mother'. Formal but indulgent. Christina's mouth twitched in a half-smile of astonishment at his ease and good humour and Nell wondered if he'd changed so much since Christina had last seen him. Nell suspected he might have.

'Nell's almost got herself set up again in her toolshed,' he told Molly. 'I haven't started at our place yet.' He hugged his sister, who widened her eyes at the spontaneous affection. 'Great stuff that you've managed to find Nell a caravan.'

'I'm a bit overwhelmed, Molly,' Nell said quietly. She still felt as if she didn't deserve something other people could have used. 'You sure no one else needs it more than me?'

'There are other vans out there for other people, Nell.' Molly was happy again, her sadness forgotten for a moment. 'You'll have to go and see Mavis. She just arrived back with Mum's neighbours; they've given her their caravan. Archie is very excited.'

People are so kind, Nell thought, and realised what a vastly different take she had on 'people' since she'd arrived two months ago. Good people stick together – like farmer's friends.

Chapter Forty-six

Mavis

A month later

Mavis loved a good wedding.

'Archie, sit still,' she whispered. He'd been good for the first half-hour, but his attention span had expired and he'd caught sight of one of the other boys he usually ran wild with. Although Archie really liked Jed and Gracie, he couldn't stop shifting on the pew beside her, impatient to disappear as soon as he could.

Mavis breathed in the whole occasion like that first frothy sip of beer on a really hot day. The scent of candles, the heavy aroma of the flowers Molly had brought from town, the litanies and homilies, and of course the vows. Mavis wished they could have done the whole traditional wedding with the bride in white and the groom in a tuxedo and the ceremony in Latin, maybe a nuptial mass, but she suspected she'd be the only one. Including the priest. It was stinking hot in here.

There. They were kissing.

Archie rolled his eyes in disgust, and Mavis withheld a snort.

It wouldn't be long before he'd be looking at kissing in a whole different light. Heaven help her.

The bride put her hand on the groom's muscled arm and turned to the church full of happy faces. Gracie wore a deceptively simple, ankle-length, palest-green, almost white, dress with pink flowers on it, and she resembled a glowing spring, not a hot summer.

Of course, Christina had made the dresses and shirts.

The groom wore new blue jeans and an open-collared white shirt with a new pair of boots. Mavis thought she'd be able to see her face in the shine of his RM Williams. The man had huge feet.

Father stepped forward and spread his fingers towards the newly married couple. 'I present Mr and Mrs Joshua and Gracie Sparke-Edwards.'

Everyone heaved to their feet and cheered. Mavis was darned sure that applause rocked the high ceiling and Archie whooped beside her.

Jed's smile split so widely that Mavis shook her head. His other hand came up to cover his wife's small one, as if to reassure himself Gracie really was at his side in a church, and they began to walk back down the aisle.

Gracie beamed her Gracie smile at everyone, her gaze roaming the eager faces with a delight and joy that brought tears to Mavis's dry old eyes for the second time in a long time. Indeed. It was a very good day the day these two came to Featherwood.

Molly's brother, Liam, handsome when he smiled, which seemed more often now, his own shirt matching Jed's, offered his arm to young Nell, who looked like a model in a pale-pink ankle-length frock that matched the flowers on Gracie's dress. She carried the wee baby as easily as a football under her arm, and they followed the newlyweds outside.

Apparently, everyone had to surge to follow.

Archie disappeared in the crush and Mavis stood back, shaking her head at the youth and savouring the moment. The old church hadn't seen so many people for years and they had a lot to be thankful for. She had a lot to be thankful for.

Over a thousand people in the area had been displaced and had to seek refuge. Local people, groups and businesses had all offered such amazing support. She'd never seen the likes of it.

Mavis's gifted caravan had a big steel shed over the top of it now and she had water and electricity. Liam had found some of her cattle that had taken to the ridges and there was a bunch of blokes on horses following a bigger herd up in the hills. A month later!

She'd see if she had any of hers in that mob when they came down.

The boy's mother had come and asked if he wanted to go back to Sydney. Archie had looked at her like she was mad, and Mavis had tried not to laugh.

The insurance company promised them a new house, but it would take many weeks for all the assessors, and the council and all the paperwork things to be even able to start, so until then they had their van, the tractor, the car and good friends.

Liam had been very helpful in the early days, but now the volunteer fence people, BlazeAid, had set up camp in the showground at Featherwood and she'd have real fences again soon.

There were so many kind-hearted people. She'd been offered furniture she couldn't fit in a caravan and the boy had a new pushbike and helmet because apparently, people wanted to give.

Life was good – it sure beat the alternative. Her eyes went straight to the altar at the front of the church. 'Thank you for my blessings, Lord,' she murmured, and breathed out the emotions from the day and even the last month.

By the time Mavis descended the wooden steps of the little church opposite the rural store and stopped to say hello to the priest again, well, the smiles of the crowd outside shone brighter than the December sun.

The wedding party was having church photos and the rest of the guests all swirled across the road past the Farmer's Friend store, over the cattle grid. Mavis smirked at some of the high heels trying to navigate that.

A trail of happy, noisy people tromping past the ribbon-decked Farmer's Friend, along the river-pebble drive, through the black paddock and down to the little house that had survived it all.

Acknowledgements

Thank you, dear reader, for choosing *The Farmer's Friend* to spend time with. I am truly grateful and honoured by your support. Without you – well, there'd be no books like this to share. Nowhere for me to channel my imagination and dreams of creating fictional worlds from the real world, to offer insight and adventure in Australia from my house to yours. I've loved living in Gracie and Nell and Mavis's world. I hope you did too.

The Farmer's Friend is not just a story about friendship and healing but an acknowledgement for those who lived and died through the bushfires of 2019 and 2020 over the whole of Australia. And for those volunteers and servicemen and women who fought for others at personal cost.

Of course, Featherwood is an amalgamation of all those places, a fictitious town in my mind, melding with Ebor, west of the Dorrigo plateau towards Armidale in northern New South Wales and the small townships of Willawarrin and Bellbrook, closer to the coast in the Macleay Valley near my home. Like many towns, all three suffered drought and then the fires that ripped through their communities. This year those places have lived through floods and landslides.

Some of the more personal aspects for this story came from people from the Macleay Valley. I'd like to mention Jutta and Terry Flynn who lived through a situation very similar to Mavis's and escaped with their lives, though they lost their home, their possessions and their dog. I spoke to Jutta and Terry a year later, and it was their resilience and gratitude for the support of their community that became the real theme for this book and I appreciate being privy to their firsthand experiences.

We hear of the sacrifices and relentless efforts of the rural fire service volunteers, and there can never be enough ways to highlight their bravery. The description of the 'flashover' is my interpretation and imagining after watching fire surround a red truck full of RFS men in the video from Parma, south of Nowra, on New Year's Day 2020.

A big thank you to Brian Condon, an RFS volunteer with more than twenty years of turning up for rural fire service emergencies in Bowraville and the district. Brian answered my questions or knew who to ask when I needed to know if something was possible, and was a fabulous resource to me during writing. Any inconsistencies with the RFS are my own, not Brian's, and occurred after consulting him.

Thanks to Macleay Valley Rural Supplies, the inspiration for my rural store, though I made lots of things up, including adding the farmhouse behind for Gracie and Jed to live in! Andrew and Loretta are not Gracie and Jed, but their store was one of the hubs for the community in Willawarrin after the fires and thankfully they didn't mind me describing their products and their business.

When I began to think about this book, I read an old court case about a young midwife caught up in tragic circumstances with a homebirth, and I wondered at the fallout from something that certainly would have begun as a whole-hearted loving service provision before becoming a nightmare for the parents and midwives involved. My anti-hero midwife was a figment of my imagination. Current homebirth services, both government and non-government funded, provide incredibly impressive statistics for safe birth and satisfied clients and if I was having my babies now, this is a service I would trust.

Liam's backstory came from the stories of so many of our returned servicemen and women, soldiers to whom we owe so much, and yet who suffer from PTSD, often in isolation.

As always, I would love to thank the team at Penguin Random House. My awesome publisher, Ali Watts, my wonderful editor, Amanda Martin, who follows up all my questions, the fabulous cover designer, Louisa Maggio, and the super Sofia Casanova in publicity who works so hard to let readers know my book is out in the world. Thanks also to Alex Nahlous and Sonja Heijn for your insight and polish.

Thanks to my amazing agent, Clare Forster, who is never too busy for me, is the person I turn to for career advice and is my sounding board for new ideas. Thanks, Clare – you rock!

Special appreciation to my writing friend cheer squad, Bronwyn Jameson, Trish Morey, Jaye Ford and Marie Miller, for your amazing input with that first draft. I love your sense of humour in dealing with me. You are great mates. And lastly, Annie Seaton, you make me say, 'If she can, I can.' You are an inspiration and always have time for me. To my writing friends in RWAus, where

ACKNOWLEDGEMENTS

I found our lovely Maytone group, and RWNZ, who always provide forward motion when I lose my way – thank you.

Then there's my hero. No acknowledgement would be complete without the man who is, as the song goes, the wind beneath my wings. Dearest Ian, my love, my best friend and my biggest fan – I am *your* biggest fan. Thank you.

Yes, it takes a community to write a book. And that's what I love about writing – we give, we learn and we share, so that we can create books that touch our readers, share magic moments and inspire the joy and satisfaction that comes from writing and reading a story we love. I hope, dear readers, that you loved *The Farmer's Friend*. I loved creating it.

Thank you for your wonderful support. xx Fi

Book club notes

1. The Farmer's Friend is a central meeting point for many in the Featherwood community. Discuss its importance to the characters in the story. Is there a place or business that fulfils this role in your hometown?

2. Gracie is more practical than Jed, and Jed is more optimistic than Gracie. Are you more like Gracie or Jed? In what ways?

3. The Featherwood community put a lot of work into their fire plans. What experience have you had with preparing for natural disasters in your own community and how does it compare?

4. Nell wonders: 'Could some of the shame and self-reproach strip from her soul?' At what point in the story do you think Nell starts to forgive herself? How does she begin to trust herself again?

5. Mavis thinks, 'Young ones these days baffled her,' but she and Archie are very close. How do they help each other throughout this story?

6. Gracie and Jed have a strong relationship but clash over their different approach to money. Do you think this is common between couples? How do you feel about how they both handled their arguments?

7. Nell and Liam are both experiencing post-traumatic stress from events in their lives. Does this shared experience help or hinder their growing attraction? Why?

8. 'Family were people who supported you and believed you over others, especially when you were innocent.' What role does the idea of chosen family play in this story, and in your own life?

9. Gracie describes 'a horrid something's-going-to-happen feeling' to Nell and asks if she's ever had that. How does each character's intuition drive the decisions they make in this story?

10. The drought takes a huge toll on the farming families of Featherwood. What emotional effects did you pick up throughout the story?

11. Several characters lose their homes during the story's events. What do you think helps people keep going under those types of circumstances?

12. If you have read any of Fiona McArthur's other books, what similarities and differences do you notice between them and *The Farmer's Friend*?

Discover a
new favourite

Discover a
new favourite

Visit penguin.com/ournewbook